PLAYING CHESS WITH GOD

BY VERNE R. ALBRIGHT

Hellgate Press Ashland, OR

Playing Chess with God
©2018 Verne R. Albright

Published by Hellgate Press
(An imprint of L&R Publishing, LLC)

Hellgate Press
PO Box 3531
Ashland, OR 97520
email: info@hellgatepress.com

Interior Design: Sasha Kincaid
Cover Design: L. Redding
Cover Illustration: San Francisco's Niantic Hotel (Library of Congress, Prints & Photographs Division, CA-1719-1) Built 1850 - Destroyed by fire 1851.

Cataloging In Publication Data is available from the publisher upon request.
ISBN: 978-1-55571-919-7 (paperback)
ISBN: 978-1-55571-920-3 (ebook)

Printed and bound in the United States of America
First edition 10 9 8 7 6 5 4 3 2 1

OTHER VERNE R. ALBRIGHT BOOKS AVAILABLE THROUGH HELLGATE PRESS:

THE WRATH OF GOD (SEQUEL TO *PLAYING CHESS WITH GOD*)

PROLOGUE

A hundred and fifty miles northeast of San Francisco, in California's Sierra Nevada foothills, John Sutter's new sawmill was ready for its first test. Water—brought from the American River in a manmade ditch—briefly rotated the huge main wheel then backed up, unable to exit the mill fast enough. The tailrace canal needed to be wider and steeper.

For the rest of the day, workmen dug and blasted the hard, rocky soil. That night, flood gates were opened to wash the channel clean. While inspecting their progress the next morning, Superintendent James Marshall found a shiny metal flake. Compared to a five dollar gold piece, its color was identical.

For the rest of that week Marshall and his men found fragments and finally a nugget big enough to be bitten, hammered, boiled in lye, and melted on hot coals. These tests left no doubt. The perplexing yellow metal was gold. Workers searched the river and found plenty more.

John Sutter feared a gold rush would threaten his fifty-thousand-acre agricultural empire, but it was too late to keep the news secret. First to take advantage were Mormons who had fled persecution and violence in Missouri and Illinois. Men from the Mexican War's Mormon Battalion left Sutter's Mill and his other businesses that employed them. More came from Mormon Island, bringing wives and children to work alongside them.

"Soon there won't be anyone involved in any other activity," Marshall told Sutter when the latter complained his workers were deserting him.

"Not with gold being scooped up at the rate of two thousand dollars a man per day."

But there were other ways to get rich during a gold rush. Back when San Francisco was called Yerba Buena, Sam Brannan had brought two hundred fellow Mormons to California. He now owned stores in the Sierra Nevada foothills and learned about the momentous discovery when customers began paying for purchases with gold.

A natural-born promoter, Brannan hired local craftsmen to fill his stores with prospector's tools and supplies—then hurried to San Francisco. Running up and down the streets, he waved his hat with one hand and rattled a bottle of gold with the other.

"Gold! Gold! Gold from the American River!" he shouted over and over.

Soon Brannan's stores were supplying four thousand '48ers, so-called because it was 1848. Most found so much gold they feared an oversupply would drive the price down to almost nothing. When there were no more nuggets to be picked up off the ground or plucked from creeks, men needed only a knife to pry more from rocks. Or a pick and shovel to dig sand, dirt, and gravel so gold could be washed from it.

In the midst of this madness *Portales*, a Chilean schooner, put in at San Francisco to find the city deserted except for the aged and infirm, who eagerly passed along the momentous news. But their tale was suspect because of how easily they revealed information that could bring outsiders to compete with their friends in the Gold Country. Only two of *Portales's* crew jumped ship. The rest brought the questionable tale to Talcahuano, halfway down Chile's long coastline.

CHAPTER ONE

THE '48ERS

Talcahuano's principal attraction was dark-eyed, pigtailed whores. *Portales's* crew enjoyed them for two days and then continued their voyage. As they left, a gangly young Prussian named Henning Dietzel ran down the gangplank from another freighter and hurried toward the House of Smiles. He didn't want anyone to claim Encinas Peralta before he got there.

Five months earlier, Henning had stopped outside the bordello's door long enough to finger comb his thick blond hair. Inside he paused again and waited for his eyes to adjust to the dim light in a room with a busy bar against a purple wall. A tall, shapely girl rose from a couch of scantily clad ladies and ground out a cigarette in an abalone shell. To his delight, she glided up to him, her tight pink dress emphasizing a wasp-like waist.

"You have the nicest smile I've seen in the House of Smiles," she said, "and the bluest eyes."

"Thank you." Embarrassed by the accent he was trying to lose, Henning felt his face flush. "As pretty as you are, I'm sure you've seen more than your share of smiles."

She touched his arm with a manicured hand. "Are you here to enjoy women's bodies or practice your Spanish? You seem in need of both."

"Will you help me with my pronunciation if I buy you a drink?"

"We don't teach languages here. We pleasure lonely men."

"I'm looking forward to that too." His eyes were drawn to her cleavage.

"You don't have to tell me." She kissed his cheek. "I know men."

"My name is Henning."

"Mine's Encinas." She took his arm and guided him toward a private table.

When the waitress came Encinas ordered a *ratafia*, brandy with fruit juice and almonds.

"What can I bring you, my love?" the waitress asked Henning.

"I don't drink alcohol, *Fräulein*," he replied, finishing in his native German.

"You have to if you sit with a girl," the waitress said.

"Bring him a *ratafia* without brandy," Encinas broke in. "Even nuns can drink that."

Henning's urge—insistent when he'd come in—gave way to fascination with Encinas's easy laughter and surprising intelligence. He'd never thought about what prostitutes might be like aside from their specialty.

"You seem softer than the other girls," he said.

"Are you saying I'm fat?" she asked.

"In case you're not teasing, I meant being with you is nicer than being with other girls."

"Who else have you been with?" Her eyes flashed flirtatiously.

Reddening, he looked down. "No one. I don't know what to do."

"I'm well qualified to teach you, but I want to know you better first."

For hours they explored their mutual interest in books, nature, travel, and the art of making money. A man paused beside their table and tried to start a conversation. Encinas said she was taken. When other girls slinked past with movements designed to tempt Henning, she put her hand protectively over his and said, "He's with me."

"To them you're nothing more than a source of money," Encinas said, leaning closer. "But this profession has given me special insight into humanity...well, men at least. And I see you as especially kind and thoughtful."

"Thank you."

"You're also extremely shy and I sense you're uncomfortable with my praise," she continued. "But I can't help it. I love your height and uniqueness. Look around. Everyone here has black hair. Yours is the color of wheat in the fields. Everyone else has brown eyes. Yours are bluer than a cloudless sky."

"You talk like a poet."

"I read a lot of poetry."

Henning wasn't so innocent he believed her compliments. Expensive drinks were coming fast. She'd leave as soon as his wallet was empty, but he couldn't hold back a smile or stop his eyes from participating.

"You should do that more often," Encinas said. "Your teeth are perfect and white as pearls. Any other man would flash them often and to great advantage."

"Smiling makes me look boyish."

"What's wrong with that?"

"No one takes boys seriously."

"It's the other way around for females. We get more attention when we're young."

By midnight they had discussed songwriters and whether they used words as well as poets...fathers and whether they were ever as kind as mothers...food and whether God had intended for humans to eat three times a day or once every three days.

Without being asked, the waitress brought one refill after another. With several untouched drinks on the table between them, Encinas sent the next round back. Annoyed, the bartender marched to their table and told Henning, "If you're going to take this lady's time, you have to buy drinks."

"Don't be bad, Juanito," Encinas purred. "My shift ends soon. Let the gentleman stay until then. Please."

The bartender turned sullen. "Just this once. Never again. Understand?"

When they were alone, Henning reached for his glass. Encinas grabbed his hand in midair.

"Know what I like best about you?" she asked. "You weren't upset when I didn't invite you to one of the rooms on the second floor. I didn't want to because those are for sex, and I like you too much to have sex with you. But we can make love after my shift ends."

Later Encinas took Henning to her fastidiously clean one room cabin and lit its hanging lantern. In one corner a pot-bellied stove sat beside logs and tinder. Green curtains bracketed the only window. Below it, a wilting flower in a whiskey bottle sat on a bookcase stuffed with poetry. A pillow and open book rested on the red blanket covering a mattress on the floor.

Encinas closed the curtains and undid her pigtails. Released from its tight braids her black hair fluffed full. With long flowing strokes she brushed it into a dark frame around her face. Then she unbuttoned her dress and let it slide to the floor, revealing the whitest skin Henning had ever seen. In corset and pantalets she knelt to untie and remove his shoes. Before wriggling from her undergarments, she helped him shed his shirt and pants.

Henning had never seen a woman's naked body. Seeing his first only increased the mystery. He stole glances at her firm bottom, pink nipples, and thick pubic hair as she led him to the mattress. When he was on his back she swung a leg over him and perched on his torso. Leaning forward, she put her hands on opposite sides of his face and touched her lips to his.

"I hope I don't taste of burning tobacco," she said. "I've been sucking on mints since I snuffed out my last cigarette. Should I not kiss you?"

"Only if you want to punish me." Henning usually found smoking offensive, but Encinas's cigarettes were only a tiny flaw.

During a series of increasingly passionate kisses, her long hair formed a tent, isolating them in a private world where she made Henning's first lovemaking exciting and memorable. Afterward she gave him luxuries her customers didn't get, a home-cooked dinner and a night's sleep with a warm, soft companion.

He woke up with Encinas already awake and nestled close. Sleeping through the night was a rare pleasure because he stood the night watch at sea. She made it obvious she wanted him again. He'd been told orgasms were best after long abstention, but this one—on the heels of his best ever—was even more intense.

When Encinas tried to get out of bed he wrapped his arms around her and held her against him, back first. She ran her fingertips along his arms, then recoiled from a jagged scar.

"How did you get that?"

"I was in a situation where someone else's safety took priority over mine."

"Which means?"

"I stopped a crewmate from attacking our captain with a knife."

Rolling over and staring with special intensity, Encinas said, "I'd gladly have your baby if you could guarantee your blue eyes and golden hair." She was clearly flirting, but not for money. She hadn't asked him to pay and would be offended if he offered.

Overwhelmed with loneliness after his ship sailed that afternoon, Henning soon hired on with another vessel, one that regularly called at Talcahuano.

******

Today was the five-month anniversary of their first meeting. At the House of Smiles Henning found Encinas arguing with men at the bar.

"The news brought by *Portales's* crew is too good to be true," one of them insisted.

"Before you can have a dream come true," Encinas replied, "you have to have a dream."

When she saw Henning, her brown eyes sparkled and a smile puckered her cheeks. As always when he saw her with other men, he felt betrayed. His jealousy evaporated after she draped her arms around his neck and her disappointed former companions went looking for other girls.

"You look wonderful," he told her.

"And your Spanish will be perfect as soon as you start rolling your r's," she teased. Glancing at his mouth she added, "Show me your real smile—not that little half-grin."

"If you want people to make changes," he said mischievously, "you have to praise their first steps."

She led Henning to a table and breathlessly told him about the gold that was the talk of Talcahuano. Disappointed by his lukewarm interest she said, "I'll take the night off. Let's go where there aren't any distractions."

"I'll be more distracted if we go to your room," he teased.

"We'll do that first and then talk," she said.

Her simple, lumpy mattress seemed like a cloud far above the rest of the world. There they made passionate love, then talked. And every time he changed subjects, she brought the conversation back to California's gold.

"Go to San Francisco," she urged before they fell asleep. "At worst you'll lose a few months' salary and the cost of a ticket. At best you'll find enough gold to open your store now instead of someday."

Henning spent shore leaves in other towns among merchants who told him what they could sell if only they had it. During his subsequent travels he found what he could and brought it to them, earning almost nine hundred dollars in three years. He'd saved every penny—along with most of his wages—hoping to open a store in Chile's capital, Santiago.

The next day Encinas was up before dawn. Henning woke to see her dicing onions, bell peppers, cheese, and ham for omelets. He lay in bed reveling in her graceful efficiency.

"How long have you been watching?" she asked, noticing he was awake.

"I was enjoying you too much to keep track of time." He stood and stretched, then pulled on his pants. "Why are you up so early?"

"I have things to do." She poured their omelets into a frying pan. "Since we last saw each other, the owner put me on trial as manager at the House of Smiles."

"Manager. That's an honor."

"Especially for someone my age." Encinas—like Henning—was eighteen. "I'm earning more money, which is nice. But the best part is that now I only have to lie down with the man of my choosing—you. Be patient with my long hours. I want to keep this promotion."

"You will." He crept up behind and kissed her neck. "I've never seen you do less than a Prussian job."

"What's that?"

"According to my grandfather it's the best job possible. If I did anything less, I got his cane across my backside."

After breakfast, Henning walked Encinas to work. On the way, sailors leered at her and the town's ladies glared. But businessmen took off their hats and greeted her respectfully. Talcahuano prospered when its bordello did, and under her leadership the House of Smiles was bringing more ships. Her newest innovation was a room for captains, first mates, and ships' surgeons. Inside its wood-paneled walls they relaxed in easy chairs beside tables offering complimentary paper, envelopes, pens, cigars, rum, and sweets.

Seeing Talcahuano's worthiest citizens confirm his lofty opinion of Encinas, Henning gave more weight to her insistence he go to San Francisco. Back at the ship he asked a fellow deckhand's opinion.

"Haven't you learned that ports are full of wondrous yarns that are never true?" his friend replied. "If there's gold in California, why didn't *Portales's* crew jump ship?"

His other crewmates were equally discouraging.

That afternoon, Encinas answered his knock on her cabin door wearing a provocative maroon and gold dress. It left the top of her bosom bare and clung from neck to ankles. She'd worn it to please, but he would've preferred something less revealing.

Once inside, he saw an overstuffed chair she'd added to her sparse furnishings.

"I borrowed it from my new office," she explained. "You can read there while I'm at work tomorrow."

"How did you get something that heavy clear across town?"

"Pulled it on a cart. I want you comfortable on what may be our last day together until you get back from California." She gestured for him to sit at the table. "You're going, right?"

"Maybe I should wait until the rumors are confirmed."

"By then California will be overrun." She set a plate of steaming spaghetti in front of him. "News will travel to America's Atlantic coast by ship, a three month voyage. Leave now and you'll get there six months before Americans start flooding in."

"It's a long way to California and there's no guarantee I'll find gold even if it's there." He rolled a mouthful of spaghetti onto his fork. "I could be away from you for a year or more."

"On a sailor's wages, it'll take ten times that long for you to save enough money to open a store," Encinas said gently. "When you have your own business, I'll work for you and we can be together every day instead of two or three nights a month."

He sighed. "Okay. You win. I'll go."

"Good." She grinned. "That was easier than I expected."

On Henning's last afternoon in Talcahuano, a sudden inspiration sent him rushing to town. In the market he selected a dozen tightly closed roses. At the general store he bought glue and sheets of thin white pasteboard.

Sitting at the table back at Encinas's cabin, Henning cut an irregular piece of pasteboard, then folded and glued it, making a small lidless box. He poked a hole in the bottom, threaded a rose stem through it, and pulled until the bud was nestled inside. After repeating this eleven times, he put the roses in a pail of water and hid them under the porch.

The next morning, Encinas accompanied Henning to the dock, making him the envy of his shipmates. Before going aboard he stared at her for a long time.

"You've stopped blinking," she said, embarrassed.

"I want to remember exactly how you look right now," he said. "God I'll miss you."

"Write to me as soon as you find a ship to California." Encinas wasn't sure she'd ever see him again. Her doubts faded as his big, calloused sailor's hand took a dozen red roses from their hiding place in his knapsack—each bud protected by an individual white box.

"I didn't want them squashed," he explained. "A perfect girl deserves perfect flowers."

She buried her nose in the roses and inhaled, then looked up at him and promised, "I'm going to stop smoking. Next time you kiss me I'll taste better."

CHAPTER TWO

PROFESSOR VON DUISBURG'S DAUGHTER

As soon as Henning's ship reached Valparaiso, he started looking for someone going to California. Someone who'd bring him along and show him how to find gold. But he couldn't find anyone who took him—as young as he was—seriously.

"When you're older and look in a mirror, you'll see your father looking back," his grandfather had once promised. Henning could hardly wait. His father had been dashing and dangerous. Everyone had paid attention to him.

Sitting alone in a waterfront saloon, Henning was joined by five men. One climbed up on the table and addressed the other patrons in a booming voice.

"I'm Roberto Flores. Me and my friends," he gestured to the men around him, "are going to California. We need a man to do our chores. In return we'll show him how to pan gold."

"Sounds like you need a sucker to do your dirty work," an onlooker heckled.

"When he gets back from California with bags of gold," Flores said, "you'll wish you'd been that sucker."

"What do you know about gold, let alone California?" the heckler challenged.

"I was in Minas Gerais, Brazil, during the big strike there."

"In that case why aren't you rich?"

"Because I got there too late, but this time you'll be the one making that mistake…if you ever work up the gumption to go." Flores got down from the table, moving with exaggerated care to mask his inebriation. He rapped a shin against a chair, then cursed, "*Maldito* sea."

"Is it true?" Henning asked the man sitting beside him. "Are you going to California?"

"Why?"

"I might be interested in joining you," Henning replied.

"My name is Eduardo Vásquez."

"I'm Henning Dietzel."

"Nice to meet you. I'll introduce my friends later if there's any point in it."

Vásquez was over six feet with broad, level shoulders. Perhaps because Henning was taller yet, though little more than a boy, he pulled himself erect and threw back his shoulders. Studying Henning's threadbare clothes, he said, "It'll cost four hundred U.S. dollars for supplies and passage to California. Do you have that much?"

"I can pay my way."

"Your Spanish isn't bad. How's your English?"

In English Henning answered, "It's passable."

"What's your native tongue?"

"Prussian."

"If you can learn three languages, you can learn to pan gold. We'll teach you if you work for us without wages and make a deposit to guarantee you won't take off before putting in your time."

"How long would I have to work for you?"

"What do you suggest?"

"Half-days for a month."

"Negotiations seldom succeed if the opening bid is unreasonable," Vásquez growled. "Would you like to start again?"

"Isn't it your turn now?" Henning asked.

"Dawn to dusk for three months."

"If I agree to that, the gold will be gone before I can gather any for myself."

"Gather?" Flores snorted drunkenly. "Sounds like you expect it to be scattered on the ground where girls could frolic around on their tiptoes filling their aprons with it."

"Two months," Vásquez broke in, holding up that many fingers.

Henning crossed his arms over his chest. "Why would I spend four hundred dollars to go where everyone but me will get rich?"

"The only ones getting rich will be those with the necessary skills." Vásquez covered a yawn with his fist. "The others will be wasting their time."

"How about six weeks?"

Vásquez waited in vain for Henning to improve his offer, then said, "Your deposit will have to be at least four hundred dollars to discourage you from taking off before living up to your side of the bargain."

"You have a deal." Henning extended his hand.

"We leave for California tomorrow," Vásquez said as they shook hands. "Meet us at noon in front of the cathedral and bring your money."

"If there's really gold in California, what are our chances of finding it?"

"Prospecting is like playing chess with God." Vásquez flashed a conspiratorial wink. "You can't win unless He lets you, and you don't know if He will until you try."

******

Slow to fall asleep that night, Henning relived the changes in his life after his mother died of cholera. He had been thirteen, living in Hamburg, Germany. Unable to force himself to attend her burial he'd walked a solitary pilgrimage to her favorite places, imagining her beside him.

The next day he was sent to live with his father's father. Grandpa Dietzel sharecropped a worn-out patch of land belonging to wealthy Lord Marcus Herr Becker who provided seed, tools, and living quarters in exchange for a share of the profits. His grandfather put him to work but otherwise ignored him.

Henning's loneliness eased when a stray black and white dog adopted him. For two days it furiously wagged its tail when it saw him and slept by his feet at night. After his grandfather complained that he had no food to spare, the dog disappeared. Henning suspected the old man had killed it.

Peasants like Henning weren't entitled to an education. Because his father was in the Prussian cavalry, he'd previously attended a military school. No such facility was available near Grandpa Dietzel. But Herr Becker saw something special in Henning and enrolled him in the exclusive Maximilian Academy for Boys. And since Henning's twelve-hour work days saved his grandfather the expense of a hired hand, Herr Becker had to force the old man to let Henning attend.

On the eve of his first day at the Academy, Henning looked forward to something for the first time in months. Starved for the company of other boys and eager to make a good impression, he begged his grandfather to cut his hair. Begrudgingly the old man slapped a bowl over his head and snipped off the protruding locks with scissors.

Next Henning washed his shirt and trousers. Already tall, he was still growing. Frayed at the cuffs, his shirtsleeves ended well above both wrists. And baggy, patched pant legs left his bony ankles exposed. But these were his only clothes and he ironed them, knowing the shirt's wrinkles would return and the trousers' creases would disappear during his walk to school.

At the academy, senior class president Hans Krüger made himself the center of attention in a hallway full of students who wore the latest styles and were professionally barbered.

"I hereby dub thee the foul and pestilent congregation of vapors," he pungently greeted Henning. Turning to his audience, he added, "That insult was the only useful thing I learned in my Shakespeare class."

A week later, schoolbooks Henning needed to study for his first exam vanished from the locker for which he couldn't afford a lock. They reappeared after he flunked the test. He was positive Krüger was the culprit.

One of that seemingly endless year's rare pleasures was Professor von Duisburg's gorgeous daughter, Christiane. Henning's secret infatuation with her didn't rise to the level of unrequited love because she didn't know he existed. And when she finally detected his interest, she responded with callous public mockery.

Shunned by his peers, Henning felt lucky if even the teachers and staff spoke to him. The one exception—*Fräulein* Lange, the librarian—sensed that characters in books were his only friends. She recommended two novels with poverty stricken protagonists who were otherwise superior to those who ridiculed them.

"Like the main characters in these books," she said, handing both to Henning as the library closed one evening, "you shouldn't be embarrassed by your economic standing. That's only one measure of a person, and a poor one." Reminding Henning of his mother she gently asked, "Are you open to a little advice?"

"From you...yes," he replied.

"Your devotion to Professor von Duisburg's daughter, Christiane, is touching, but I sense that you don't think you deserve her. The truth is the other way around. She isn't worthy of your exceptional mind and compassionate heart."

Though embarrassing, Fräulein Lange's words were comforting.

CHAPTER THREE

THE DUEL

Henning almost quit school after his freshman year. But with foresight unusual for boys his age, he decided four miserable years were preferable to a lifetime of poverty—Hans Krüger notwithstanding. Krüger, a Prussian general's son, was the underclassmen's most persistent tormentor and had taken special interest in Henning.

Tired of being bullied, Henning enrolled in the Academy's boxing class.

"Your physical skills are adequate, *Herr* Dietzel," his instructor told him early on. "Your attitude, however, is all wrong. Why do we learn to box?"

"To be able to defend ourselves," Henning replied.

"Would you like to make another feeble guess?"

"No, *Herr* Instructor."

"We learn boxing to help us project confidence so we don't have to fight."

The Friday before final exams, Henning rushed through his work in the fields and hurried to the school library where he studied furiously. By the time the library's doors closed behind him, he was exhausted. Trudging down an otherwise empty hall he rounded a corner and saw two boys in front of his open locker. One, Hans Krüger, held Henning's year-end essays in his meaty hand, reading aloud while his constant companion, Helmut Meyer, chuckled contemptuously.

"Those are mine," Henning cried out. Half his annual grade depended on those pages. They had taken months to research and were due before final exams on Monday.

Briefly Henning and Krüger stood eye to eye, then Henning looked away. They were the same height, but Krüger was older and much more substantial.

"I'm going to read these to my other friends," Krüger said, cramming Henning's essays into his coat pocket.

"Give them to me or I'll tell the headmaster you stole them."

"Whiny babies run to headmasters. Men stand up for themselves," Krüger snarled. "And calling me a thief slanders my good name, obliging me to do this." He slapped Henning's cheek with a glove as though challenging him to a duel.

"This is the Maximilian Academy—not the University of Heidelberg," Henning said, convinced Krüger was joking.

Heidelberg's students often settled disagreements with sabers. The antagonists wore leather armor and steel goggles, and tried to draw first blood from their opponents' faces. To many, the resulting scars were sought-after badges of honor. But dueling with swords was forbidden in pre-university schools.

"Heidelberg's duels usually end quickly," Krüger said. "Here, however, we use wooden canes instead of swords and the head is out of bounds. Our contest will continue until you yield unless you're afraid to face me."

"Where and when?" Henning asked.

"In the gym in a half hour. Don't be late."

"*Herr* Krüger has been the Academy champion four straight years," Meyer needled as Henning turned away. "You'd better bring an assistant in case you need stitches."

Twenty minutes later Henning entered a white gymnasium with a high ceiling supported by massive timbers. Krüger was warming up, a protective leather suit clinging to his barrel chest and tapered torso. His hardwood cane hissed as he swung it. Rumor was, the tip had been drilled and a weight inserted to deliver a heavier blow.

"Where are my essays?" Henning asked with bravado he didn't feel.

Krüger pointed to wads of paper on the floor. While Henning gathered them, Helmut Meyer slammed down a wicker basket of dueling canes and commanded him to, "Choose your weapon and pay me."

"I don't have any money," Henning said.

"Pay by this weekend." Meyer handed over the shortest cane.

"I won't have money by then either."

"You'd better find some."

The Academy required protective pads and adult supervision for these contests. In the absence of either, Krüger sent Meyer outside as a lookout. Alone now Henning and Krüger raised their canes in the mandatory salute, then began circling, their footsteps echoing in the big empty room.

Krüger was cat-quick. Powerful. Unpredictable. Henning never knew where the hardwood blade would pound him next. First, his thighs were crisscrossed by stinging welts. Then his shoulders. Finally his elbow—with no cushion between skin and bone—was split open.

Dripping blood, Henning swung until exhausted. Sometimes he missed because his cane was too short, but usually for lack of skill. Frustration and anger replaced his fear. He wanted Krüger to pay for being a bully. To feel pain. To doubt himself.

"It's time to cry uncle, whiny boy," Krüger goaded.

"Not yet."

Conserving energy, Henning swung his cane less often. Krüger stepped up his attack. Burning spasms radiated from blows to Henning's hip, shin, and forearm. In total command now, Krüger hadn't yet been hit. But he had to open his mouth to suck in enough air. And he was no longer enjoying himself.

"You've had enough. I'm declaring victory," Krüger proclaimed. Sweat glistening on his forehead, he turned away. Henning's cane touched him for the first time. Just the tip. Gently, between the shoulder blades.

"I think you're the one," Henning managed between breaths, "who's had enough."

Krüger whirled and raised his wooden sword.

The gym door slammed against the wall. Without coming inside, Meyer gasped, "Headmaster's coming."

Krüger dashed outside. His victory had been absolute, but Henning's refusal to yield seemed to have disheartened him.

Fighting for breath Henning made his blood on the floor less visible by smearing it with his shoe. His wounds throbbed but the pain was tolerable. Never again would Krüger back him down with the threat of physical punishment. The humiliation that came from being pushed around was far worse.

Bathed in sweat, Henning slid the rented cane down his pant leg as footsteps in the hallway grew louder.

"Good evening, Headmaster Klein," he greeted the formidable man who came in.

"I'm surprised to find you here at this late hour, *Herr* Dietzel." The headmaster paused, waiting for an explanation.

"I'm just leaving, sir."

"For good reason, you're required to wear exercise clothes here," Klein said with a disgusted glance at Henning's sweat-soaked shirt.

"I don't have any."

"Buy some."

Facing his bloody sleeve away from the headmaster, Henning started for an exit.

"Why the stiff leg?" Klein asked.

"I twisted my ankle, but it's not serious."

******

That weekend, Henning cut wheat fourteen hours a day while his grandfather stacked it in shocks to dry. He also stayed up most of both nights, neatly copying the essays Krüger had wrinkled and smudged. Monday he handed them in and took his final examinations, then rejoined Grandpa Dietzel in the field.

Though the afternoon was chilly, the hard work soon overheated him. He removed his shirt. Pausing to inspect his itchy, throbbing elbow he saw thick yellow pus in a violently red gash.

"You should have the school nurse take care of that," his grandfather told him.

"If I do, she'll ask who did it," Henning said. "When I refuse to tell her, I'll be suspended from school."

"Make up a story."

"Can't you please buy some iodine?"

"Why would I buy something you can get free? If you're too proud to lie to a nurse, you can steal some."

"I'm not a thief."

"And I'm not rich."

Later that day, Herr Becker saw dried blood on Henning's sleeve and insisted on examining his elbow. Pressed to explain the festering split there, Henning briefly described the duel, without names. Becker bought him iodine, a padlock, and three changes of the nicest clothes he'd ever owned— adding to previous kindnesses and making Henning feel he wasn't alone in the world.

Before padlocking his locker that afternoon, Henning opened it and found a note demanding he return the dueling cane and pay by Friday. 'If you don't,' the message ended, 'what you owe will double every day until you do.'

Henning rushed to the library. Breathing in the aromas of old leather bindings, furniture polish, and incense he studied until alone. Then he searched for coins beneath cushions on sofas and chairs, lifting them gingerly because touching velvet gave him chills. Almost done, he heard voices and turned to see Hans Krüger standing behind him.

"Well if it isn't the foul and pestilent congregation of vapors stealing money that belongs to his betters," Krüger snarled. "How much have you found?"

Henning opened his hand, displaying three *pfennigs*. Then he closed it into a tight fist and said, "I almost have enough to pay the rent on my dueling cane."

Krüger held out his palm. "Those must have fallen from my pocket. I recognize them."

"They're for *Herr* Meyer." Henning slipped the coins into his pocket.

"Do you honestly think I'll let you pay for your dueling cane with my money?" Krüger stepped forward aggressively.

Henning held his ground, face showing the steely determination it had during their duel. Krüger retreated a step.

"Pay your rental fee by tomorrow night or you'll be sorry," he growled, a clear attempt to regain any respect he might have lost by backing off.

As Krüger ambled away, Henning realized his boxing instructor had been right about the advantages of confidence. But poverty had no advantages. He resumed his search for coins, vowing that one day he'd have all the money he could possibly want.

Now, four years later on the other side of the world, Henning had an opportunity to fulfill that pledge. But he had doubts about Eduardo Vásquez,

Roberto Flores, and their companions. He could've found out whether or not they were trustworthy if they'd been from Valparaiso, but they weren't.

For all he knew they planned to take him to California, ditch him, and steal his deposit.

CHAPTER FOUR
GUESTS IN SOMEONE ELSE'S HOME

At noon the next day Henning was in front of Valparaiso's cathedral. The Chileans arrived an hour late.

"Ready to go shopping?" Eduardo asked, as calmly as if this were an ordinary day.

Setting out, they passed two black-robed nuns with faces surrounded by starched white wimples.

Block after block of booths bordered the market's narrow streets. In one area their occupants sold everything from axes and buckets to clothes. In another they offered fresh vegetables, fruit, and meat. Here and there restaurants gave off the aromas of baking bread, frying meat, and simmering sauces.

Henning stayed behind at the shop where his companions purchased shovels.

"Pine breaks easily," he told the man behind the counter. "Do you have any with hardwood handles?"

"I have some tucked away for discerning customers." The man took one from a closet. "Mind you, they cost twice as much."

"I can buy better shovels for much less." Henning handed it back.

"I'll give you a twenty percent discount," the merchant offered.

"Make it thirty and I'll buy two." Henning took out his wallet.

The merchant shook his head, then changed his mind as Henning started for the door.

New shovels across his shoulder Henning caught up with Eduardo's group and tagged along, buying what they bought. Towering, blue-eyed, with sunlight catching his golden hair, he stood out. When the number of curious little boys tagging along had doubled, he bought six chocolate bars, broke them into thirds, and passed them out—ignoring the imp who'd gotten back in line after receiving his share.

Back at the docks Eduardo and the other Chileans bought passage to San Francisco on *Portales*, the ship that first brought news of California's gold. The new captain, a German named Schulz, was trying to replace a crewman he'd discharged after hearing the man intended to jump ship in San Francisco.

"I'd apply for the job but I too plan to stay in California," Henning said, in English out of courtesy to the Chileans who spoke it but not German.

"Goot. You honest." Schulz slapped Henning's shoulder. "Job is yours. This is my first time on *Portales*. I hire extra man. By time ve in San Francisco, I don't need you longer."

Portales wouldn't sail for hours so the Chileans left for their favorite saloon. Henning went back to the market. Earlier he'd seen something irresistible, a man selling books. Finding none about gold, he bought several written by naturalists, a new breed of scientists who were expanding man's knowledge of his world.

With what he'd saved by not paying passage Henning bought rum and tobacco, to be sold at a profit in California. Then he returned to *Portales*. From its deserted deck he watched the ocean rise and fall while breathing its tangy combinations of seaweed, iodine, salt, and something he couldn't identify. He was nostalgic about leaving Encinas by the time Eduardo's group returned.

Eyeing Henning's latest purchases, Eduardo groused, "You'll have to carry that shit when we hike from San Francisco to wherever the gold is. Don't expect us to slow down for you. Taking goods to sell is worth the effort, but you need to get rid of the books."

"If I had to give up one or the other," Henning said, "the choice would be difficult."

The first mate showed Eduardo and the other Chileans to passenger cabins, then locked up Henning's rum and tobacco. Assigned a narrow upper berth in the ordinary seamen's tight, stale quarters, Henning climbed into it.

As usual his fellow crewmen were Hispanic. Most were outstanding physical specimens who neglected their health and hygiene. Flushed faces and trembling hands suggested some drank excessively. Others had dry raspy coughs, most likely caused by smoking vegetable greens scavenged in markets because they couldn't afford tobacco.

Sitting on a crate, one was filing a chunk of wood into a club. Seeing Henning's interest, he explained. "I felt naked after the new captain took our weapons."

A man putting an edge on a strip of rusty iron said, "Myself, I prefer a blade. How about you, kid, you got a way to defend yourself?"

"No." Henning's exact copy of the long knife Jim Bowie had used at the Great Sandbar Duel wasn't a weapon. It was a memento of his childhood hero and now reminded him of his mother who'd hoarded bits of her grocery money for months to buy it for him.

Someone slammed the room's only door and a group huddled together, organizing a fist fight with bets riding on the outcome.

"Keep your voices down," one said. "Cap'n Schulz promised a whipping for anyone caught gambling." With a sliver of coal he wrote down wagers as men whispered them.

The man with the club frowned when Henning pulled a book from his knapsack. Like most of Henning's past crewmates, he seemed suspicious of people who could read.

Henning yawned. He had enjoyed a sailor's life, but Encinas was right. He should put his mind to better use. And with luck California would provide the perfect opportunity.

******

When *Portales's* sails needed adjusting, sailors climbed into the rigging and manned lines that turned, raised, or lowered yardarms. Having done everything possible to avoid this backbreaking job, Henning's crewmates were amazed every time he volunteered.

"My reason is simple," he answered one puzzled man. "I want to be in the best possible condition when I get to California."

Former crewmates had used Henning's wiry physique and mild manner to obtain good odds when matching him against boxers from other ships. He lost his first fight then won five straight, earning a reputation for toughness. Rather than lose his shipmates' admiration, he'd hidden his intellect. Sailors didn't trust cerebral people, and he'd wanted to fit in.

Hungry for a friend with whom he could be himself, Henning admired Eduardo's flair for language and the enjoyment he got from discussing the why of thinkers as well as the how of doers. But so far the man's gruffness and the difference in their ages had kept him at arm's length.

Eduardo was all smiles as he came on deck the third morning of the voyage.

"You don't seem to realize that prospecting is hard work," he teased as Henning climbed down from adjusting sails. "Otherwise you'd conserve your energy, rather then squander it on the hardest job this scow offers."

Eduardo's playful tone encouraged Henning's response. "Begging your pardon, your honor, but I'm getting myself in better condition—which is hardly a waste of energy."

"Energy is like fine wine," was Eduardo's elegant rejoinder. "Squander it and you won't have enough when you need it."

"That may be true for men of advanced age," Henning shot back. "For the young, however, energy is like muscles. The more we use, the more we have."

Their sparring continued throughout the voyage. Holding his own more than once, Henning sensed mutual respect and even affection developing, as it often did when men met worthy opponents.

******

After paralleling Alta California's coast for days *Portales* made a sweeping turn east. Under a clear sky and bright sun Henning and Eduardo stood together at the rail as their ship navigated a gusty channel between cliffs. Emerging into a large bay they scanned the barren shoreline, searching for the city that had dominated their dreams for weeks.

Portales headed for a rundown wharf. Not having been lowered, an anchored windjammer's shredded sails snapped in the breeze. Henning eyed the weather-beaten shanties on the shore behind.

"San Francisco," the first mate announced. "It's probably not as grand as you gentlemen was expectin'."

After helping dock *Portales*, Henning stood beside Eduardo watching men on the wharf.

"If there's gold," Eduardo whispered, "why aren't those guys looking for it?"

The answer was obvious as soon as they started down the gangplank. The waiting men were elderly, unsound, or in poor health.

"Welcome," one boomed, despite his frail appearance. "I'm in charge of receiving freight. I 'spect you got a delivery fer me?"

"Ya," Schulz replied with his thick German accent. "Ve unload now. How you pay?"

"In gold," the agent said.

Winking at Henning, Eduardo whispered, "That's a relief. Apparently California's gold isn't a figment of someone's imagination."

"Vare you vant freight?" Schulz glanced back at his crew, gathered along *Portales*'s rail beyond earshot.

"There." The agent stabbed a finger toward moisture-stained crates at the dock's far end.

"No varehouse?" Schulz asked.

"Nope, and no one to build one. Everyone but us is in the Gold Country."

"Then it's true that gold has been discovered?" Eduardo asked in excellent English.

"Yup," the agent said. "Cain't say how much or exactly where, but—"

"Please to have this conversation later," Schulz interrupted.

"You worried your crew will jump ship?" Eduardo needled.

"Vare vent men from vindjammer?" Schulz asked.

"You're wasting your time," Henning said in German. "The crew already knows about the gold."

"No sense in making it any more tempting," Schultz countered, more comfortable in his native language.

"Can you please deliver this next time you're in Talcahuano?" Henning handed Schulz a coin and a thick envelope addressed to Encinas.

"I'll see to it." Schulz went aboard, then strapped on a sidearm and focused his attention on the men taking cargo ashore.

"Has anyone come back after going to the goldfields?" Eduardo asked the freight agent.

"Some merchants been back to pick up supplies."

"What did they say?"

"Just that there's a bonanza in the Sierra Nevada Mountains, east of here. They been back twice to order supplies and leave gold to pay for 'em. They're due any day now to pick up the cargo that came on that windjammer."

"Hopefully we'll see them along the trail," Eduardo said. "Do you know which way they'll come?"

"Ain't but one trail to the Gold Country." The agent pointed at the far shore. "It begins this side of them three knolls over yonder."

"Looks like we have to cross ten miles of water to get there," Eduardo said.

"More like fourteen," the agent observed. "You can tip *Portales's* captain to take you."

"As soon as his ship weighs anchor, he'll head for the ocean rather than give his crew a chance to jump ship. Can we hire you to take us across?"

"We ain't got no canoes or rowboats. Not even a raft. They all got left on the other shore during the stampede outta here."

"Got any horses or mules for sale?"

"There was precious few to start with and they're all in the Gold Country now."

"How'd they get across the bay?"

"They din't. They went around. You'll hafta do the same." The freight agent stepped off the dock and knelt to draw a map in the sand. "You're on the tip of a peninsula with the bay on one side and the ocean on the other. The Gold Country is east of here, but you hafta go fifty miles south to get around the bay. After that the trail goes north on the opposite shore and then curves east near them three knolls I showed ya."

"Much obliged for your help." Eduardo rotated toward his companions. "Time to get our oars in the water, gentlemen."

"The day's half-gone," Roberto challenged. "If we're smart, we'll get a good night's sleep and leave in the morning. That way we—"

"We're leaving now," Eduardo interrupted. "I want a head start in case *Portales's* crew jumps ship."

Keeping the bay in sight, they hiked through rolling country covered with sunbaked ryegrass and tinder-dry scrub brush. Fast afoot, Eduardo left the others behind. Henning kept up with everyone else despite carrying more weight. As they made camp, the heat remained oppressive. Rather than light a campfire, they ate bread and cold sausage.

At sunset thick pearly fog crested the coastal hills to their west and flowed toward them, hugging the ground and cooling the air. Refreshed, they slept soundly.

After breakfast the next morning, Henning was the only one who bothered to shave.

"You won't find any fetching girls out here," Eduardo teased, starting down the trail.

"Never hurts to be prepared," Henning called after him, folding his straight razor.

Eduardo steadily pulled away as they continued south under a blistering sun. By midday the others, drenched in sweat, had fallen behind Henning. As the sun slid below the horizon, he came upon Eduardo, sprawled on the ground, asleep at the campsite he'd chosen. Worn out, Henning shed his heavy pack.

"Where are the others?" Eduardo asked, sitting up.

"About three miles back," Henning replied.

"Don't give me that. They're fast on their feet if you don't compare them to me." Eduardo stood and studied the trail, then shrugged. "It's true. They're way back there."

As twilight darkened, the others reached camp and collapsed. By then Henning and Eduardo had eaten three sandwiches apiece.

"Henning's work on *Portales* put him in good shape," Roberto acknowledged begrudgingly. "Considering the weight he's carrying, he was impressive today."

"A compliment from Roberto Flores?" Eduardo asked with mock amazement.

"He better enjoy it," Flores grumped. "It's the last he'll get from me." He ate two of the sandwiches Henning had made and piled on tin plates, then fell asleep on his bedroll, fully dressed.

"You remind me of me," Eduardo told Henning. "If I have a son somewhere, which is a distinct possibility, I hope he's like you."

Henning lowered his eyes. From a man like Eduardo any compliment— no matter how flippant—was appreciated.

******

Midway through the third day, the faint trail rounded the bay's southern tip and became a well-beaten track going north. Soon after that, Eduardo stopped on a hilltop. When Henning and the others caught up, they looked back and saw riders coming.

Eduardo greeted the horsemen as they raced past. They swiveled their heads and glared.

"Go back where you came from," one shouted.

Later another unfriendly group passed.

"Apparently the call of gold is bringing men from southern California," Eduardo said, "and their hostility means they don't welcome foreign competitors. We'd best keep our mouths shut when Yankees are around so they don't hear our accents."

The trail swerved east near the three knolls they'd seen from the bay's other side. The hills of San Francisco were no more than fourteen miles away, but Henning and his companions had hiked a hundred miles to get there.

Another day's trek brought them to the Carquinez Strait, where they got in line behind riders and wagons waiting for the ferry.

"Anyone on foot?" a deckhand asked.

Eduardo's group raised their hands.

"We can fit you into nooks and crannies too small for horses or wagons," the deckhand said, waving them to the head of the line.

"Them damn furiners should go last—not first," a man in a stovepipe hat shouted.

"First come, first served," another yelled. "What makes them bastards any better'n us?"

Roberto had heard all he could stomach. "The next idiot who makes a stupid remark," he fumed, rolling his hands into fists, "will have to back it up."

"When you're outnumbered hundreds to one in someone else's country, you need a sense of humor," Eduardo said, grabbing Roberto's arm and steering him toward the ferry.

They paid full fare and were ordered to cram themselves under a wagon.

"There's not enough room under here," Roberto complained.

"Enough for Mexicans," the deckhand growled.

"It'll just make them angrier if you tell them we're Chilean," Eduardo cautioned. "To Yankees, all greasers are the same."

On the opposite shore, Eduardo no longer had to prod his companions. Not wishing to be overtaken by their tormentors they sped up without urging. When riders finally passed, one respectfully touched a finger to his hat brim and told Henning, "Can't believe you're makin' such good time carryin' a pack that size."

"Why don't you lighten my load by buying some tobacco and rum?" Henning asked with a saleman's grin.

Slowing his horse the man brightened, but his friends refused to stop.

Three days later in the Sierra Nevada foothills, Eduardo's group passed five prospectors headed west, away from the Gold Country. They had ragged clothes, bushy beards, and long hair held in pony tails by leather thongs. Their heavy, lumpy packs indicated they'd struck it rich.

"Where you headed?" Eduardo asked, breaking his own rule against speaking to strangers.

"Back to San Francisco," one replied. "You're too late. The gold played out last week."

CHAPTER FIVE
A PROMISE KEPT

His enthusiasm sapped by the news, Henning dropped his heavy pack and lowered himself to the ground. The Chileans did likewise—except for Eduardo who roared, "Get up and put your packs back on. We don't have time to fritter away."

"What's the hurry?" Roberto asked. "We're too late."

"You believe those half-wits?"

"Why would they lie?"

"They're not lying. They're telling the truth as they see it. There's no gold left in plain sight, but what was found so far is nothing compared to what's still here."

"How do you know?" Roberto asked.

"Because it was that way in Brazil and every other strike I've ever heard of. That fool and his friends were spoiled by finding nuggets lying on the ground or in shallow water. They don't know how to pan streams and soil. I do and that little secret will make us rich, but not while you sit on your backsides."

Eduardo started down the trail. His analysis made sense to Henning. The men returning to San Francisco were carrying enough gold to make them wealthy. Tired of living as if destitute, they weren't willing to sweat for more of what had come so easily.

Henning stood and shouldered his pack, then told Roberto, "Eduardo's right. We're wasting time."

Looking back and seeing Henning close behind, Eduardo gave one of his exaggerated winks. One by one the others scrambled to their feet and followed. On his way past Henning, Roberto turned his head and scowled— not for the first time.

Four days into the hills they reached a stream that slid across a yellow meadow carpeted with buttercups and golden poppies. Eduardo ordered them to search the area. After Henning found a nugget, half buried in mud, everyone staked out a claim. Then the Chileans exploited Henning's discovery while he set up camp.

The following morning everyone else stockpiled gold while Henning washed laundry, trapped rabbits, cooked beans, and baked biscuits. In the afternoon he dug a fire pit and lined it with stones before chopping fallen trees into firewood.

For two more days Henning's companions panned gold while he built lean-tos and cooked. At week's end he had made a place to eat by chopping the branches from two fallen trees, parallel and six feet apart. At lunchtime the Chileans sat on the logs, facing each other, tin plates on their laps, chuckling in appreciation of the crude Dining Room sign Henning had carved in a nearby tree. Then Roberto shouted for Henning to hurry up and serve their meal.

Dishing out bacon and biscuits, Henning told Eduardo, "In exchange for my labor you promised to show me how to pan gold. Can we start tomorrow?"

"We've been slow to keep our part of the bargain, haven't we?" Eduardo said.

"The rest of us have no obligation to this boy," Roberto barked as if Henning wasn't there.

"Oh yes you do," Eduardo contradicted. "In exchange for doing our chores, we agreed to teach him to pan gold."

"You agreed to teach him. I was drunk at the time," Roberto fired back. "But if you'd spelled out the details the next day, I'd have told you not to give him such a one-sided deal."

"Have you forgotten we get everything he pans for six weeks?"

"That won't be much. By the time he's any good at panning, he'll be out on his own competing with us."

"Why did you wait until now to object? You weren't drunk when he gave us his deposit."

"We could teach him a few things, I suppose," Roberto conceded.

"A few things? To properly repay this boy for working as hard as he is, you'll have to be this open with him." Eduardo's fist sprang open, palm up, fingers wide apart.

"Let's compromise. We'll teach Henning if he gives us everything he pans for three months."

"We already agreed on six weeks. If you and the others don't live up to that, you'll lose the benefits along with the obligation."

Impressed by Eduardo's forceful defense, Henning followed the voices back and forth as if watching a tennis match. Only his mother and Herr Becker had ever stood up for him. And that was long ago.

The next morning Roberto and the others again refused to teach Henning so Eduardo took him to the stream.

"Panning isn't as easy as it looks," he began, then demonstrated the proper technique.

After scooping up a mix of sand, gravel, and water, Henning swirled his pan attempting to create a current that would carry lighter materials over its sloping sides while the heavier gold settled to the bottom. But when the sand and gravel were gone, Henning's pan was empty. He tried again with similar results.

Twice during that time, Eduardo poured more yellow dust and flakes into his pouch.

"Keep trying," he encouraged. "You'll get the hang of it."

By midafternoon Henning was contributing pinches of gold to Eduardo's hoard. After dark he cooked rabbit for two while everyone else sat on rocks glumly eating beans.

Roberto left his group and stormed to the so-called dining room. Glaring at Eduardo and Henning, he fumed, "We brought this boy to do chores so we could use our time for panning. But after giving him too good a deal, you're the only one not fending for himself. That stinks."

He whirled and rejoined his friends.

"Because of me," Henning said sadly, "he's challenging your leadership."

"It won't get him anywhere. I know more about gold than he ever will. His friends will remember that as soon as they stop sulking."

******

Over Roberto's strenuous objections, Eduardo revealed some hard-earned secrets while he and Henning panned the river at sunrise.

"There's no end of useful little tricks that most prospectors never learn," he began. "I'll give you two every day you pan at least a half-ounce of gold."

"Which I did yesterday," Henning said.

"Until you get better at this, you should swirl the last of each panful above a metal tub to recapture gold that washes out. And wash your hands every hour so oil from your skin doesn't float on the water and prevent gold dust from settling."

A week into Henning's apprenticeship, he and Eduardo moved to a section of creek near madrone trees with shiny red leaves and papery, peeling, orange-red bark.

Eduardo broke a long silence. "What was your dad like?"

Henning didn't like personal questions but couldn't disappoint the man who'd lost friends standing up for him. Staring at his pan's swirling contents he replied, "I hardly knew him. He was stingy with his time."

"Was it painful when he left you with your grandfather?"

"He had joined the cavalry to get away from farming and knew I detested that life as much as he did. So yes, it hurt."

"Did he abandon you?"

"Not altogether. Some years he came to see me. He always brought wonderful gifts but what I wanted was more of his company."

Having finally managed to draw Henning out, Eduardo now responded in kind. "My father disappeared when I was nine, but I didn't miss him. He was one of those men who go silent for days if you displease them, and I was forever doing that."

"My father would drift away in the middle of conversations," Henning said. "I spent more time interpreting silences than words. He was always happiest on the day he returned to his regiment."

While he worked for Eduardo, Henning's only income came from selling the rum and tobacco he'd brought from Chile. He charged exorbitant Gold Country prices but had to pay the same for food and other necessities. He was nearly broke by the time he finally satisfied his obligation to Eduardo.

Now that everything he panned was his, Henning quit shaving his sparse, straggly beard even though it still made him look like an adolescent in the midst of an anxious puberty. Why waste time shaving when he could be adding to his wealth? Overnight he went from a hard worker whose efforts benefited someone else to a fanatic whose reward depended on his own efforts.

To his surprise—but not Eduardo's—he had a full-blown case of gold fever.

CHAPTER SIX
GREENER PASTURES

Henning was panning three hundred dollars a day when Eduardo—tempted by rumors of richer strikes—had his companions pull up stakes three times in three weeks. The first new diggings were inferior to those they'd left. The second location was no better. The third was producing plenty of gold. But every inch along its rushing river and the ravines feeding into it had already been claimed.

Hoping to find available ground, Henning and Eduardo spoke with a *Californio* who told them, "Last week, I was thrown off the best diggings here. It didn't matter that I was there first and descend from a man who was among California's first settlers. So I staked a claim in the *Californio* camp higher up, but there was no gold there."

Camps along the lower river housed unwelcoming communities of white *gringos* in tents, lean-to's, and structures of interwoven pine boughs covered with canvas. At Camp Betsy Ross, Eduardo's group passed a photographer who was taking people's pictures with the Stars and Stripes dramatically waving from a tree in the background.

"You're looking at a banner of freedom brought from an abandoned ship in San Francisco Bay by a patriotic sailor," the photographer told Eduardo. "He climbed the highest cedar here and nailed the flag to its top. Then he sawed off every branch on his way down so the damn foreigners can't take it down. Fer ten dollars I'll take your picture with it."

"No, *gracias.*" Eduardo's use of Spanish wasn't a slip of the tongue. He was sick of being treated like an outsider in a land where English-speakers had only recently arrived.

"*Gracias?*" The photographer jerked his thumb over his shoulder. "These prime diggings aren't for your kind. Take your ass upriver."

Crossing the next camp, they passed men bringing gravel from pits to rockers, wooden boxes resembling baby's cradles. These separated gold in greater quantities than pans did.

"We picked you as our leader because you claim to know everything about gold," Roberto sneered, glaring at Eduardo. "But the Yankees' method is faster than yours."

"Not for a group our size," Eduardo snapped. "Where would we get saws, hammers, and nails to build a rocker? How long would it take to cut trees into lumber? And how much gold would we produce with only six men? It takes several times that many to build and operate a rocker. For us, panning is better…unless you can charm the *gringos* into letting us join them."

All around, Henning saw men with red-blue, pinprick size spots at the base of corkscrew shaped arm hair. Having seen those symptoms at sea, he always went out of his way to eat fruit and vegetables. But those were expensive and seldom available. As a result many prospectors had scurvy. And their health deteriorated for other reasons, too. In camp after camp they ate spoiled food, stood all day in icy water, wore filthy clothes, and relieved themselves near the same river where they drank.

In Mormon Camp Henning passed a pine box containing the first corpse he'd ever seen. Noticing his interest a man said, "Josiah came all the way from Salt Lake City."

"How'd he die?" Henning asked.

"He was sick when he got here. Whatever he had killed him three days after his partner lost his footing and drowned."

Farther along, angry miners had surrounded a Peruvian aristocrat and his South American Indian servants.

"You can't use slaves, and that's final," a Yankee shouted.

"What gives you the right to make rules?" the Peruvian demanded.

"The same thing that gave us the right to run *Californios* and their Ohlone Indian laborers off the Feather River," the Yankee snapped. "And the same thing that'll give us the right to kick out southerners who bring niggers. This is America's gold and if you outsiders want some, you'll have to do as we say."

No law governed the size of claims, who could stake them, or under what circumstances. Each community made its own regulations. Like all Gold Country rules, these were written, interpreted, and enforced by whoever imposed his will.

Eduardo and Henning passed a tent filled with tables and men playing cards. Twice a man hovering near the entrance started in and then restrained himself. Studying Eduardo he tentatively asked, "Eduardo? Eduardo Vásquez?"

Eduardo brightened. "Pedro. I didn't recognize you with the beard. So you came to California after all. How are you?"

"I'd be a lot better if I stayed out of these public houses. Three nights ago I won thousands playing monte. Next day I lost everything. This morning I worked myself half to death on the rockers and filled this pouch." He held it up. "And now I'm resisting the urge to get rich the easy way."

"There is no easy way," Eduardo said. "You'll lose a fortune trying to find one. Why don't you join up with us instead?"

"Maybe I'll come looking for you later." Red-faced, Pedro ducked into the tent.

Henning shifted his weight from one foot to the other.

"In a hurry?" Eduardo asked.

"Tired of wasting time. Let's go upstream and stake out claims."

"Learning that gambling can be a sickness was worth a few minutes, wasn't it?"

"No. Games of chance don't tempt me. I like things I can control."

"In that case, you must not like many things."

Finally Eduardo and his group reached unclaimed ground where they panned promising samples of sand, gravel, and dirt. Called prospecting, this process evaluated potential claims and had given gold rush miners their nickname, prospectors. This time, the results were dismal.

They worked their way up to where bushy, chartreuse wolf lichen clung to the trunks and branches of redwood trees. There Roberto found a speck of gold and the group spread out. Eduardo and Henning worked together as usual, as did Roberto and his friends. None found what they sought.

"This is the only good thing here," a neighbor said, stuffing wolf lichen into his pack. "It's an excellent poison for wolves and coyotes. Their pelts will sell for big money once it turns cold."

"Panning here will get us nothing but backaches," Eduardo told Henning. "Time to move on. Word is there's a big strike up north."

Rising to his feet Henning said, "The creek where we started is still the best place we've found. Why don't we go back?"

"Do you know what a bonanza is?" Eager to make his point, Eduardo answered his own question. "It's a strike that yields thousands of dollars a day—not hundreds."

"Before we started moving around, we were each averaging three hundred dollars a day. That's more than I used to earn in a year."

"You're too easily satisfied. Faced with the opportunity of a lifetime, all you want to do is put the tip of one toe in the water. Don't be content with a pittance. There's a jackpot out there and we're gonna find it."

"Leaving a proven claim to chase bonanzas is gambling, and as I said earlier..."

"Pack up." Eduardo buckled the straps on his knapsack and slid his arms through its straps, then faced Henning and asked, "Ready?"

"I'm not going with you." Henning squared his shoulders. "The way I see it, our first claim was a jackpot and we shouldn't have left. I'm going back. How much of my deposit will it take to release me from my remaining obligation?"

"Are you serious?"

Looking ready to rub his hands together with glee, Roberto asked Eduardo, "How many times did I tell you this kid would be a bad investment?"

Living with a grandfather who never let him make up his own mind, Henning had resolved to never again be pushed around. Despite that he'd followed Eduardo three times, against his better judgment. And he now had three thousand dollars less than he would have had if he'd trusted his instincts.

"I'm tired of chasing rumors," he said gently. "I prefer a sure thing. Is there any way I can convince you to go back to our first claim?"

"Absolutely not. To reap big rewards, a man has to take risks. I'm moving on."

Looking into the eyes of the man who'd been his defender and friend, Henning said, "I hope you find a bonanza that makes you the richest man in Chile. You deserve it."

Eduardo wheeled around and stormed away. "We're no longer friends," he shouted over his shoulder without looking back. "If you haven't taught my secrets to the Yankees by the next time we see each other, I'll return a third of your deposit."

Roberto's only goodbye was an obscene hand gesture.

Henning shouldered his belongings and began the long trek. Glad to be free of the surly Roberto, who'd never warmed to him, he already missed Eduardo. And still considered him a kinder, less-distant version of his father.

******

Completely alone for the first time in his life, Henning reached his original claim in two days. Relieved no one had moved in, he set up camp on a hillside covered with greenish-gray shale. For days he wondered if his former companions were amassing mountains of gold while he wasted time on a molehill. But after a week of panning three hundred dollars a day, he was satisfied with his decision to come back. Not, however, with being alone.

Beside his glowing campfire he wrote his first letters in weeks. For Encinas—the only woman he'd ever loved—he described the future he wanted to give her. And he told his grandfather about prospecting and life in the Gold Country. When he had nothing more to say, he stared at the blur of smoke above his fire, clearing his mind for sleep.

When merchants passed through, Henning paid them to dispatch his letters by ship next time they picked up goods in San Francisco. Correspondence sent that way could easily go astray. He liked to think that was why his letters to Grandpa Dietzel hadn't brought answers.

In fact, the only letter he'd received since leaving his grandfather's farm had come from Maximilian Academy's librarian, *Fräulein* Lange. Mostly full of praise, it also informed him that Professor von Duisburg's daughter had married a man who treated her as shabbily as she had Henning.

One afternoon a merchant told him, "San Francisco's postal service is offering private boxes, where mail can be received. I can put one in your name and bring you the key for a hundred bucks."

Having a return address would make it possible for Encinas to write him. And though a hundred dollars had recently been six-month's wages and still sounded like a lot, it now represented only a few hours' work.

"Sign me up," Henning said. "I'm dying to hear from my lady."

Being out of touch with Encinas for months had made him uncertain she still loved him. But if she did, his days would soon offer much more than gravel, sand, and gold flecks swirling in a pan.

CHAPTER SEVEN
FRENCHIE'S CANYON

Unhappy with the amount of gold he was now finding, Henning worked his way upstream. For a week he panned narrow ravines near a jagged rock formation that resembled a compound fracture. Still not satisfied, he followed the river up to a gorge labeled Frenchie's Canyon on his newly bought map.

There, a section of rain-swollen creek had recently rerouted itself. Starting with the first panful, sand and gravel from its former bed yielded enough gold to satisfy even Eduardo Vásquez. To take full advantage before competitors found out about this bonanza, Henning resolved to stay through the winter.

November's rains swelled Sierra Nevada creeks and rivers, making them dangerous and driving other '48ers from the Gold Country.

"We'll hole up in San Francisco and resume prospecting in the spring," one of a group said as they passed Henning's camp. "You should do the same. Winters here are brutal."

As far as Henning knew, he was the only one who stayed behind. Day after day he panned until it was too dark to see, then sat in his lean-to reading or writing letters he couldn't mail until spring because traveling merchants too had quit the Gold Country.

These two nightly pastimes ceased after he ran out of whale oil for his lantern.

The first night of sub-freezing temperatures, he spread oilcloth and both his coats over his sleeping bag, then crawled in and hugged both knees to his chest. Still cold, he pulled his head inside so his breath would warm his shivering, tightly curled body.

Henning had a rule against wasting daylight on anything but finding gold. Granting himself a one-time exemption he spent an afternoon in his lean-to, building a stone fireplace. As darkness fell, he lit a pile of twigs to make sure his crude stick-and-mud chimney drew the smoke outside. Next he added logs. The resulting blaze brought warmth, light, and the cheery crackling his grandfather had called 'companionable.'

With his lean-to again illuminated at night, Henning resumed his reading and briefly forgot his worsening hunger. He'd bought food from prospectors on their way out of the Gold Country and supplemented it by trapping rabbits and squirrels. But with no firearm, he had to limit himself to two small meals a day. The grouse around his camp and elk bugling in the distance were beyond his reach.

To increase his gold production, Henning salvaged a battered metal tub and four nails from a burned-out lean-to. He pounded the dents out with a rock and scrubbed the rust away with sand, then drove the nails through the tub's bottom and into the side of a log. Rocked from side to side, his jury-rigged device functioned as a gold pan but processed more material.

He watched water swirl in the tub day after day, alert for what prospectors called color. Bored into a stupor, he stared through his reflection without seeing it and lost sight of his appearance. His beard became greasy and matted. His hair—no longer tied back because he wanted it to warm his neck and ears—twisted into straggly knots.

He knew something was wrong when he finally noticed his eyes, sunken in dark wrinkled sockets. For too long he'd pushed himself too hard. Now his thoughts were filled with the nonsense that occurs to those whose minds have no stimulation. Images of his tedious daily routine haunted him after he closed his eyes at night, preventing desperately needed sleep.

Perpetually cold, exhausted, and ravenous, he began to fear he was going crazy—never more than when he tried to figure out where the white in snow went as it melted. With all his heart and soul he longed for the day when he'd be able to eat his fill in a warm house shared with a wife—preferably Encinas. Losing more often that he won, he played countless variations of 'If that bird lands before it's out of sight, it means Encinas still loves me.'

Then he had a dream in which the woman with him wasn't her. He was sharing his happy future with someone else.

******

Americans called them camp robbers. They were squirrels and birds made bold by hunger. The one that targeted Henning near the end of that cruel, harsh winter was a whiskey jack, a long-tailed gray bird with black markings. No matter how often Henning chased it away or how well he secured his food, Jack always came back, hungry, hopeful, and noisy.

Before Henning ran out of flour, they shared scraps of dry bread while he talked and his guest seemed to listen. When Jack brought his mate Henning gave them tiny morsels of fat, which they received so enthusiastically that he almost offered more. But the small mammals he trapped were also losing weight, and he needed their fat to help his body warm itself.

One crisp morning Henning was awakened by something crashing against his lean-to. Outside he found Jack on the ground, knocked senseless. He'd read that wild birds could die of fright if they regained consciousness in human hands, so he sat on an upside down bucket, hoping for the best. A feathery blur flashed past. A hawk. Unwilling to abandon the prey it had chased into the side of Henning's shelter it winged skyward, Jack hanging from its talons. Henning's lunge missed.

That night he feared he'd finally lost his mind. What else could explain crying himself to sleep over a bird?

******

Henning's ordeal ended in early March when a merchant passing through Frenchie's Canyon sold him supplies. The man shook his head in disbelief when Henning said he'd been there all winter. After an hour of catching up on news from the outside world, Henning went back to working the exposed creek bed.

Now nineteen he'd grown his first acceptable beard, was emaciated, and breathed with a wheeze that was going away thanks to warmer weather. The merchant's respect had indicated he no longer seemed boyish. He certainly felt more like a man—and a wealthy one though he found it difficult to think of himself that way, living as he was.

When other prospectors saw Henning's leather pouches, stuffed like sausages and stacked like firewood, they staked out claims near his. They expected another year like the last, but newspapers back east had published letters sent to family and friends by '48ers. Those were read by farmers who cleared three hundred dollars a year, laborers who earned a dollar a day, and ex-soldiers still unemployed after the war with Mexico. Shortly after that, President James K. Polk officially confirmed the previous year's astonishing discovery in his State of the Union address.

The rush to California brought people from everywhere to the middle of nowhere. Ships from the East Coast delivered as many as eight hundred a day. Wagon trains brought thousands more, transforming the Oregon, Santa Fe, Gila River, California, and Mormon trails from faint paths into thoroughfares visible for miles. And no one had any idea how many foreigners were en route.

During the spring of 1849 Northern California's population doubled and redoubled. The '49ers were answering the call of quick and easy riches, but many were also escaping lives gone wrong. They included gamblers, prostitutes, liquor merchants, thieves, con men, and murderers. A year earlier gold had stood unprotected in the camps. Now it had to be guarded at all times.

Successive waves of restless Easterners and Southerners worked claims near Henning's and moved on, chasing rumors of easier pickings. By fall, Henning and five other foreigners were alone in Frenchie's Canyon.

For the first time since parting with Eduardo, Henning had friends who stimulated his mind and helped when a job was too much for one man. At night they got together, hungry for social contact and curious about one another. Among them, they spoke enough languages for all except Lee Wong, the Chinaman, to communicate.

Nonetheless Lee joined them, sitting quietly and laughing on cue though he didn't always seem to know why. Henning quickly came to respect this simple, thrifty, industrious man who bought only as much food as his body required and regularly sent money to his family in China.

The same age, Rodolfo Peschiera and Henning became constant companions. Cheerful and friendly, like other Italians Henning had met, Rodolfo had a talent for making people feel good. Every day before sunrise, they met at the creek and worked side by side, talking and joking. After dark they cooked over a common campfire and whispered together long after the others were asleep.

Henning had never known a man who did so little to hide his feelings. Every morning—as if they hadn't seen each other for weeks—Rodolfo gave him a hearty *abrazo*, the backslapping hug with which Latin men greeted each other. Embarrassed at first, Henning soon found himself looking forward to this pleasant ritual.

One afternoon a deer straggled into camp. Rodolfo shot at it from close range and missed. The deer trotted ten yards and stopped. Rodolfo fired again and it scurried out of sight.

"Are you a good shot?" he asked Henning, red-faced.

"My father was in the military," Henning replied. "He taught me to shoot."

"Could you have hit that deer?"

At such short range Henning could have hit it in the eye, but he sidestepped the question. "Maybe your sights aren't properly aligned or something's wrong with your ammunition."

"No need to go easy on me." Rodolfo flashed a self-deprecating grin. "Every Prussian I've met is direct to the point of rudeness. It's your birthright to be that way."

"Being direct with Italians isn't wise. Most are pretty thin-skinned."

"You Prussians are terrible at quick, clever repartee."

"Probably because we hate superfluous words, and repartee is quick and clever by definition. May I see one of your bullets?" Inspecting a paper cartridge that looked like a hand-rolled cigarette, Henning said, "Looks good. Let me see your rifle."

It was the first Colt Paterson Henning had seen. In the breech above the trigger was a rotating cylinder like those found in the pistols known as revolvers. This meant it could shoot five times in rapid succession, making it the world's fastest-firing rifle.

"That should help," Henning said after adjusting the rear sight with his knife. "But tell me something. This rifle can hold five cartridges. Why do you load only one?"

"Colt Patersons have a nasty habit of misfiring," Rodolfo replied, "which sets off all five chambers at once. "When that happens, the four bullets that don't go through the barrel amputate the hand supporting it. Hence the nickname, Colt's Revolving Wheel of Misfortune."

After setting a discarded tin can on a boulder, Henning returned and said, "Stand sideways and hold the stock firmly against your shoulder and cheek." He demonstrated. "Then close your left eye and line up the sights with your right. Take several deep breaths, let the last one halfway out and shoot.

When Rodolfo pulled the trigger he also moved the rifle, causing the bullet to miss it mark.

"Try it again with your feet farther apart," Henning said. "Then close your hand on the trigger. Don't jerk it."

Rodolfo loaded a single chamber and squeezed off a shot. The can flew from the rock and tumbled end over end.

"One dead can," he said, smiling broadly, "but if we ever need protection, I'm not the man for the job." He extended the Colt Paterson toward Henning. "It's yours."

"Keep it for hunting. I'm moving to the side canyon tomorrow."

"Come on. You don't have a gun and we may need someone who can hit what he shoots at. Please. Take it. I can live with not being able to shoot dinner. Can you live with having it be your fault if someone steals our gold?"

Henning scooped up a panful of gravel and water.

Rodolfo squatted beside him. "Hard-headed Kraut. If you ever need a rifle you'll find this one and plenty of ammunition under my lean-to. Anyone else would have taken my gift and been glad to get it. You're the most selfless man I ever met."

Staring at the whirlpool in his pan, Henning said, "I think that's because my father gave me things instead of what I really wanted, his time and approval."

Henning's father had praised him only once. Studying Henning's latest practice target, he'd said, "I didn't know you were such a good shot."

Smirking, Henning's uncompromising grandfather had pointed to the hole outside the bull's-eye.

"He'll get better," Colonel Dietzel said. "Practice makes perfect."

"No, it doesn't," Henning's grandfather snapped. "Perfect practice makes perfect. Doing something wrong doesn't lead to perfection even if you repeat it a thousand times."

Grandpa Dietzel's words spoiled a special moment, but Henning concealed his feelings. The old man would ridicule a show of emotion with his own version of some proverb. He had an unlimited supply. His favorite was, "Better late than never, but never late is better."

******

The Gold Country's camp followers were relentless. Some went so far as to strip down to undergarments and dance provocatively on tree stumps. 'Anything for a buck,' a camp newspaper had called their attempts to inflame the passions of potential customers.

With only six men in Frenchie's Canyon, the much talked about bedrooms on wheels didn't come there. When Henning's neighbors went where the girls were, he and Lee stayed behind. Lee feared he'd be unwelcome. Henning wanted Encinas to be faithful to him and couldn't justify being otherwise to her. But when his urges increased and his resolve weakened, he went along—just for the hike he told himself.

Presently he, Rodolfo, and the others reached a hand-painted sign that garishly screamed 'Good Time Girls.' Beyond, Henning saw a meadow with a canvas-covered wagon and five tents.

A man at the end of one of the lines breathlessly told them, "The macks brought in new girls and are rotating them from camp to camp to provide variety."

Leaning toward Rodolfo Henning whispered, "Macks?"

"That's what they call pimps around here."

Off to one side, Rodolfo watched the permanent occupants of the tents and wagon escort their previous customers out and welcome the next.

"How do you pick someone without even getting to know her?" Henning asked.

"These are soiled doves, not brides," Rodolfo quipped. "According to your taste you choose the biggest tits, best legs, roundest ass, or prettiest face."

While Rodolfo and the others waited in lines, Henning stayed where he was. When he looked at the girls he didn't see cleavage, curves, or alluring faces. In the Chinese, he saw a painfully shy girl, probably indentured and clearly terrified. The two Hispanics looked twelve at most and had almost certainly been unable to read the contracts that brought them to the Gold Country. The shapeliest white girl looked charmingly innocent, as if she was an enslaved orphan. All were graceless. Not one had done anything to make herself attractive. They didn't have to. Deprivation brought more than enough clients.

Rodolfo chose the blonde, who was the star attraction and held court in the wagon. After coming out he told Henning, "Choose someone besides the queen bee. She was a waste of money, charming and coquettish before being paid—then frigid. She barely stopped short of reading a book while I took care of my needs. I paid her a fortune and she humiliated me... hardhearted bitch."

To Henning the girls weren't unfeeling. In fact, they probably felt more than they could bear. Beneath their hard exteriors, they were no more than ports in a storm, to be used and left behind. One customer expressed his depressing outlook as, "The four f's: find 'em, feel 'em, fuck 'em, and forget 'em."

The Good Time Girls' lonely, monotonous lives couldn't help but feel meaningless. According to a camp newspaper, they were frequently beaten by clients and mutilated by the macks if they tried to run away. One of the girls they'd replaced had killed herself.

The macks had made one of life's great gifts unspeakably dirty and mechanical. Henning wanted no part of further degrading their girls...or disgracing himself.

******

As fall turned chilly, Henning and his neighbors set up benches around a fire pit so their evening conversations could continue. They no longer complained about California's high prices or described hardships endured on the way to the Gold Country. Now better acquainted, they talked about their thoughts, feeling, and families.

Ignoring rumors of bonanzas, they worked long and hard. Only Rodolfo and the Frenchman continued to spend money on Good Time Girls. The others saved every penny to take home to their wives and children. Close-knit and grateful to be alone in their out-of-the-way canyon, they liked being able to pan wherever they wanted without encroaching on other claims. That they'd be safer if more numerous was driven home one rainy morning.

Henning had moved to a side canyon. No longer able to see his neighbors, he thought the gunshots meant Rodolfo was shooting tin cans. He dived into bushes when men on horses galloped toward him. Oozing menace, they slid their horses to a stop beside his lean-to. Heart pounding, he flattened against the ground, mouth open to silence his breathing. But he couldn't stop rain from loudly splattering on his canvas coat.

Speaking with Mexican accents, the intruders tore his lean-to apart and found what they wanted, apparently more than they'd anticipated. They crammed his gold pouches into oversize saddlebags, then mounted up and mercilessly spurred their horses back toward the main canyon.

Henning raised his head and memorized details that might help identify the bandits later. They disappeared around a corner. He sprinted to where he could see them again. If only he'd accepted Rodolfo's rifle. Without it he could only watch as the Mexicans ransacked his friends' shelters.

Saddlebags bulging, the Mexicans charged away. Henning abandoned his hiding place. Stumbling at a dead run in tall grass, he landed eye to eye with Lee's corpse. He'd tripped on the Swiss man's remains.

Near the fire pit he came across another body. Then found Rodolfo face down in the creek. Grabbing both feet, he dragged the body clear. Felt for a pulse. With rainwater cascading from his hat brim and beard, he trembled. Never again would he hear this good man's voice.

In Prussia he'd have reported the murders. But in the Gold Country, men settled their own scores. He'd bury his dead companions later, after avenging them.

Henning crawled into Rodolfo's cramped shelter, past the familiar daguerreotype photograph of the wife who now a widow. Caught unaware when it was taken, she and their son hadn't struck the usual serious pose. Henning couldn't bear to look. But after closing his eyes, he still saw their beaming smiles and obvious mutual affection.

Under a floor board he found the Colt Paterson and two boxes of ammunition. To keep them dry he rolled both in oilcloth.

Rain came down harder as he dashed to his lean-to. Inside, he dropped the ammunition in a knapsack with jerky and a wooden canteen. Around his neck he hung his last souvenir of his father, a Prussian military spotting scope. Made of cylinders that slid inside one another, it was remarkably compact. His father's commanding general had given it to him at the funeral.

"Your dad put this to excellent use," the general had said. "Make sure you do the same."

He would if he caught up to the men who'd cold bloodedly murdered his friends.

******

Carrying the oilcloth-wrapped Colt Paterson in one hand—horizontal and thigh-high—Henning stormed outside and hurried up the trail the bandits had taken. The steep climb out of Frenchie's Canyon soon had him winded and second-guessing himself. The Mexicans had a head start and were on horseback. He'd never catch them—not on foot.

But Henning's Teutonic temperament wouldn't let him quit. What he wanted to do was difficult—not impossible. He was traveling light while the bandits' horses carried riders and saddlebags full of heavy gold. He could eat on the move. The horses had to stop and graze or go hungry. He was fresh and could go thirty-six hours without sleep. The bandits' mounts had been already been lathered and worn out when he first saw them.

Best of all, the Mexicans didn't know he was coming.

Around noon the rain stopped, leaving puddles and slick mud. Several times Henning saw fresh marks where fast-moving horses had skidded. Then he came across an imprint where one had fallen. After that, their strides shortened. They'd slowed down.

Henning passed a poster tacked to a tree and addressed to 'Prospectors Who Are Not U.S. Citizens.' Charging past another, he read enough to know it was a proclamation ordering foreigners out of the goldfields—no doubt posted by vigilantes. California was overrun with self-proclaimed lawmen who made rules as they saw fit and enforced them with guns.

Henning had spent his savings getting to California, then risked his life by staying behind in the Gold Country during a savage winter. He'd worked without rest for sixteen months. He'd lost Eduardo Vásquez's friendship. And when he'd finally accumulated enough gold to open a store, Mexicans had stolen it. Now he'd been ordered out of the only place on earth where he could earn more than a dollar a day. Before leaving, he had to get his gold back.

CHAPTER EIGHT
COLT'S REVOLVING WHEEL OF MISFORTUNE

An hour later Henning saw men on horseback in the distance, facing him and watching their back trail. Ducking behind a bush he put the spotting scope to his eye. Magnified, the Mexicans seemed to be looking right at him. Tense seconds later, he decided they were too relaxed to have seen him, then realized he was holding his breath and quietly exhaled.

What would he do if and when he caught them?

Like all Colt Patersons, Rodolfo's had a minuscule gap between the barrel and rotating cylinder. This allowed energy to escape as gunpowder in its cartridges exploded—reducing the distance its bullets traveled. But it could fire five times in rapid succession while the bandits' rifles had to be reloaded after every shot. And their fast-firing hand guns couldn't reliably hit a target beyond ten yards. If Henning could attack from just beyond pistol range, the Colt Paterson would be more accurate than their revolvers and would shoot faster than their rifles.

Of course, none of this would mean anything if the bandits saw him first. They'd simply speed up and he'd be left far behind. But when a hawk—circling high above—screamed, they continued on without urgency.

Where they'd followed switchbacks down a steep canyon wall Henning squatted, buttocks against his heels. On his boot soles he slid straight downhill in slick clay-rich mud, repeatedly crossing the trail while traveling a fraction of its length. By the time he reached the bottom, brush had clawed bloody scratches on his arms, a small price to pay for gaining ground.

He soon came upon an opportunity to gain more. A log bridge, undermined by the stream it crossed, had collapsed. The Mexicans had veered left, leaving the trail to look for shallows where they could ford. Henning tied his rifle horizontally across the top of his pack and picked up a five-foot-long stick. Then he lowered himself down the sheer bank and waded into the fast, waist-high torrent.

The water's rapid flow was almost overpowering. He faced into it and angled his stick against the bottom. Leaning against it, he created a tripod. Moving one leg, then the other, then the stick was slow going. He went through the rotation several times and seemed no closer to the other bank.

His foot caught between boulders and wouldn't come free. Off balance, he was dragged under. Ice-cold water burned his sinuses. The rifle came loose. He grabbed it but lost his stick. Planting his other foot he thrust his head above water, gasping for air, blinking water. He slid the rifle through his pack's shoulder straps. Barely kept his balance by spreading both arms above the rushing water.

Henning's trapped foot anchored him. When he freed it, he'd probably be swept away. But he had no choice. He pulled, then pushed. The rock bit into his ankle. He tugged until the pain was almost unbearable. Finally he jerked. Hard. Pain stabbed up his leg. His foot popped loose. He thrust it to the bottom as the current twisted him around. Legs wide apart he stayed upright. Should he turn back? He glanced one way, then the other. Both banks were equally far. Might as well keep going.

Breath roaring between wide-open lips, he reached shallow water. Hands on knees, ribs violently expanding and contracting, legs numb in icy water, he was still in danger. If the bandits reappeared he'd be one against six and they'd have the high ground.

He climbed the bank, using exposed tree roots for handholds. At the top he checked his gouged, bleeding ankle, then his rifle and bullets. Inside oilcloth, his reserve ammunition was dry. But the paper cartridges in the Colt Paterson's cylinder had disintegrated, depleting his meager supply. He blew the chambers dry and reloaded.

Once across the creek the bandits would circle back to the trail rather than go cross-country in heavy timber. Depending on how long it took to find a ford, they were probably still ahead. If not they'd see him from behind before he saw them.

Henning proceeded cautiously until he came upon fresh, familiar hoofprints, then alternated between a brisk walk and a jog. At a meadow, his natural caution warned him to skirt its edge, using the trees for cover. But the bandit's tracks went straight across. Rather than lose time he did the same.

Farther along, the trail snaked into a narrow canyon. Partway to the bottom he saw riders on the opposite wall. He crouched behind a fallen tree and studied them through his spotting scope, making absolutely certain they were the men he wanted to kill. Their *sombreros*, bandoleers, saddlebags, and horses were the ones he'd seen at Frenchie's Canyon.

Blood pounding through his temples Henning aimed at the nearest rider, then remembered why the Colt Paterson was known as a revolving wheel of misfortune. He rested its barrel on the log in front of him, pulled his left hand behind the cylinder, and squeezed the trigger.

The Colt Paterson slammed against his shoulder. Unable to find the hammer with his thumb, he looked down. The Mexicans were off their horses and out of sight when he refocused his eyes on the canyon.

Apparently confused by an echo, two bandits were huddled on the wrong side of a boulder, their backs to him. He squeezed off two more rounds. Both men disappeared. Had he hit them? Or only sent them diving for cover? At worst he was still outnumbered six to one. At best those odds had been cut in half.

Henning reloaded and crawled away. Not knowing how many men they were up against, the bandits would stay put. If he moved fast he could get ahead and set up another ambush. Out of sight now, he began plowing through brush and scrambling over boulders.

He'd circled the Mexicans' position by the time it hit him. The horses. He should've shot them, leaving his enemies afoot with all that heavy gold. Tempted to go back and correct his oversight, he decided not to. They'd be ready this time.

From the crest of a hill he studied the terrain, trying to figure out where the bandits would go next. All day they'd traveled south toward Mexico, the only destination that made sense. Behind them were five murders for which they'd be hanged if caught. The way east was blocked by the rugged Sierra

Nevada Mountains. To the west were Monterey and San Francisco, where thousands of Mexican-hating Americans were pouring into California, bringing fresh memories of the war.

Henning's attention kept returning to a deep, v-shaped notch in the ridgeline blocking the way south. That's where the trail would cross. Based on a Wild West novel he'd read, he named it Ambush Pass and set out to beat the Mexicans there.

******

Seven hours later in bright moonlight, Henning reached Ambush Pass. Emerging from the forest he saw that a steep outcrop in the middle had recesses large enough to conceal him. He scrambled up its closest incline and found a vantage point from which he'd see the bandits long before they rode past. Whether they passed on his left or right, he'd get a good shot because the area was bracketed by cliffs.

Struggling to stay alert, he laid out a row of cartridges behind a boulder. A rock tore loose from a cliff. The sound of its crash on the pass's granite floor reverberated. If the Mexicans came, the clatter of horseshoes on rock would be equally jarring. Henning gave himself permission to sleep. He didn't expect the bandits for a while yet. After his first ambush, they'd probably hidden until dark and then made their way cautiously.

Awake as soon as the sun came up, Henning stood and stretched. The tension he'd felt for twenty-four hours was gone. It returned as two riders emerged from the trees, single file at a trot. The one in the lead with his arm in a sling had been among Henning's earlier targets. He and the man behind watched the outcrop warily, zigzagging to make themselves difficult to hit.

Two more men rode out of the trees. The one in the lead also made evasive maneuvers. The one behind didn't. Obviously the leader, he had his men out front—offering them in return for early warning of an ambush. He rode a palomino and led two riderless horses with bulging saddlebags slung across otherwise empty saddles.

At Frenchie's Canyon, there'd been six riders. Now there were four, with one wounded. And the bags once distributed among six horses were now grouped on two, making them easier to take back.

The first two bandits passed to Henning's left. He let them go. The next two galloped by on opposite sides. He snugged the Colt Paterson to his shoulder, left hand steadying the barrel in front of the cylinder despite the danger of a misfire. Sights lined up on the rider to his left, he squeezed the trigger. Face first, the man dropped to the ground.

Henning pivoted, cocking the Colt Paterson's hammer. The other Mexican had turned his packhorse loose and was clinging to his mount's far side, using its body as a shield. Henning aimed and snapped off a shot. The horse staggered, then kept going. Henning glanced over his shoulder. The first two riders were out of range. He searched for the man whose horse he'd shot. The rising sun blinded him. And tugging his hat brim lower didn't stop the reflections from dew-covered boulders.

He rushed downhill, staying low. Submerged in shade he turned right. When he could see the area he wanted to examine he stopped. Off to one side, the packhorses had joined the palomino near its downed rider. That left one horse unaccounted for.

Henning found it with his scope. The animal had run a hundred yards after being shot and now lay at the base of a cliff, all four legs pointed at the outcrop. The empty rifle scabbard on its saddle said its former rider was ready to fight.

Repeatedly Henning scoped the area. Finally his persistence paid off. The man he sought was on his stomach, shielded behind the dead horse. The cliff protected his back and the barren floor of the pass offered no cover.

An assault would be perilous. Henning could leave empty-handed or risk his life. Or improvise. The cliff behind the bandit leaned toward him. Its angle would redirect bullets rather than stop them.

"With ricochets you can shoot around corners," Henning's father had taught him.

Resting his rifle barrel on the rock in front of him, he aimed. Squeezed the trigger. A distinctive whine said the cliff had deflected his shot downward. He fired again and heard another ricochet.

The bandit's upper half appeared above his horse's corpse. He snapped off a wild shot and ducked. Henning held his fire. Shooting without aiming was a waste of ammunition. And firing again so soon would reveal that he didn't need to reload between shots.

Thirty yards away, a side canyon beckoned. In the Mexican's predicament Henning would have tried to get there while his attacker reloaded. Immediately after the next ricochet, the bandit bolted. Henning aimed. Rotated his shoulders to keep pace with his target. Pulled the trigger.

The bandit went from dead run to dead.

CHAPTER NINE
GERMAN ACCENTS

Henning stood beside the first bandit he'd shot. The man wasn't breathing and his face was twisted with shock.

"Don't look so surprised," Henning growled. "You had it coming."

Every time he got close to the dead man's palomino horse, it sidled away. Finally he set the Colt Paterson on the ground and approached slowly, hands empty. This time the animal allowed itself to be caught.

Henning grabbed his rifle, mounted up, and crossed the pass at a gallop—gently rocking in the saddle. He scanned the cliff tops. The remaining bandits would come at him from there. And soon. Stopping beside the last man he'd shot, he didn't bother to dismount. No one could be alive with so much of his blood thickening on the ground.

As he closed in on the packhorses and their precious cargos, one snorted and trotted off. The other continued chewing dry, stunted grass a better-fed animal would have disdained. Leaning in his saddle Henning grabbed the dangling halter rope. Slamming both heels against the palomino's sides, he pushed it into a canter.

Henning tied the packhorse in a nearby grove and returned to the pass. Unable to locate the other packhorse and its gold, he dismounted at the outcrop and hurried to its top. There, he shaded his eyes but still couldn't see the two bandits he'd allowed to escape. Rather than give up their loot, they'd circle back. Time to clear out.

In the trees again and spurred by thoroughness more than doubt, he confirmed that the saddlebags were packed with pouches of gold. The missing packhorse carried at least as many. But Henning had more than before the robbery, and pushing his luck could get him killed. He was ready to bury his friends in Frenchie's Canyon.

As Henning rode up the far side of the canyon below Ambush Pass, a stick snapped behind him. Looking back he saw nothing. But sticks didn't break by themselves. Hearing an iron-shod hoof hit rock, he yanked his rifle from its scabbard. Then veered off the main trail and headed up a steep incline, concealed in tall brush.

Noisily, the horse behind followed.

Henning's mount refused when he demanded more speed. Every time he reached the apparent summit another horizon appeared, higher and farther away. Finally at the top, he sprang from his saddle and hugged the ground behind a boulder.

His pursuer was so loud that Henning suspected one bandit was holding his attention while the other snuck up on him. He scanned his surroundings and saw nothing unusual. Then caught a glimpse…of what? It was just a blur between trees. A glimmer. Then another…closer. Aiming his rifle where the trail came out of the brush, he took a deep breath and held it.

The bay packhorse that had disappeared at the pass trotted into view. Still carrying three saddlebags it nickered and rushed toward its companions. Henning ignored the noisy equine reunion behind him, watching instead to make sure his visitor hadn't led the Mexicans to him.

When certain he was safe, Henning caught the bay and unbuckled the flaps on its saddlebags. He knew what he'd see inside but gasped anyhow.

A lonesome horse had brought him a fortune.

******

Hours later, Henning was still miles short of Frenchie's Canyon and desperately needed sleep. His spirits rose as he sighted pillars of smoke, clearly from a settlement large enough to offer lodging. Distracted by the prospect of a hot bath, good meal, and warm bed, he was slow to hear someone coming up behind. Startled, he flinched when a red-haired man came alongside, dressed in homespun clothes and riding a small mule.

"You like to zell one horze?" the stranger asked in heavily accented English.

"They're not for sale." Henning needed them to carry his gold.

"I sink your aczent iz Cherman, like mine?"

"Yes, I'm Prussian."

The man switched languages, to German. "I'm Franz Wulfe from Bavaria. Have you heard about the foreign prospectors shot dead in Frenchie's Canyon? Apparently a countryman of ours stole their gold after murdering them. Vigilantes are taking a close look at anyone who's tall and sounds German. I've already been questioned three times."

"Strange. Vigilantes don't usually concern themselves with crimes against foreigners."

"It's not the murderer they want. It's the gold. The victims had no known friends or family, so it'll belong to whoever recovers it."

"Do they have the killer's name?" Henning asked, face expressionless.

"Not yet."

Three men sauntered past. They greeted Wulfe, then looked back over their shoulders at Henning. Suddenly a meal, bath, and bed weren't worth the risk of going into town—not with saddlebags full of gold and a German accent.

"My place is off the beaten track, less than a mile away," Wulfe said. "I can offer a good meal and a place to sleep. All I want in return is a chance to buy one of your horses."

"I told you they're not for sale. I need them to carry my supplies."

"I'm a farmer. With the price of food around here, I'm doing well. But I'd do better if I had a horse for plowing, instead of this little mule. I'll trade my mule plus cash for one of your horses. Spend the night at my place. You can try the mule in the morning. He doesn't have the bulk to pull a plow, but he can carry plenty."

Bavarians and Prussians were both Germanic. In the old country, however, they hated each other and had fought wars. Wulfe's offer of hospitality seemed strange, all the more so with a murderer on the loose. But Henning needed to rest and plan his next move.

"Lead the way," he said.

Near a clearing planted with beans, corn, and wheat, Wulfe swerved toward a ramshackle cabin that didn't look like its owner could afford

Gold Country prices for a horse. Halfway there, Wulfe dismounted and went inside a crude barn. Moments later a boar and several pregnant sows charged out.

"You wouldn't believe what miners pay for pork," Wulfe said. "I usually keep my hogs locked up, but they can defend themselves against the predators around here. And your horses look like they need a comfortable rest."

The elaborate hospitality increased Henning's suspicions. But with no reasonable alternative, he led his horses into the unexpectedly clean barn.

"You'll find a cot and blankets up there." Wulfe pointed to the loft. "Throw your horses some hay and make yourself at home. I'll bring dinner later."

Wulfe rode to the cabin. The sun was down, but he left his mule saddled and tied to a hitching rail. This all but confirmed Henning's worst fear: the Bavarian wasn't interested in a horse. He suspected Henning of the murders in Frenchie's Canyon and wanted the stolen gold. If he got a chance, he'd try for it on his own. Otherwise he'd ride for help during the night.

Henning put the horses in stalls—never looking way from Wulfe's cabin. Did it have another door or a window he couldn't see? He loosened his horses' cinches but left them saddled so they'd be ready on short notice.

After feeding and watering, Henning sat on the ground and leaned the Colt Paterson against the wall. He was struggling to stay awake by the time Wulfe returned with a rifle.

And two pie tins of beans mixed with meat cubes, one of which he handed to Henning.

"I always carry a gun at daybreak and twilight," Wulfe explained, sitting on a well-stuffed gunnysack with his weapon across his lap. "That's when deer raid my crops. I've shot several but they keep coming, which is fine by me. Venison fetches a good price."

While they ate, Henning slid closer to the Colt Paterson. Seeing this, Wulfe leaned his rifle against a stall. Still alert, Henning hungrily spooned beans and meat into his mouth.

"You can try my mule in the morning," Wulfe said after they'd eaten.

Rifle in hand Wulfe returned to his cabin, clearly having decided against a shoot out. He'd likely go for help while Henning slept. If he did, Henning would go in the opposite direction. He turned out the lantern, then paced back and forth in the dark, forcing himself to stay awake.

But he'd hiked and ridden seventy miles in thirty-eight hours. And slept less than three. Beyond his limits, he sat down. Wulfe's mule was still tied to the hitching rail. Glancing at the moon he calculated the time at past midnight. His eyes closed. He wouldn't sleep. He'd just...

When Henning woke the sky was dark and the mule was gone. Leaping to his feet he peered between the barn's planks. A distant whinny chilled him. Wulfe didn't have a horse. Or neighbors. There was only one explanation for what he'd heard.

He tore away the cobweb curtain in front of the door in the back wall. It swung silently on leather hinges. No one was visible outside. Saddles scraping the doorjamb, his horses squeezed through the opening. A hundred yards into the forest he tightened all three cinches.

Once mounted, he jumped the horses into a gallop until certain he wasn't being followed. His only crime had been to recover stolen gold from bandits who'd slaughtered five innocent men. Yet he was a fugitive, much more likely to be shot on sight than allowed to explain what really happened in Frenchie's Canyon.

******

Two days later Henning reached the rolling grassland that stretched from the Sierra Nevada foothills to San Francisco Bay. When he and the Chileans had hiked through on their way to the Gold Country, they'd admired a sea of green ryegrass being baked golden brown by an intense sun. Since then the vegetation had been reduced to ashes, cinders, and occasional blackened, leafless trees.

'49ers by the tens of thousands had camped there on their way to the Gold Country. Most were best described by the American word tenderfoot. They knew nothing about living outdoors. Their cooking fires sometimes got out of control and raged until they burned out.

Winds relentlessly prowled the resulting wasteland, raising gray-black powder that coated everything it touched. The only travelers Henning saw were going the long way around, sticking to country not yet burned. Pushing straight ahead he gained time, ignoring the bitter dust that invaded his nose, burned his eyes, and left a vile taste in his mouth.

Having decided to go to Chile, Henning was on his way to catch a ship in San Francisco. He had enough money to open a store. It wouldn't be the emporium it might have been if he'd kept prospecting. But foreigners had been ordered out of the goldfields, and he was wanted for murder. Too, he'd been away from Encinas sixteen months, long enough.

That morning Henning had bought hay from a farmer and paid him to draw a map showing The Burn's waterholes. Then he'd ridden hard and stopped late. With no fuel for a fire he sat in the dark chewing jerky, in a dismal mood, his skin black with soot.

Never had he been in a place where authority belonged to whoever seized it. Or where the men motivated by self-interest more than justice decided who to suspect of crimes, then arrested them, reached a verdict, and imposed a penalty. If he fell into vigilantes' hands they'd hang him and keep his gold.

Henning's racing mind conjured up the photograph of Rodolfo's widow, hair piled high, dark eyes proudly fixed on the chubby boy in her lap. They'd soon be destitute, along with Lee's family and those of the others murdered in Frenchie's Canyon. Some of the gold he'd recovered was rightfully theirs. It would go to them if only he knew where they were.

He'd held another unpleasant thought at bay during most of the chase, gunfight, and escape from Wulfe. Now it barged into his consciousness. He'd killed four men. Yes, murderers deserved to die. But their deaths seemed like a damn shame—not a triumph. Had his father felt that way fighting Prussia's wars?

He slept fitfully, worried vigilantes would sneak up on him while he was defenseless.

CHAPTER TEN
THE GHOST FLEET

Henning's mood improved two days later as he left The Burn and crested a hill covered with golden ryegrass. Below, he saw a familiar body of water shimmering with reflected sunlight. Beyond its broad expanse, San Francisco looked tantalizingly close but was three days away. He turned south for the long trip around the bay.

At a spring surrounded by lush grass, he stopped and let his horses graze. Underfed for days, they frantically bit off tender shoots, chewing while Henning flung water into his eyes, washing out specks of grit.

He was filling his canteen when he saw a vessel coming across the bay. Made of logs surfaced with planks and pushed by a motorized paddlewheel, it carried a wagon, horses, and men. Passengers for its return trip were waiting in a stagecoach at the landing below. If Henning took that ferry to San Francisco he'd avoid three days of hard riding. But his fellow passengers would've come from the Gold Country in those coaches. Noticing his height and hearing his accent, they might suspect him of the murders. Even if they didn't, the ferry would deliver him to the heart of town where his horses and bulging saddlebags would attract unwanted attention.

That, however, was no worse than what he'd face if he didn't get to San Francisco for another three days. By then news of the slaughter in Frenchie's Canyon would have arrived and been published, along with his description.

He mounted up and started downhill toward the landing.

******

Near San Francisco Henning saw hundreds of ships, anchored near the waterfront like the fleet of an invading army.

"They call it the Ghost Fleet," the ferryboat captain explained. "The crews are in the goldfields. God knows what'll happen to the ships. I expect the owners will send men to retrieve the ones that are seaworthy. Our new harbormaster tells me every last one of Chile's merchant ships is out there, along with most of Peru's."

Rather than reveal his accent, Henning didn't reply. He felt conspicuous enough with tangled hair to his shoulders, a long grimy beard, and a tattered brown canvas jacket hanging from his gaunt frame. Looking around, he was comforted to see his fellow passengers looked much the same.

"Appears you did well in the Gold Country," the captain said studying Henning's bulging saddlebags. Still waiting for a response, he was called to supervise the ferry's landing.

Henning turned his attention to San Francisco, bigger and disappointing as ever. The few decent houses were along shore. Behind were thousands of tents, shacks, and lean-tos.

Shuddering as its paddlewheel reversed, the ferry stopped then rocked beside its berth. Once the ramp was secure, Henning rode ashore and squeezed through congested streets. With almost everyone on foot, he stood out and would continue to do so until he cashed in his gold and sold the horses.

If news of the murders had arrived, the sale of this much gold would raise eyebrows. Rather than attract attention by selling it all in one assay office, Henning decided to use several. But every time he went inside, the saddlebags on his horses outside would be unprotected.

His dilemma was solved when he saw a prospector lead a mule and its cargo into the Wells, Fargo & Company Assay Office. No one paid any attention. The trick, it seemed, was to tip the clerk for his forbearance.

"Nice doin' business with ya. Come back anytime," the clerk called out—gratuity in hand—as the prospector and mule left.

Henning loaded all six saddlebags on one saddle, overburdening one of his two packhorses but making it unnecessary to lead both into assay offices. Then he started exchanging gold for banknotes issued by Eastern banks that redeemed them on demand for gold or silver coins. Most people preferred precious metal to paper money, which became worthless if the bank standing behind it went broke. Nonetheless, printed currency was common in San Francisco where men frequently dealt in sums that would have amounted to wagonloads of coins.

By the time he'd sold all his gold, Henning's largest saddlebag was stuffed with banknotes. As he tied it behind his saddle two men approached.

"How much for the palomino?" one asked.

"Fifteen hundred," Henning replied.

"Are you crazy? Not even a champion race horse is worth that much."

"You'll more than get your money back when you reach new strikes faster than prospectors on foot."

Passersby joined the bargaining and the price climbed, reaching two thousand dollars. Henning sold each of his three horses for that price, then slung his bulging saddlebag over one shoulder and headed for the hotel district. On the way he passed Yankees of every stripe as well as Chinese, Mexicans, South Americans, Australians, British, Italians, French, Scandinavians, and Hawaiians. Men of like nationality banded together. Language, dress, and cooking odors varied from one neighborhood to the next.

Looking at his reflection in a window, Henning saw a nervous-looking, hollow-cheeked man he didn't recognize and wouldn't have trusted.

******

Following its two-year war with Mexico, the victorious United States had seized territory stretching from Texas to the Pacific Ocean, doubling the young nation's size. American troops and political authorities were dispatched to replace those withdrawn by Mexico. In California, they deserted their posts and went to the goldfields, leaving no one to enforce the law. Henning couldn't have found a better hiding place. Or one where he'd have been as uncomfortable with so much cash.

Since San Francisco had no banks Henning did the same as other prospectors. He deposited his money with a merchant who charged to keep valuables in his safe. Then he scrubbed himself at a bathhouse, got a shave and haircut, and bought new clothes.

Next time he saw his reflection, it bore no resemblance to the prospector who'd worked Frenchie's Canyon. Now at ease with his appearance, he ate two steak dinners at one sitting.

"Every room in town is taken," a hotel desk clerk told him. "However, the tenpin alley rents sleeping spaces on its lanes after closing. Better reserve one fast though."

As Henning waited in line at the alley's counter, he heard a Frenchman say, "I don't have American money. Where can I exchange francs?"

"You can't. There's a shortage," the clerk replied. "Don't worry. We take francs, doubloons, pesetas, shillings, florins, rupees, guilders, and privately minted coins…as well as gold in the form of dust, flakes, or nuggets."

By the time it was Henning's turn, only one space remained. Three feet wide by five feet long, it would be cramped but better than nothing.

"Bein' a forner, y'all will be innerested in the latest news," the clerk said, repeating what he'd told the man ahead of Henning. "Turns out you people kin stay in the Gold Country if you pay a tax. Be careful though. It's often collected by imposters who keep it for themselves."

On his way to breakfast the next morning Henning passed the first female—other than the Good Time Girls—he'd seen since Chile By the time he went around the block for a second look, the sidewalk was crowded with men who'd slowed their headlong rush to gawk at her.

"Long time since I was that close to a decent female," one said, as she disappeared around a corner. "It's a wonder I didn't faint."

Henning hadn't been in danger of fainting, but being reminded of Encinas had increased his longing for her.

He went through a doorway with no door into a restaurant that never closed. During a breakfast of pork chops and fried potatoes, he eavesdropped on a nearby conversation.

"A recent strike near Downeyville produced gigantic nuggets worth up to twenty thousand dollars each," one man claimed.

"I ain't gonna tell you where," a second man said, "but my frens and I was diggin' a grave for a departed comrade and turned up shovelfuls of gold. Before we was done, we filled a gunnysack."

"I was workin' near a flume outside Placerville," another man piped up, "when a plank broke, releasing water that eventually dug up a quarter million dollars in fist size nuggets."

Henning routinely discounted prospectors' tales by ninety-five percent. But after they left, one of the men who took their places said something that rang true.

"I was a clerk in Sam Brannan's store at Sutter's Fort, and I know for a fact it nets thirty thousand dollars a month selling flour at four hundred dollars a barrel, eggs at two dollars apiece, and…" he quoted a list of other prices comparable to what Henning had paid in recent months.

Because gold seekers were arriving in a flood while supplies trickled in, California's merchants earned unimaginable profits selling the world's most expensive goods. Henning was eager to open a store in Chile where he and Encinas could work together. But here was a once-in-a-lifetime opportunity to earn infinitely more than he could anywhere else in the world.

With his knowledge of South America he could bring supplies in a fraction of the time needed to import them from the East Coast. While putting his first shipment together he'd be gone long enough for news of the murders to grow stale. When he got back he'd sell to prospectors far from Frenchie's Canyon and unlikely to give a damn about what had happened there. He might even open a store in Angel's Camp, a town civilized enough for Encinas to take care of his customers while he went for more merchandise.

Going from shop to shop in the commercial district, Henning made a list of what was in demand. It soon included flour, beans, corn, rice, coffee, cooking utensils, boots, work clothes, tents, cigarettes, tobacco, matches, rum, shovels, picks, canteens, soap, and lanterns, along with whale oil to burn in them. As an afterthought, he added mules.

He also discovered that society's normal restrictions on women didn't apply in San Francisco. Even those who were decent had irons in the fire. Some operated laundries and for washing a dozen shirts earned more than men elsewhere did in a week. Others ran boarding houses or restaurants. The latest *Alta California* newspaper said one hardy soul had gone to the goldfields where she baked and sold eighteen thousand dollars worth of pies in a few months. Her husband was quoted as having said, "She was born feeling compelled to do everything people say women can't do, a characteristic that served her well in this particular case."

At four-thirty a man rushed down the street brandishing newspapers and shouting, "Five miners shot dead in the Sierras. Read all about it in today's special *Alta California* edition."

Henning bought a copy. Beneath the six-inch headline was an article by a reporter who'd fluffed up a few facts to fill three columns that concluded with, 'Prospectors say the murderer was tall and spoke with a barely detectable German accent.'

Henning hurried to Clark's Point and booked passage on an outbound clipper ship. Eager to leave San Francisco, he was in an equal rush to return with his merchandise. More and more supply ships were arriving. His list of what was in demand would soon be outdated.

CHAPTER ELEVEN
A BACKLOG OF YANKEES

Henning had chosen a clipper because they were the fastest of all ships. Their development had been spurred by demand for speedy transportation to San Francisco. Going from the East Coast to California—around South America's southern tip—had taken six months before these speedy vessels earned their name by clipping that time in half.

The wharf at Clark's Point was being rebuilt and a man in a rowboat took passengers out to the *California Clipper*. Anchored offshore, she was the first such vessel Henning had seen. Beneath towering masts that reached for the heavens, her streamlined hull and graceful overhanging bow gave the impression she was racing across the water even while standing still.

While the crew winched up the anchor Henning turned in his rifle as required by ship's regulations. Then a sail was unfurled and the ship leapt forward. Listening to the whisper of water sliding along the hull, Henning was impressed by the burst of speed. He looked forward to another when more sails were unfurled outside the bay's crowded confines.

Passengers on an arriving schooner had climbed its rigging, seeking the earliest possible view of their destination.

"Is the gold gone?" one bellowed between cupped hands

"There's still plenty being found," a man on *California Clipper* shouted.

The incoming passengers cheered. Like them, Henning had high hopes, an uncertain future, and sketchy plans. He knew Santiago, Chile had the merchandise he wanted. But Acapulco, Mexico and Lima, Peru were closer.

Regrettably, he'd never been to either and didn't know if they offered the goods and quantities he needed.

"Since the war," Captain Mortimer answered Henning's inquiry, "Mexico's economy has been in shambles. There's no way to know what's available, but we'll find out soon enough. Our larders are depleted and little food was available in Frisco. We'll have to put in for supplies at Acapulco, and I don't look forward to that. Other American vessels have had problems there."

While the crew worried about Acapulco's perils the next day, Henning sat on deck enjoying warm sunshine and writing to Encinas. Though she should have long ago received the letter with his San Francisco post office box number, she still hadn't written.

'I hope you will come to the Gold Country and run my new store so we can be together,' he wrote, 'but first I must find the merchandise I need and get it back to California while it's still in short supply.'

Alerted by hissing water, he saw a whale spout after breaching. It avoided the *Clipper*, but sea lions sought her out and performed tirelessly, twirling in the water and slapping their bellies. The crew threw them undesirable portions of an ocean sunfish the cook had caught in San Francisco Bay.

Not yet mature the unearthly fish had been a fraction the size of its gentle, slow-moving companion. That one was about ten feet long, nearly as tall, and probably outweighed two Clydesdale horses. Looking like a gigantic disembodied head with puckered mouth and huge eyes, it had caught the cook's attention while on the surface, letting birds feast on its parasites.

As Henning had discovered at dinner the previous night, the leathery insipid meat was unappetizing, even with barnacles and worms scraped away. Passengers and crew had eaten it sparingly. But the sea lions fought over it.

******

Two thousand nautical miles south of San Francisco, *Clipper* entered a bay sheltered by a semicircle of hills. At the foot of steep slopes Henning saw Acapulco, a port through which Spain had once traded with Asia.

After docking his ship, Captain Mortimer led Henning and a dozen men ashore to buy food. On the pier, they were blocked by an angry mob led by a fat man with a holster and pistol on each hip.

Shaking their fists, the Mexicans chanted, *"Fuera yanquis de Mexico."*

"Yankees, get out of Mexico," Henning translated for the man beside him.

"Return to the ship," Mortimer ordered, "but don't show your backs."

Still facing the crowd, the shore party retreated across the dock. Speedily they untied *Clipper's* mooring lines, then charged up to the deck and pulled the gangplank aboard.

"I want armed sentries along the port side," Mortimer shouted to the first mate. "Tell them to hold their fire and keep their weapons in plain sight."

The first mate fetched an armload of rifles from the storeroom.

"Mister Dietzel," Mortimer shouted. "The truth please. No modesty or exaggeration. Are you any good with that rifle we're keeping for ya?"

"Yes, sir," Henning answered.

"Give him his rifle," Mortimer ordered the mate, "and assign him a place on the rail."

Clutching his Colt Paterson Henning looked down at the dock and saw men with burlap bags join the mob. His pistols holstered, the fat man was looking at the sentries and their rifles with concern. His followers reached into the bags and counted, *"Uno dos, tres, ahora."*

A volley of egg-size rocks all arrived at once. Dodging them was next to impossible. One barely missed Henning. Another hit the cook, splitting his forehead open. Immediately a cabin boy held cold ashes against the wound to speed coagulation. The cook was on one knee, rifle to his shoulder.

"I didn't hear an order to take aim." The speaker had snow white hair. A passenger, he'd sprinted across the deck amidst a second rain of rocks.

"Goddamn greasers," the cook snarled. "Guess we're gonna hafta kick their arses again."

"If you shoot, we could wind up facing Mexican warships." Henning joined the debate without knowing if Mexico even had a navy.

"Those backward bastids don't have nothin' fast enough to catch a clipper."

"How about a cannon ball?" Henning pointed to artillery on a cliff.

The cook lowered his rifle. Braving more flights of rocks the crew raised the anchor and unfurled sails. *Clipper* inched away from the pier. Another volley drummed on her deck before she was out of range.

"It took backbone to speak up like that," the white-haired passenger told Henning with soft South American vowels.

"You spoke first," Henning replied. "It's easier to follow than lead."

"My name is Tómas Sánchez. Pleasure to meet you."

"Henning Dietzel. The pleasure's mine."

Clipper dropped anchor in the harbor's center.

"I want sentries on both sides of the ship all night," Mortimer announced. "First thing in the morning, I'll ask the authorities for an armed escort so we can buy food."

"Is there any reason I hafta be next to this goddamn Mexican lover?" the cook asked, glaring at Henning.

Mortimer sent Henning and Tómas Sánchez to the other rail, where Henning asked, "Are you Mexican?"

"Peruvian by birth, but I live in Ecuador."

"Looks like people here are still bitter about the war," Henning said.

"Rightfully so, but that's not what has them riled up."

"What then?"

"Filibusters, private American citizens bent on taking over portions of Mexico and Central America by force. One group just got run out of Baja California, but others will come and the Mexicans know it."

******

At dawn's first light Henning notified Captain Mortimer of an oncoming rowboat. The rising sun highlighted the craft's standing passenger. In a military uniform he cupped his hands around his mouth and shouted, "I'm aide-de-camp to General Vilchez, Acapulco's *comandante*. Permission to come aboard please."

"Granted," Mortimer boomed.

After climbing aboard and shaking Mortimer's hand, Vilchez's aide said, "I imagine you're here for supplies."

"That we are, but a mob forced us away from the dock. I'm hoping General Vilchez will have soldiers escort us to the outdoor market this morning."

"The general can fill your larders from our military warehouse."

"I prefer to have his men protect us while we do our own shopping."

"There's hardly any food in the market."

"What can General Vilchez offer?"

"*Tortillas* along with sacks of rice, dried corn, and dried beans."

"How much will he charge?"

Even compared to Gold Country prices, the quote was outrageous.

"Your general should wear a highwayman's mask," Mortimer sputtered.

Calmly the aide said, "You *gringos* say San Francisco's merchants are smart when they charge high prices. Why does doing the same make General Vilchez a thief?"

"Because I suspect he steals his merchandise from the Mexican army. For all I know, he also sent the mob that kept us away from the outdoor market."

"After your accusations, the general won't sell you anything." The aide turned to go.

"Unless I pay his asking price. Right?"

"Possibly. That's up to him."

Henning saw no sign either of these proud men would give in. But if one did, it would be Mortimer, who had the most to lose.

"Tell the general I accept his terms," Mortimer said, "and be so kind as to keep my other comments to yourself."

"Please?" the aide asked.

"Please. Here's a list of what we need."

Hours after *Clipper* had again tied up at the pier, General Vilchez came aboard. Short and sturdy with flat cheeks and wide jaws, he demanded Mortimer confirm their agreement, and then waved to a soldier on the dock below. Military wagons came around a corner and clattered toward *Clipper's* berth. A crowd appeared out of nowhere and blocked them.

The man beside Henning at the rail silently prayed for the officer in charge to prevail as he and the fat man with two pistols negotiated. The soldiers turned their wagons and retreated.

"We can't shoot our friends and neighbors just to do you a favor." Vilchez's tone said those friends and neighbors would regret spoiling his golden opportunity.

As *Clipper* left Acapulco Bay, Mortimer ordered the cook to put the crew and passengers on half rations. The cook made sure Henning's portions were even smaller, which troubled Henning less than the prospect of losing more time looking for food in other ports.

******

Ten days later they put in at Central America's only deepwater port. Puntarenas had become a hub for sea traffic to and from San Francisco. Its stores and markets were sold out. Mortimer reduced everyone to quarter rations and pushed on to Panama City, a sleepy little village seldom visited by vessels as grand as his.

The dock and surrounding beach teemed with angry, menacing men. Hundreds more streamed from town.

"What the hell is this?" Mortimer asked no one in particular. "I've never seen more than a handful of men here."

Clipper dropped anchor offshore and firearms were issued to the men who'd been sentries in Acapulco. Mortimer followed as they descended rope ladders and manned a rowboat.

"I'd steer clear of this if we weren't almost out of supplies," he grumbled.

Rowers picked up oars and pulled toward the dock in unison. Men on shore waved their hats and chanted boisterous hip-hip-hurrahs.

"Avast," Mortimer commanded.

The rowers stopped. Henning heard men on the dock speaking English with accents he'd heard in the goldfields, American accents.

"Is your ship owned by the Pacific Mail Steamship Company?" someone shouted.

"No," Mortimer answered through his speaking trumpet.

"Are you going north?"

"South."

"We'll pay handsomely if you take us to San Francisco."

"My employer's instructions are to return to New Orleans, and that's what I'll be doing."

The crowd's mood soured.

"I'm not going ashore among men who might hijack my ship," Mortimer whispered to his first mate.

"That might not be any more dangerous than resuming our voyage while critically low on food," the mate replied.

Facing the dock Mortimer asked, "Why are there so many Americans here?"

"We were sold a bill of goods by ticket agents who promised to get us from New Orleans to San Francisco in thirty-seven days," came the answer.

"Thirty-seven days," Mortimer scoffed. "That's ridiculous."

"Actually it's not. Side-wheel steamships can make Panama from New Orleans in nine days. It takes a week to cross the isthmus, and California is three weeks from here."

"How'd you cross Panama?" Mortimer asked.

"The ticket agent said there'll soon be a railroad makin' the trip in five hours. Maybe that's true, but until then it's a seven-day crossin' by canoe and mule through the worst jungle you can imagine. When we got here, we found too many men arrivin' and too few leavin'. Turns out there are plenty of ships bringin' men to Chagres, on the Atlantic coast, and very few to take us the rest of the way. So we're waitin' our turns, sleepin' on bare ground, and buyin' half-rotten food at prices that have us near broke."

"How long have you been here?"

"Over a month. Can you sell us some eats?"

"We're out of food ourselves," Mortimer replied. "I was hoping to buy some here."

"Forget it. None of us has had a decent meal in weeks."

"We fed too much of that sunfish to the sea lions," Mortimer told his first mate.

******

Taking the only available option, Captain Mortimer cut his crew's rations to almost nothing. When not on duty crewmen slept to forget their hunger. Henning dealt with his by reading books from the officer's library.

Once *Clipper* had docked in Guayaquil, Ecuador, Mortimer called the crew together under an ominous black sky. Tersely he ordered the cook and four crewmen ashore.

"Buy anything edible," he commanded. "Pay as little as possible but as much as necessary."

Watching from a distance Henning waited until the captain was alone before approaching him to ask, "May I join the shore party?"

"The cook won't welcome you," Mortimer said, "but you get along with Hispanics better than he does and we need this town's goodwill. Our backs are against the wall. We can't leave here with empty larders."

Once ashore, Henning and his companions found that California-bound ships had emptied Guayaquil's markets. At the only restaurant still open, they bought what little remained in its pantry for many times normal price.

"What now?" the cook asked when they were back on the street. "We've gone through every nook and cranny of this godforsaken dump."

Apparently every nook and cranny means something different to you. , Henning thought, then pointed to a residential neighborhood and said "Let's see what we can find there."

"Idiot." The cook rolled his eyes. "What can we possibly do there? Go door to door and buy rice by the spoonful? With the markets empty, the locals won't have anything to spare."

"The captain said we can't leave without food," Henning said.

"And I say we won't find any until we come back with guns and more men."

Evidently the cook was willing to take what they needed by force. Shouldering their purchases he and the other crewmen headed for the dock. Henning went in the opposite direction.

An hour later on a little-traveled cobblestone street he came upon a wagon loaded with two live pigs, plus crates of potatoes, vegetables, and fruit. Two men, gray-haired and elderly, stood beside it. One wore a professional driver's hat and gloves. The other was dressed in beige slacks and a pistachio colored *guayabera* shirt. They were inspecting the shattered spokes on one of their vehicle's rear wheels.

"I haven't seen you before," the man in the green shirt said. "Are you a sailor?"

"No, I'm a passenger," Henning replied. "The captain of the ship that brought me will pay well if you sell him some food."

"Sorry this isn't for sale. It's for a *fiesta* I'm having this afternoon."

"What will you do with the leftovers?"

"There's a spare wheel under the wagon. If you take this one off and put that one on, I'll give you what's left after my guests finish. Don't worry, there'll be plenty."

"Where did you get all this?" Henning asked, rolling up his sleeves.

"It's from my farm. My name is Mariano Martinez by the way."

"Can you bring more food to sell us?"

"My farm is in Quito. I won't receive more shipments for weeks, and they're all sold."

Changing the wheel was a two-man job, but at their ages Martinez and his driver could only offer encouragement. Henning unloaded enough crates to lighten the wagon, then removed the spare from its underside. After supporting the axle, he replaced the broken wheel.

Weak with fatigue and hunger, he briefly sat on one of the crates before reloading them.

"Come to my house late this afternoon," Martinez said, handing over bread, cheese, and a map he'd sketched while Henning worked.

******

Following a dismal search for more food, Henning found his way to Martinez's mansion.

"*Señor* Martinez told me to expect you," the butler announced at the front door. Stepping outside, he led Henning to an enclosed side yard where a cook basted two freshly slaughtered pigs roasting over grease-fed flames. His assistants stirred the contents of kettles hanging above other fires.

Henning was politely asked to wait in a corner.

Later, servers carried heaping platters to the adjoining yard. Stomach rumbling, Henning peeked through a triangular opening in the wall. Elegantly dressed guests were seating themselves at long tables covered with platters of white pork, brown rice, yellow potatoes, chocolate-brown beans, and purple plum sauce. Torches kept swarms of tropical insects at bay, and bronze-colored songbirds in wrought-iron cages provided soothing music.

Twice guests piled their plates high and the staff replenished the serving dishes. By then Henning was uncomfortably eager to deliver the leftovers before the cook convinced Captain Mortimer to do something rash.

Martinez's driver overfilled a plate and offered it.

"It wouldn't be right to eat before my shipmates," Henning said.

"In that case let's get going," the driver responded, as hoped. "We can't have you starving to death."

While Martinez escorted guests into his house, the driver brought a wagon. Henning helped load it with what turned out to be far more leftovers than he'd anticipated.

On the way to *California Clipper* the driver turned in at an icehouse.

"Do we have to stop?" Henning asked. "I'm in a bit of a hurry."

"This is important and won't take long," the driver replied. "Whatever you don't eat today will spoil if you don't keep it cool."

Inside an insulated room, a man with tongs dropped transparent, radiantly blue chunks into gunnysacks.

"Where does he get ice so close to the equator?" Henning asked.

"It's harvested with axes and saws from a glacier on the Cotopaxi volcano near Quito." The driver signed an invoice, charging the purchase to his employer.

At the dock, still-warm pots and pans were rushed to *Clipper's* galley.

"This has to be carefully rationed," the cook told Henning, generously sampling the food while spooning it onto tin plates.

Henning made sure Mariano Martinez's pots and pans were returned to his driver. He was enjoying a meager but welcome meal in the passengers' dining room when the first mate stepped in and said, "Come with me please."

Henning stuffed his mouth with what remained on his plate and did as requested. Still chewing when they reached the captain's quarters, he swallowed before going inside.

The ship's officers raised their glasses and Captain Mortimer proposed, "A toast to a resourceful young man who earned our everlasting gratitude today."

"I was in the right place at the right time," Henning said. "It was pure luck."

"That's what the cook said." Mortimer grinned. "I told him he too would be lucky if he had your determination and ability to get along with people."

That night, Henning couldn't sleep. The search for food had prolonged *Clipper's* voyage by a week, during which several freighters would have unloaded in San Francisco. For all he knew, they had delivered enough to saturate the market for everything he planned to take there.

CHAPTER TWELVE
NO WAY TO TREAT A CUSTOMER

As usual Lima's port city was enveloped in *garúa*, a mist that coated everything with a slippery film making it difficult for the crew to climb the ratlines and lower sails.

Combing his white hair, Tómas Sánchez stopped beside Henning who was admiring the row of large cannons at the fortress protecting the harbor.

"I get homesick every time I come here," Sánchez said. "My father was Peruvian and I grew up in Lima."

"Are Lima's markets likely to have these items in large quantities?" Henning handed over his shopping list.

Glancing at it, Sánchez replied, "Back when Lima was the most important city in the Spanish empire, its markets were as good as any in the New World. Things had gone downhill by the time I lived there and I'm sure they're even worse now. The only way to know for sure is to go inland and see for yourself."

Henning's next question was cut short when Captain Mortimer stormed past, cursing as *Clipper* dropped anchor in the middle of the harbor.

"Why are we stopping?" Henning asked.

"Peru doesn't let ships dock without permission," Mortimer replied, "and there won't be anyone to give that 'til tomorrow."

"I've never been in a port that requires permission to dock."

"It's Peru's way of discouraging smuggling," Mortimer explained.

"Will you be here long enough for me to find out what's available in Lima?"

"No. I'll leave the instant the larders are restocked. We're ten days behind schedule. That's enough to get me fired."

Henning faced a treacherous choice. Should he stay or go? If Lima offered the goods on his list, he'd be back in San Francisco weeks sooner than if he continued on with *Clipper*. But otherwise he'd be forced to find a way to Chile after *Clipper* had left. That would be next to impossible with most of the area's ocean going ships abandoned in San Francisco Bay.

******

With dawn an hour away, Henning came on deck. Captain Mortimer and *Clipper's* other officers were already there.

"If you leave now," Mortimer said, handing documents to his purser, Fernando Acosta, "you'll be first at the customshouse."

Neither Henning nor anyone else onboard—except possibly the cook—had eaten for two days. Stomach growling, Henning stood at the rail as Acosta's slow-moving launch grew faint in the gloomy *garúa*. Stomach growling, he willed Acosta's escorts to row faster.

He stayed until the deck was deserted. Then until the harbor was engulfed in white haze. Finally the haze burned off revealing faraway mountains, each higher than the one in front. In the foreground Lima's bell towers beckoned, making it almost physically painful for Henning to be idle at the pleasure of petty officials.

At noon, Acosta returned, his expression sour.

"Oranges," he said, handing the cabin boy a well-stuffed burlap bag. "Give some to Captain Mortimer and then distribute the rest."

"Do we have permission to dock?" Mortimer asked.

"The authorities asked to see our bills of lading."

"We don't have any," Mortimer bellowed. "The only thing we're carrying is ballast."

"I told them that and also mentioned that we're out of food. They bought those oranges and sold 'em to me at a hefty profit, then demanded an affidavit signed by you and swearing that we're not carrying cargo. We'll also have to pay a special fee."

"For what?" Mortimer demanded. "Damn Peruvians are worse thieves than Mexicans. They steal time as well as money. Hell, you took enough papers to satisfy any other port on earth."

Mortimer went below to prepare the requested document. He soon returned, a bottle of rum cradled in each arm, and slid them inside the bag where the oranges had been.

"A bribe should speed things along," he told Acosta. "Let's go."

"Why so early?" Acosta asked. "It's *siesta* time. Customs won't open for two hours."

"I don't want to be at the end of a long line."

******

When Mortimer and Acosta returned they were smiling.

"We're cleared to dock," Mortimer told Henning, "and a purveyor is bringing food. I asked him about the merchandise you need. He says you'll find it in Lima, but don't be too sure. Peruvians think it's courteous to give you the answer you want—even if it's not true."

"Guess I'll take my chances in Lima," Henning said.

"Good luck."

Powered by a light breeze *Clipper* glided into a berth. As the ramp was lowered, Tómas Sánchez called Henning's attention to a line of coaches beyond the docks.

"Those *calesas* are the only transportation available," Sánchez said. "Avoid the ones in bad condition. A breakdown will make you easy prey for bandits between here and Lima."

Henning hid his Colt Paterson by detaching its stock from the barrel and sliding both inside his bedroll.

"It's against the law to carry firearms in Peru," Sánchez whispered. "If you're caught, there's a local custom you'll find useful. It's called bribery."

"Much obliged," Henning said. "You've been extremely helpful."

Going down the gangplank Henning stayed to his right, avoiding stevedores bringing bags of food aboard.

"This way to customs." A man in uniform said, pointing to the door beneath an *Aduana* sign.

Inside, Henning stopped at an inspection table beneath a hanging flag with three vertical stripes—red, white, red—and Peru's coat of arms centered in the white one. An inspector pried the lid from Henning's wooden crate. Extending an index finger he counted twelve bottles of whiskey, then said, "You can only bring two of these into Peru."

"What if I pay the tax?" Henning asked.

"That can be arranged." The inspector set four bottles behind his counter.

In San Francisco fine scotch whiskey cost well over a hundred dollars a bottle. Knowing he'd need favors, Henning had brought a dozen. He wanted to keep them and pay the tax at the official cashier's window, but didn't insist. Distracted by the chance to steal something desirable, the inspector hadn't gone through his bedroll and saddlebags. Or seen his rifle and cash.

Outside, a moneychanger rushed up. Henning exchanged enough dollars to get him to Lima, where Sánchez had promised a better exchange rate. Stopping at a vendor's cart he bought bananas and mangoes. A meal in a restaurant would've been preferable, but he was in a hurry.

A bell clanged as Henning took his place in the line waiting for Lima-bound *calesas*.

"What does that mean?" he asked the man ahead.

"It means the *calesas* stop running in an hour and won't start again until tomorrow," the man replied.

Late arriving passengers unashamedly crowded into line. Henning spread his arms to stop them. In San Francisco this would've provoked fist fights. But in Callao people simply took a wider path around him.

Calesas were freight wagons with benches and sunshades. Used hard and neglected, they were pulled by too few mules and were all the slower because drivers rode their lead animals to make room for another paying fare. One after another, vehicles rolled in, disgorged passengers, then reloaded and headed out. Still far from boarding after a half hour, Henning joined the pushing and shoving, gaining ground he soon lost to people ruder and equally determined.

Last week he'd finished reading *Voyage of the Beagle* in which Charles Darwin recounted his famous five-year, around-the-world trip. On his way to the Galapagos Islands—where he'd made observations that became the basis for his theory of evolution—the famed British naturalist had described Callao as filthy, ill-built, and foul smelling. And had characterized its inhabitants as every conceivable mixture of European, Negro, and Indian blood.

Things have only gotten worse, Henning thought.

When his turn came, the first of four waiting *calesas* pulled forward. Seeing Henning waiting alone, the driver said, "If I don't have a full load by six o'clock, I won't go to Lima until tomorrow. With bandits as active as they are, I refuse to be out after dark."

"How much to hire your entire vehicle and leave immediately?"

"Twenty dollars."

Henning protested. Tómas Sánchez had said the normal fare was less than a dollar per passenger. And this *calesa* could carry only six.

"The price is higher for non-Peruvians," the driver explained. "Foreigners carry money and valuables, making it more likely *bandidos* will rob them and delay me. But if you hire a guard I'll only charge fifteen dollars." He waved to a cluster of men.

A swarthy half-breed stepped forward, beat-up pistol shoved behind his belt. He quoted a fee so low that Henning's concern about his honesty became doubt about his competence.

Sensing this, the driver said, "Santos works here when he's not on duty with the *Guardia Civil.* He's a policeman and very well-trained."

Though not yet hired, Santos loaded Henning's luggage and reached for the saddlebags slung across his shoulder.

"I'll put those aboard," he offered when Henning pulled back.

"No thank you." Henning stepped toward the *calesa.*

To stop him from boarding, Santos threw out an arm. "Allow me," he said, then dusted the seats with his handkerchief and lowered himself onto the rearmost. Henning sat on the other, facing backward so he could watch his bodyguard.

With five empty seats, the driver dismounted from his lead mule and sat beside Henning.

"Why doesn't the *Guardia Civil* get these bandits under control?" Henning asked as the *calesa* rolled out of town.

"The bandits are corrupt policemen," the driver replied. "Look around. If there was a serious attempt to capture them, they wouldn't have a prayer of getting away."

"I see what you mean," Henning said. Like giant pointing fingers, plumes of dust hung over everything that moved across the surrounding countryside's flat, barren surface.

"There's talk an English company might build a railway between Callao and Lima," Santos offered.

"That should put the bandits out of business," Henning said.

"Bodyguards and *calesas* too," the driver added glumly.

Santos made a show of watching their surroundings, but his gaze constantly returned to Henning's saddlebags. Henning slid the Colt Paterson from his bedroll, then reattached the stock and laid it across his lap, barrel pointed toward Santos.

"It's illegal to carry firearms in Peru, *señor*," the bodyguard said, eyelids no longer at half-mast, hand closer to his pistol.

"I have a permit," Henning lied, turning his rifle so its barrel pointed the other way.

After an hour Santos jerked his thumb toward a roadside statue of a lady, her arms extended in blessing.

"This is La Legua," he said. "We're halfway to Lima and past the danger. You can put your rifle away."

"In a little while," Henning replied.

Later the *calesa* crossed a bridge over the Rímac River and sped toward an opening in the adobe wall around Lima. The driver stopped so Henning could read a plaque. It said the wall had been built by Viceroy Melchor de Navarra in 1684 to protect the city from raiders the English called privateers and Peruvians called pirates.

Piled inside the wall, stinking garbage also encircled Lima.

"Why did they put the dump so close to the city?" Henning asked.

"People are supposed to take garbage outside the wall," Santos replied, "but no one bothers."

Traveling an avenue between weeping willows, Henning heard dogs barking, children shouting, and the cries of poultry. He disassembled the Colt Paterson and put it back in his bedroll. They entered Lima's business district through a portico guarded by a stern policeman who waved to Santos.

Noticing Henning's interest in the portico's plaster figures, the driver pointed and said, "That one's a copy of a life-size wooden statue representing death in human form. The original was carved by Manuel Chili, an Indian woodcarver. It's so awe-inspiring that he died of fright when he woke up beside it the morning after he finished."

"Because he'd done a good job?" Henning asked, raising an eyebrow. "Or a bad one?"

Lima's downtown was even more disorderly than San Francisco's. More than half the people jamming narrow sidewalks were Indians and half-breeds with skin the color of raw sienna. Most women balanced pails of water or baskets of fruit on their heads.

A wagon with a broken wheel blocked traffic. Taking advantage of this captive audience, an organ grinder had set up on a nearby curb. His two tufted monkeys wore clown suits. Tails entwined, they did a creditable imitation of a waltz. When finished they approached their audience with cups and paused longest in front of cooing women.

The driver detoured down a side street past two vultures fighting over rubbish. Nearby, a *Quechua* woman hurried along carrying a perfectly good wheelbarrow on her back.

"I read that South America's Indians are one of few peoples who didn't invent the wheel," Henning said. "Looks like they still don't have much use for it."

A chuckle rumbled out of Santos. Henning handed over a Spanish copy of his shopping list and asked, "Where can I buy these in large quantities?"

"You can buy food in the outdoor markets and mules from peasants," Santos answered. "For large numbers of the other items, you'll have to go to craftsmen who make them."

"It's too late to accomplish anything today." The driver nudged Henning with an elbow. "You may as well go to the *Alameda de los Descalzos* and enjoy the parade of *Limeñas*. I can take you there if you like."

According to a book Henning had read, *Limeñas*, Lima's women, were reputedly the most attractive in South America. In certain neighborhoods they put on their finery and came outside to be admired every afternoon.

"If you're going, we should get started," the driver said, "Bullfights and the promenade of *Limeñas* are the only events in Lima that start on time."

"After three days without eating, I'm more interested in a meal," Henning said. "Can you recommend a hotel with a dining room?"

"There's one near the *Plaza Central.* I'll take you."

Lima had once been splendid. Now the ornate fountains were dry. Streetlights had been stolen from their posts, and church towers had no bells. Buildings from the city's elegant past had Moorish balconies and intricate wrought-iron grilles over every window. But their exterior plaster needed paint and was crisscrossed with cracks.

The *calesa* stopped.

"End of the line, the *Plaza Central.*" The driver jumped from his seat and placed a wooden stool in the street so Henning could step down.

Pointing to a majestic three-story building, Santos said, "The best hotel in Peru."

Elegantly dressed people were going and coming through its unique revolving door. After Henning's spartan life in the goldfields and during his voyage, a room there would be worth its price. Unfortunately, he wouldn't be welcomed.

Early that morning, he'd tried to make himself presentable. Using a sliver of soap, a rag, and a basin, he'd managed a bath of sorts, then shaved with the dirty water and trimmed his hair with a straight razor. His clothes had been clean before the *calesa* ride, but shabby even then.

"Can you take me someplace less exclusive?" he asked the driver.

"I know just the place."

A few blocks away, outside a lesser hotel, Santos said, "*Adiós.*"

"I'm glad you turned out not to be a bandit," Henning told him, causing Santos's thick lips to curve upward. "I'm starving. Can you recommend a restaurant around here?"

"They're all good, but they close between lunch and dinner."

Too hungry to wait, Henning locked his luggage in his room and threw his saddlebags over his shoulder. He'd seen vendors selling food in the *Plaza Central.*

CHAPTER THIRTEEN
WOMAN FROM ANOTHER WORLD

Huge ficus trees shaded the *Plaza Central*. At the intersection of diagonal walkways dividing the block into four triangles, the statue of a horse and rider honored Francisco Pizarro, the *conquistador* who founded Lima. To Henning, the avenue between him and the plaza seemed like a barrier, much like streets that separated upper from lower classes in his native Hamburg.

His tattered clothes wouldn't be well received by the stylishly dressed gentry sitting in the plaza's cool shade, enjoying their city's relaxed pace. But he'd be welcomed by vendors hawking beverages and hot food. Unable to resist the provocative aromas Henning crossed the street, avoiding holes where paving stones were missing.

From a grill six inches above the sidewalk, a man sold him *anticuchos*, small shish kebobs served with tangy green chili sauce, corn on the cob, and sweet potato. The stones supporting the metal where they'd cooked had obviously been pried from the street.

From another peddler Henning bought four *empanadas*, small pastries stuffed with meat, rice, onions, and raisins. A woman in Indian garb sliced two avocados in half and removed the pits, then asked if he preferred salt or sugar. From a wooden pail balanced on his head, a peddler sold him milk and pineapple ices and wafer cookies. Next he downed a glass of pure orange juice, far tastier than San Francisco's watered down version.

Eager to eat more but knowing he'd regret it, he set out for a clothing shop he'd seen from the *calesa*. The tailor inside looked offended when he inquired about ready-to-wear clothes.

"We don't offer that kind of merchandise, *señor*," he sniffed. "Everything we sell is made to order. With good cause, the British refer to mass-produced clothing as slopwork."

"How much for two trousers, four shirts, and a suit?"

"Pick the styles you want and I'll give you a price." The tailor pointed to a stack of sketches. While being measured Henning thumbed through them. Most were from Rome, Paris, New York, or London. The style he preferred was captioned: 'Worn by San Francisco's Most Discriminating Men.' Apparently he wasn't discriminating. He always wore ready-made clothes called all-done outfits.

Henning made his selections and asked, "How much?" The tailor quoted an unbelievably low price. Dispensing with the normal haggling, Henning asked, "Do you accept dollars?"

"No, *señor*. You have to exchange your money at a bank, and while you're at it you should buy your fabric. I'll write down the amounts you need."

So much for the bargain price. "If I bring this right away, how soon can you have my order ready?"

"Two weeks."

"Are you sure? I won't be in Peru any longer than that."

"Your clothes will be ready on time, *señor*."

At a bank full of customers and crisp echoes, Henning eventually reached the head of a long line. A bored clerk filled out a document and sent him to an even longer line. Twenty minutes later another clerk checked Henning's dollars for counterfeits, initialed the document, and pointed to a third line. When Henning's turn came, a supervisor sauntered to the vault and returned with Peruvian banknotes. He counted them multiple times before sliding them under the wrought-iron grill.

In San Francisco Henning had sold eighty thousand dollars' worth of gold in less time.

At the fabric shop he selected cotton shirting—a white, two blues, and a green—plus linen for his trousers—chocolate brown and charcoal. Next he chose gray alpaca wool for his suit.

Handed a bill before his order was cut from the bolts, he protested, "You've made a mistake. These prices are higher than the ones posted."

"We charge foreigners more," the proprietor replied.

"Do you take me for a fool?" Henning shot back.

The proprietor asked another customer if he could help her, evidently willing to lose the sale rather than back down. Henning left but soon returned. He hadn't found any fabric he liked in other shops.

When he took his material next door, the tailor was cutting a length of thread on a broken tooth. Once his mouth was available he said, "You forgot to buy lining and thread."

"You didn't tell me to."

"I didn't think it was necessary. Everyone knows you can't make a suit without them."

******

By the time Henning returned, the *Plaza Central's* gaslights were lit. Seated among lilies and shrubs, people were enjoying leisurely conversation—a sight never seen in San Francisco where time was a commodity to be converted into money. Henning sat on a bench with missing slats.

Still caught up in the Gold Country's urgency, he wanted to gain time by asking men around him where he could buy the goods he needed. But Peruvians of status looked down on people who earned a living with their hands, and his were calloused and discolored. He slid them into his pockets. Like his threadbare clothes and scuffed saddlebags, they were beneath the plaza's tone.

A street urchin with impressive dignity, sad brown eyes, and straight black hair stopped in front of him.

"I'm looking for work," the boy said. Years younger than Henning he was a *cholo*, part Indian and part Caucasian. As such, he had more status than pure Indians but lived on the fringes of polite society, as Henning once had.

"What's your name?" Henning asked.

"Alcalino Valdivia, *señor*. At your service."

"Well, Alcalino, my name is Henning Dietzel."

Henning stood and offered the much shorter boy a handshake. Alcalino stifled a grin as his hand disappeared inside a much larger one. Henning sat and gestured to the empty spot beside him. Alcalino remained standing. Like the Indians in California, he knew his place.

"Can you help me make some purchases?" Henning read his list aloud and then said, "I need everything by the fifties and hundreds."

"You can get food in the market," Alcalino replied. "You'll have to order the other items directly from men who make them."

"And where do I find such men?"

"In villages south of town. I can take you there."

"Will your parents object if you work late?"

"I'm fifteen years old. I go where I want when I want."

"What wage are you asking?"

Alcalino lifted his shoulders and let them fall. "I'll leave that to your discretion, *señor*."

"What time do the stores and markets open?"

"Nine o'clock."

"Meet me here at eight tomorrow morning. If you're a good worker, I'll give you two week's work at good pay."

"I'll be here."

"Eight o'clock at the latest," Henning said firmly. "If you're late I'll hire someone else."

"I understand, *señor*," Alcalino glanced at Henning's saddlebags, then added, "You should have those over your arm—not across your shoulder. Otherwise thieves with razors will cut them open from behind. You won't feel a thing until it's too late."

"Thanks for the warning." Henning lowered the saddlebags to his lap.

An adobe wall blanketed with flowering vines surrounded the plaza and dampened the sound of passing traffic. Henning's attention was called to two men on the other side. Visible from the shoulders up, they mysteriously floated through the air as if on rails.

At the plaza's entrance the men swept into view aboard high-stepping horses with manes past their shoulders and long tails that resembled shimmering waterfalls. Heads thrust high they vibrated with energy. Every man in the plaza rose to his feet applauding, a surprising display from such a dignified audience.

Alcalino's fingers brushed Henning's elbow. "Take off your hat, *señor*, when the ambassador leaves his carriage."

A splendid coach stopped behind the riders. The driver and his assistant scrambled from their perch, opened the vehicle's door, and stood at attention.

The man who got out wore a cloak made of *vicuña*, a Peruvian wool more costly than silk. Had he entered a theater in the middle of a play, the audience would've looked away from the stage to admire him.

Reluctantly exposing his ragged, self-administered haircut Henning removed the broad-brimmed that had shaded him before sunset.

"Who is that?" he asked, leaning toward Alcalino.

"*Don* Manuel Prado, *señor*. The horses you were admiring are his. He's taking them to Argentina's president as a gift."

Don was a title reserved for very important men and Prado looked the part. He was tall and thin with a high forehead, piercing eyes, and a neatly kept beard. According to a nearby conversation, his walking stick was three hundred fifty years old. Its ornate white handle had been carved from the hip bone of Francisco Pizarro's horse and its shaft had been part of Lima's first flagpole. Over the years countless hands had rubbed its wood with oil, imparting a glow more elegant than varnish's garish glare.

Lima was famous for its ladies and the plaza was full of men accustomed to the best. Nonetheless, every voice went silent as Prado helped a woman from the coach. She was stunning—breathtakingly gorgeous. With her at his side the ambassador glided into the plaza, flourishing his walking stick in rhythm with his body. She moved with courtly elegance. Loose brunette curls hung almost to her waist. As she came closer, Henning saw expressive green eyes and full pink lips. She was younger than he'd first thought.

"Is she the ambassador's wife?" he whispered.

"No, she's his daughter and unmarried even though she's seventeen." Alcalino's tone said this was scandalous. "*Don* Manuel's wife is dead. He and his daughter—her name is Martine—came here last week from his estate in the north. They're about to leave for Argentina, where he'll be Peru's new ambassador."

Halfway across the plaza Martine Prado lapsed into a loose jointed, sassy strut that somehow managed to be feminine as well as athletic. When she stopped, young men gathered around. Latin males took pride in putting women under their thumbs, but there was no hint of subservience in this one. Instead, her admirers looked eager to please.

She shook her head, apparently rejecting an invitation. Her suitors wouldn't be refused and succeeded in getting her back inside the coach.

The coachman and his assistant unhooked the horses and led them aside. The dandies stepped into the horses' former positions and pulled the coach forward. Physical exertion was normally beneath their social class, but they didn't stop until they'd taken *Señorita* Prado all the way around the *Plaza Central*. Back where they'd started, they paused to catch their breath, then opened the coach door and welcomed its passenger outside.

"What was that about?" Henning asked Alcalino.

"It's a way of showing admiration."

The swains who'd pulled the wagon weren't alone in their fascination with *Señorita* Prado. No man there—young or old—looked away from her more than briefly. Though most were no doubt married, none seemed to feel as guilty as Henning. He was glad Encinas would never know he'd been fascinated by another woman—however briefly.

The ambassador and his daughter sat on a bench and were instantly surrounded. As demanded by the Spanish-speaking world's code of conduct, the younger men listened while their elders did the talking. Now and again one of the older boys was sent to the bar across the street to fetch drinks.

When *Don* Manuel and his daughter boarded their carriage, Alcalino whispered, "If you're lonely, I can take you where there are other beautiful girls."

"Girls that are for sale?"

"No." Alcalino grinned impishly. "For rent."

"No thank you. I have someone waiting for me…at least I hope so."

The ambassador's carriage disappeared around a corner. Henning slung his saddlebags across his shoulder and said, "I'll meet you here at eight o'clock sharp tomorrow morning."

After a few steps he looked back and saw Alcalino following, obviously concerned.

"It's difficult to break old habits," Henning explained, lowering the saddlebags over his forearm where no one could cut them open from behind.

CHAPTER FOURTEEN
THE ARISTOCRAT'S IMPOVERISHED SON

Henning reached the *Plaza Central* before eight the next morning. Alcalino was already there. Again Henning was struck by the boy's thinness. In daylight, he looked undernourished.

"Have you had breakfast?" Henning asked.

"I don't eat in the morning," Alcalino replied as if the decision was voluntary.

Henning led the way to a restaurant where he offered a generous tip if Alcalino's breakfast was served quickly.

"Today I want to go through as many shops and markets as possible," Henning said as Alcalino finished a double serving of eggs, beans, rice, and bacon. "Tomorrow I'll place orders with the artisans whose work I like best."

Alcalino led the way to a patch of bare ground inside a square of side-by-side wooden booths. In one Henning saw a row of handmade boots. When he took a pair off the shelf he saw the leather had been properly cured, then sewn with impressive craftsmanship and waterproofed with beeswax.

"I'll pay you to tell me who made these," he said as a man appeared from behind a curtain.

"How much?"

"Sixteen *reales.*"

"That's not enough."

"Are you sure?" Henning placed two eight-*real* coins on the counter between them. The man slid both over the edge into a cigar box, then wrote an address on a scrap of newspaper.

Back outside, Alcalino asked, "Why did you show your money before he accepted?"

"To make my offer more tempting."

"I was surprised he changed his mind."

"I expected it. People respond one way to what they hear and another to what they see."

Ten hours later Henning's mood was expansive for a man normally stingy with words. He'd gotten two dozen addresses and had greatly enjoyed teaching Alcalino about human nature.

"Eat breakfast before we get together tomorrow morning," he said, handing Alcalino a coin as they parted company.

He stopped at a bathhouse and was ushered to a tub of gray water and soap scum.

"If you want hot, clean water," the attendant said, "you'll have to pay double."

"Clean the tub before you refill it," Henning said, imagining Martine Prado's pert nose wrinkled in disgust.

After being scrubbed, the tub was half filled from a nearby ditch. Then the attendant topped it off with buckets of steaming water. Using a brush and lye soap Henning washed so thoroughly his skin stung.

Freshly combed and shaved, he hurried to the *Plaza Central. Don* Manuel Prado and his daughter were already there. After a day of wondering if she would still be as beguiling, Henning found her more so. Everything about her fascinated him—the way her mouth moved, her sparkling eyes, the way she tilted her head as she listened, the crisp ring of her laughter. A maroon dress covered her from neck to wrists and ankles. It added an aura of purity, but also clung in a tantalizing way.

Henning's arrival was followed by that of a young gentleman riding a horse and leading another that carried an empty sidesaddle. With well-polished courtesy he invited *Señorita* Prado to ride. She declined as two elderly men seated themselves beside Henning.

"They say she's an excellent rider but refuses to use a sidesaddle," one whispered gravely.

"She rides astride?" the other exclaimed.

"Yes, and in public no less. I'm afraid *Don* Manuel permits her more freedom than is wise with daughters."

"That would mean…" the speaker paused, searching for adequately delicate words, "she wears trousers in public."

"So I'm told. Of course *Don* Manuel has the good sense not to allow her to do that in Lima. However, a friend of mine in the Chiriaco Valley has seen her riding astride, without a chaperone and wearing her dead brother's trousers."

"I hope *Don* Manuel won't regret his failure to properly discipline her," the other man said with inflection that didn't match his words.

Lying in bed that night Henning tried to imagine Martine Prado in trousers but found it difficult to picture her at all. He'd seen her only twice, from a distance. Why had she made such an impression? He arranged his pillow as a backrest and lit the lantern on the nightstand. Periodically licking his fingertip he turned the pages of *Don Quixote*, the book he was currently reading. Finally he found the passage he sought: 'All kinds of beauty do not inspire love; there is a kind which only pleases the sight, but does not captivate the affections.'

Henning put out the lamp and sat in the dark. He felt as he had during his boyhood fascination with Professor von Duisburg's daughter. *Fräulein* Lange had cautioned him that such infatuations were unhealthy. But he'd survived his first and was very much enjoying his second.

******

Next morning Henning and Alcalino rode rented horses to the hamlet of Barranco where streets were lined by one-story adobe structures with common walls. Along the *Avenida Central* they passed signs advertising blacksmiths, glassblowers, woodworkers, tent makers, and cobblers. Turning down a side street they saw businesses belonging to men who refined whale oil, distilled liquor, rolled cigars, roasted coffee, and made sulfur matches.

As Henning set out to find the men whose work he'd admired in Lima, Alcalino said, "You'll get better prices by offering U.S. dollars. Peruvians prefer them because North American money holds its value better than ours."

In the establishments they visited, craftsmen lived and worked with their families. Not as sophisticated as Lima's merchants, they quoted their standard prices even though Henning was a foreigner. When he offered to pay in dollars, their eyes lit up.

"I'll give you a bonus," Henning told one after another, "if you hire additional help and finish my merchandise in ten days."

On the way to visit craftsmen in nearby Chorrillos, Alcalino said, "You're buying with dollars and in large quantities. You should pay less than the asking price—not more."

"Under normal circumstances, yes. But right now, time is extremely important." Normally secretive, Henning liked training a protégé and expanded his explanation. "I'm giving these men incentive to work fast because everything I ordered was in short supply when I left San Francisco. If someone brings more before I do, I'll be forced to sell for less."

******

Every morning for ten days Henning revisited the craftsmen and did everything possible to keep them on schedule. This usually involved sending Alcalino to track down employees who hadn't reported for work. Meanwhile Henning handled other problems, and there were many. Metal for pickaxes didn't arrive as scheduled. Leather came to the bootmaker improperly tanned. The tentmaker opened a crate from his supplier and found rotten canvas.

"Shall I find wagons to take your merchandise to Callao?" Alcalino asked as they rode back to Lima one evening.

"I'm going to buy mules instead," Henning replied. "They bring good money in California, and before I sell them they can take my merchandise to the goldfields."

"Can ships carry mules?" Then Alcalino remembered. "Of course they can. Ambassador Prado's horses are going to Argentina by ship."

"Vessels at sea often carry livestock and poultry, keeping them alive until it's time to cook them. That way the meat doesn't spoil."

"But if you take mules, you'll want them to survive." Alcalino smiled. "I can be useful in that regard because I know how to care for them. And how to load a packsaddle."

Henning slowed his horse. When Alcalino came alongside, he looked the boy in the eye. "Are you offering to go to California with me?"

"*Sí, señor.*"

"What about your family?"

"I have no family. I live in a tack room at a stable in exchange for cleaning stalls."

"Someone brought you up."

"My mother was the servant of a wealthy *patrón*. He raised me as much as anyone. I think he was my father, but I hated the way he treated me after my mother died so I ran away."

"You know a lot about business. Did he teach you?"

"He wouldn't, so I learned by watching him. How did you learn, *señor?*"

"I was born with a knack for commerce, and my grandfather worked for a wealthy man who sent me to an academy. The other students were from prosperous families, and in Prussia rich boys are taught to make money."

"But if they're rich, they already have plenty."

"Enough for you perhaps, but not for them."

"Take me to San Francisco, please," Alcalino said, pleading with his gentle brown eyes.

Henning's merchandise would be more than he could handle alone. And in California he'd have to hire the world's most expensive workers. But should he take Alcalino where people of his race were mistreated…and worse?

His first year in California, Henning had seen '48ers trick Ohlone Indians into trading gold for worthless trinkets. When the natives caught on, they took their gold to assay offices. There, clerks stole as much as they paid for by substituting two-ounce weights for the one-ounce size normally used on their scales.

When the '49ers arrived, they didn't bother to fleece Indians. They found it easier to rob them at gunpoint and faster to simply shoot them.

"Most Yankees won't treat you well," Henning told Alcalino.

"I've worked for *yanquis*," the boy replied. "I know how to keep from offending them. How old were you when you left Prussia?"

"Younger than you are now."

"Then why won't you take me to California? You won't regret it."

******

After making his temporary employee permanent the following afternoon, Henning bought thirty mules. Alcalino turned out to know a great deal about their care but couldn't balance cargo on their backs. He'd seen it done, but found it more difficult than he'd anticipated.

Disappointed, Henning hired an expert to teach them both. After several lessons Henning could load a packsaddle, but Alcalino still couldn't. Henning paid the muleteer to help him transport his merchandise to a Lima warehouse.

After turning his mules loose in a rented corral Henning told Alcalino, "Watch them until I get back."

"Where are you going, *señor.*"

"To buy hay."

"That's what I thought. You should take me with you."

"Why?"

"I want to make up for not being very good at loading packsaddles."

"How will you do that?"

"Let me show you, please," Alcalino replied eagerly.

Henning gave in.

In the far corner of an outdoor market, they saw stacks of hay and a sign quoting Abel Costa's per-pound price.

"I bought from him once before, but I doubt he remembers," Alcalino said quietly as they tied up the mules brought to carry their purchase. "When you order your hay, make him think you're not coming back."

Henning did as requested and Costa lifted four bales onto a scale, then put several iron discs on its counterweight hanger. When he excused himself to greet another customer, Alcalino cut the twine on one bale and pried it open. Inside, it was damp.

"He'd never do this to a regular customer," Alcalino whispered, "but when Costa gets a buyer he won't see again, he sells them hay where he poured water to increase its weight." Alcalino opened a second bale releasing the sour, earthy smell of mold. "That's what happens after he wets hay down for several days while waiting for strangers."

"Have you got four fresh, dry bales?" Henning asked when Costa returned.

Caught red-handed, Costa didn't attempt to explain. He pushed a cart to a nearby stack and brought more bales. Broken open, they proved to be dry and mold free.

"What kind of discount do I get if I buy five tons?" Henning asked.

"I don't have that much."

"Can you get it?"

Costa plunged his eyebrows into a V. "Yes, if you can wait for two days."

"How much?" Unhappy with Costa's answer, Henning asked, "Is that the best you can do for such a large sale?"

Costa lowered his quote.

"That includes delivery to the docks in Callao, right?"

Costa's cheeks inflated and he blew out a sigh. "*Sí Señor.*"

Alcalino struggled to hold the corners of his mouth down when Henning said, "Bring twine so you can retie the bales after *Señor* Valdivia inspects and approves them."

Back at the mules' corral Henning handed Alcalino a crisp, red banknote and said, "Today you made up for fibbing about your ability to load a packsaddle. And earned this bonus."

Unable to hide his delight, Alcalino stashed the bill in his shoe.

When Lima's far-flung outdoor market opened the next morning Henning, Alcalino, and the muleteer were waiting with seven mules each. Henning zeroed in on the man behind the counter at the largest stand and said, "I need a half dozen hundred pound bags each of coffee, flour, dried beans, corn, rice, wheat, and oats at a good price."

"For a sale that big, I'll give you a sensational price," the shopkeeper replied, dispatching employees in several different directions. "But first I need to collect some of your order from other vendors. It won't take long."

Before Henning paid the bill, Alcalino had a bag of rice poured into a bin.

"You'll have to hire people to clean those rock chips from the rice, oats, and wheat," he told the shopkeeper.

"That's not included in my price," the shopkeeper said.

"It is if you want to make this sale," Henning silenced him. In a gentler voice he asked Alcalino, "How did you know to look for those?"

"My mother's *patrón* insisted I have them removed when I bought grain for him."

After years of threshing wheat on bare ground in his grandfather's fields, Henning knew such impurities were inevitable. But he hadn't thought to check for them because grain in Germany was sifted before going to market.

"I appreciate your diligence," he said, dropping three coins on Alcalino's palm. "Like your *patrón*, my customers won't appreciate breaking their teeth."

By then the shopkeeper had hired every boy in sight to clean the grain. While they worked Henning bought a trunk and the clothing Alcalino would need in California.

******

Thirty minutes from the market, Henning's group stopped their mules outside the rented warehouse where he stored his merchandise. He left Alcalino and the muleteer to stack his latest purchase in its dingy interior, lit by shafts of light filtered through dirty windows and cobwebs.

Twelve kilometers later, Henning was in Callao trying to find a San Francisco-bound ship. For the fifth time in five days, he failed.

"Are your mules' crates ready yet?" the harbor's freight agent asked as they stood near a freighter's busy gangplank.

"Any day now," Henning replied.

"Give the builder a push. Ships bound for San Francisco will continue on without you if you can't load your mules immediately."

The carpenter shop was closed.

Back in Lima, Henning told Alcalino, "Before coming to work in the morning, get yourself ready to travel. We may have to leave on short notice."

Back in his room after a bath and a visit to the tailor, Henning dressed in his new gray alpaca suit. On his way to the *Plaza Central* for what could be the last time, he went down the hotel stairs, imaging how he'd introduce himself to Martine Prado if only he was brave enough. Shy with females, he'd exchanged very few words with any but Encinas, his mother, and *Fräulein* Lange.

Self-conscious in his new suit, Henning wondered if he looked as ridiculous as he felt. But as he passed the lobby's full-length mirror he saw a dashing figure in a jacket and trousers that both fit his long limbs perfectly. His face was angular and defined, a welcome change from its boyish roundness. And his ever more muscular body was nearly in proportion to his height.

Looking more closely, he realized Grandpa Dietzel's prediction had come true. He looked like his father.

CHAPTER FIFTEEN
A VERY EXPENSIVE MISTAKE

The *Plaza Central* was nearly empty.

"I've never seen so few people here," Henning told a man on a bench. "What happened?"

"Everyone left after Ambassador Prado sent word that his trip was moved up. He and his daughter sail tomorrow. We're all invited to see them off in Callao."

"What time and where?"

"Three p.m. Pier One."

That night Henning drifted in and out of sleep, trying to decide which appealed more, *Señorita* Prado's beauty or her vitality. He'd always liked women with energy, and she sparkled with it. He had to see her one last time.

Next morning he was aboard the first *calesa* to Callao. At nine o'clock he checked on his shipping pens. They were ready. At noon he inspected two fishing boats, newly converted for passenger service to meet the demands of the gold rush. He booked space on *Pescador* because it looked faster.

In an exclusive bathhouse he scrubbed with a soft, luxurious wash cloth and then dried himself with a fluffy, heated towel. Ten minutes later he was at Pier One in his new suit and tie. The wharf was packed. One man carried a sign that read: *"Vaya con Dios Embajador Prado"* (Go with God Ambassador Prado).

Martine and her father weren't among those who first boarded the Argentina-bound ship.

"Can you tell me when Ambassador Prado will go aboard?" Henning asked the officer in charge of a nearby police detachment.

"I have no idea," the man replied curtly.

"Could you please find out?" Henning pressed.

The officer looked at Henning for the first time. Apparently impressed, he respectfully said, "My men and I accompanied the ambassador and his daughter to their suite ahead of the other passengers. When the ship is ready to sail, they'll come topside and wave goodbye." Turning toward the crowd, he raised his voice. "Step aside please." When people didn't move fast enough he ordered, "Clear this gentleman a path to Pier One."

Two *Guardia Civil* officers ushered Henning through the crowd, not stopping until they reached people so important they didn't move aside even for policemen.

Later Ambassador Prado and Martine stood near the quarterdeck, waving to well-wishers until their ship left. As the crowd dispersed, Henning dashed to the pier's edge and watched the vessel clear the harbor.

He blew out a robust sigh. If only Martine could have seen how good he looked in his new suit.

******

An hour later Henning suffered another disappointment, this one at a counter in Callao's customhouse. His cargo and mules required an export permit, which would take two weeks to issue. And in Peru two weeks meant three or more. Fresh from California where not even imports needed permits, Henning was infuriated. When he'd inquired a week earlier, another official had assured him no permits were needed.

"It may be insufferable," the man in charge said when Henning protested, "but it's also unavoidable."

By law, export formalities were handled by customs agents, who had more business than they could handle. Two days later Henning finally found one willing to take on another customer. But Ricardo Rivas was worn down by thirty years of dealing with a notoriously stubborn bureaucracy. He moved slowly. And rather than pay for cabs—cabriolet carriages for hire— he walked everywhere he went.

"I'll pay four times your normal fee if you get my permit in a week," Henning offered after the first day. "I'll even hire a carriage so you can get around faster. And I'll go with you so you don't lose time bringing documents for my signature."

"The price I quoted includes the customary bribes," Rivas replied. "Getting your permits faster will require larger amounts, and you'll have to advance me the money."

Bribes were customary in Latin America but Henning had never paid one. "I prefer not to do anything dishonest," he said, "and—"

"Actually," Rivas interrupted, "you've greased several palms already. I did it on your behalf, of course, but with your money. Without that incentive the only way to get your stuff out of Peru is to smuggle it, and smuggling is a crime whereas bribes are an accepted part of doing business. Government employees couldn't feed their families without them."

"How much will it take?"

Surprised to learn officials could be bribed for amounts that hardly justified their loss of integrity, Henning handed Rivas the money. For days they visited buildings where doors were chained shut before closing time and remained that way long after they should've reopened. The offices were understaffed and the clerks slow. They moved faster after Henning gave their bosses bottles of scotch whiskey from San Francisco.

Night after night Henning tallied his expenditures, fed-up with a process that had no purpose beyond collecting taxes, fees, and graft. With the permit almost ready, *Pescador* sailed with other men and cargo in Henning's place. Henning found another ship, *Lágrima*. She'd been a whaler and her foul stench had discouraged all but the most determined passengers.

The next day Henning, Alcalino, and ten armed guards brought a caravan of heavily laden mules from Lima to Callao. At the entrance to the docks, they were met by a flatbed wagon and stevedores.

"You'll have to transfer your cargo to our vehicle," the dockmaster said.

"My cargo is going aboard that ship." Henning pointed to *Lágrima*, fifty yards away. "My mules can take it the rest of the way."

"Outside transportation is forbidden on the docks, *señor*."

"These mules aren't outside transportation. They're mine and they're traveling on *Lágrima*. See that hay near the gangplank? It's for them."

"Don't worry, *señor*. Our services are cheap."

Henning stifled an exasperated protest that would only make matters worse, and the stevedores started transferring bags and boxes from his mules to their wagon. When the first load was heavy enough to flatten the vehicle's worn-out springs, the dockworkers' mules dug in and pulled it toward the waiting ship. Partway there a wheel shattered with a resounding crack. Finding and installing a replacement took the rest of the day.

Henning's cargo was loaded the following morning. Shortly after noon the first mule was hoisted then lowered onto the deck with a hand-operated block and tackle. To Henning's amazement the animal didn't struggle. One by one the others hung in their slings, heads down, watching the dock below as they went up and studying *Lágrima's* deck as they came down. But they weren't so docile while being led to their pens on the ship's stern, where the stench of butchered whales was strongest.

******

Lágrima's captain kept her at half-speed and within sight of shore after clearing the harbor. Within an hour, two ships—traveling farther out—overtook and passed her. Either or both might be carrying trade goods that would make San Francisco's shortages into gluts before Henning got there.

"I just took command of this tub," the captain said when Henning complained. "I want to be absolutely certain she's seaworthy before I take any chances."

"Pray for the Lord's protection, then hoist the rest of the sails, and take her farther out," grumbled a burly Peruvian with a thick moustache. "If you continue at this speed and follow the shoreline all the way to California, the gold will be gone by the time we get there."

Clearly appealing for good luck, the captain knocked several times on a wooden rail and said, "I never tempt God by taking unnecessary risks—even though I don't believe in Him."

Next day, *Lágrima* moved away from the coast and began making better time. North of Panama City she passed a clipper going the other way.

"You coming from California?" the captain bellowed through his speaking trumpet.

"Aye, from San Francisco," the clipper's captain answered.

"What's the latest news?"

"California is joining the Union as a state."

"Slave or free?"

"Free."

Henning felt like cheering. He couldn't believe the so-called Land of the Free had countenanced slavery for more than two centuries.

At Puntarenas a lanky Costa Rican came aboard with goods to sell in San Francisco. He wouldn't say what was in his crates and kept to himself except for repeated attempts to buy Henning's mules. Finally he offered five hundred dollars apiece. Having seen mules sold for seven fifty in the Gold Country, Henning turned him down.

When *Lágrima* tied up in San Francisco, the wharves were congested with crates, barrels, and bales.

Amazed, Alcalino said, "California is a land of plenty."

"Let's hope there isn't plenty of what we brought," Henning replied.

While stevedores unloaded his mules and merchandise, Henning learned that schooners were taking passengers and cargo up the Sacramento River to the Gold Country in a fraction of the time needed for overland travel. Leaving his shipment in Alcalino's care he went to find out how much the trip would cost. Partway across the docks, he noticed Alcalino following him.

"Why aren't you watching my merchandise?" he asked.

"I'm too small to stop a thief."

"Just being there will stop them. They don't operate in broad daylight with people watching."

But Californians had no respect for so-called inferior races. In a rush to get his goods to market, Henning had forgotten how dangerous it would be for an Indian to enforce rules in San Francisco.

"You're right," he said, reversing course. "I'll hire a guard so you can come with me."

Later Henning's mules and merchandise were crammed aboard *Lucky Lady*, minus a crate of lanterns stolen during Alcalino's absence. The schooner crossed the bay, passed Benicia, and sailed through the Carquinez Strait. As it entered the Sacramento River, buzzing mosquitoes enveloped the ship, distracting passengers' attention from elk—several with huge antlers—on both banks.

"This ain't nuthin'," a deckhand with an Irish brogue hollered. "At times the mosquitoes here are so thick they turn day into night. Last week I balanced a quart of whiskey on a stick and raised it into a swarm. When

I withdrew me stick, the bottle stayed up there. The females was holdin' it while the males fought to see who'd have the honor of takin' the first drink."

"Tragic waste of good whiskey," another Irish-accented voice piped up.

"Naw. It wasn't good Irish whiskey but English swill that poisoned every mosquito dumb enough to drink it."

At Sutter's Landing in Sacramento, newly constructed wharves and warehouses were protected by private guards, the first law enforcement Henning had seen in California. Smaller than San Francisco's docks, these were also less crowded. Henning had done well to save time by taking *Lucky Lady*. San Francisco's glut of freight hadn't yet reached Sacramento.

Two strangers approached. "I'm Perry Miller," one said. "If the price and quality are right, I'll buy everything you've got, wholesale."

"I'm selling retail," Henning replied.

"You'll find it difficult to compete with my eight stores. And you'll make more money by selling to me wholesale and going for another shipment."

Miller's claim had merit. Henning could go to Peru and return in the time it would take to retail his merchandise. In the process, he'd probably earn more. And be beyond the reach of vigilantes.

"That's an interesting possibility," he said.

"Do you have an inventory of your goods?"

Henning handed over the Peruvian export permit. Miller scowled and said. "I've seen some real crap come outta Peru."

"You won't find better quality than this. See for yourself."

Miller's assistant opened random crates and pawed through their contents.

"I hope you don't have an inflated idea of this stuff's value," Miller haggled. "Remember, I'm buying wholesale not retail."

"The mules alone will bring seven hundred and fifty dollars apiece," Henning said.

"Eight months ago maybe. Not now. Mexicans have been pouring in from Sonora with mule trains, and the wholesale price is down to a hundred fifty dollars. What about this grain? Is it fulla grit like most from Peru?"

"I had it cleaned," Henning replied. "Take a look."

Miller's assistant found nothing to help beat down Henning's price.

"How much for everything but the mules?" Miller asked.

After several offers and counteroffers, Henning heard a price he could accept.

"I'm finding it difficult to get merchandise," Miller said as he paid. "Can you bring me another shipment exactly like the one I just bought?"

"That would be risky," Henning replied. "How do I know someone else won't bring all you need before I get back?"

"Don't worry. My stores sell everything I can get, and I'll pay the same price as this time."

"You willing to shake on that?"

"Don't be insulting." Miller turned and waved.

Responding to this signal, men drove up in four large wagons and started loading.

"If I bring an identical shipment," Henning clarified, "you'll pay no less than you did for this one? Right?"

"No more either. If I guarantee my price, you'll have to guarantee yours."

"You have a deal. How do I contact you when I get back?"

After Miller left, other merchants came to bid on the mules. None would top Miller's offer and only one would match it. Seeing the abundance of other mules on the dock, Henning accepted.

During the return voyage to San Francisco, Henning and Alcalino were in very different moods. Astonished by the sum he'd seen Miller count out, Alcalino was upbeat. Henning couldn't stop brooding over his failure to sell his mules to the Costa Rican. He'd intended for them to transport his merchandise and then be sold for a hefty profit. But thanks to *Lucky Lady*, they'd added to the freight bill they were supposed to minimize. And thanks to Mexicans, they'd sold for less than they cost.

Bringing mules had been stupid as it turned out. Earlier, before leaving Sacramento, Henning had learned that Mexicans were flooding the market even before his trip to Peru. Prior to leaving, he should have made sure they were still in demand. But he'd broken even anyhow. And he had a buyer for his next shipment, a giant step toward realizing a longtime dream and becoming a merchant.

******

Between the docks and the hotel district Henning and Alcalino passed through San Francisco's notorious Sydney Town. Also known as the Barbary Coast, it was ruled by ex-convicts from Australia. Their much feared gang, the Sydney Ducks, committed most of the area's crime and controlled its vice.

Rain had reduced the streets to deep, sucking mud. Last year, merchants had hired teamsters to stabilize them with wagonloads of chaparral and sand. When that didn't work storekeepers had heaved empty crates, hogsheads of spoiled tobacco, bags of weevil-infested flour, and sacks of stale coffee into the muck outside their businesses—to serve as stepping stones if they stopped sinking.

Planked sidewalks were found only in San Francisco's better neighborhoods—except for Barbary Coast's block-long promenade where streetwalkers paraded, high heels clicking seductively. Henning wasn't surprised that Alcalino couldn't stop gawking. The only prostitutes he'd ever seen were part or pure Indian and had olive skin, black hair, and brown eyes. A *cholo* like him could only dream of lying with a pink-skinned, light-eyed woman who had blonde, red, or brunette hair.

One girl spit in Alcalino's direction. The others looked away with disgust. Knowing the Sydney Ducks would beat an Indian senseless if they caught him showing interest in their girls, Henning sped up and didn't slow down until they reached a quiet neighborhood.

"In a perfect world," he said, "people wouldn't have to stick with their own kind. But here in San Francisco it's a good idea. Going back to Sydney Town could get you killed."

"I understand," Alcalino replied.

Later, looking disappointed, Henning came out of the downtown post office and led the way into a smoky restaurant. Waiting for their barbecued ribs and baked potatoes, he noticed Alcalino's eyes seemed less prominent after weeks of regular meals. The boy also seemed unruffled by the streetwalkers' contempt. But rejection was always painful, as Henning's empty post office box had reminded him. The difference was Alcalino's loneliness could be soothed by any reasonably acceptable woman while Henning needed one in particular.

"If you want," Henning offered, "I'll take you where you can find companionship."

"Will I be welcome?" Alcalino asked.

"There's a place called the Black Cat. It's run by a Peruvian whose girls are from Lima."

"Do we have time?"

"We'll make time."

In the sprawling tent city called *Chilecito*, Little Chile, the flashiest landmark was the Black Cat, a two-story bordello. A man at the bar seemed offended when Alcalino came in, but held his tongue. No less prejudiced than Yankees, Hispanics were gentler.

In a large room with threadbare yellow couches and dusty silk roses in ceramic vases, eight dark-haired, brown-eyed girls lined up for Alcalino's inspection. He went upstairs with one who was astonishingly shy considering her profession. Forty-five minutes later they still hadn't returned. Apparently the Black Cat's girls weren't like their Barbary Coast sisters, who were notorious for competing to see which got the most men in and out of her room in the least time.

Sitting alone on a lumpy couch, Henning was targeted by a voluptuous woman who strutted past, skintight low-cut gown dragging the floor. She pretended to lose a shoe in front of him and lifted her dress to put it back on. Henning caught a glimpse of sheer stockings and feet squeezed into tight high-heel shoes. Peruvian men had a fetish for feet, especially small ones. Displaying them was a special favor.

Henning declined that invitation and others. He was saving himself, but for whom? Encinas Peralta? Martine Prado? He'd never see Martine again. And his post office box hadn't received a single letter, though he'd sent its address to Encinas months ago.

By the time Henning and Alcalino went outside, the streets were overrun with rodents. Mice scurried from one hiding place to the next. Rats sauntered as though they had a right to be there. A man came out of a warehouse and locked the door behind himself.

"Damned rats," he shouted, throwing a rock at one that had ventured too close. Seeing Henning he complained, "Blasted vermin damage thousands of dollars' worth of merchandise. Every time I trap one, two more take its place. It's impossible to get rid of them."

Financial incentive discourages use of the word impossible, Henning thought, sensing potential profit.

CHAPTER SIXTEEN
SURPLUS MOUSERS

Back in Peru with another shipment ready to go, Henning was shepherding his customs agent, Ricardo Rivas, through the process that would eventually yield an export permit. Eager to get back to San Francisco, he was beginning to hate Callao.

The miserable little seaport offered no comfort or entertainment. It was filthy and had neither plumbing nor sanitation. The stench of human waste and garbage fouled its air. People constantly came out of miserable shacks and dumped wash basins and garbage pails in the streets. If there was a paradise for rats and mice this was it. Yet Henning hadn't seen any.

On the way to his hotel one night, he noticed several half-wild cats, slinking in the shadows. Like most hunters they were going about their business without attracting attention. Henning asked around and learned that they'd been brought in to keep rodents under control. Since then they'd multiplied to where they were having trouble feeding themselves.

******

The chief of Callao's *Guardia Civil* played his famous trick on as many foreigners as possible. He'd ask one to lunch or dinner, then stuff himself and wash his food down with expensive wine. After dessert he'd tastefully suggest his guest had broken this or that law—providing an opportunity to bribe him by paying the check. Rumor was that one had held out until locked in a cell.

Like most potential victims Henning had been warned, but went the chief one better and invited him to dinner. The savvy chief accepted—no doubt wondering why a man who'd studiously avoided him would inexplicably change course.

They went to the Blue Moon, the only restaurant in town with glass in its windows, tablecloths, and tile rather than dirt floors. The headwaiter seated them at a corner table where the comings and goings of others wouldn't disturb them.

When customers came in or went out, cats snuck in before the doors closed. A street urchin, apparently hired by the restaurant, was catching these moochers and taking them outside. Though working at top speed, he soon ran afoul of Callao's supreme legal authority.

"*Cholo*," the chief roared, kicking a cat that had rubbed against his leg. "Do your job. Get rid of this parasite."

The boy bagged his prey and carried it outside.

"What does he do with them?" Henning asked.

"He takes them to a wall down the street," the chief answered.

Henning had seen that wall. There the feline intruder would be transferred to a bloodstained bag and bashed against unyielding bricks—not a pleasant thought during dinner.

"Damn cats are a worse nuisance than the rats they were brought in to control," the chief complained. "I'd do this town a favor if I had my men shoot half of them."

"If you like," Henning remarked casually, "I'll take some with me to California."

"So that's why you asked me to dinner," the chief said. "Give me a dollar apiece and take as many as you want."

Delighted with that amount Henning negotiated anyhow. The wily chief refused to budge, but became less likely to raise his price later.

The next morning Henning located the owner of an abandoned poultry farm on Callao's outskirts. He rented two large coops and hired six boys. When they reported for work he gave them cloth masks, brooms, shovels, mops, buckets, and hammers.

"I'll be back as soon as possible," he told Alcalino. "When the boys finish cleaning and scrubbing, have them patch the walls. Don't spare the lumber or nails. I bought plenty because these coops have to be so secure that not even a cockroach can escape."

"The job is done," Alcalino said when Henning returned.

"Is it done well?"

"*Sí Señor.*"

Alcalino and the boys watched, looking more embarrassed with each board Henning nailed over the openings they'd left.

"Come back tomorrow," he said after paying them. "If you're here by eight o'clock, I'll give you a chance to earn much more than you did today. And I'll give you a dollar for every friend you bring."

******

Driving his rented carriage to their hotel, Henning told Alcalino, "I booked space on a vessel that leaves in a week. Before we sail, you and the boys have to catch three hundred cats and I have to look over Ricardo Rivas's shoulder while he adds them to my export permit."

Early next morning at the poultry farm, Henning handed Alcalino a bag of canvas gloves.

"When the boys get here, give them these for protection and tell them I'll pay three U.S. dollars for every cat they catch. I'm told they'll find plenty at that dump over there."

Waiting in a government office with Ricardo Rivas, Henning designed a cat trap. While Rivas ate lunch, he took his sketch to a carpenter.

"I'll pay double for every trap you make by tomorrow morning," he offered.

"How many do you want?" the carpenter asked.

"As many as you can make by eight o'clock."

"In that case I'll hire help and work through the night."

"I was hoping you'd say that."

Later at Ricardo Rivas's office, Henning was surprised when Alcalino arrived to report, "The boys have only caught three cats. They want to be paid by the hour."

"That would leave them with no incentive." Henning explained how he wanted the situation handled, stressing, "There's no time to lose. We need three hundred cats in a week."

He hired Alcalino a cab and said, "On your way back to the dump, buy a bag of anchovies for the boys to use as bait."

The driver brought Alcalino back to report, "They insist on being paid by the hour."

Henning sighed. "I'll talk to them."

With swinging arms and long strides, he led Alcalino to his carriage. It had no springs and punished them while violently bouncing along the rutted road to the dump, where Henning counted thirty-two boys sitting in the dirt. He gathered them around, speeding up the process by passing out candy.

"Every boy who brings in at least two cats today," he announced, "will get a trap tomorrow. With it, he can catch ten cats a day. At that rate he'll earn two hundred and ten dollars this week—more than his father gets paid for three months' work."

"When I told them the same thing, they laughed," Alcalino said as the boys began hunting with renewed energy.

"Did you emphasize what we want from them more than how much they can receive for doing it?"

"No. I told them they can earn a fortune."

"It's hard to visualize a fortune. That's why I gave them an exact amount and compared it to their fathers' wages."

Next day, the boys baited their traps with anchovies and caught almost a hundred cats. But some had mange and others were missing eyes, ears, tails, or toes—imperfections that would make them less saleable.

When Henning paid the boys that evening he announced, "Starting tomorrow, I'll pay twice as much for females in good condition and nothing for those that are defective, or for males under seven kilos."

"Why?" the oldest boy asked.

"Because they're useless to me and we'll have to turn them loose."

"Why don't we kill them instead?" the boy asked. "If we let them go, we'll wind up catching them again."

"I'll have someone prepare another chicken coop so we can put them there until we're finished," Henning replied.

"Why go to all that trouble? Are you like those monks who can't step on an ant?"

An image of the horse he'd shot in Ambush Pass flashed through Henning's mind. He'd also killed men that day, but they'd deserved it. The horse had simply been in his way, much as the imperfect cats were now.

"Someday I might want more cats. It's in my interest to leave plenty of breeding stock," he said, to silence the boy's objections—not because it was true. This would be his only shipment of cats. He planned to take mostly females, which would sell for better prices because they could produce a litter of kittens every three months.

Like Callao, San Francisco would soon have all the cats it needed.

******

In 1848 San Francisco had been a cluster of shanties around Yerba Buena Cove. By the time Henning returned with his second shipment, the shelf between the bay and the hills was crowded with businesses and residences. And more building sites had been created by sinking abandoned ships in coves, then covering them with rocks and dirt.

Drawn by the world's highest prices, shiploads of lumber arrived almost daily from mills in California as well as the Oregon and Washington Territories. Even so, there was never enough for the carpenters nailing it together at top speed.

'No large city on the west coast of the Americas has less to fear from earthquakes,' a developer's advertisements boasted. He was right. With the exception of San Francisco, those cities had been built with adobe. During earthquakes their heavy buildings collapsed and crushed people. San Francisco's flexible, lightweight, wooden structures didn't come down as easily and inflicted fewer casualties when they did.

But San Francisco faced another, equally deadly threat.

******

Henning was fast asleep in a hotel room when a hand touched his shoulder. He looked up and saw Alcalino, a red glow reflecting from his dark eyes.

"What is it?" Henning asked.

"I'm not sure, *señor.*" Alcalino's attention was riveted to something beyond the window.

Henning heard clanging bells. A split second later someone hammered the door and a gravelly voice shouted, "Fire. The whole town's in peril."

"Be right out." Henning leapt to his feet. Pulling on his pants, he heard the same announcement next door. Then farther away.

"You'll find buckets in the lobby," someone in the hall yelled. "Bring two per man and be quick about it."

Looking through the window Henning saw flames above distant rooftops and tar colored smoke being blown toward the warehouses where his shipment was—including the cats.

Henning and Alcalino joined men sprinting down the hall. In the lobby each grabbed two wooden pails. An excited stampede pushed them toward the fire where a man was organizing a bucket brigade to bring water from the bay. Unable to understand English, Alcalino copied what Henning did.

One after another, pails of water were speedily passed from a stranger to Alcalino to Henning to the man ahead of him, who wore a blue sailor's blouse. A scarlet sash intertwined with linked gold nuggets held up his leather pants.

"Dis my fourth fire," he said with an unnaturally calm New Orleans accent. "When she broke, I wuz tendin' bar at de Bucket of Blood Saloon. It burn ta da groun'. Tomorrow, I be needin' new job."

"Sorry to hear that," Henning said.

"No lacka jobs," the man said philosophically. "I more worried 'bout de house me and ma friends own."

"Where is it?"

"Tree blocks behind us. If it burn, dis gonna be second time."

"We'll save it."

"Don't tink so. Dis de worst fire I seen, and I seen lots. Dis town oughta rebuild with brick. But before de ashes done gone cold, builders be makin' wood houses, same as always." The bartender wiped his brow. "I sworn dis water heavier dan when we started."

An injured firefighter was carried between the line passing water and the one returning empty buckets to the bay. His stretcher was followed by men leaving the head of the brigade—unable to endure the heat any longer, coughing, rubbing their eyes, spitting black phlegm.

Henning and Alcalino were thrust closer to the flames, near enough to see the brigade's buckets being emptied into a pumper wagon's reservoir. The wagon's team had been unhooked and was being held down the street.

"Horses unpredictable around fire," the bartender explained.

Above the pumper's water tank, two volunteer firefighters perched on a platform and teeter-tottered a handle that forced water into a hose. A bulky man clung to the nozzle at its other end, battling the recoil. Hundreds of individuals, including Henning and Alcalino, were producing a feeble stream of water. Most turned to steam before reaching its target.

Unearthly screams dwarfed men's guttural shouts. Released from a livery stable, terrified horses charged in every direction, some toward safety, others toward certain death. Buildings collapsed. The inferno's heat ignited wood without touching it. Planked streets burst into flame. Embers rained down, bringing yelps of pain when they landed on flesh.

"Fall back," the fire chief roared.

The drain valve on a pumper jammed. Loaded with tons of water, the huge vehicle didn't respond to frantic pushing and pulling. Henning, Alcalino, and others lent a hand.

"Damn it," the chief bellowed. "You're pushing at different times. Work together on my count. One…two…three…push."

The pumper rolled a few feet, stopped, and wouldn't budge. The chief grabbed Alcalino's collar, yanked him away, shoved a bigger man into his place. The wagon gathered momentum until screeching brakes said it had gone far enough.

Henning and Alcalino returned to the brigade just before the first explosion.

"De firemen dey blastin' a line trew da neighborhood behind us," the Bucket of Blood bartender observed. "Dey go clear cross da city if dat whaddit takes."

"They just blow up houses and buildings?" Henning couldn't believe it.

"Dat or lose da whole town."

Another blast hurled debris skyward. Henning's cats weren't far behind the still incomplete fire line.

"What with fires, blasting, and newcomers, it's a great time to be in the lumber business," a familiar voice said.

Henning whirled and saw the man who'd taught him to pan gold. Eduardo Vásquez's soot-blackened features were scarcely recognizable beneath a fireman's helmet. There was no trace of the anger he'd shown when they'd parted. Instead he gave Henning one of those artful winks reserved for his close friends.

CHAPTER SEVENTEEN
HOUNDS, DUCKS, AND REGULATORS

"Eduardo," Henning exclaimed, continuing to pass buckets.

"I thought that was you." Eduardo said, teeth unnaturally white in his blackened face. "We have a lot to talk about. Meet me at the Double Diamond Saloon after the fire's out. Make it the Naked Lady if Double Diamond burns." He sprinted away before Henning could reply.

The battle was won at the fire line. Lying on the ground, wood burned slower than standing structures, giving the pumper trucks time to do their jobs.

Later, saloons still standing were overrun by exhausted men who wouldn't be able to sleep until the excitement was out of their systems. Henning and Alcalino confirmed the cats were unhurt and went to meet Eduardo.

Double Diamond's knotty pine walls were covered with newspaper clippings and hunting trophies—deer, elk, pronghorn antelope, and a massive golden bear head. Unusual bottles and antique muskets hung from the high ceiling.

No one had objected when Alcalino helped man the bucket brigade. Now he drew hostile stares. Eduardo and Henning exchanged an *abrazo*, reaching around to slap one another's backs. Eduardo had lost weight in the year since they'd parted. He seemed less aggressive too, but his jutting chin still warned against disagreeing with him.

"You filled out while I did the opposite," Eduardo said, slapping a wad of banknotes into Henning's hand. "That's the deposit you gave me in Chile. I should've returned it when we parted."

Henning found it hard to believe such a sum had ever seemed important. "Why did you return my entire deposit?" he asked. "You're entitled to at least half."

"You idiot. I'd been taking advantage of you. By the time I felt a twinge of conscience, we'd parted ways and it was too late to do the right thing." Eduardo raised a hand to stop Henning's protest. "Tell you what. Buy me dinner, and we'll call it even."

"You've got a deal." Henning introduced Alcalino, then asked, "Are all fires as hard to fight as this one?"

"No, thank God." Eduardo made the sign of the cross. "After most fires, the volunteer companies turn their hoses on each other to empty the water left in the pumpers. New Englanders against New Yorkers and so forth. It's a great way to cool off and break the tension, but this time we barely had the strength to open drain valves."

"Does anyone know how the fire started?" Henning asked.

"It was set on purpose and headed straight for Little Chile before the wind shifted. I'll bet that broke the arsonists' hearts. But I'm sure they consoled themselves by looting while everyone else fought the fire."

"It's hard to believe anyone would intentionally set a fire."

"You don't know the Hounds. They're looking to punish us Chileans for refusing to pay protection money."

The Hounds were a gang, like the Sydney Ducks and Regulators. Most were from New York or British penal colonies in Australia. They'd been responsible for rampant theft on the docks before warehouse owners started hiring them as guards. Proving they learned quickly, the Hounds now demanded protection money from everyone with anything to lose.

"I can't understand why the government hasn't at least made an effort to establish law and order," Henning mused, watching the bartender work his way toward them.

"It isn't the politicians' job to take care of us. It's ours." Eduardo pounded the table with his fist. "I, for one, am glad the government leaves us alone. Public officials in other countries would've diverted California's gold into their own pockets, especially since it's coming from public land." He raised his glass and proposed a toast in a voice loud enough to be heard across the room. "God bless America." The saloon echoed with clinking glasses. "But not all Americans," Eduardo added under his breath.

"Any plans for after you get some sleep?" Henning asked.

"I'm going to the bear and bull fight. Want to come along? The Mexicans are bringing a grizzly and a bull for a fight to the death. Believe me, you've never seen anything like it."

"I've read grizzlies can weigh a ton and carry a steer as easily as a coyote carries a rabbit. How do Mexicans get their hands on an animal like that?"

"With four ropers. Each one catches a paw. Then they flip the bear on his back, let him struggle 'til he's exhausted, and put him in a wheeled cage." Eduardo took a sip of beer. "The trick is to rope both front paws first. If you only get one, a grizzly can grab the lasso and pull a horse right up to him."

"What's the point of having a bear fight a bull?"

"The point, my dear fellow, is to sell tickets and provide opportunities for wagering. I'll give you a tip. Always bet on the grizzly. There's no better fighter on earth."

"Some make that claim for the African lion," Henning said.

"A few years back, a grizzly was taken to Mexico City and matched against a lion. They met in a bullfight arena. Tickets sold for upwards of five hundred dollars apiece, and it turned out the lion isn't King of Beasts after all."

"Five hundred dollars a ticket," Henning exclaimed. "I wouldn't have paid five cents."

"That's because you're a puritan and only interested in work, which is probably why you look so prosperous. What are you doing these days?"

"Bringing supplies from Peru and selling them to a store owner in the Gold Country."

"Why Peru? You'd get better quality in Chile."

"I see you're still the custodian of all truth."

"Custodian hell. I'm the sole owner," Eduardo retorted. "What are you selling?"

"Whatever's in demand. This time I brought three hundred cats among other things."

"You're the one who brought the cats?" Eduardo gave a thumbs-up. "If you price them right, you'll have more customers than you can handle."

Henning switched to English. "I never discuss business in front of Alcalino. He can't keep a secret."

"Then send him away so we can talk freely."

"I can't. It's dangerous for *cholos* to be alone in this town. We'll have to speak English for a while. How much do you think I can get for my cats?"

"Up to two hundred dollars apiece."

"At that price I'll be lucky if people don't fight over them."

"You think you can get more?"

"A lot more."

"Wanna bet?"

"Time to feed the cats," Henning said. "I'll meet you here at eight for dinner. Hope your grizzly wins his fight."

"He will. Good luck selling your mousers for over two hundred bucks. You'll need it."

******

Reaching the warehouse, Henning and Alcalino found several men gathered at its door.

"We heard you have cats for sale," one said. "Can we see them?"

"I'll bring some out here," Henning said, unlocking the door with the key he'd been given. "The owner doesn't want me to let anyone in."

He was more than happy to enforce that rule. If potential buyers saw how many cats he had they'd hang back, waiting for a better price.

Inside, the recently completed warehouse smelled of recently sawed pine and fresh paint. Coarse metal grills covered its windows, restricting incoming light. Holding a flickering lantern, Ralph Milo, the owner, stood by the cat cages.

"How much of a discount do I get if I take three males?" Milo asked.

"You drove a hard bargain when you rented me space," Henning replied. "It's only fair you pay full price."

"Who's gonna pay five hundred dollars for a cat? Even if the damned things do catch a rat once in a while."

"Males cost that much because I have only ten and their owners can charge to have them breed the females. But if price is your only consideration, I'll sell you a female for three hundred."

Milo stamped into his office.

Henning and Alcalino displayed two dozen cats in a cage on the sidewalk and put up a for sale sign. A crowd collected and soon people were buying so fast that bringing replacements kept Alcalino in constant motion.

Less than fifty cats remained when Milo came outside and told Henning. "You win. I'll take three males at five hundred each."

"You're too late," one of the buyers said, reaching into the cage. "The price went up to eight hundred just before I bought this guy, leaving only two available."

"Sometimes the law of supply and demand works for you and sometimes against you," Henning told Milo, grinning.

Earlier Milo could have bought three cats for less than the pair he wound up buying.

After all the cats were sold, Henning took the proceeds to his hotel room. While Alcalino slept, he sat on the floor arranging banknotes in piles according to denomination. Originally he'd considered bringing only male cats, so the new owners couldn't breed them. Females in their prime could produce up to twenty kittens a year, enough to saturate the market.

He'd changed his mind, anticipating that buyers would pay much more if they could look forward to selling offspring. It was as good a decision as he'd ever made. His cats had brought in nearly a hundred thousand dollars, enough to buy a clipper ship—not that he wanted one.

Lying on the couch and closing his eyes didn't stop Henning from wondering what he should import next. The answer was far from obvious. Large East Coast companies were sending shiploads of merchandise— eliminating shortages and driving prices down. Small operators like him were being forced to look harder for fewer opportunities.

Henning left Alcalino asleep and made his way to the docks on deserted streets. After fighting the fire most of the night and celebrating their eventual victory all morning, San Franciscans were napping. The wharf was empty except for a short, balding man Henning recognized as John Bartlett, the dockmaster.

Wearing his trademark bowtie and formal three piece suit, Bartlett was staring at a mudflat littered with bolts of calico and silk that would be underwater when the tide came in.

"Bringing cats was a damn good idea," he said when Henning stopped beside him.

"How'd you know about that?"

"I'm the dockmaster fer chrissakes. To tell the truth I wish I'da beaten you to the idea. Those cats are gonna sell like hotcakes."

"They already did."

"Then why aren't you in a bar celebratin'?"

"I'm not much for drinking."

"What are you doin' down here?"

"Making a list of things in high demand and short supply."

"A little research goes a long way." Bartlett pointed to the bolts of cloth. "Those were sent by East Coast speculators unaware that women are few and far between out here. They wound up being thrown away because there's no market for ladies' cloth and warehousing costs a fortune. We get more than our share of ill-advised shipments—razors for a population that doesn't shave, saddles for which there are no horses, stoves for a city where cooking is done over open fires. Unlike you, a lot of speculators leap before they look."

About to mention his fiasco with the mules, Henning was knocked forward by Bartlett's congratulatory thump on the back.

"Of course," Bartlett continued, "some speculators have had spectacular successes, the most notable being houses made with walls fabricated back east."

Henning had seen such houses. The walls arrived by ship and were taken to building sites, then assembled, sold, and occupied in a single day. Built by the dozens they'd pushed the tent cities and shantytowns into the hills behind town.

"Being the dockmaster," Henning said, "you know this town's shortages and surpluses better than anyone. What would you recommend I bring next?"

"At the moment there's a surplus of necessities," Bartlett replied, "but if you bring the right luxuries, they'll sell. San Francisco's fulla men with money in their pockets. Carpenters are turning up their noses at wages ten times higher than can be had anywhere else. Cooks' incomes tripled because they were being hired away from restaurants by groups of miners who didn't wanna spend time preparing food." Bartlett switched to a personal tone. "I've been watching you. It's nice to see a young man work hard and use his head for something besides a hat rack."

This second round of praise from the normally unfriendly dockmaster surprised Henning.

"Bring me some *pisco* from time to time," Bartlett added, "and you'll be the first to know about shortages and oversupplies."

"What's *pisco*?"

"You really aren't much of a drinker, are you? *Pisco's* a Peruvian brandy distilled from muscat grapes. And it's a lot better'n whiskey or rum."

Bartlett went on his way and Henning hurried to the rapidly growing commercial district. Since he'd last been there, it had doubled in size and added a livery stable, brewery, and three banks. He deposited his money in the one with the best reputation, San Francisco Mercantile.

Going through stores, he found the widest selection and lowest prices he'd yet seen in California. Good for customers, but bad for him.

******

Eduardo and Henning met for dinner at the Double Diamond saloon and sat at a small, round table in the dining area.

"How was the bear and bull fight?" Henning asked.

"With most of the town asleep after the fire, the Mexicans postponed it," Eduardo replied. "Looks like the fire interrupted your routine too. You didn't shave this morning and have a good start on a beard. Let it grow. You'll never be taken seriously while you look as young as your Indian boy, who couldn't generate facial hair if his life depended on it. Where'd you find him?"

"In Lima, Peru."

"You treat him like a protégé."

"My high hopes have been replaced by doubts. In Peru he kept himself busy and was full of information and useful advice. But that changed when I took him out of his world."

"That's how it is with Indians," Eduardo said. "Been to bed since the fire?"

"No. After I left you I sold my cats and spent the rest of the day trying to figure out what I should bring next."

"Seeing you yesterday was a godsend. I've found a once-in-a-lifetime opportunity. Problem is I can't exploit it because I don't have any money. With you as my partner, though…"

Dodging the implied question Henning said, "I was hoping you'd ask about the cats' prices."

"Your enthusiasm was answer enough."

"What are you doing these days?"

"After the *yanquis* forced Roberto and me out of the Sierras, we discovered that bricklayers in San Francisco earn twenty times what we'd get in Chile. Every time there's another fire, the demand for brick buildings increases. We work seven days a week and make more money than most prospectors."

"I'm glad you're doing well."

"I wouldn't call it doing well. People no smarter than me are making ten times what I am," Eduardo said, then smoothly reopened the subject Henning had avoided. "I've found a golden opportunity and you have the money to exploit it. That combination could make for a mutually beneficial partnership."

Henning hadn't forgotten the outburst provoked when he wanted to pan a proven area and Eduardo preferred to look for a bonanza. If they worked together with Henning's money, Eduardo would have to accept a subordinate role. Could he do that?

"What do you have in mind?" Henning asked.

"I'll tell you tomorrow after I look into the details."

"Let's make it Friday. Tomorrow I take the rest of my merchandise to Sutter's Landing."

"Okay. Come to my house when you get back. From now on, you and Alcalino can stay there whenever you're in town."

Next day on Sacramento's docks, Henning showed his goods to Perry Miller, the man who'd bought his first shipment and ordered another. Miller offered less than he'd paid before.

"You agreed to pay the same amount as last time," Henning reminded him.

"There wasn't as much merchandise available back then," Miller snapped. "Now I can pick and choose, so I'm buying from whoever has the best price."

"Are you charging your customers less?"

"Of course not."

"Then why should I lower my price?"

"Because I bought my competitors' stores, making me the only wholesale customer you'll find," Miller sneered. "You can read an excellent discussion of supply and demand in Adam Smith's *Wealth of Nations*."

"That book also contains a description of the moral code Smith called rational self-interest—as opposed to greed."

As Miller stormed off, a man standing nearby stepped forward.

"Couldn't help overhearing," he said. "My name is Fraser Ashton. Perry Miller doesn't know it yet, but I'm his new competitor. I plan to take my merchandise to the diggings rather than make customers come to me. Perry won't much like that aspect of supply and demand. How much do you want for your merchandise?"

Happy with what he'd seen, Ashton later handed over a stack of banknotes and said, "If Miller had kept his promise to you, I might not have been able to find merchandise for weeks. He doesn't often pay a price for breaking his word, but this time he will. He shouldn't have skipped over the moral considerations in *Wealth of Nations*."

"I read them twice," Henning said, "but next time I'll pay closer attention."

CHAPTER EIGHTEEN
PROUD TO BE A GREASER

At Eduardo's house, no one answered Henning's knock. Having expected to sleep there that night, Henning and Alcalino hurried downtown. Too late. Every hotel still standing after the fire was full. They finally found sleeping quarters above a store, where partitions of calico—salvaged from the mudflats and pulled tight across wood frames—divided a room into cubbyholes no bigger than the cots inside.

The next morning Henning went to the post office, hoping to find his first letter from Encinas. Disappointed, he took Alcalino to check Eduardo's house and found it still empty.

At noon they made the rounds again. Still no letter from Encinas, but Eduardo was back.

"Sorry I'm late," he told Henning as they sat on wooden crates in his living room. "My return from Monterey was delayed, but the trip was a huge success. We're in business."

"What business are we in?" Henning asked guardedly.

"Most of Northern California's bakers are Chilean," Eduardo said. "The ones in Little Chile supply San Francisco's bread and pastry. The ones in Monterey take care of that area. At the moment they can only get American flour, but they prefer the kind from their country. If you bring it, they'll buy exclusively from you. I have orders for a shipload, which will cost a hundred twenty thousand dollars wholesale. Do you have that much?"

"Yes, but I haven't agreed to this yet," Henning replied. "Did you collect deposits?"

"If these guys could afford deposits, they'd band together and import their own flour. They'll have to pay after delivery, in installments."

"A lot could go wrong with this deal." Henning crossed his arms over his chest. "What happens if they don't pay?"

"They'll pay. I'll personally vouch for them."

"What if someone in Chile sends flour before I get back?"

"How?" Eduardo boomed. "Chile's merchant fleet is rotting in San Francisco Bay, and every vessel coming this way from elsewhere is full. You, on the other hand, can charter one of the ships that leave here empty."

"What if bakers buy from someone else before I get back?"

"If making money was easy, women and children would do it," Eduardo grumped. "Look, you stand to triple your money. Don't worry. I'll see to it that the bakers don't buy more than it takes to tide them over until you get back."

"Losing a fortune on mules showed me the pitfalls of having all my eggs in one basket."

"Jesus," Eduardo exploded. "Are you afraid people will stop eating bread? This sounds like the disagreement that led us to go our separate ways last year. If you want big rewards, you can't play it safe. I told you that before. Remember?"

"Yes," Henning said. "I also remember that we split up because you searched for a bonanza while I stuck with a sure thing. And that's why I have the money to implement your plan while you don't."

"How about this?" Eduardo said, arrogance gone. "Instead of being your partner, I'll work for you. You make the decisions and I'll settle for a third of the profits. That's only fair since you're putting up the money."

"Having regular customers sounds wonderful and so does working with a friend." Henning paused, then added, "I'll take you up on your offer. But when we disagree I want you to always present your arguments as vigorously as you just did."

"Count on it." Eduardo's wink was exaggerated.

"But I only want to hear them once," Henning clarified.

"I fixed up a room for you and Alcalino. It's not fancy, but from now on my house is your house as we say in Chile."

Henning chartered an Argentine ship, *Nuestra Señora del Rosario*, named after a flagship in the Spanish Armada. Hours before sailing, he checked his post office box yet again. Finding it still empty, he didn't mail his most recent letter to Encinas. She hadn't written because she'd lost interest. He needed to accept that.

******

Worried about his new venture, Henning slept badly during his voyage and arrived in Valparaiso worn out. Determined to fill *Rosario's* hold quickly, he hurried down the gangplank only to have the dockmaster inform him that none of the area's mills could fill such a large request in less than a month. Without stopping to eat, he frantically ordered flour from every mill within miles.

Worn out after dinner, he sent Alcalino back to their noisy cabin aboard ship and splurged on a night in a hotel. He needed to be alone but even in his room's peace and quiet, he couldn't concentrate on reading his new copy of *Wealth of Nations*.

Long after turning out the lantern and stretching out on a bed with life-size roses carved in its headboard, he was wide awake. He'd never been on such a comfortable bed but would gladly have traded it for the lumpy mattress on the floor of Encinas's simple cabin in Talcahuano.

He and she were in the same country for the first time in two years and he desperately wanted to see her. But going three weeks out of his way just to confirm he'd lost her would be insane, especially since he'd gambled a fortune on a speedy return to California.

And why waste time and money on a trip that would only worsen the emptiness he felt after losing the only woman he'd ever loved?

******

Before *Rosario* sailed, Captain D'Arcy replaced two ordinary seamen who'd jumped ship in San Francisco. The new crewmen, Dario and Mateo, had worked with Henning on *Portales* during his first voyage to California. They hung around him when off duty, eager to hear how a former deckhand had risen to where he could charter a ship.

Dario and Mateo—like Henning—were worried his flour would add to surpluses in Monterey and San Francisco, ruining him financially. In Monterey they lowered the gangplank and waited at its bottom as if for a famous man.

"Good luck," Dario said, shaking Henning's hand enthusiastically. "Don't lose heart no matter what happens today."

"I appreciate the encouragement," Henning replied.

"We're encouraging ourselves—not you." Mateo's half smile was higher on one side. "To us you're proof that one day we too might better ourselves."

Ashore, Henning learned the gold rush was now bringing thousands of prospectors a week. Monterey's bakers were out of flour and bought enough to fill their storerooms. On his recommendation, one hired Dario and Mateo. Captain D'Arcy refused to release them until Henning found qualified replacements.

As Dario and Mateo carried their duffle bags across the dock toward what they hoped would be a better future, Henning called out. "Next time we meet I expect you to own a bakery."

"Don't worry, we'll buy our flour from you," Dario responded, looking back.

Near San Francisco, Captain D'Arcy scanned the shoreline with growing frustration.

"Son of a bitch," he exclaimed, lowering his spyglass.

"He can't find the Sentinels," the first mate told Henning.

"The Sentinels?"

"Captain D'Arcy likes to be original. Most people call them the Navigation Trees."

Henning had seen them on previous voyages. Thought to be the world's tallest living things, they were two enormous redwoods, probably thousands of years old, on a hill beyond San Francisco. Towering above a forest of giant redwoods, they could be seen for miles. Navigators used them to find the bay's narrow entrance and then miss a treacherous submerged rock near Yerba Buena Island.

"They're gone," D'Arcy bellowed. "Loggers must have cut them down. Bastards. The two largest trees on earth are gone forever so some jackass could put a few coins in his pocket. That's the problem with a culture where everything is dollarable."

Dollarable. Henning's fascination with word tinkering had come from Latin Americans, who were experts. Long pushed around by Yankees and their dollars, Hispanics frequently made hilarious use of the similarity between their words for dollars, *dólares*, and sorrows, *dolores*.

Dollars were indeed two-edged swords. They provided an alternative to force when people dealt with one another. And their allure encouraged progress. But to get them, men who loved money above all else did things they shouldn't. With consequences that were often unintended but usually bitter.

******

Not long after Henning went ashore at Clark's Point, Eduardo arrived with a line of freight wagons.

"How'd you know I was here?" Henning asked, stepping back from their *abrazo*.

"I gave John Bartlett, the dockmaster, fifty bucks to notify me whenever a shipment of flour came in," Eduardo replied. "This is only the second since you left. I had the bakers buy the first a little at a time, in case you got back sooner than expected. With the number of men arriving these days, I should be able to sell two shiploads next time, provided the Hounds don't shut down the bakeries."

"Why would they do that?"

"For the same reason they set fire to Little Chile after you left. Because we refuse to pay protection money. The men who started the fire were imprisoned on a ship in the harbor, but only because what they did threatened the whole town. There's still no law and very little order. I guess it's foolish to hope for anything else in a city with no jail and tens of thousands of young, undisciplined men. Did you bring the pistols I ordered?"

"Four dozen of the latest Smith & Wessons, with ammunition." Henning pointed to a crate. "But I worry that the Hounds will arm themselves if you and your friends do."

"Let 'em. We'd rather risk death than live as stooges."

After stevedores unloaded *Rosario's* last sack of flour, Eduardo ushered Henning and Alcalino aboard the lead wagon.

"There's talk," he said once the convoy was underway, "about forming a vigilance committee to deal with the gangs, but nothing will come of it. This town can't even prevent the landing of ships bringing convicts from Australian penal colonies. And a vigilance committee would undoubtedly persecute foreigners. Hell, I bet you left the Gold Country because Yankees noticed your accent and ran you out."

"Actually I left because I was accused of five murders."

"You're suspected of murder, yet you come to San Francisco without a second thought. What does that say about this city's law enforcement? Last year we had more killings than the rest of the United States combined. Only two of the men responsible were hanged, and only because they were Mexican." Deep wrinkles appeared on Eduardo's forehead as he added, "How'd you manage to get blamed for five murders?"

"Aren't you going to ask if the accusation is true?"

"I already know that answer."

Henning described the events in Frenchie's Canyon, and his subsequent revenge. Hearing the story for the first time, Alcalino squirmed. More than once he'd passionately expressed opposition to violence, no matter what its purpose. He was clearly disappointed.

The disappointment was mutual. Time had shown that Alcalino lacked the wherewithal to be Henning's protégé. And they'd never be close. Friendship could survive disappointments but couldn't be built on them, and there had been too many. Alcalino shunned responsibility and couldn't keep a secret—crucial failings in the business world. Despite Henning's help and encouragement, he understood little English and spoke less. Instead of showing initiative after finishing jobs, he sat waiting for Henning to bring further instructions.

A hard worker who rarely complained, he'd lost his once-bright promise.

******

Henning was appalled by Little Chile's so-called recovery from the fire. Too poor to afford better, most residents had replaced tents with cloth draped over poles. A few had cobbled together half-breed structures made with canvas stretched across wood frames. And business owners had replaced charred wooden buildings with more of the same.

The fire had shown how quickly flames race through canvas and wood. It hadn't killed anyone but had been a powerful warning. Nonetheless *Chilecito* had been rebuilt into a tinderbox that had flammable dwellings and businesses packed more tightly than ever.

While delivering flour, Henning also distributed Smith & Wessons to bakers who had ordered them. Afterward, he put the remaining revolvers in three knapsacks. Shouldering one each, he, Eduardo, and Alcalino set out on foot to sell them.

As they passed the rebuilt Black Cat brothel, a girl came outside. Fastening a red gauze carnation in her shiny black hair, she stepped in front of Henning and asked, "Want to smell my flower?"

He bent at the waist and sniffed. The fake blossom smelled of perfume.

"Nice," he said.

"There's more elsewhere," she purred.

"Maybe next time." Henning continued on his way.

"You always say that," the girl called after him. "But next time never comes."

As Alcalino shambled past, she crooned, "My name is Rosa," "Have you ever been kissed below the belt?"

Hiding grins, Henning and Eduardo kept walking, eyes pointed forward. A block later Henning's attention was attracted by angry voices. Hounds—six of them carrying chains, axe handles, and rubber hoses with protruding nails—had surrounded Alcalino and Rosa.

Looking like his newspaper photos, the Hound's notorious Michael Keyes scowled at Rosa, who was glaring defiantly, hands on hips.

"If you was to lay down with this 'ere Indian," Keyes said with a thick Cockney accent, "you'd likely come to serious 'arm."

"What authority do you have in *Chilecito*, your lordship?" Halfway through her curtsy she spit on the ground.

"We're the committee for public 'ealth." Keyes brandished a knife. "It's our duty to make sure this city's white citizens don't unknowingly put their dicks where an Indian 'ad 'is."

"There's nothing you can do about that," Rosa shot back.

"You're wrong. We're about to teach this redskin a lesson. When you see how he looks with no ears and half a nose, p'raps you'll wish you'd ignored 'im. Tell you what though, we'll overlook your transgression—just this once—if the Black Cat's owner buys our insurance."

"I'm not sure how these things work, but I think I got it right," Henning announced, spinning the cylinder of the revolver he'd just loaded. As the clicking stopped, he aimed the pistol at the ground and cocked its hammer.

The Hounds spread out.

"You'll regret it if you point that at us," Keyes threatened.

"You'll regret it even more if it accidentally goes off six times." Henning's tone added no menace to his words. He didn't want the confrontation to explode. And it wouldn't if the Hounds had time to think about the price they'd pay for rushing him.

"That's the latest model Smith & Wesson," Keyes said. "Where'd you get it?"

"It?" Henning asked. "I brought four dozen for merchants you gentleman are harassing here in Little Chile."

Keyes squinted. "I seen you before with that Indian and these papists. One day we'll show you what 'appens to people who 'ang around with redskins and followers o' the Pope."

"That would've been easier before I stopped importing pots and pans and started bringing six-shooters."

"I never once seen you with a beard," Keyes muttered. "Clean-shaven men are better with pens and ledgers than with pistols."

Henning heard the crisp click of Eduardo cocking another revolver. Keyes and his men did an almost military about-face and swaggered away.

"My money says they went for reinforcements," Eduardo said. "Let's get these sold before they come back."

Henning sold his remaining revolvers exactly as he'd sold the others—at cost, even though he could have gotten many times more in other parts of town. Twenty-two of Little Chile's grateful residents wore their new pistols in plain sight while guarding Eduardo's house that night.

******

After a late breakfast Henning was at the desk in Eduardo's living room, entering expenses in his ledger.

"There was a riot downtown last night," Eduardo interrupted, turning the page of his newspaper.

"The Hounds again?" Henning asked.

"No. Hungry prospectors protesting food prices. The authorities needed help from greasers to get 'em under control."

"What greasers?"

"How much do you know about the *Gamarra*?"

"Only what I've read in the *Alta California*." Henning stood and stretched.

Gamarra was a Peruvian warship anchored in San Francisco Bay. The mayor had angrily referred to it a "foreign military presence." Its captain insisted he was there to repair Peruvian-owned vessels in the Ghost Fleet and send them home or auction them off. That's all they'd done so far. But a crewmember interviewed by reporters had let it slip that *Gamarra* had a second mission—to intervene if San Francisco's Yankees continued to abuse Peruvians. Published, his revelation had made the ship more unwelcome than ever.

"After yesterday's looting broke out," Eduardo said, "the mayor asked *Gamarra's* commander, José María Silva Rodríguez, for help. The man was good enough to send marines who disbursed the rioters and earned an official commendation."

"Must make you proud to be a greaser." Henning grinned.

"It was definitely gratifying. On one side were Yankees—dressed in rags, and breaking the law with no clear idea as to how that might help them. And keeping them under control were South Americans—disciplined, groomed, uniforms creased, knowing exactly what they were doing and why. Not the usual stereotypes."

Holding a dishtowel and plate, Alcalino joined them from the kitchen.

"Was anyone hurt?" he asked. "Or killed?"

"From what I read," Eduardo said, "the marines were sorely provoked but accomplished their purpose without firing a shot."

"Which means they did their job without violence," Alcalino said, approval in his voice. "Bet we don't see much abuse of Peruvians while *Gamarra* is here."

"We wouldn't see any at all if they'd shot a rioter or two," Eduardo challenged.

"That would depend," Alcalino replied, "on whether those rioters' friends and relatives tried to get revenge."

Eduardo drew breath for a retort that didn't come.

"Admit it," Henning teased. "Alcalino has a point."

******

El Pórtico de Mauricio, Mauricio's Porch, was *Chilecito's* busiest bar. After the fire set by the Hounds destroyed it, the latest version had been cobbled together with a combination of new and salvaged wood. Inside, Mauricio Pérez—affectionately known as *El Gordo,* fatty—waddled up to Henning with a glass of light-brown liquid in one hand and a bottle in the other.

"*Cola de mono,* monkey's tail," he said, handing Henning a glassful. "It's the Chilean equivalent of eggnog and very popular at Christmas. How much more alcohol should I add?"

Pérez had prepared his specialty with coffee, milk, cinnamon, and sugar—adding a splash of *aguardiente* before garnishing it with orange peel.

Henning took a sip and said, "Perfect."

"You're just being polite," Pérez said. "It has almost no *aguardiente.*"

Any was too much for Henning's taste, but rather than offend he said, "It's fine. Really."

All around them, Little Chile's residents were enjoying their annual Christmas Eve party. At one end of the bar was a *pesebre* with crude figurines representing baby Jesus, Mary, Joseph, a donkey, and an ox.

Ramon Cruz, a baker, came out from behind a table of pastries with a slice of *pan de pascua,* spice cake with rum, nuts, and golden *sultana* raisins. He handed it to Henning and raised his glass high.

"May I have your attention please," Cruz boomed. "Christmas is for celebrating the birth of Jesus Christ. It may be blasphemous to mention the son of God and Henning Dietzel in the same breath. But without the revolvers he sold us at no profit, we'd be paying protection money. At the very least, we owe him a toast."

Glasses clinked and a roomful of baritone voices crisply said, "*Salud.*"

Henning took his last bite of cake as three young men marched up to him.

"We're bricklayers on some of San Francisco's biggest construction projects, which puts us in a position for a little tit for tat," their spokesman said in flawless English. "The tit we offer isn't as nice as those found on women, but we'd like to show our gratitude by introducing you to potential customers. Are you available tomorrow?"

"Have you forgotten tomorrow's Christmas?" Henning asked.

"We and the men we'd like you to meet work seven days a week, including holidays. What else can you do in a town with so few ladies?"

The next day Henning met the bricklayers, each at a different job site. They recommended him to a shopkeeper who needed merchandise for his soon-to-be-finished store, a man looking to buy furniture for a hotel he had under construction, and Andrew Larsen, a San Francisco contractor desperate for building material. All three gave Henning large orders.

Two days later the bakers paid for their flour and ordered more. That night Henning chartered *Liberty*, the largest freighter in port, and went with her to Valparaiso. He filled her with flour and the goods ordered by his new customers, then stayed behind with Alcalino while she took her cargo to San Francisco.

Waiting for *Liberty's* return, Henning roamed Valparaiso buying plows, harrows, grain shovels, and mechanical planters. California now imported less food, closing one door but opening another because the state's fledgling farmers desperately needed tools.

With nothing more to do until *Liberty* returned, Henning resorted to killing time. Lonely, he considered going to the House of Smiles but again pride stopped him. Even if Encinas was still there, visiting her after she didn't answer his letters would be a mistake.

And it made even less sense that Martine Prado kept coming to mind. She was in Argentina, out of his life forever. And even if she weren't, he didn't have the nerve to approach a woman of her status and beauty.

******

Three more times Henning sent flour for the bakers, building material for Andrew Larsen, and merchandise San Francisco's shopkeepers had ordered from Eduardo. Twice *Liberty* returned with orders for more. The third time, her captain handed Henning an envelope from Eduardo and said, "Bad news I'm afraid."

'San Francisco's shops are overstocked,' Henning read. 'Large East Coast companies are sending better construction supplies than ours, as well as flour at a price we can't match. Grateful as *Chilecito's* bakers are, they can't buy their basic ingredient for more than competitors pay. When you get back, we'll figure out what to do next.'

Eduardo had enclosed a list of goods currently in demand—chandeliers, office furniture, harnesses for carriage horses, and printing presses. Henning bought those and filled *Liberty's* remaining space with prospectors eager to join the gold rush.

You'll have to pay for a round-trip, Valparaiso-San Francisco-Valparaiso," *Liberty's* owner, Rodrigo Salazar, insisted when Henning was ready to depart.

"Why?" Henning asked. "I don't need *Liberty* after she unloads at Clark's Point."

"Pay for a round-trip or find another ship," Salazar said. "There's no freight coming out of San Francisco, and I'm not going to waste money sailing a ship with nothing but ballast."

"You've done that often and made a good profit every time."

"Not as much as I could have."

"But more than you ever did before." Henning's voice grew louder. "What about the contract we signed."

"Null and void."

"Your signature means nothing?"

"Not since I noticed the shortage of San Francisco-bound ships with space available. You can pay for a round-trip—in advance—or take your merchandise off my ship and try to find another before the gold rush is over."

"What about the passengers who bought passage?"

"I'll sell them new tickets after you refund their money."

"Never thought I'd see the day a Chilean would screw the man who saved Little Chile."

"What the hell are you talking about?"

"Forget it."

Nothing Henning could say would change Salazar's mind. The man was a shameless opportunist, but he turned out to be right about one thing. Henning had no choice—not with a fifteen month backlog of cases clogging up Valparaiso's courts.

Liberty's captain disappeared hours after Henning signed a roundtrip charter and paid in advance. His replacement was James Morgan. Henning had never mistrusted anyone as quickly or completely.

CHAPTER NINETEEN
A SHORTAGE OF COFFINS

When *Liberty* came alongside San Francisco's pier at midnight, no dockhands jumped forward to secure the mooring lines. The lone man on the wharf wore a bandanna across his face.

"Do you need a physician to care for your sick?" he shouted through a speaking trumpet.

Captain James Morgan cupped his hands around his mouth and bellowed, "We have no sick. Who the hell are you?"

"John Bartlett, the dockmaster."

"This is the first time I've been welcomed to a port by the dockmaster."

"I'm not necessarily welcoming you. Any deaths during your voyage?"

"Where are the men to help us tie up?"

"Answer my question." Bartlett pointed to an iron bell. "Otherwise I'll sound the alarm and armed men will prevent you from landing."

"There were no deaths."

"Any sick? Crew or passengers?"

"Everyone's healthy," Captain Morgan thundered. "Why wouldn't they be?"

"Because there's cholera."

Henning felt a chill. His mother had died of cholera. She'd wakened one morning feeling fine and breathed her last agonizing breath before bedtime.

Every conversation on *Liberty's* deck stopped. Passengers and crew gathered along the rail staring past the wharves toward town—not knowing what to look for. The world's most efficient killer had finally caught up with them.

For months Europe had waited in terror as an outbreak in India spread to the Far East and ravaged populations along trade routes into Afghanistan and Russia. From there it struck Poland and left tens of thousands dead in Hungary, Austria, Germany, France, and England. Americans hoped the Atlantic Ocean would protect them, but cholera killed a hundred fifty thousand in New York. Then more than fifteen hundred died in wagon trains on their way to California's goldfields. And now the blue death had reached San Francisco.

"My crew and passengers are in excellent health," Captain Morgan emphasized.

"Very well," Bartlett replied. "Tie up, but no one comes ashore until physicians examine your vessel and everyone aboard. If they give you a clean bill of health you can unload."

"Are there precautions we should take?"

"Cover your mouths and noses with fabric," Bartlett said, "and avoid anything that raises your respiration and makes you breathe more miasma."

Liberty's crew and passengers dropped what they were doing to search for cloth.

Bartlett stood guard at the foot of the gangplank while two doctors inspected the vessel from stem to stern. Finding nothing suspicious, they lifted the quarantine.

"You low on food or water?" Bartlett shouted.

"Yes. Both," Morgan replied.

"You'll find stores and seep wells up that street. Most open at six a.m."

Henning had often bought the brackish water from those shallow, hand-dug holes.

"You'll do well to send someone at five," he told Morgan. "By six there'll be lines of people waiting for owners to unlock the covers and start selling the water that collected overnight. You don't want to be one of the disappointed customers who have to wait hours for more to ooze out of the ground."

Morgan blew his whistle. When he had everyone's attention he said, "We'll shove off as soon as we replenish our food and water. I want my crew to stay aboard except as necessary to unload and re-provision. Any passengers wishing to return to Valparaiso can come with us, but you'll have to pay passage."

"Wait here," Henning told Alcalino in Spanish. "I'm going ashore to look around. If things are as bad as they sound, I'll send you back to Valparaiso." Switching back to English, Henning asked Morgan, "When will you unload my cargo?"

"At first light."

"I'll leave Alcalino here while I go ashore. In the morning I'll let you know whether he returns to Valparaiso or stays aboard."

"If he goes with me," Morgan said, "he'll have to pay passage."

"My charter doesn't end until you get back to Valparaiso," Henning replied, eyes cold. "I have a copy of the contract to prove it."

"Show it to me later. I'm busy."

"Let me come with you, *señor*," Alcalino said. "I don't understand what's going on, but the look on your face says it's bad."

"You'd know what's happening if you'd bothered to learn English." Regretting his abruptness, Henning placed a reassuring hand on Alcalino's shoulder. "You'll be better off here than with me."

Cloth masks tied around the lower halves of their faces, Henning and other passengers trudged down the gangplank.

"How bad is it?" the man in front of Henning asked John Bartlett.

"Nearly two thousand have died in Frisco, Sacramento, and Placerville," Bartlett replied.

Several passengers went back up the ramp.

"I brought you a whole case of *pisco* this time," Henning told Bartlett.

"So far our arrangement hasn't worked out for you," Bartlett said. "You keep bringin' *pisco*, but I haven't told you anything you couldn't have found out for yourself."

"Not for lack of trying. Don't worry. Someday you'll give me information worth a lot more than a few bottles of *pisco*."

"I can do that now, provided you have molasses."

"I brought my usual thirty cases."

"Good. You can sell it for five hundred dollars a jar."

"Another ship's coming in," a voice filled with urgency shouted.

Bartlett hurried away.

"Why would anyone pay that much for molasses?" Henning called after him.

"I'll explain later," Bartlett shouted over his shoulder. "Whatever you do, don't sell for a penny less than five hundred."

If that was indeed the current price, Henning's thirty cases were worth twice as much as the ship that brought them.

******

Liberty's other passengers headed downtown in a cluster, as if numbers would protect them. Henning set out for Little Chile, alone and in the opposite direction. From a deserted sidewalk near Telegraph Hill he looked up at the semaphore on its summit. The arm on the horizontal crossbar was raised, announcing the arrival of a ship. Normally that brought retailers stampeding to the docks. But not tonight.

Long after Henning knocked, Eduardo's door swung a few inches inward. His face appeared in the opening, mouth and nose covered with cloth, normally expressive eyes lifeless. Half-asleep and still collecting his wits, he looked at Henning's mask and said, "I see you heard about the cholera. I was hoping you'd stay away until it runs its course."

"You're not sick, are you?"

"Not yet anyhow. But yesterday Roberto Flores took ill in my living room. Remember how stubborn he was about teaching you to pan for gold? He was the same about going to the hospital. He died shortly after I put him over my shoulder and carried him there."

"Sorry to hear that."

"Where's Alcalino?"

"I left him aboard ship. Didn't think I should bring him ashore."

"Get him out of here and go with him. Men are kicking the bucket at the rate of two to three hundred a day, and that number will go higher because doctors are dying right along with everyone else."

"Sorry to bring up my petty problems at a time like this," Henning said, "but I need to know what arrangements you've made for my merchandise."

"I reserved space in our usual warehouse."

"Can we get stevedores to unload in spite of the cholera?"

"Of course." Eduardo tried shaking himself awake, like a dog. "This town will starve if it stops unloading ships."

"What can you tell me about cholera?"

"I volunteered at the hospital after Roberto died," Eduardo said, "but still have a lot to learn. You should talk to Doctor Mossman. He was in London during the outbreaks there and probably knows cholera better than anyone else on earth. Give me a second to get dressed and I'll take you to him."

"At this hour?"

"He's on duty twenty-four hours a day. But be warned. He's long-winded. For him, there's no such thing as a simple answer."

"We'll go in the morning," Henning said. "You need your sleep."

"I've had all the sleep I'll get. I start work in an hour."

While Eduardo washed and dressed, Henning waited on the couch marveling at his friend's charity.

"You're special," he said as they left for the hospital. "Damn few Chileans would've volunteered as a fireman and then a hospital aide after the way San Francisco has abused them."

"I volunteered because many of my friends are in that hospital."

"They're treating people from Little Chile?"

"Not due to any sudden spirit of brotherhood. Dr. Mossman insisted and no one wanted to get on his bad side—not while he's saving more lives than all other doctors combined."

Eduardo's long, flowing strides created his usual breakneck speed. It was all Henning could do to keep up.

The town's usually boisterous streets were silent. No cooking fires or prostitutes. No drunks or bragging prospectors. Everyone was inside as if locked doors and closed tent flaps protected against cholera. The only sound was a violin, faint and wailing in Germantown. Abruptly its morose chords were drowned out by a lively fiddle in the Irish district.

"It amazes me that people can think about commerce at times like this," Henning said as a convoy of wagons slogged past. "I guess I shouldn't be surprised. In the morning, I'll be doing the same."

"What are you talking about?"

"Tomorrow I'll take my merchandise to town the way those men are taking theirs."

"Merchandise? Those are corpses going to the cemetery."

"In cloth sacks?"

"San Francisco ran out of coffins the day people started dying."

******

Henning and Eduardo stepped into a tent crowded with patients who'd been brought in after every bed and floor in the hospital was full. Apologetically, they passed between rows of cots where men lay with openings through the canvas beneath their buttocks. Buckets caught discharge gushing from those too weak to make it to outhouses. The horrific odor brought bile to Henning's mouth.

On the ground at the head of each cot was a basin. When there was vomit in these or diarrhea in the buckets, aides in white recorded its volume and sent the container to be washed. Volunteers in street clothes went from victim to victim, giving priority to those who'd lost the most fluid. When men could be revived, their heads were elevated and they were encouraged to drink a dark liquid. Otherwise it was infused directly into their veins.

Small and frail, Dr. Bertrand Mossman was at the center of this activity. Not someone who would normally command respect, he'd become San Francisco's ultimate authority. Seeing Henning's pinched expression he said, "It's a bit malodorous in here, but you'll get used to it."

Malodorous. The word was new to Henning. It seemed too elegant.

"This is Henning Dietzel, my partner and best friend," Eduardo told Mossman. "He has a couple of questions if you're not too busy."

"Hope you don't mind if I work while I answer." Mossman continued from cot to cot, making notes on patients' charts.

"I'm a wholesaler and I just brought a shipment," Henning said. "If there's anything I have that you need—"

"I desperately need molasses," Mossman interrupted. "Hard to believe something so simple counteracts the world's most terrifying disease, isn't it? But it's so effective that it sells for five hundred dollars a jar."

Seeing rows of men—all in agony, some near death—Henning hesitated to ask his questions. They seemed unimportant with so many suffering so horribly. His eyes were drawn to a nearby cot with its occupant facing away.

He didn't realize she was a woman until he saw her feet. Petite with high, feminine arches, they made her suffering more poignant.

"I have thirty cases of molasses on a ship at Clark's Point," Henning told Mossman. "They're yours free of charge. I'll send them in the morning, or do you need them sooner?"

"We have enough for tonight." Thick lenses on Mossman's glasses magnified his eyes. "In this town people take advantage of every opportunity to make money. Generosity like yours is refreshing. How can I repay you?"

"When you have a moment, you can tell me about cholera. I left my employee on a ship at the wharf, and I'm trying to decide whether to bring him ashore or send him elsewhere."

Mossman yawned. "Sorry. I need fresh air, and we shouldn't talk in front of the patients." Outside near volunteers pouring human effluent into trenches, he continued, "No disease kills as fast as cholera. The first symptoms are cramps, nausea, and fever. Later diarrhea and vomit explode from the body under pressure. Three to four gallons of water—weighing twenty-four to thirty-two pounds—are expelled from the victim during the first few hours, leaving the skin loose and puckered."

"I remember that," Henning said. "My mother died of cholera. Eduardo tells me your treatment is remarkably effective."

"I got the idea of using salt from the writings of Dr. Rhinelander in New York. I've had good results with a hundred minims of salt and eight hundred minims of molasses dissolved in a liter of boiling water. In layman's terms, that's a three finger pinch of salt and a handful of molasses in a whiskey bottle of water. If you keep two jars of molasses and two pounds of salt, you can bring your man ashore without undue risk. There'll almost certainly be cholera wherever you send him anyhow. And his treatment will be better here than in most places."

"Is it possible to avoid whatever causes cholera?"

"We have no idea what the cause is," Mossman said. "There are lots of theories, none satisfactory as far as I'm concerned. The one given most credence is miasma."

"Miasma?"

"Miasma is air that's become unhealthy after too many people breathe it, or because it's mixed with vaporous emanations from slaughterhouses, cesspools, decomposing garbage, marshes, or rotting corpses. Miasma is also blamed for malaria. In fact the word malaria comes from the Latin *mal aire*, meaning bad air. But if both have the same cause why do these two diseases have different manifestations? On the other hand, miasma would account for why cholera strikes population centers rather than rural areas. It would also explain why Irish and Negroes suffer more often, since they usually live where the air is worst." Mossman took off his glasses and rubbed his eyes. "There are other theories too. An Englishman named John Snow has advanced the notion that some sort of invisible living agent may be the cause."

"Sounds farfetched," Henning said.

"Yes, it does."

"I'll bring you more molasses in my next shipment. What else do you need?"

"Will you be in Peru anytime soon?"

Henning glanced at Eduardo who said, "Turns out I brought you back here for nothing. Cholera on the East Coast is playing hell with shipments of merchandise. I have stacks of orders. You should leave for Peru immediately."

"Can't believe my good luck," Mossman exclaimed. "Peru has a medicine called cinchona that comes from the bark of a special tree. In the 1600s a viceroy's wife was stricken with malaria and recovered after an Indian medicine man recommended it. Later she took samples to Europe where malaria has killed more people than any other cause—even war. After proving effective in Italy, cinchona became the world's best-known medicine. I treat lots of malaria and can use two hundred pounds if you can get it."

"Is cinchona useful against cholera?" Henning asked.

"It has no effect whatever, but it cures malaria faster and more reliably than any medicine cures any other disease."

"I'll do my best to find some." Henning's curiosity was aroused. He'd seen men die from malaria contracted on the way to San Francisco. And he'd read the writings of Alexander von Humboldt, a Prussian naturalist who'd discovered vast cinchona forests in the Andes Mountains.

"You were right," Henning told Eduardo after Mossman went back inside. "His answers aren't simple. But they sure are interesting."

******

Next morning Henning and Alcalino set aside molasses for themselves, then loaded the rest on a stagecoach and sent it to the hospital. Of little note a month ago, the thick brown syrup was now worth enough to require shotgun-toting guards.

Turning his attention to Alcalino, Henning said, "We're leaving on *Liberty.*"

"Good." Alcalino's grim look faded for the first time since Henning had said they might go separate ways.

As Henning's remaining merchandise was unloaded, he told Captain Morgan, "Alcalino and I are going as far as Lima with you."

"I checked my copy of your contract," Morgan said. "You're right. I have to take you and your man at no charge. All other passengers, however, will have to pay."

"No. I'm giving free passage to anyone who wants to return home," Henning said.

"That's not your decision. I'm in command here."

"And I have *Liberty* chartered until it's back in Valparaiso."

"In emergencies like this," Morgan said, "maritime law grants captains complete control of their ships."

"Maybe so, but you obviously intend to pocket the fares you take in and I'll make sure your employer finds out." Henning let his threat sink in, then added, "My guess is he'll force you to turn over every penny you collected before he has you thrown in jail."

"You're asking me to pass up several thousand dollars in easy money. Tell you what. I'll give you half."

"Half? I'm entitled to every penny *Liberty* earns while under contract to me."

"You want it all?"

"No," Henning replied. "I just gave away molasses worth a hundred and eighty thousand dollars. Why would I squeeze a few thousand out of men fleeing for their lives?"

CHAPTER TWENTY
VANDERBILT ROAD

"Untold thousands died of malaria while the Catholic Church suppressed knowledge of cinchona because it was discovered by heathens," Lima's Doctor Ignacio Vargas told Henning. Leaning back in his mahogany chair he surveyed his sunlit, wood-paneled office, then continued. "Ironically cinchona's effectiveness at the Vatican—where malaria's victims had included popes and cardinals—brought it to Europe's attention. Since then there have been constant shortages."

"Why?" Henning asked.

"Bad management. The Indians harvested cinchona bark without killing the trees. But when demand increased, collectors started felling and stripping trees as they lay on the ground. That's faster but it forces workers deeper into the jungle in search of new trees. To make matters worse, malaria is now treated with quinine, a preparation refined from cinchona. Quinine is more effective but producing it requires more raw material."

Henning sighed. Apparently people in the medical profession were incapable of brief, to-the-point answers.

"Surely I can find a mere two hundred pounds," he said.

"Not a chance. I have a hard time getting any."

Later, Henning visited a combination laboratory and workshop that reeked of industrial alcohol. There he asked his question of Ruperto Ostos, a reputedly honest cinchona trader.

"I have cinchona for sale right now," Ostos replied, "but it's concentrated extract—not the bark that buyers are accustomed to."

"I thought only Europe or the United States could process cinchona."

"That was true until engineers from Scotland finished my new treatment facility last month." Ostos pointed to rows of metal vats. "Now I can reduce thirty tons of bark to one ton of the substance from which quinine is purified. As a result my customers will spend less for shipping and I'll be able to charge a higher price. Buyers, however, are waiting for someone else to try my extract first. If you want to be that someone, I'll give you a very special price."

"How much do you have?"

"Four tons, the equivalent of a hundred twenty tons of raw bark. You'll have to buy it all."

Dr. Mossman had ordered a mere two hundred pounds.

"I couldn't sell that much in a thousand years," Henning said.

"That's because no one in San Francisco produces quinine. But several New York companies do. One of their buyers dispatched a hundred tons of bark on a clipper, Mercury, several weeks ago. And he's buying more because New York has run out. If you get there before Mercury does, the need will be acute and you'll make a massive profit."

Henning asked for paper and a pencil. Bending over a desk he did calculations, then crossed his arms and considered factors he couldn't reduce to numbers. Mercury had a head start, but her cargo was too big for the direct, much shorter route across Central America. She had to sail all the way around Cape Horn at South America's southern tip. With Ostos's concentrate, however, Henning could make good use of the shortcut. And if he beat the clipper to New York, he'd take in a million dollars—an enormous sum considering that two hundred acres of prime U.S. farmland could be had for a thousand.

"How long does it take to get an export permit?" he asked.

"Two weeks normally." Ostos stepped closer. "But these delays exist so exporters can avoid them by paying bribes, and my friends in customs can have you on your way in no time."

After confirming the extract's purity at two laboratories, Henning decided this was a worthwhile gamble.

"Keep these crates dry at all times," Ostos warned as Henning's purchase was loaded on wagons. "Moisture leaches away cinchona's potency and causes decomposition."

Ostos had packaged fifty-pound cakes in a hundred and sixty wooden boxes, then had each sewn inside latex-coated cloth.

"The protective covering is water resistant—not waterproof," he stressed. "Keep these on pallets and cover them with tarps."

"I'm not familiar with pallets," Henning said.

"They're portable wooden platforms, several inches high and used where water might collect. I can give you as many as you'll need."

******

Henning booked space on *Triton*, an ocean-going side-wheel steamer that was faster and more watertight than other available ships. Since she was scheduled to leave as soon as Henning's cargo was aboard, he offered a bonus for a fast job. While stevedores stacked the last of his crates in *Triton's* hold, the captain came through the door and announced, "Our departure is indefinitely postponed. Several of my crew are in the hospital with cholera."

Leaving Henning and Alcalino alone in the hold, the captain and stevedores missed a rare demonstration of Henning's ability to curse in Spanish.

"*Chingada*." He hurled his brand-new Panama hat to the floor. "This could keep me from getting to New York before *Mercury. Carajo.*"

Alcalino looked stunned, probably because he'd never heard Henning swear or known him to handle something expensive with so little regard. Embarrassed, Henning picked up his *jipijapa* hat and shook it. Made of flexible, delicately woven strands of palm fiber, it returned to its original shape.

After climbing the ladder to the deck Henning leaned on the rail, face etched with concern, watching incoming waves rise up, droop forward, and collapse into boiling foam.

"I should be ashamed of myself," he told Alcalino, speaking for the first time since his tantrum. "Those sailors have far worse problems than mine."

He visited *Triton's* hospitalized crewmen, bringing molasses and salt. The doctors declined to use either one and assured him they had better treatments for cholera.

Six of *Triton's* stricken crewmen died. Finding replacements took a week.

******

As *Triton* got underway Henning and Alcalino stood between her side-wheels, located one on each side amidships. Powered by separate engines and measuring thirty-three feet in diameter, these would rotate an astonishing twenty times a minute once they reached open water.

Outside Callao's harbor the wheel on their left sped up, turning the ship north.

"I thought you were taking your cinchona to New York," Alcalino said.

"I am."

"Shouldn't we be going south around Cape Horn?"

Henning had kept his plan secret because Alcalino was inclined to blab. He liked attention and couldn't be made to understand that competitors and thieves were always looking for information. But with cholera on the rampage there were no other passengers aboard *Triton*.

"Before getting to San Francisco, this ship will stop in Nicaragua," Henning said. "I'll get off there and cross to the east coast, then catch a ship to New York."

"If we're not together how will I know what to do?"

Disappointed yet again by Alcalino's slavish dependence, Henning said, "Your only tasks will be to keep Dr. Mossman's cinchona dry and make sure his bottles of molasses don't get broken. In San Francisco Eduardo will deliver them and take charge of the other merchandise. He'll send you back to Peru with a list of what we should bring next. When you get to Lima, go to the Hotel Republica every evening and ask the desk clerk if I've checked in yet."

After dinner Henning and Alcalino descended a ladder into the dank hold, carrying lit lanterns. In the room with the extract they made sure all crates were still on pallets and covered. As the ship rocked, tiny rivulets of water ran back and forth, leaving wet lines on the floor.

Back in their cabin Henning told Alcalino, "Our cinchona is on the ship's manifest as seed potatoes so it won't tempt thieves. Not even the captain knows the truth. Don't tell anyone."

"Don't worry."

"Your answer was casual. But this is the most important secret I've ever asked you to keep," Henning emphasized.

Later he left Alcalino in their room and snuck back to the hold with an armload of bedding so he could sleep on his crates.

Finding the captain alone the next morning, Henning said, "I brought hasps so I can lock the storeroom where my crates are. Do you mind if I bolt them to the door?"

"Who the hell's gonna steal seed potatoes?" the captain growled.

"Probably no one, but I want to make sure." Henning held out a shiny American double eagle twenty dollar gold piece.

"Good point." The captain pocketed the coin. "I can't have thieving on my ship, can I?"

Twice every day Henning made sure the crew was elsewhere and opened the padlock on the storeroom door. Though he never saw anything untoward, he invariably counted crates to confirm none were missing, then felt for moisture beneath the bottom row.

On the voyage's twenty-third day he was locking the door behind himself when the sound of crewmen dashing across the deck above announced they were getting ready to dock at San Juan del Sur on Nicaragua's coast.

******

Gangplanks were portable bridges, occasionally used to get from one ship to another but normally used to go ashore. Depending on the dock's height relative to that of the ship's deck, the angle could be steep. But the one at the Vanderbilt dock was almost level.

Before crossing to shore, Henning handed Alcalino a sealed envelope and explained, "This is for Eduardo."

He'd begun the letter inside, 'You have relentlessly encouraged me to take risks and I have found one worth taking.' The next paragraph outlined his plan. In writing, it seemed riskier than it had in his head.

As Henning and Alcalino parted company they saw their immediate futures differently. Alcalino stood at the ship's rail, shoulders sagging under the weight of unwanted responsibility. Henning went across the gangplank with a lively step, looking forward to the challenge ahead.

He'd had a choice of two competing routes across Central America, one in Panama, the other in Nicaragua. Neither could handle large quantities of freight. Until Panama's railroad was finished, that route couldn't handle shipments the size of Henning's. But Nicaragua's Vanderbilt Road could.

The Vanderbilt freight agent weighed the crates, then filled out a bill of lading and said, "You'll be traveling with a group of homeward bound argonauts."

Henning hadn't heard that nickname for a while. It was used in the Gold Country to describe prospectors and was based on Jason's Argonauts, heroes of a mythical search for the famous Golden Fleece. The latter day versions with whom Henning would travel looked as if they'd spent their last dimes for passage home.

"They look hungry," Henning told the agent, holding out a coin. "I'd better keep an eye on my seed potatoes. May I ride on the wagon carrying them?"

"Of course."

The next phase of Henning's trip began with a surprise. Courtesy of Cornelius Vanderbilt, Nicaragua had a road paved with crushed rock and tar.

"This is the first macadam road I've seen," Henning told the driver as he watched the wagon's shadow slide along the blacktop. "Not even San Francisco or Lima has one."

"Commodore Vanderbilt," the driver said proudly, "is usually ahead of everyone else."

The wagons rumbled past rich, green pastureland. Wearing no shirts or shoes, children stampeded from occasional thatched huts waving and shouting, their smiles huge and white and their dark eyes sparkling with joy.

Later the convoy rolled through Rivas and reached the docks at Virgin Bay on Lake Nicaragua. *Orizaba*, a paddle-wheeler, was building up steam.

"Passengers will board as soon as all cargo has been loaded," the first mate shouted.

Stevedores shouldered two of Henning's crates each and trudged up the gangplank. He weaved through them, leaning his shoulders and swivelling his hips. Reaching the top first, he made sure his cinchona was stacked where the main deck was sheltered by the one above. Then he counted and began covering his crates with canvas.

"My name is Nicanor Moncayo," the part-Indian first mate said, lending a hand. "Apparently it's important to keep these dry?"

"That it is," Henning replied.

"You're lucky. Before these docks were finished last month, steamers stood offshore while passengers and cargo were ferried back and forth in dugout canoes that often overturned." With a sympathetic look Moncayo added, "You're in for a rough time. The San Juan River has four impassible rapids and each has an overland path to a ship at the other end. Your crates have to be transferred by hand, and thanks to an outbreak of malaria we don't have enough porters."

That was but one of Henning's worries. Water could seep through seams in the latex-coated cloth protecting his cinchona. And where he was headed, rain fell in sheets—not drops.

Halfway across Lake Nicaragua, the overcast lifted revealing cloud-capped mountains to the south. Twenty miles later, near San Carlos, *Orizaba* accelerated and started zigzagging.

"Take cover, *señores*," Moncayo shouted, herding argonauts away from the rail.

They crouched behind Henning's crates. He climbed on top to better protect his cinchona. Watching Moncayo stare without blinking, Henning saw that the boy's attention was directed toward the fortress guarding the entrance to the San Juan River. A puff of smoke appeared above one of its cannons.

A geyser erupted off the port bow.

"Why are they firing on us?" someone hollered.

"There's a civil war going on," Moncayo explained, staying low. "An American brigade under William Walker is fighting against the side that holds Fort San Carlos. Walker's volunteers come here on Vanderbilt ships, so the fort's commander uses us for target practice."

"Were they actually trying to hit us?"

"If they had better cannons you wouldn't have to ask."

The argonauts cowered where they were until *Orizaba* entered the San Juan River. After they returned to the rail, Henning joined them and saw his first jungle. Each passing mile brought more mangrove trees, flowering vines, and orchids. Soon clouds darkened the sky and a downpour drove everyone back to Henning's crates.

He breathed easier when the sun reappeared and passengers hurried to the rail, from where they saw harpy eagles and boat-billed herons flying beneath a triple rainbow. Hearing monkeys, Henning saw three on a branch above the river.

Pointing to one at a time, Moncayo said, "That's see no evil, hear no evil and speak no evil."

He pushed his fist upward and pulled it down. In response, *Orizaba's* pilot tugged the cord above him. A burst of white steam screamed through the ship's whistle. The monkeys exploded like a string of firecrackers, frantic then gone.

Near Toro Rapid the paddle wheeler put in at a crude dock. *Gold Hunter*, a gray steamer with an unpainted repair on its bow, waited at the end of a long portage. The porters on duty grabbed the argonauts' luggage. Their supervisor informed Henning his cargo would be stacked on the dock and sent on when more men were available.

Henning reached into his saddlebags and pulled out a handful of silver coins brought for such emergencies.

"I'll pay one of these," he announced, "for every box delivered to *Gold Hunter*."

Indians shouldered crates and headed along the riverbank past white-faced monkeys watching from trees.

"Keep an eye on those guys." Moncayo's tone was urgent. "They don't work for the company."

Soon some of Henning's cinchona was aboard *Gold Hunter*, some remained on *Orizaba*, and the rest was in transit. Unable to see all his crates from any one place Henning rushed back and forth, frantically trying to keep track. Each box was worth six thousand dollars, enough to support a whole Indian village for generations.

"I'll keep an eye on *Orizaba* and the first half of the portage," Moncayo offered. "You watch the other half and *Gold Hunter*."

They didn't see each other again until all Henning's cinchona had been transferred.

"Ordinarily I'd stay with *Orizaba* and return to Lake Nicaragua," Moncayo said as they spread tarpaulins on the crates. "But I have next week off and am on my way to Greytown."

Being short, most *cholos*—fascinated by Henning's height—latched on and pestered him with endless questions. But Moncayo had been polite and helpful. Henning looked forward to more of his company.

Later *Gold Hunter* stopped at a rapid beside a hill topped by an abandoned fortress.

"*El Castillo*," Moncayo said. "The Spanish built it to stop Caribbean pirates from sailing upriver and raiding towns around Lake Nicaragua. Later they and then the English were driven out by malaria, which is still a threat. Notify the ship's doctor immediately if you feel feverish."

CHAPTER TWENTY-ONE
TAKING RISKS FOR MONEY

Near *El Castillo,* the river became a leaping, roaring avalanche. *Gold Hunter* continued at full speed toward forbidding white water and protruding boulders. Passengers stepped back from the rail, taking hold of banisters, life-preserver holders, anything solid. The helmsman spun the wheel. At the last possible moment the ship swerved toward a dock. And the delighted crew erupted in laughter, as if this was the first time they'd played their dramatic prank.

Sir Henry L. Bulwer, a red-hulled steamer, waited at the rapid's far end. Again Henning handed out tips to get his crates transferred. Preoccupied with supervising, he stopped swatting mosquitoes. On *Bulwer's* deck as she got underway, he scratched bites on both arms.

Moncayo handed over two *limónes.* "Their juice repels mosquitoes," he explained. "Rub it on your skin."

Compared to lemons, *limónes* were smaller, more sour and green instead of yellow.

Gazing at a moonlit sky Moncayo said, "Luck is with us. We normally drop anchor at dark, but tonight we have a full moon and no clouds, so we'll keep going."

"That's the best news I've heard in weeks." Henning's smile made his cheekbones more prominent. "I'm in a hurry."

"I noticed." Moncayo handed over more *limónes* and headed toward the crew's cabin.

Henning cut a *limón* in two, then rubbed his arms with the halves and squeezed the remaining juice on a cloth. He lay down on his bedroll beside the crates and draped the cloth across his face. The engine's steady throb and *Bulwer's* gentle rocking lulled him to sleep.

When Henning woke, the motor was no longer running and clouds hid the moon, making the night too dark for travel. He swatted a mosquito, leaving a bloody spot on his arm, then drifted in and out of sleep.

At dawn the crew restarted the engine. Henning could still see *El Castillo*. He'd hoped to be far upriver by then.

Just before noon, a dugout canoe shot from beneath a thatched hut on stilts. Its Indian paddler seemed hell-bent on crashing into *Bulwer*. Suddenly he dug his oar into the water. Thrown into a quarter turn, his craft slammed broadside into the steamer.

Henning unrolled the blanket concealing his Colt Paterson and cocked the hammer. The man in the canoe tossed his bow and stern ropes over *Bulwer's* rail. Moncayo pulled both tight and tied them.

"I am Agapito," the man announced. "I brought food."

A toothless smile on his ancient face, Agapito began selling chicken, rice, and plantains—a banana-like fruit, seasoned, wrapped in leaves, and baked. Henning bought meals for himself and a half-dozen argonauts who couldn't afford them.

Grabbing the grease soaked rag from under the chickens, Agapito threw it in the river. A dark shadow pulled it under, leaving traces of froth.

"*Tiburón*," the old Indian said under his breath.

"A shark?" Henning was skeptical. "In fresh water?"

"Sí, *señor*. There are many in this river."

As Agapito pushed off, his hollowed-out log started to roll. Newly aware of the danger beneath the river's surface, an argonaut at the rail shouted, "Be careful."

Deftly Agapito shifted his weight, keeping the dugout upright.

"Don't worry," he chirped in English. "I've done this many times, and the sharks never got so much as a taste of this magnificent body. I'll be back with more meals and derring-do when *Bulwer* comes in the opposite direction tomorrow."

"How did an Indian in the middle of a jungle learn to speak English like that?" Henning asked the captain.

"A few years back," the captain replied, "a promoter took him to be a special attraction at the United State's seventy-fifth birthday celebration in Philadelphia. Little bastard stayed for years and obviously has a knack for languages."

Downriver at Machuca Portage there was no one to transfer luggage and cargo. The argonauts carried their battered trunks to a ship waiting beyond the rapid. Those who'd eaten Henning's free lunches came back to help with his crates. Burdened by two each, they rushed through the first round-trip then slowed to Henning's and Moncayo's more moderate pace. After the job was done, they refused Henning's tips.

"One good deed deserves another," one explained. "A free lunch was payment enough."

"No," Henning insisted. "Without your help I'd have been in trouble up to my eyes. I'll never forgive myself if you gentlemen miss another meal before getting home."

He went from one to the next, slapping coins into their palms.

Charles Morgan—a barge with scaffolding that supported three tiers of platforms under a leaky roof—was a step down from *Bulwer*. Henning untied a fraying hammock, hung it near his crates, and enjoyed its gentle swaying as he slept. Urgent voices woke him after dark. Word was, Nicanor Moncayo had come down with malaria and been isolated.

Henning sought out the ship's doctor and asked, "How's your patient?"

"He'd be better if I could give him quinine," the doctor replied, "but my supply disappeared, probably stolen by a destitute prospector who later sold it."

"I have cinchona extract. Will that help?"

"If it's pure enough. How much do you want for it?"

"Nothing. But whatever you do, don't tell anyone where you got it."

"Got what?" the doctor asked, looking relieved.

******

Coming into Greytown, a bustling settlement on Nicaragua's Caribbean coast, the San Juan River divided into three channels. *Charles Morgan* followed the one leading to the wharf, where a worried-looking man came aboard.

"*Star of the West* will take you the rest of the way," he announced between cupped hands. "Unfortunately, she's been delayed by engine trouble. Until she gets here, you can live on the *Morgan* and we'll feed you at no charge."

Everything Henning had was riding on his race with *Mercury*. After losing eight days during Lima's cholera epidemic he couldn't afford this delay. He spent hours looking for another New York-bound ship. Finally convinced he was fretting about something he couldn't change, he hired a guard to watch his crates.

At the hospital where *Morgan's* doctor had sent Moncayo, a nurse told him, "He's recovering but isn't well enough for visitors."

When *Star of the West* anchored offshore, eight days later, Henning still hadn't seen Moncayo.

"You'll be taken out in bungoes," *Morgan's* captain told passengers who had gathered at his ship's rail to gawk at the world's largest side-wheel steamer.

Dugout canoes tied up nearby and the Negro in charge climbed aboard, sculpted muscles rippling beneath glossy blue-black skin.

"Moses is my name," he said in melodious English that identified him as a former Jamaican slave. "My men and I are here to escort you to the Promised Land. We'll take half now and the other half when we get back. Then we'll transfer your luggage and cargo."

Bungoes weren't suitable for ocean use. Before his cinchona went aboard one, Henning wanted modifications. But ex slaves—tired of being told what to do—were often less amenable to suggestions than men born free. If Moses was that way, he and Henning would butt heads.

On their first trip to *Star of the West*, the bungoes were repeatedly swept off course. Coming back, one capsized spilling its crew. For ten minutes they bobbed in churning water while gusts tore spray from the tips of waves around them. Finally they succeeded in righting their craft and squirming aboard.

Passengers back on the dock refused to board that bungo.

"Load it with these crates," Moses ordered, pointing at Henning's cinchona.

"Those are seed potatoes," Henning said. "Salt water will kill them. The bungo that carries them will need outriggers to keep it from rolling over."

"We don't use outriggers for people and aren't going to do it for potatoes." Moses's tone was clearly intended to discourage debate.

"Perhaps we can stabilize two bungoes," Henning said, "by lashing them together, side-by-side."

He'd suggested outriggers—a more difficult solution—to make this simpler task seem like a compromise.

"We have plenty of rope in the main warehouse," a voice came from behind as Moses's face clouded over. "How much do you need?"

Henning spun. "Nicanor," he exclaimed, using Moncayo's given name for the first time. "I went to the hospital twice a day, but the doctors wouldn't let me see you. You look well."

"I wouldn't be if you hadn't—"

"My pleasure," Henning interrupted before Moncayo could mention his cinchona.

Moses hefted one of Henning's crates. "*Sangre de Cristo*," he cursed. "These are heavy. It will take better men than mine to row bungoes tied together and carrying this much weight."

"Perhaps your men can make two trips." Henning scooped a jingling handful from his saddlebag. "I'll compensate them for the extra effort."

Without waiting for an answer he began handing out silver coins.

******

After delivering half the cinchona, Moses's men had returned and loaded the rest. Ready to go, they sat in their roped-together bungoes waiting for Henning to come aboard.

On the dock Moncayo told Henning, "Hope we see each other on your way back to Peru."

Henning pulled an oilskin bag from his pocket and handed it over.

"More cinchona," he whispered, "just in case."

"I can't afford this."

"Just make sure it stays dry."

Moncayo's eyes widened. "No wonder you're so concerned about your crates getting wet. They're full of cinchona."

"Keep that to yourself." Henning bent at the waist to give his friend an *abrazo* and receive one in return. The Negro rowers reacted as though they'd never seen a Caucasian show fondness for a dark skinned man.

******

By nightfall, *Star of the West* was steaming north along Nicaragua's Mosquito Coast. Henning was in his cabin trying to figure out if he was ahead of *Mercury*. The clipper's trip had been far longer, but she'd left Lima weeks earlier and Henning had lost eight more days in Greytown. His cinchona—potentially worth a million dollars if it reached New York during a shortage—would sell for little more than he'd paid if *Mercury* got there first.

Poring over charts borrowed from the captain, Henning felt certain he was ahead. But by how much? Had *Mercury* made stops? Had she been forced from the most direct route to find trade winds? Even if his lead was substantial, he could still lose this race. Under ideal conditions clippers were faster than steamers.

Exhausted, he was too worried to sleep. Long past his usual bedtime he stood at the rail, intent on the phosphorescent foam churned up by the paddlewheels.

*****

Henning didn't like the sound of *Star of the West's* port engine as she put in at Havana, Cuba. Soon after she docked, the captain confirmed his worst fear.

"We have mechanical problems again," he told his passengers. "Repairs could take days or weeks. We won't know until mechanics open the motor. If you want, we'll refund your unused passage so you can take the mail boat to New Orleans and find another ship from there."

Going that way doubled the distance to New York, but few ships called at Havana while New Orleans was among the world's busiest ports. Henning took the mail boat. Four days later it tied up at wharves piled high with cotton bales and jammed with passengers. He charged across the pier hoping the steamer warming up was bound for New York.

It was going to California.

"The earliest scheduled New York departure is next week," the ticket agent said. "But there's no way to communicate with vessels at sea and we frequently get unscheduled ships. Sometimes they don't stay long. If I were you I wouldn't get far from the docks."

Henning stored his cinchona in a warehouse and checked into a nearby hotel. Six times that night he got out of bed to see if the semaphore had announced an arriving ship. Only one came, and it was bound for England. By morning his mood was foul. With no motor to break down, *Mercury* was undoubtedly closing in on New York while he was twice as far away as he'd been four days ago.

CHAPTER TWENTY-TWO

SPLAT!

For a week Henning met every vessel that put in at New Orleans. *Little Rascal*, a fast packet ship, was the first bound for New York City. It found favorable winds and whisked him there—along with its cargo of urgent letters and packages—in six exhilarating days.

The crew lowered two sails, cutting their vessel's speed as it entered the East River.

"That must be Manhattan," a Peruvian deck hand marveled. "It's only part of New York City, but if you put Lima in there, it would be no more than a small neighborhood."

Energy pulsed from the East River's bustling docks. Standing at the rail and gliding past seemingly endless wharves, Henning felt his chest suddenly tighten. *Star of the West* was tied up at the Vanderbilt terminal. She'd beaten him there.

When *Little Rascal* docked, Henning rushed ashore and asked a stevedore if *Mercury* had arrived.

"Never heard of her," the man replied.

"She's a clipper that carries cinchona from Peru to New York."

"Forgive me," the man growled sarcastically. "With hundreds of ships comin' and goin' from so many different wharves, I haven't yet learned all the names, cargoes, and routes."

Henning hired an equally testy Pinkerton guard to watch his cinchona, then hailed a Hansom cab, a two-wheeled cabriolet pulled by a single horse.

The driver sat on an elevated seat behind the passenger compartment. A porthole in its roof allowed him to talk with customers.

"I need to get to Smith Pharmaceuticals fast." Opening a door that read: 'Arno Ungar at your Service,' Henning climbed aboard.

The initial pace was typically sedate. Most cabs were driven by their owners who babied them for obvious reasons. But when offered twice as much for a speedy trip Arno Ungar began taking advantage of every opportunity to pass other vehicles.

"In spite of all the fools who've run off to hunt for gold in California," he yelled through the porthole, "New York is the fastest-growing city in history. Twelve thousand foreigners land here every month, and you'll have a hard time finding one who doesn't thank God he's in the land of opportunity."

Ungar handed a square of Mexican *chicle* through the porthole. One of Henning's favorite treats, it was sweet natural gum produced by trees on the Yucatan peninsula. Chewing faster as the cab slowed in congested traffic, Henning observed that New Yorkers—like San Franciscans—worked at a frantic pace, as though commerce was the sole purpose of life.

The first idle men he saw were standing outside an employment agency.

"Immigrants looking for jobs," Ungar explained.

One looked out of place in short leather breeches, coarse wool shirt, and wide suspenders.

"Bet he's German," Henning said. "I'm from Prussia, myself."

"Never would've guessed. You don't have an accent. I'm Hessian and you undoubtedly noticed mine even though I came here as a boy."

"The number of Germans in this country is amazing."

"There are more of us than any other nationality."

"We outnumber the British?"

"Them and everyone else."

Henning liked New York. People in New Orleans had been friendlier but dedicated to idleness and chatter. Those in New York were full of purpose and contagious enthusiasm.

His good mood faded after he told the purchasing agent at Smith Pharmaceuticals' counter that his cinchona was partially processed.

"Tell you what, mack," the agent said, using the title that referred to pimps in the Gold Country. "We only buy cinchona bark, but give me a sample and we'll test it."

Reappearing almost two hours later, the agent slid a lab slip across the counter and snarled, "Your cinchona is garbage."

Henning checked the bottom line and exclaimed, "Something's wrong. I had tests done in Lima, and the readings were much higher."

"Wouldn't be the first time someone in greaserland falsified results. Or made a dumb mistake."

Or maybe, Henning thought, *buyers were right to be suspicious of Ostos's extract.*

"I had tests done at Lima's best laboratories," he said, calmly as he could. "And on top of that, a doctor in Nicaragua used my extract to cure a man who'd come down with malaria."

"According to the test we ran, he must have gotten better on his own." The agent wiped his nose with the back of his hand. "Anyhow we're not buying cinchona right now. We just received fifty tons."

"Did it come on a clipper named *Mercury*?"

"I can't give out that information."

"Not even after wasting two hours of my time testing cinchona you never intended to buy?" Henning slapped the counter. He'd had his fill of New Yorkers. The only friendly one he'd met was Arno Ungar, a fellow German.

Apparently persuaded by Henning's size and mood, the agent opened a filing cabinet and pulled out a folder.

"Yes," he said, glancing inside, "our latest shipment came on *Mercury*."

Bad news. That meant Acme, New York's other large pharmaceutical house, had also received its share of *Mercury's* cargo. Henning turned to go.

"Tell you what," the agent intoned. "I'll pay half what you're asking."

"How about ninety-percent?" Henning countered.

"Fifty's my best offer, and that's a damn good price considering the test results."

"I'll give you my answer tomorrow."

"Now or never."

"What difference does it make if you steal my cinchona today or tomorrow?"

Henning stormed outside and heaved an anguished sigh. Evidently he'd gambled everything and lost. Or had he?

A parable popular at Maximilian Academy had began with a young man on his way to success when suddenly knocked down. Splat.

"Success isn't down that road," he told his father afterward.

"You didn't find it," his father replied, "but it's there."

"No. I tried everything and still failed."

"How did you know you'd failed?"

"I was flat on my back."

"You're not a failure because you get knocked down," his father had replied. "You're a failure if you don't get back up. Success is usually found on the far side of setbacks."

In that case, I must be getting close Henning told himself glumly, then asked the waiting Ungar, "Do you know of any independent medical labs?"

"You just came out of a place that has a lab. It's not independent, but—"

"I need a test that's impartial," Henning interrupted.

"How about Acme Pharmaceuticals? It's not far."

"I'll give you a bonus to get me there fast," Henning said.

A test done at Acme would tell him if Smith's results had been inaccurate, which he strongly suspected. And with luck he might even sell Acme his extract, though they wouldn't pay as well right after receiving their share of *Mercury's* shipment.

※※※※※※

Waiting in Acme's lobby, Henning saw Smith Pharmaceuticals' purchasing agent rush in. Without knocking he barged into an office. Minutes later he hurried past and left without noticing Henning. Then a man from that same office introduced himself as the purchasing agent.

"I have four tons of cinchona extract that was tested in Lima," Henning began, placing a lab slip on the counter. "If you're interested, you can verify these results in your laboratory."

"We've never used extract," the agent said, "but might be interested in trying yours at half the price of raw bark."

"I'll dump it in the East River first." Henning resisted an urge to walk out.

"No one pays top dollar for low-grade cinchona," the agent said firmly.

"What makes you think it's low-grade?" Henning demanded. "Did your friend from Smith Pharmaceuticals tell you to say that so you can buy it for less than it's worth?"

Back on the street Henning asked Ungar to take him to Babish & Sons, the city's only other pharmaceutical house.

"It'll be closed before we get there, *mein Herr*. Why don't I drop you off at a hotel and take you in the morning?"

"Make it a cheap hotel. My money might have to last a while."

On the way, Henning asked Ungar to pull over at a drugstore. Its well-lit interior had white walls displaying garish posters. These threatened dire consequences for people who didn't use the advertised products.

"What brands of quinine do you have?" Henning asked the druggist.

"Acme, Smith, and Babish & Sons," the man replied. "They're the only ones available."

"Do you have other products containing cinchona or quinine?"

"Most patent medicines contain one or the other." The druggist unlocked a glass case.

"Do these sell well?" Henning asked.

"Better'n anything else I have. They have preventative as well as curative powers and are used by sick and healthy alike."

In California, patent medicines competed with herbal remedies sold by Chinese. Henning read labels on the wide selection of tonics, bitters, balms, elixirs, syrups, pills, and salves. To the druggist's disgust he left after writing down the addresses of those made by local companies.

In a district Ungar called The Bowery, Henning locked his luggage in a cheap hotel room. At a nearby hole-in-the-wall restaurant he bought the least expensive sandwich available and took it to his hot, muggy room. He devoured the first half, then savored the rest while marking the locations of patent medicine manufacturers on a map. Briefly opening the room's only window, he got the stench of garbage and the clatter of traffic instead of fresh air.

Still hungry after skipping lunch and eating a small dinner, Henning returned to the restaurant and bought a half sandwich. On his way back to the hotel, he saw a policeman stop beside a vagrant sleeping on a bench and tap his nightstick across the man's worn-out soles.

"Move along," the officer growled.

Shuffling away the vagrant swiveled his head and looked down an alley, probably for a secluded place to sleep. If Henning didn't sell some cinchona tomorrow, he'd be in a similar predicament.

******

In early morning's soft light Babish & Sons looked deserted except for a short, round man sweeping the sidewalk and whistling cheerfully.

"Is the buyer here yet?" Henning asked.

"I'm John Babish, owner, janitor, receptionist, and buyer. What can I do for you?"

"I have cinchona for sale."

"I've been having trouble getting it." Babish's enthusiasm showed no talent for driving a hard bargain. "Our main competitor is much bigger than we are. Recently its owner threatened to blackball suppliers who sell to us, and now none do. How much have you got?"

"The equivalent of a hundred twenty tons of raw bark, but it's extract."

"Perfect." Babish rubbed his palms together. "I have a rush order. That will save time."

Henning quoted his price and Babish said, "That's a lot but I'll pay it without quibbling if I like the result of our potency test."

The results were soon ready. Handing over the lab slip, Babish said, "Your cinchona is extremely high quality."

Suspicion confirmed. Smith Pharmaceuticals had falsified its test results hoping to buy at a low price.

"How much do you want?" Henning asked.

"I'll buy half of what you have as soon as I convince my banker to loan me the money."

"Until the bank approves your loan, I'll be open to other offers. Being in business yourself, I'm sure you understand."

"I stand to make a good profit," Babish said. "Reserve me half for three days, and I'll pay an extra ten percent."

"Give me a small, nonrefundable deposit and you've got a deal."

Babish lifted his hand, took aim, and thrust it into Henning's.

"And the deposit?" Henning left his palm extended.

In the lobby, Babish finalized their agreement with twenty dollar gold pieces from a cigar box behind the counter.

At least I won't have to sleep in alleys now, Henning thought.

Back outside, Ungar was leaning against his cab reading a newspaper. He looked up when Henning asked, "Can I hire you for the day?"

"That would be to my liking." The corners of Ungar's mouth moved higher. A wide gap between his upper front teeth spoiled the dapper appearance created by his top hat, black gloves, and red livery coat.

"Take me to these locations please." Henning handed over the map he'd marked.

Barely underway, Henning saw a sign identifying a building's occupant as Johnson's Quinine Water. He had Ungar pull over and went inside.

"Yes, our product actually contains quinine," the receptionist answered him. "It's very popular where fevers are a problem. We're the only company in the world that makes it."

"May I speak to whoever does your purchasing?"

"Have a seat. I'll tell Mr. Johnson you're here."

"Your price is fair," Elmer Johnson said after Henning explained his visit's purpose. "Can you come back tomorrow morning? I have to consult my partner."

By late-afternoon, three patent medicine manufacturers had also expressed interest without committing themselves. Still without a single sale, Henning returned to Babish & Sons.

"The bank agreed to finance my purchase," Babish told him. "But first, they want a letter from the War Department certifying that the army's order for quinine tablets is irrevocable."

"Does your banker always complicate things this much?"

"For large loans. But when he gives his word he keeps it, which many bankers don't."

"Doing business here can be an ordeal." Henning was accustomed to San Francisco where buyers lined up—cash in hand—and transactions were completed in minutes.

Over the next week, Henning signed contracts to sell his remaining cinchona to Johnson's Quinine Water and four patent medicine manufacturers.

He toured New York City while their banks processed loans. When he'd seen enough, he slept in to shorten the days.

Every afternoon he was first in line when *Frank Leslie's Illustrated Newspaper* hit the newsstand near his seedy hotel. The gaudy periodical— full of lurid drawings and vivid dispatches from the scene—was setting New York's streets abuzz with accounts of William Walker's exploits in Nicaragua.

Walker, a filibuster from Tennessee, commanded American mercenaries fighting in Nicaragua's civil war. Spurred by his promise of five hundred acre farms if they won, his men had repeatedly triumphed. Rumors said he intended to declare himself Nicaragua's president.

That afternoon Henning saw boisterous rowdies headed for the docks to join Walker's brigade. Their loud bragging seemed foolish because they were still within reach of a government that disapproved of their mission. But their fellow New Yorkers clearly considered them heroes.

Henning couldn't decide if soldiers were evil or admirable. They destroyed but didn't create. They imposed their will by force and often fought for the highest bidder no matter what his cause. The worst were merciless killers, yet the best were godlike. No one suffered as terribly or gave more for less. Of all professions, theirs most severely tested a man.

The day Henning collected his final payment, he left New York—his venture a resounding success he could never repeat. With the quality of Ruperto Ostos's extract now beyond question, Acme Pharmaceuticals' president had left for Peru—undoubtedly with an offer to buy all Ostos could produce.

CHAPTER TWENTY-THREE
VEILED LADY

With his million dollars Henning could retire and live in luxury, but he wasn't tempted. For one thing, he didn't feel secure with only that much. For another, business was the most satisfying activity he'd ever known.

Back from New York, he found Lima's businesses closed for *Carnaval*, the weeklong pre-Lent holiday. Unable to shop for the merchandise on Eduardo's latest list, he gave Alcalino the week off. And soon discovered that thousands of costumed children celebrated *Carnaval* with water fights during which passersby were often drenched.

Lima's normally demure women also misbehaved during *Carnaval*. The least of their self-indulgences was pouring water from balconies onto unsuspecting pedestrians. After one such soaking, Henning sought refuge in his hotel room.

On the way to a restaurant that night, he saw coquettish *Limeñas* in masks and costumes. Returning to his hotel later, he walked between two who met his eyes and swayed their hips, then looked away. They were searching for someone who'd show them a good time and had initially liked Henning's height. Their next reaction had reminded him of Encinas's long-ago advice, "Show that gorgeous smile instead of looking stern all the time."

Dreaming of Martine Prado had sustained Henning since he'd lost Encinas, but tonight he was unbearably lonely. Seeing three *Limeñas* with dazzling white smiles, he continued walking toward them, passing his hotel and the uniformed man opening the door for him.

These particular *Limeñas* wore generously revealing blouses embroidered with sterling silver thread. Lace flounces hung from their skirts, providing glimpses of stockings so sheer the flesh showed through. As they passed, one locked eyes with Henning. He looked away.

Over his shoulder, Henning saw a man with a pointed beard swagger up to them and say, "If this were a beauty contest and I were the judge, all of you would win."

They giggled. Henning missed the man's next words but the ladies looked spellbound.

A block later Henning passed young men in costumes, leaning against a building.

"Where are you from?" the one dressed as a pirate asked.

"Prussia, by way of Chile and California," Henning replied.

"Were you in San Francisco during the gold rush?" the pirate asked.

"Yes, and I'm still in business there."

"Why don't you join us? There are plenty of fine young ladies where we're headed."

Henning traipsed the streets with his new companions, answering their questions about Chile's whores, Prussia's soldiers, and California's millionaires. Their inquiries ceased when they reached a neighborhood with narrow streets and sidewalks.

"Get ready," the pirate said. "This is where we got lucky last year."

They strolled beneath balconies as if unaware of the possible consequences and were finally rewarded. Dripping wet, Henning looked up and saw giggling ladies refilling pitchers from a tub on a balcony. More rushed out of nearby houses armed with hand-held water pumps.

"We must respond to this unprovoked attack." The pirate gave Henning a handful of brightly decorated eggs. They'd been prepared according to custom—drilled, drained, filled with perfumed water, and sealed with wax.

Henning squared off with a woman across the street. One by one his eggs hit her, but so softly that several bounced off and didn't break until hitting the street. When he was out of ammunition, the lady rushed forward and soaked him with her water pump. She was masked, but clearly older than the girls attacking the pirate and his men.

Out of water, she retreated back across the street with a throaty chuckle. One of the younger ladies declared a truce, then sashayed up to Henning's companions and started a conversation. The woman who'd engaged Henning backed into the shadows.

Squinting, he stared harder. A scarlet mantilla accented her pink blouse and her supple hips swung a dark green hoop skirt. *Tapada*-style, a black silk hood covered her head and neck, leaving only one eye exposed. This severe veil—brought to Peru by the Spanish—was usually a sign of extreme piety. But an editorial in that morning's Catholic newspaper had said *tapadas* increased dramatically during *Carnaval*. 'Their headgear,' the author had written, 'sometimes conceals the identities of women bent on misbehaving.'

From doorways, men—evidently the girls' fathers—sternly called them inside.

"You coming, Henning?" the pirate asked.

"No thank you," he replied.

"Good luck."

Henning's companions continued on their way. The *tapada* stayed where she was, restoring order to her disheveled garments. Henning crossed the street wondering what he'd say to her. Closer now, he detected a flowery scent, then a musky hint of the woman's exertions. Her damp blouse clung to breasts that swayed in perfect unison when she moved.

"I fear I'm lost," he said. "How do I get back to the Hotel Republica?"

Her exposed eye focused on him. "I like your face, broad shoulders, and narrow hips," she teased. "But I'm also looking for a perfect smile. May I see yours?"

Henning mustered his best, wishing he'd worn something more flattering than the ready-made suit chosen because he didn't mind if it got wet.

Taking his hand, the *tapada* said, "Nice smile. I'll show you the way to your hotel."

"Thank you. That's extremely kind."

"Where are you from? I don't recognize your accent."

"Do I have one?"

"It's more your way of speaking than an accent."

"I'm from Prussia."

"I've never met anyone from there. My name is Pilar."

"Can you please pronounce it again?"

"Pea-lar," she enunciated.

"I'm Henning."

"Hope you didn't mind the soaking. During *Carnaval* we *Limeñas* get a little wild." Her eye sparkled as she asked, "Do all Prussians have honey-colored hair and blue eyes?"

"Far from it."

When they reached a commercial area with crowded sidewalks illuminated by gaslights, Pilar released his hand.

Hoping to prolong his time with her, Henning stopped in front of a café, held the door open, and asked, "Would you like something to eat or drink?"

"Let's take a look at the menu," she suggested, going inside.

A waiter took them to a table near the fireplace. Pilar requested one in a secluded corner.

"I shouldn't have invited you here," Henning said when they were alone, "I forgot about your veil."

"If I see something I want, I'll take it off." She picked up a menu. "Oh, good. They have *chicha morada*. Have you tried it? It's a beverage made from purple corn boiled with pineapple, cinnamon, apples, and some secret ingredients we Peruvians are forbidden to reveal."

Henning ordered two. When Pilar sat down after returning from the ladies' room, she was unveiled. Older than he, she had almond-shaped eyes and lips that became fuller when she smiled. Her springy, now-unrestricted curls were charmingly mussed up.

Henning took a sip of *chicha morada*. "Delicious."

"My favorite drink." She looked at him across the top of her glass.

"Can I entice you to divulge the other ingredients?"

"Why do you want to know?"

"So I can enjoy *chicha morada* even when I'm not in Peru."

"If I don't tell you, you'll have reason to come back."

Henning touched her empty glass. "Another?"

"Please."

He ordered two more. No doubt cultivating a tip, the waiter sped across the room nimbly avoiding collisions. A man and woman sat down at the next table. Turning her back toward them, Pilar uncrossed her legs. Henning heard the provocative sound of silk stockings rubbing together as she hurried to the ladies' room, leaving her second *chicha morada* untouched. She returned wearing her veil. Facing away from the couple at the next table, she remained standing until Henning realized she was worried about being recognized.

Back on the sidewalk she fell in at his side. Too soon they were in Hotel Republica's lobby.

"This is the first time I've been in a hotel," Pilar said. "Peruvian women live protected lives. May I see your room?"

Henning's eyes caught hers and darted away. "They don't permit guests."

"How will they know? There's no one at the desk."

They scrambled up the staircase. In the top floor's hallway they leaned back against the wall, out of breath and laughing like children. Two men exited a nearby room. Henning unlocked his door and swung it open, expecting Pilar to stand there looking in.

She went inside. The men in the hallway stared as Henning followed. He left the door open as demanded by propriety, then lit the lantern. The small room had two narrow beds beside a washstand, pitcher, and basin.

"I would have had the maid put a pedestal in here if I'd known you were coming," Henning joked nervously. The men looked in as they strolled past.

Pilar checked the hall and closed the door. "During *Carnaval*, it's okay to be a little naughty." She removed her veil and boldly met Henning's eyes.

"I have something to show you," Henning said, looking away. "It was my father's." He reached into the haversack beside his bed, then touched Pilar's elbow nudging her toward the window There he showed her how to use the spotting scope.

"Lima looks romantic from up here," she said, scanning lovers on benches below. After she returned the scope he stabbed it against his chest, closing it with a series of clicks.

"I like your blond hair and blue eyes," she purred. "Do you resemble your father?"

"Yes."

"Does he look as dangerous as you?"

"He was a soldier. He didn't just look dangerous."

"As I said before, I get a little wild during *Carnaval*." She looked at his mouth the way Encinas had when she wanted a kiss. "Do you want me to go?"

"Absolutely not."

"Do you ever get a little wild? Or are you always this formal."

"I resist the impulse to do spontaneous things. It's a habit I'd like to break."

"Maybe I can help." She leaned over and dimmed the lantern.

Henning slid the beds together and lay on his back, fully clothed. Pilar stretched out on top of him. Her mouth tasted of *chicha morada*. She let her hair down and swept its cascading curls to one side. Their next kiss was longer, more eager.

Straddling Henning's stomach, Pilar helped him out of his shirt, then slowly undressed, teasing but with hints of shyness. Her hard pink nipples contrasted with porcelain skin. She caressed his biceps, breathing harder. When she flattened against him, he savored her neck's warmth, her hair's smell, the pressure of breasts spreading against his chest.

Less nervous than he and in more of a hurry, Pilar guided him inside her. He hadn't been with a woman since Encinas, two years ago. He held his excitement in check as long as possible.

"Should I pull out?" he whispered with his last shred of discipline.

"No. I'm sterile."

Her thrusting sped up, became more insistent. He went rigid, then shuddered and felt his eyes roll up. When he opened them, Pilar came in focus—restless, still in need of something. Henning knew what that was but didn't know how to give it to her. Encinas would have been satisfied more than once in the amount of time he'd held out.

Later Pilar woke him.

"Hungry again?" he asked.

"Still hungry," she corrected.

This time, their lovemaking lasted longer but ended as before, with him panting and her disappointed. He asked what else he could do. She looked away without answering

When Henning woke again, Pilar—if that really was her name—stood beside the bed, dressed and veiled, hands thrust above her head. She finished stretching and touched his lips. He knew better than to ask why her exposed eye looked sad.

She told him anyhow. "Not all women like men to be so gentle and controlled."

Buttocks alternately contracting beneath her dress, Pilar crossed the room and let herself out. Having failed her, Henning would never see her again. He didn't even know her last name.

A sheet of folded pink stationary on the washstand had his name written on it with flowery flourishes. Inside he found the recipe for *chicha morada*.

He'd hoped this night would be a beginning, but it had left him feeling even more alone.

******

Henning read most nights but found time during the day only on occasional Sundays in Eduardo's living room. An editorial in this morning's *Alta California* newspaper predicted two hundred thousand San Franciscans would soon be a half-million. It also said booming construction was driving lumber prices sky-high.

"The paper says wood is California's most profitable commodity," Henning said.

"Ever think about getting into that business?" Eduardo asked.

"No. Sawmills are expensive and all but the largest will have to shut down when the population stops growing."

"I'm not talking about construction lumber. Andrew Larsen is building a theater and needs hardwood for its interior. There's plenty of oak available, but his client wants something more exotic. Didn't you once work on a ship that transported mahogany from Ecuador?"

"Yes."

"Would you be interested in renewing our relationship with Mr. Larsen?"

Later Henning, Eduardo, and the beefy, red-faced Larsen reached an agreement from stools near a drafting table in the contractor's office.

"At the moment," Larsen told Henning, his overactive mouth chewing each word, "I need first class tangare mahogany for Tom Maguire's new theater. And please be sure to bring samples of other Ecuadorian hardwoods. I'll soon be building hotels, taverns, and mansions for clients who want and can afford something no one else has."

Henning hired a woodworker to help him select prime mahogany. After delivering it, he stopped by the Jenny Lind Theatre whenever he had a free moment. Watching Larsen's carpenters put the finishing touches on San Francisco's most elegant interior gave him a feeling of accomplishment he hadn't gotten from bringing food, clothing, and tools.

After the new Jenny Lind opened, Henning's mahogany was the most talked about feature in what instantly became a San Francisco landmark. Soon Larsen had other theaters under construction. To the city's ever more cosmopolitan population this meant plays in five languages. To Henning it meant orders for teak, *mascaray, jatoba, chanul,* and other hardwoods.

******

With well over a million dollars in the bank, Henning continued to shave himself, eat at modest restaurants, and otherwise resist Eduardo's efforts to raise his standard of living.

"You won't go broke if you indulge yourself a little," Eduardo lectured as they entered a restaurant one morning. Underscoring his words, he tipped the waiters to set up a table for three on the outside patio near a bougainvillea-covered lattice arch.

Eduardo continued their conversation once they were seated. "You're the thriftiest millionaire ever seen outside an insane asylum."

The argument he was trying to provoke—and, of course, win—was postponed when Andrew Larsen joined them.

"I'm afraid I have bad news, "Larsen said. "I'll have to stop buying tropical hardwood and start using oak from the East Coast. My clients aren't as free with their money these days."

"Not that I fear the challenge of landing on my feet after things change," Henning murmured, "but once in a while I wouldn't mind some stability."

"You'll soon have more than you want," Larsen said. "This town's boom is over."

"I've heard that before," Eduardo scoffed.

"This time it's true," Larsen said. "Thousands of prospectors are returning home poorer than when they left. Their stories will discourage others from coming."

CHAPTER TWENTY-FOUR
GOD'S FAVORITE CHILDREN

Despite Andrew Larsen's pessimism, new strikes kept the gold rush alive. By 1851—Henning's third year in California—gold had been found near Mariposa, a hundred and sixty miles south of the original discovery. There a merchant, Steven Joyce, had opened stores and put out word he'd pay more than normal wholesale for merchandise.

Henning visited Joyce's San Francisco office and left with a list of what the man's stores needed. Tucking it in his shirt pocket, he followed a newly built wood sidewalk past a whirlwind of swirling trash. Near the intersection of Market and O'Farrell, he ducked into a restaurant.

"Any luck?" he asked, joining Eduardo at a table.

"Business opportunities are rare as rocking horse shit," Eduardo replied.

"I know. Looks like I'll have to bring merchandise for Steven Joyce's new store."

Eduardo stopped tapping his foot in time with music from the bar next door and said, "After making a half-million dollars on cinchona and sixty thousand on hardwood, why go back to wholesaling? You'll be lucky to make five thousand dollars for two months' work. Take some time off and wait for a better opportunity. You've been working too hard for too long."

"Three years ago I was earning fifty cents a day," Henning said. "I haven't gotten to where I turn up my nose at twenty-five hundred dollars a month. Besides, I feel like I'm wasting time when I'm not making money."

"Why? You spend next to nothing on yourself. Your money just sits in banks."

"One of these days I'll need it for something important."

"Be careful or you'll die with a fortune, wishing you'd spent more on life's good things."

Henning took a deep breath. "Right now I enjoy business more than anything else. When I'm older I'll find time for life's other so-called pleasures."

******

Over Eduardo's objections, Henning and Alcalino sailed to Acapulco in Mexico. They traveled on an Ecuadorian ship and were welcomed, unlike Henning's previous arrival under the American flag, when a rock-throwing mob had greeted his ship.

For days they scoured markets buying food, boots, and other items from Steven Joyce's list. Then stevedores put their purchases aboard one of the ever-more-numerous ships headed for California with space available.

In Monterey, a hundred miles south of San Francisco, Henning and Alcalino loaded the shipment on rented mules and set out for Mariposa.

Twelve hours and eighteen miles later, they made camp. While Alcalino cared for the mules, Henning scrubbed laundry in a wooden bucket. Almost done, he saw cattle lumbering toward Monterey. Wild as elk, males and females alike had horns.

The herd was no doubt owned by one of the *Californios*, men of Spanish descent who had immense herds on estates granted to their forefathers by Spain and Mexico. Before the gold rush, their cows had been worth three dollars a head. Since then, hungry prospectors had driven the price up to five hundred.

Vaqueros escorting the herd wore *sombreros* garnished with tinsel cord and tassels. Filigree trinkets hung from their deerskin vests and their form-fitting leather pants had a row of metal buttons down the outside of each leg.

Without warning, a huge bull dashed from the herd. Giving chase, a *vaquero* leaned from his saddle and grabbed the animal's tail. When its rear hooves were airborne he pulled its hindquarter sideways. Thrown off balance the bull tumbled end over end, then regained its feet and tamely submitted when driven back where it belonged. Henning had never seen a rider as skilled or a horse as superbly trained.

The *vaqueros* held the cattle in place while three riders galloped their mounts toward Henning. Unmindful of squirrel holes—in which horses could break a leg—they jumped a gully, then a line of downed trees. When they were closer Henning realized two were women. The younger brought her horse to a sliding stop.

Henning pulled his hands from the laundry water. The young lady had skin the color of a ripe peach and held a coiled lariat. Her blue eyes flashed wickedly as she looked at the soapsuds on his arms. Evidently this reversal of male and female roles amused her.

"Every day we see more *gringos* out here," a deep voice boomed.

The speaker was a cheerful looking, gray-haired man who clearly loved excess. He was overdressed for a cattle drive, had a potbelly, and reeked of cologne even at a distance.

"Domingo Santa María at your service." He dismounted and shook Henning's hand, then added, "The lovely ladies are Isabel, my wife, and Makayla, oldest of our twelve children."

"Makayla is a distinctive name," Henning told the girl. "How is it spelled?"

Looking like she'd answered that question too many times, she dutifully said, "In Spanish, it's normally M-i-c-h-a-e-l-a, but my parents used a Hawaiian spelling, M-a-k-a-y-l-a, because it changes the pronunciation in a way they like."

Studying Henning, *Don* Domingo said, "I've seen you in San Francisco. You stand out because you treat your companion with courtesy few Americans extend to his race."

"I'm Prussian—not American."

"According to everyone, you're also one of very few honest merchants in California."

Which makes me rare as rocking horse shit. Spoken, those words would probably have made the old man laugh, but with women present Henning said, "I hope my reputation is as good as you say."

"Don't worry. It is. Will you join us for dinner?"

"Please, join us instead." Henning didn't want to leave his merchandise unguarded. "Alcalino's making a Peruvian specialty, *butifarras*, a masterpiece of a ham sandwich with sweet onion relish. We can also offer *chicha morada*, a beverage made from purple corn boiled with fruit and spices."

"Sounds better than *tortillas* and beans," *Don* Domingo enthused.

The ladies nodded their agreement. *Don* Domingo fired a shot in the air. Cupping his hands around his mouth he shouted, "Make camp and have supper. We'll eat with these gentlemen." Facing Henning, he added, "I trust you'll let us repay your hospitality. Salamanca, my *rancho*, is a half-day's ride from here. We'll be back there tomorrow. It would be our pleasure to have you and your man as our guests for as long as you'd like."

"Thank you, but we're on our way to the Gold Country and our merchandise will sell for less if a competitor gets there first."

"On the other hand," *Don* Domingo said, "perhaps someone is selling similar goods right now and the value of yours will increase if you don't arrive until demand builds up again."

"That would be an exception to the rule."

"What you don't sell today you can always sell tomorrow, but your mind is obviously made up. Why don't you stop by on your way back to Monterey? My wife wants to order furniture and there's good profit to be made. We have a large house and she wants only the best."

Henning had heard *Californios* were freely spending their new wealth.

"We'll arrange a *fiesta* in your honor," *Señora* Santa María offered.

"Our parties are famous," Makayla added.

Henning couldn't help but notice her twinkling eyes.

"Salamanca is easy to find." *Don* Domingo squatted—belly protruding between his thighs—and drew a map in the dirt.

While the ladies helped prepare dinner, Henning and *Don* Domingo sat off by themselves on crates.

"Do you find intuition useful?" *Don* Domingo asked.

"I don't have any," Henning replied. "Wish I did."

"You're either born with it or you're not. Mine often brings me success while logic leads my friends from one failure to another."

By midnight they had discussed the beauty of the land, the crudeness of many Yankees, how California was changing, the benefits of the end of Mexican rule, and what qualities are most important in making a woman beautiful. Henning couldn't remember ever enjoying a conversation as much.

As *Don* Domingo and his ladies prepared to leave, another herd was driven past in moonlight so bright the steers cast shadows. Henning had delayed *Don* Domingo's herd and now a competitor would get to Monterey first—with enough cattle to drive the price down.

"I know what you're thinking," the old man said cheerfully, "but if I have to sell my herd for less, our little chat was worth it. I very seldom talk with anyone as interesting as you."

******

With Joyce's merchandise delivered, Henning and Alcalino reached Rancho Salamanca three weeks later. After passing barns, corrals, and worker housing they saw *Doña* Isabel and *Don* Domingo's twelve children near a rambling one-story house. Its front yard was bare earth, purged of weeds and debris and bordered by whitewashed, grapefruit-size rocks. On the porch an Indian woman rolled a cylindrical stone back and forth across a flat one, grinding corn.

"The *vaqueros* told us you were coming," Makayla said as Henning and Alcalino dismounted. Taller, curvier, and younger than Henning remembered, she handed them glasses of purple liquid.

"*Chicha morada*," Henning exclaimed after an exploratory sip. "This is the first I've had outside Peru."

"The day we met, you described how it's made," Makayla said. "I hope we did it justice."

"I've never tasted better."

"Then we'll prepare it every time you come, which will be often I hope."

The Santa Marías had no clocks in their home or in their heads. Lunch and dinner were eaten slowly and seasoned with leisurely conversation, in contrast to the way San Franciscans washed half-chewed food down in frenzied silence. Every time Henning looked up, one or another of the children politely asked what he or she could pass. And none took second helpings without first asking if he wanted more.

Afternoon tea was served alfresco in the backyard under a sunshade surrounded by flowers. After everyone else left, Henning and *Don* Domingo discussed the meaning of life. Henning had been brought up to believe work was man's highest purpose. *Don* Domingo placed more value on leisure. Like Yankees, he believed people were entitled to be happy. But he didn't equate happiness with money and professional success.

As the maid brought a second round of tea and pastries, *Don* Domingo summed up his philosophy with a few well-chosen words, "The idea that men have a God-given right to pursue happiness was radical when Thomas Jefferson expressed it in America's Declaration of Independence. How sad to see his noble ideal perverted into the right to chase dollars, ruin your health, and ignore your loved ones."

With every new day, Henning's admiration and affection for *Don* Domingo grew. But it troubled him that the old *Californio* didn't balance his pursuit of happiness with work. It also bothered him when *Don* Domingo sent Alcalino to eat with servants in the kitchen.

"Do you mind if Alcalino sits with us?" Henning finally asked. "He and I always eat together."

"He's at ease with that because he can see it's normal for you. However, we *Californios* have the same Spanish culture he knew in Peru. He'll be uncomfortable at our table. He's always had a certain place in life. Moving his boundaries will confuse him."

"I consider Alcalino as good as any man and—"

"I don't question your man's worth," *Don* Domingo interrupted gently. "He's welcome to eat with us if you want."

At dinner that night Alcalino sat with the family, silent and uneasy. The next morning he shyly asked if he could please eat breakfast with the servants. Though their dining table was on the other side of a closed door, Henning heard his employee's distinctive laugh several times.

******

"That painting looks more like my wife did than the mirror image she copied," *Don* Domingo said one afternoon. "Believe it or not, I prefer her as she is now. She matured into the kindest woman I'll ever know, a perfect wife and mother." Patting his ample belly he added, "And I like to think she wouldn't trade me for the boy she married."

By the time *Señora* Santa María finished her drawings of the new furnishings she wanted, her shopping list included Persian rugs for dirt floors, tapestries for walls of unplastered adobe bricks, lace curtains for windows that had no glass, a porcelain bathtub with gold fixtures for a bathroom without plumbing, and an English-style bed with an embroidered silk canopy.

Henning preferred the bed the Santa Marías already had. Its willow bedposts had been planted in the dirt floor and watered. They'd taken root and sprouted a canopy of leaves. But beds like that were common among *Californios*, and *Señora* Santa María wanted something unique. Having lived modestly before the price of cattle went up, she now aspired to the standard of luxury set by other suddenly prosperous *Californios*.

At dinner one night, she announced, "At last I'm ready to organize our *fiesta*."

"Let's postpone it until Henning brings the new furniture," *Don* Domingo suggested.

"Yes," she agreed. "That way all our friends will see our new things."

******

In Lima Henning ordered the Santa Marías' furnishings from Indian artisans. Two centuries earlier their ancestors had trained under craftsmen from Spain and Italy. Their patience and perfectionism exceeded any he'd ever seen. Astonished by the excellence of their finished products, he gave them sizable bonuses.

When Henning delivered these creations to Salamanca, *Don* Domingo's wife supervised her servants as they displayed each piece to the best possible advantage. Then she set dates for a three-day *fiesta*.

"This will be our biggest party ever," *Don* Domingo told Henning. "Everyone we invited will be there. They're all dying to see our new furniture."

He was right about his neighbors' curiosity but had underestimated their competitiveness. Seeing *Doña* Isabel's humble home transformed by its new trappings, the other wives besieged Henning with orders. After that they and their husbands dedicated themselves to what *Don* Domingo called, "activities specifically authorized in the Holy Bible—eating, drinking, and being merry."

As the sun went down, a bonfire in the backyard became the focal point for more ordering, this time by husbands. For Henning the moment was bittersweet, sweet because he was opening a new market, bitter because these delightful people's furious spending could ruin them.

******

Don Domingo's neighbors had brought all their cash but the next morning, none had enough to pay Henning's invoices.

"What should I remove from your orders?" he asked, relieved rather than disappointed.

"We'll have to think about that," one said, followed by a chorus of agreement.

Later the Santa Marías' oldest son rode to Salinas and brought back a thin, distinguished looking gentleman. *Don* Domingo escorted the man to his living room and introduced him as Navarro Lydecker, a moneylender.

Lydecker's aristocratic East-Coast accent and tweed suit made him seem trustworthy. Reinforcing that impression, he slid a curved briar pipe between his teeth and patted the outsides of his pockets until he found matches. Nimbly assisting when conversation lagged, he filled time his customers might otherwise use to consider possible repercussions of doing business with him.

Sitting at a desk, Lydecker unpacked a satchel of banknotes and piled the bundles in front of himself, creating temptation. *Don* Domingo's neighbors lined up and signed documents agreeing to pay twelve and a half percent per month and authorizing Lydecker to take their *ranchos* if they didn't repay him.

When *Don* Domingo started toward the line, Henning whispered, "With daily compounding, your loan balance will double every two months."

"Don't worry so much," *Don* Domingo said. "It's bad for the digestion."

"But how will you and your friends repay these loans?"

"By selling more cattle than usual."

"That will drive the price down."

"Cattle prices are going up—not down." *Don* Domingo replied, clearly exasperated.

"This kind of spending can ruin you. Credit has two sides and so far you've only considered the benefits."

"So you say, but every day things get better. My family and I have never lived so well. What could possibly go wrong?"

"For one thing, luckless prospectors are returning home by the thousands, which will reduce the demand and price for your beef."

"I survived just fine when cows were worth three dollars a head."

"In those days you didn't have a mortgage. If you sign one and can't make the payments, you'll lose your land along with your way of life."

Don Domingo dismissed that as he did all unwelcome thoughts, with a wave of his hand.

"Do you know anything about the cattle business?" he asked.

"Nothing, but I understand money."

"What is there to understand? A man can do four things with money— earn, spend, borrow, and repay it."

"You can also save it for the future."

A few feet away *Doña* Isabel listened intently. Henning asked what she thought. As usual, she changed the subject to avoid offering her opinion.

"It's too warm in here," she said, then closed the drapes and left.

Looking at Henning, *Don* Domingo said, "You're what Yankees call a worrywart. Tonight will be the last and best night of my party, provided that our bickering doesn't put me in a bad mood. How about a truce? We'll finish this discussion tomorrow."

"That will be too late."

Don Domingo marched to the desk. When he got to the head of the line he signed a document and left the room without counting his bundle of banknotes wrapped in elastic bands.

Henning had never met a group he liked as much as *Californios*— nor one as clearly doomed. Accustomed to a conflict-free life of repose, they had gentle dispositions compared to Yankees. The two groups had already clashed, most notably when *Californios* brought Indian servants to work their claims in the Gold Country. Objecting to what they called 'slave labor,' *gringos* had bullied the *Californios* into leaving.

That event had been a preview of what seemed inevitable. The *Californios* would be blameless victims. They had welcomed the Yankees to California, fought with them against the Mexicans, and been made American citizens by the treaty that ended that war. Now they were doing their best to adapt to their new country.

But the aggressive, gun-toting Yankees outnumbered them thousands to one and had different goals. In less than a century they and their predecessors had torn an entire continent from the grasp of Indians—drowning them in their own blood when necessary. And now they coveted the *Californio's* land.

Lending money to these simple, naïve people was the first of what would no doubt be many schemes to steal their *ranchos*.

******

After dark the *fiesta* moved to the main barn. In the warm glow of whale oil lanterns, a band materialized from among the guests. With a crude guitar, a beat-up trumpet, and a wooden box for a drum, they provided music for couples dancing on a low wooden platform.

Watching the women reminded Henning of a newspaper article, which had proclaimed the horsemanship of *Californio* men superior to that of Comanche Indians, Arab bedouins, Russian Cossacks, and Argentine gauchos. The author had also declared *Californio* women better at dancing than their men were at riding.

Henning went outside and sat on a veranda in faint moonlight. Listening to the music, he heard rustling and opened his eyes to see Makayla in a flowered blue hoop skirt and plain white blouse.

"Why are you out here?" she asked.

"Because this is the right place for someone who enjoys a good tune but can't dance," he replied, now standing.

The music slowed.

"Waltzes are easy. Let me show you." Makayla offered her right hand and left hip.

"Not tonight, thank you." Henning kept his hands to himself.

"Let me know if you change your mind. I'd love to dance with someone as tall as you."

With a saucy wiggle of her hips Makayla went back inside. Henning hated giving so little in return for her interest, but she never came to him in dreams the way Martine Prado did. In the two years since he'd first seen her in Lima's *Plaza Central*, they'd frequently talked while he slept. He'd forgotten what was said but not how good it felt to say it.

CHAPTER TWENTY-FIVE
THE BONE BUYER

Next morning a stranger arrived as Henning and *Don* Domingo came out the front door. The man dismounted, touched his hat brim without tipping it, and introduced himself by his profession instead of his name.

"I'm a chemist. My company manufactures fertilizer and animal feed. I'm looking to buy bones." As an afterthought, he added, "Harman Jones is the name."

"I sell my cattle to slaughterhouses," *Don* Domingo said. "I don't know what they do with the bones."

"They sell them to my company, and we grind them into meal for our products," Jones replied. "But we need more and hope to save the time and money needed to dry fresh ones."

Don Domingo perked up. "My field near the coast is covered with dry bones."

"How big a field?" Jones lit his corncob pipe.

"A hundred acres more or less."

Jones choked on a mouthful of smoke.

"Some of those bones have been there decades," *Don* Domingo added. "Is that a problem?"

"We're interested in their calcium and phosphorous, and minerals don't deteriorate. Would you like to sell them?"

"Depending on the price."

"We'll pay well. When can I see them?"

"Now if you like."

"Let's go." Jones held a coin over the bowl of his pipe until the tobacco stopped glowing.

Don Domingo gave Henning his best I-told-you-so look, and Henning forced a smile. At the moment, his *Californio* friend lived in a world where money was practically forced on him. He might as well enjoy his illusions of endless prosperity while they lasted.

A half-hour later *Don* Domingo and Harman Jones started for the coast with Henning and Makayla following.

"You're about to see something truly incredible," Makayla said as they rode past Indians harvesting corn. "Before the gold rush, my father sold cowhides and tallow. The leather went to New England shoemakers and the tallow was used to make candles for Peru's silver mines."

"I recently read a book about the *Californio* trade with New England and Peru," Henning responded.

The author had described *Californio vaqueros* driving cows to the coast, slaughtering them, then salting and stacking the hides. The fat was heated in kettles until it liquefied, then poured into pits and left to solidify. Ships picked up the tallow cakes and hides. The carcasses were left for predators.

"Bones have collected since my great-great-grandfather's time," Makayla explained, "and since our neighbors don't have land on the coast, my father let them use ours so they too could sell hides and tallow."

"It appears he'll be rewarded for his good deed," Henning said.

"You don't know him. If he sells those bones, he'll share the money with the men whose cattle helped earn it."

From a sand dune Henning saw caramel colored sand littered with sun-bleached skeletons. Only a small number had been torn apart by predators. Apparently the slaughters had produced more meat than the area's cougars, bears, bobcats, coyotes, and wolves could eat.

Harman Jones shaded his eyes with one hand and let out a whistle, then spurred his horse forward with *Don* Domingo close behind.

"We should wait here." Makayla dismounted. "My father doesn't like to negotiate in front of an audience."

Stepping off his horse Henning said, "Jones acted like this is the best thing that ever happened to him."

"What's the best thing that ever happened to you?"

"Tough question. How about you?"

"I'm hoping mine hasn't happened yet." Makayla looked up with big, blue, effervescent eyes. Mouth half-open, she looked mature and experienced.

Arms at his sides, Henning leaned forward and kissed her. Straightening up he saw her eyes gazing into his with undisguised adoration. That kiss had probably been her first. He should have left it for someone her age.

"Did I do something wrong?" Makayla asked.

"Not in the least."

"Then why did you pull away?"

"Because you're at an age where you long for affection and hunger to give it. You should find the right man first."

The glow in her eyes went out. "Is that how you see me?"

Scrambling to soften his thoughtless remark, he said, "No. I see you as attractive, intelligent, and caring."

"Then why…?

He resisted the urge to answer. She walked to where she could see her father and Jones.

God, life can be complicated. Ever since Encinas failed to answer his letters, Henning had longed for someone to love him. Now his wish had been granted and still he wasn't satisfied. He wanted to be struck by the same lightning that hit him when he first saw Martine Prado.

******

Six weeks later Henning returned from Lima with *Don* Domingo's second order and the first for his neighbors. He charged the Santa Marías half what everyone else paid, sacrificing his profit rather than add to their indebtedness.

That evening *Don* Domingo gave Henning a new list as they sat on his veranda watching cattle graze in spring ryegrass so tall the calves seemed to have no legs. His long list included carved hardwood doors with silver doorknobs, to replace the *serapes* hanging across his interior doorways.

"Forgive me for making your business mine," Henning said, "but your cattle and bone sales won't pay for all this."

"Don't worry. You'll get your money. I've arranged to borrow it."

"You can't run after moneylenders every time you get an urge to buy something."

"I don't run after them. They run after me."

"In his book, *Inferno*, Dante consigned moneylenders to Hell's most terrible place," Henning said, "and for good reason."

"We're not going to have this conversation again, are we?"

"No, that wouldn't do any good. Tomorrow Alcalino and I will pick up Eduardo Vásquez's latest order in San Francisco. From there we'll sail directly to Peru."

"My wife hasn't finished the drawings for our latest…" Seeing Henning's expression, *Don* Domingo paused. "Oh, I see. Well, no matter. Other merchants will be happy to sell to me."

"Let's compromise. I'll bring another order at my cost if you'll promise not to buy more until you repay your loans."

"You're treating me as if I were a child."

"I'm asking you to prove you're serious when you preach the virtue of patience."

"Meaning?"

"When you want something, wait until you have the money." Henning's smile didn't relax the tension.

Don Domingo persisted until Henning agreed to pick up *Señora* Santa María's drawings on his way from San Francisco to Peru. But even then he couldn't get the old man's promise to curtail spending.

******

Because Henning would return to Salamanca before going to Lima, Alcalino stayed behind with his *vaquero* friends. Alone, Henning rode to Monterey and took a ship to San Francisco. At Clark's Point he came down the gangplank with no sense of foreboding for the first time since the massacre in Frenchie's Canyon. Having arrived after that event, the vast majority of argonauts had never heard of it. And old-timers no longer gave it much thought.

Still seething over Navarro Lydecker's poorly disguised scheme to steal *Californio* land, Henning set out for Eduardo's house. On the way, he caught sight of another Yankee mistreating people he considered beneath him. His victims were celestials, so called because China was known as the Celestial Empire. Its people were persecuted in San Francisco, treatment that had been incomprehensible to Henning even before he'd gotten to know Lee at Frenchie's Canyon.

A crowd had gathered to watch. With a New York accent, the biggest of three bullies proclaimed the "disappointing racial inferiority" of Chinamen hurrying past with short rapid strides. Far from seeming disappointed, the man was enjoying himself.

"You celestials steal everything that isn't nailed down," he declared, snatching a carpetbag from a passing woman. "Whatcha got in there, honey?"

"Doctor," the woman said, accent heavy, eyes downcast.

"I don't think there are any doctors small enough to fit in this here bag."

The woman's tormentor rummaged through her belongings. She reddened and her male companion clenched his fists. Henning crossed the street.

"Lookee here." The bully held up an ivory carving of a naked woman. Staring between its thighs, he said, "Woowee. This doll has everything a real woman has."

"Doctor," the woman repeated without raising her eyes.

"Why would anyone but a pervert have this?" The bully held the figurine high for everyone to see.

Henning had ignored this kind of mistreatment too often. He stepped forward.

"She works for me and I've never had reason to question her decency," he lied, closing one hand around the figurine and the other around the handles of the woman's carpetbag. He didn't pull. One against three, he'd succeed only if he didn't provoke the bully's companions, who'd backed away looking embarrassed when he seized the woman's bag.

"You'd best go about your own bidness, mister," the bully growled.

"I will as soon as you return this lady's things."

"Why the rush?" The bully opened his hands, releasing their contents. "You in a hurry to be alone with her? Whatcha gonna to do 'bout her husband...or whatever this idiot is?"

Henning dropped the figurine in the bag and led the Chinese through the crowd. When no one followed them he slowed, waiting for the lady to come alongside so he could return her possessions. She and her companion respectfully remained behind him.

Pronouncing every syllable, Henning asked, "Do you speak English?"

"Doctor," the man offered a business card.

"You're a doctor?" Henning read the name on the card, Bertrand Mossman, the physician who'd saved countless lives during the cholera epidemic.

Mossman's office was around the corner. He was out front on the sidewalk.

"I was thinking about you yesterday," he told Henning. "I'm treating more malaria than ever and badly need cinchona."

"Every ounce in Peru is under contract to pharmaceutical houses," Henning said as they shook hands. "I'm not in that business anymore."

"I don't see how you can call it a business. You never let me pay."

"I charged you the same you charge indigent patients."

"I see you've met Mr. and Mrs. Yiu."

"A ruffian down the street was harassing her about a nude figurine she carries," Henning explained. "It's rather graphic, and according to the bully it shows she's a pervert."

"Actually it proves something quite different. Most of my Chinese female patients use those carvings to describe their symptoms. They're too modest to point at their own bodies."

By the time Mrs. Yiu was treated, Mossman's next patient had arrived.

"Be with you in a moment." Mossman waved Henning into his office, then closed the door and said, "The president of Mercantile Bank credits me with saving his son's life during the cholera epidemic. That's why he informed me that his bank will probably go broke due to bad loans. He doesn't want to trigger a panic so he told me to move my account and tell only one other person, someone who can keep a secret. It would be a sin not to pick you after your free molasses and cinchona saved so many lives."

"I don't have money at Mercantile, but Eduardo Vásquez does. May I warn him?"

"Of course. He was the best volunteer I ever had and deserves to know. But tell him not to breathe a word. If people panic and withdraw their money, the bank will go broke for sure."

Henning returned to the waiting room where the Yius were at the window, fidgeting. Looking past them, he saw the bully outside on the sidewalk.

The New Yorker folded his arms across his chest as the two celestials came outside, then looked away when Henning appeared behind them.

"I'll walk you home." Henning motioned for the Yius to lead the way.

Immediately Mrs. Yiu started in the direction from which they'd come. She'd either deciphered his hand gesture or understood English better than she spoke it.

Glancing back several times to confirm no one was following, Henning took the two celestials to their tiny rented room above a laundry.

******

Later at Eduardo's house, Henning left his mud-caked boots in the familiar entry hall. Lost in thought, he and Eduardo then sat on the living room's dark leather sofa facing an empty shipping crate. Used as a coffee table, it held a bowl of dark-purple plums, one with a yellow scar where its skin had burst.

"First things first," Henning began. "Dr. Mossman says Mercantile Bank's future looks grim. You should move your account at once."

"Horace Taggart, Mercantile's president, is a friend," Eduardo said. "I helped save his son's life during the cholera outbreak. He would've said something if my money isn't safe."

"If he told all his friends, it would cause a run on the bank."

"He'd tell me," Eduardo insisted. Henning let the subject drop, intending to reopen it later. All Eduardo's money was in Mercantile Bank. If it were to go broke, so would he.

Eduardo pointed to stacked newspapers and said, "I saved the *Alta California's* back issues for you."

Henning started with the missing persons notices. Most had been placed by Yankees back east and offered rewards for information about loved ones with whom they'd lost contact. Again, he found no inquiries about his friends murdered by bandits in Frenchie's Canyon. Their families must be in dire need, even though much of the gold he'd recovered at Ambush Pass was rightfully theirs. He'd gladly hand it over if only he could find them.

"How are the Santa Marías?" Eduardo asked as they sat down for dinner.

"*Don* Domingo is borrowing hand over fist from a moneylender," Henning replied. "If I can't stop him, he'll lose Salamanca."

"His finances are none of your concern. Meddling in them could cost you his friendship."

"Your way of saying I shouldn't push you to withdraw your money from Mercantile?"

Eduardo winked slyly. "Something like that."

******

The Santa Marías were partway through lunch when Henning returned to Salamanca. He joined them and after dessert handed out gifts he'd brought. Makayla loved the blue lace *mantilla* he'd found in a shop serving San Francisco's growing female population.

"It makes my eyes even bluer," she said, looking in a mirror.

The hug Makayla gave Henning was subdued, but her lush body aroused him—only slightly and briefly, but much to his distress. Later his discomfort returned when she came to the barn while he was re-nailing one of his horse's shoes.

"Oh, hello," she chirped as if surprised to see him, unlikely since her makeup was fresh.

Doing their best to suppress grins, her brothers excused themselves and left.

"I made fresh *chicha morada*," Makayla said. "You must be thirsty as hot as it is. I'll bring you some." Her skirt swished as she pirouetted and backtracked.

"I'll join you at the house when I'm finished," Henning called after her.

She didn't answer or slow her pace.

Henning sped up, but Makayla returned before he'd finished. Handing him *chicha morada* she said, "It's warm, but that problem will be solved when you bring our new icebox."

Discussing her father's finances with Makayla was a breach of etiquette, but Henning couldn't resist saying, "An icebox will cost many times its original price by the time you add the expense of weekly ice deliveries from Monterey. I was hoping your dad would pay off his loans before buying anything else."

"You don't want to make more sales?" she responded playfully.

"Of course I do. Not to your father though. Cattle prices are falling and our friend Navarro Lydecker will foreclose on Salamanca the minute your dad misses a payment."

Turning serious, she admitted, "I'm worried too. For generations our family was self-sufficient, but now we're buying dozens of things we don't need and can't afford."

Makayla's maturity didn't come as a surprise. Alone among the Santa Marías, she'd never ordered anything from Henning and had even cancelled orders placed in her behalf.

"Every time I warn your father, he becomes more determined to do as he pleases."

"When it comes to unwanted advice, *papi* either doesn't hear what you say or hears what you didn't say."

"How can I make him understand?"

"Look to heaven for help—not to me. Like all *Californio* men, my father isn't interested in female opinions. The best I can do is stop my brothers and sisters from asking for things."

"You sound as worried about his future as I am."

"I'm worried about my entire family's future. What happens to my father happens to all of us. Why don't you stop selling to him?"

"I came close once, and he threatened to buy from someone else. Any other merchant will charge at least twice what I do."

Makayla's elbow to his ribs silenced Henning as *Don* Domingo rushed in.

"Don't be planning my future without me," he pretended to scold, taking a lariat from the wall and hurrying back outside.

"He always knows when I'm talking about him." Makayla said, then changed subjects. "The fact you're not interested in me makes me like you more. It proves you're not one of those marriage-minded sharks who stalk the impressionable daughters of wealthy *Californios*."

"Are there truly men like that?"

"Haven't you noticed all the smooth talking, good looking outsiders who dawdle around the *ranchos* rather than waste their manly virility on work?"

"Has one ever courted you?"

"Not to make you jealous, but last year a handsome young Irishman found out my father has the largest herd in the area and tried to bribe our local priest to influence me in his direction."

"You deserve a man who sees who you are—not what your father owns."

"If I'm so good why do you keep pushing me away?" She held up a hand stopping his response. "Don't be diplomatic. Tell me the truth. Are you in love with someone else?"

Henning searched for a kind answer, then said, "Yes. A Peruvian lady I haven't seen for two years."

"That can't be very satisfying." She took a small step back and crossed her arms. "What attracted you to her?

"No one knows how we humans pick someone to love."

"I know exactly why I picked you."

Eager to hear more, Henning nevertheless refrained from starting a conversation that could only hurt Makayla. Instead he said, "We don't choose the people we love. We find them."

"Don't be insulted…" she paused after the words that often preceded her unfiltered opinions. "But I suspect you usually love from a distance and don't feel good enough for women worthy of you."

Having described Henning much as *Fräulein* Lange once had in Maximilian Academy's library, Makayla stormed out of the barn.

******

In deference to *Don* Domingo's pride, Henning announced his decision privately, when they were alone on wooden chairs under the veranda's thatched sunshade.

"My money's not good enough?" was *Don* Domingo's blustery response.

"Your money's as good as any," Henning said, "but not as important as my self-respect."

"If you won't bring what I want, I'll find someone who will."

"That's up to you. But I won't sell you anything more until you're out of debt."

Don Domingo stomped off and spent the rest of the day behind his library's closed door. Next morning, he had his breakfast sent to his bedroom and didn't come out when Henning and Alcalino were ready to leave.

Vaqueros brought their already saddled horses to the house.

As they mounted up *Señora* Santa María said, "Don't be offended. Domingo will get over his disappointment, and he'll regret this sulking. Come back soon and often. Please."

"I don't understand," Alcalino said when they were beyond earshot. "Why won't you sell *Don* Domingo what he wants?"

"Because I want to benefit my customers—not threaten their way of life."

"Someone else will sell to the *Californios* if you don't."

"There's nothing I can do about that."

"Are we still going to Peru?"

"No. Eduardo doesn't have enough orders to justify the trip."

For the first time in years, Henning was without plans for his immediate future.

CHAPTER TWENTY-SIX
ABSENT WHEN NEEDED

The following afternoon in San Francisco, Eduardo greeted Henning and Alcalino at his front door. Clearly excited, he hurried them down the hall to his living room. They sat on the sofa while he closed the window. With incoming wind cut off, the checkered red and white curtains went from nearly horizontal to vertical.

Bypassing small talk Eduardo said, "In the hills around Nevada City, thousands of prospectors are digging pits called coyote holes. They haul the dirt in wagons through rugged up-and-down terrain to the nearest creek and wash the gold out in chutes called Long Toms. If we dig a canal to their claims, these men will pay handsomely for water. I can get diggers. Can you bring shovels, picks, pry bars, windlasses, and dynamite from Mexico?"

Henning found a ready supply of tools in Acapulco, but no dynamite. Next he and Alcalino scoured the area for blasting powder. When they finally had enough, Henning couldn't find a ship's captain willing to transport such a fearsome cargo. In desperation, he hired an explosives expert to oversee the shipment until it was safely in San Francisco. Even at that, only one captain was interested, probably because his vessel wouldn't have been much worse-off if the powder had exploded onboard.

Two months later, the grandly named Dietzel Vásquez Canal—three feet wide by three feet deep—began delivering water from a river far uphill. Prospectors at dozens of coyote holes were soon washing more dirt in less time with a fraction of the effort. When their diggings played out, they moved to an adjoining location. Still worthwhile, it was less productive. After another move, they decided coyote holes were no longer worth the effort.

Flush with his share of the canal's profits, Eduardo returned to San Francisco. Henning stayed behind and brought tools to men who'd banded together to reroute a river so they could wash sand and gravel from its bed. That project's spectacular earnings motivated argonauts to divert other waterways. When they constructed earthen dams, Henning brought picks, shovels, and wheelbarrows. When they detoured rivers into wooden flumes, he sold crosscut saws, hammers, and kegs of nails. When they dug canals, he imported blasting powder.

Every time Henning and Alcalino returned to Acapulco, they passed Monterey and Alcalino suggested a visit with the Santa Marías.

"We can't spare the time," was Henning's unvarying reply.

Partly true, perhaps. But Henning still felt the sting of *Don* Domingo's rejection after their last visit. He also feared the old *Californio* would strain what was left of their friendship by trying to place more orders with him.

******

The man in front of Henning and Alcalino was positive the Placerville Café's cashier had overcharged him. Having consumed several beers, he tried to add up his check, lost count, and started again.

"Can we pay while this gentleman finishes?" Henning asked, offering a gold coin. The cashier made change while Alcalino selected a toothpick from a cut glass bowl.

A man in the doorway pulled in his stomach to let them pass and they stepped onto Placerville's bustling main street. For weeks Henning and Alcalino had brought supplies so prospectors could reroute the nearby American River's South Fork. The project hadn't covered costs, forcing most participants to take salaried jobs in the Gold Bug Mine's timbered shafts.

Every day more prospectors gave up. Many went home. Those who stayed took jobs for wages or farmed vacant land. On Henning's last trip from Acapulco he'd seen communities of Yankees squatting on *Californio* estates, plowing where cattle once grazed.

He stepped around the undertaker, Chalmers Nixon, who wore his usual black suit and beaver hat. Nixon and a man on a horse were staring at a bulge under canvas on a buckboard.

"I don't bury people for free," Nixon declared. "Who'll pay?"

"Don't make no nevermind to me," the other man said. "His wife give me a silver plate to bring you his corpse and that's what I done." He stabbed his finger in the direction of a regal woman with a long slender neck. "That's her and her two girls. She claims she don't have a red cent after bein' run off her estate by the squatters who shot her husband."

"Well, it'll take two hundred dollars to get his body out of your buckboard and into my funeral wagon." Nixon pointed to a hearse with his name in gold letters across its side windows. "If she doesn't have that much, she can bury him with her own two hands."

The woman's demeanor and clothes marked her as a *Californio*, definitely upper class.

"I'll pay," Henning said, stopping beside Nixon. "Write me up a receipt."

"What's the deceased's name?"

"Just a minute. I'll get it." As Henning approached the widow, she spread her arms to protect the girls cowering behind her.

"I've arranged to have your husband laid to rest," he told her.

"He should be buried on our land, but the squatters…." Her voice trailed off.

"What's his name?" Henning asked. "I'll have the undertaker write it on the receipt."

"His name is…was *Néstor Ávila*."

"Do you have a place to stay?"

"My husband's *vaqueros* are bringing a carriage to take us to my uncle's *rancho*."

"You'll need this in case they're delayed." Henning handed her a fifty dollar gold piece. "Wait here. I'll bring the receipt so the undertaker can't cheat you."

After Nixon wrote the victim's name on the receipt, Henning said, "Make a notation saying this pays the funeral's total cost, including casket, burial, and headstone."

Looking offended, Nixon did as requested. Henning took the receipt to the widow who thanked him profusely.

"My pleasure." He tipped his hat.

Dodging a fast-moving tumbleweed, Henning crossed the street and bought the latest *El Dorado Republican* from a newsboy. Beneath its headline, **Californios and Squatters at War**, an article reported clashes throughout Northern California including the Salinas area, where Domingo Santa María and his family lived.

With Alcalino close behind, Henning hurried to Wells Fargo & Company. Beside the ticket window was a life-size statue of the Roman god Mercury, speeding to an unknown destination, naked except for a fig leaf, winged hat, and sandals. On one of its buttock a prankster had drawn a kiss with women's red lip wax. Alcalino chuckled.

"Normally I would've wiped that off," the agent said, "but people have been flocking here to see it since it was mentioned in the newspaper."

"Two passages to San Francisco please," Henning said.

Sliding the tickets under the iron grill between them, the agent cautioned, "Stay close. The Frisco coach arrives soon and won't stay long."

As Henning and Alcalino waited on an outside bench, clattering and a fog of dust announced the stagecoach. Prospectors crowded around as the driver handed out mail. The man riding shotgun announced that the day's clash between squatters and *Californios* had killed five.

Checking Henning's ticket, the driver said, "This is your lucky day. You gents will have the whole passenger compartment to yourselves. Most times I have a full load before I get this far, but right now people are sittin' tight, waitin' to see if the squatters and *Californios* is gonna keep throwin' lead at each other."

"Think they will?" Henning asked.

"I'd bet on it."

Henning gestured for Alcalino to board, then sat across from him. The extra space was comfortable, but a full load would have made for a faster trip. With seats available the driver would turn in at every settlement along the way, looking for passengers.

As the coach left for Shingle Spring, Henning closed his eyes. Worried about *Don* Domingo, he couldn't sleep.

The driver picked up a passenger in El Dorado and two in Sacramento. Hours later he made an abrupt stop near Fairfield, where the road was blocked by boulders with armed men crouched behind them. A giant with riotous red hair and tobacco-stained teeth disarmed the security guard and ordered the passengers outside. He was much taller and huskier than Henning.

"You a *vaquero?*" he asked.

Having been forbidden to respond to strangers' questions, Alcalino searched Henning's eyes for permission to answer.

"He works for me," Henning said, "and he's not a *vaquero*. Why do you ask?"

"The first time my friends an' me tried to farm this land," the man drawled, "a *Californio* named Antonio Elias claimed we was trespassin' an' his *vaqueros* run us off. This time we brung sixty men, but we been told Elias's *Californio* friends is sendin' *vaqueros* to help 'im. We're gonna stop 'em before they join forces. We spent the whole summer buildin' houses and plantin' crops. We ain't gonna leave. We'll shoot to kill if need be."

"Do that and you'll end up in jail if not hanged. You're trespassing on *Californio* land."

"Goddamn forners don't deserve this land."

"They're not foreigners. They were made U.S. citizens by the treaty that ended the war with Mexico. And for your information, that treaty also recognized their land grants."

"You tellin' me our guvmint give them greasers the best land around?"

"No. The Mexicans and Spanish gave it to their forefathers generations ago."

"Guess you ain't heard the latest." The redhead sneered. "The courts done invalidated two o' them grants 'cause one was forged and the other was messed with to include extra land. Them decisions cast doubt on all *Californio* titles. The way I see it, we're entitled to kill the bastids if they try to push us out."

With renewed urgency Henning motioned for Alcalino to board the coach, then followed. Men like the redhead were undoubtedly going broke near *Don* Domingo's *rancho*. If they hadn't already squatted on Salamanca, they soon would.

******

Henning and Alcalino arrived in time for supper at Eduardo's new oak dining table.

"Bought it last week," he said proudly, "along with a real coffee table to replace that shipping crate in front of my sofa."

"Are Yankees squatting on *Californio* land near Salinas?" Henning asked, sitting down.

"Probably." Eduardo passed a bowl of beef stew. "There's been one hell of a fuss since someone discovered two fraudulent grants—so much so that the Land Commission has scheduled hearings where *Californios* have to document their titles or forfeit them. Word is most will lose at least some of their land. Those grants were never surveyed. The maps describing them are crude and open to broad interpretation."

"In that case I'll hire the best attorney I can find to represent Domingo Santa María."

"Too late. The Land Commission already held hearings down where he is."

"Did they uphold his grant?"

"My new job with Andrew Larsen keeps me so busy I've lost track of everything else."

"You're working for Larsen?"

"Yup. He's putting up brick buildings one after another and I'm overseeing his crews."

******

Next morning Henning and Alcalino boarded a southbound ship. Hours later in Monterey, Henning rented a room and bought horses. By dinnertime, he and Alcalino were ready to leave for Salamanca at first light.

Hungry after skipping lunch, they joined other guests for dinner at their boarding house's community table. Alcalino sat beside a man called Rattler who plainly disliked Indians and showed it with unpleasant sidelong glances.

"Have any of you heard the results of the Land Commission hearings?" Henning asked.

"Them greasers got no right to the best land in California," Rattler said. "I'm glad the Land Commission is takin' a hard look at their grants. An' the moneylenders is overjoyed because *Californios* is borrowin' lotsa money fer lawyers. Poetic justice, by Christ. Even if the grants is upheld, they'll lose their land when the loans comes due."

"That land is legally theirs," Henning said. "Wouldn't it bother you to see them lose it?"

"It bothers me ta work myself half ta death tryin' ta get by while they sit on their asses and live better'n I ever will."

"Way I hear it," another man added, "dem bastids fought with Mexico and agin' us durin' the war."

"You're wrong," Henning said. "The *Californios* fought on the American side. Anyone know what happened at Domingo Santa María's hearing?" Responding to Rattler's wrinkled brow Henning added, "He's a dignified, gray-haired gentleman who wears too much cologne. Back when men in this town were ready to eat their boots, he barbecued a steer for them every time he brought a herd to Monterey."

"Don't know him," Rattler said.

"Hell you don't," another man broke in. "I seen you at his barbecues, stuffin' yer face. He's the one whose wife and daughter came along on his drives."

"Now I 'member. The daughter was a pretty lil morsel with great tits."

"Suppose she's lost her cherry?" someone asked.

"Don't make no never mind," Rattler said. "She still got the box it came in."

As the room filled with lecherous snickers Henning clenched his fists under the table, then said, "Does anyone know anything about her father's hearing?"

"Mister, we ain't heard nothing. Cain't you get that through your skull?" Rattler's face contracted into an unpleasant expression. "You a Mexican lover or sumpin'?"

※※※※※

Henning had bought the only horses available. Both were in bad condition and tired quickly. He and Alcalino reached Salamanca long after sundown and found the grounds deserted and the buildings dark. The only lights anywhere were the moon and its rippling reflection on the creek behind the barn.

Henning hurried to the house and knocked—politely at first, then insistently. He was hammering the door with the heel of his hand when he noticed a poster and struck a match to read it. The Land Commission had ruled *Don* Domingo's grant was fraudulent. The poster gave an address where interested parties could apply to homestead forty of his now-abandoned acres.

Holding the match in midair, Henning forgot the flame until it singed his thumb. He'd been delighted when California's legal system put vigilantes out of business. Now he was appalled by how easily the law's high ideals could be manipulated.

Alcalino followed Henning around the house. Looking in window after window, they saw canopied beds, wall hangings, and Persian rugs with only mice to enjoy them.

"We should have come sooner, *señor.*"

Alcalino built a fire, then cooked beans and cornbread rather than one of his usual sumptuous dinners. Henning's food grew cold as he stared without seeing. He'd lost touch with *Don* Domingo because the old man hurt his feelings. Fourteen splendid people had lost their home and livelihood because of his childish pride.

Wakened by morning's unseasonable heat, Henning slid out of his bedroll, and sat in the shade of an oak. Hugging his knees to his chest he remembered conversations with *Don* Domingo and relived memories so vivid he could almost taste Makayla's *chicha morada* and see *Doña* Isabel working at her easel. They had taken him into their family. He'd repaid them by letting them down.

He'd probably never again see them or even know where they were.

******

On Henning's first day back in San Francisco, dockmaster John Bartlett invited him to dinner. They took a cab to the Navigator Restaurant, built by pulling an abandoned ship ashore, then gutting it while leaving its weathered exterior intact. Dark wood and mirrors covered the interior walls. Every stool at the long bar was occupied. Bartlett asked the waiter to seat them in an alcove, away from prying eyes and ears.

"I have no idea how you can exploit this," he told Henning quietly, leaning forward, "but I just heard about an extraordinary business opportunity involving bird shit." He raised both hands defensively in a hear-me-out gesture. "Peruvian guano is the world's finest fertilizer and a rich source of the basic ingredient in gunpowder. I learned about it from Alfred Benson, a shipping magnate whose vessels return to the East Coast empty after bringing passengers and freight to San Francisco. He calculates he could make millions by loading them with guano on their return voyages."

"Millions?" Henning asked skeptically. "Did I hear right?"

"Millions, with an s." Bartlett adjusted his bowtie. "Plantations and explosives manufacturers back east pay premium prices for guano and buy all they can get. Benson wanted to load it at the Lobos Islands, in international waters. Since Peru claims them, our government promised the U.S. Navy would back him up if he took possession. But when he planted our flag, Peru impounded his ships and arrested their captains. We backed down rather than risk war with England, which supports Peru's claim."

When Bartlett's plate was empty, Henning's was still half full.

"Looks like you lost your appetite over a measly few million dollars," Bartlett teased.

"My hunger disappeared the instant you mentioned shit—hardly an appetizing topic."

"So you say, but I suspect you can't eat and think about potential profit at the same time, which explains why you're so thin."

"What else can you tell me about the guano business?"

"I've told you everything I know. You need to talk with Francisco del Solar. He used to be a guano trader, but nowadays he's here in San Francisco."

"Where can I find him?"

******

In Little Chile's most congested area, Henning finally found Francisco del Solar's crude windowless shanty. Lanky and courtly, del Solar invited him in with typical Latin graciousness. They sat on wooden crates in faint candlelight. Del Solar had come down in the world since his days as a guano baron. According to Bartlett he'd been luckless in the goldfields and didn't have money for passage back to Peru.

"Guano is the world's most sought-after resource—even more so than gold," he said in answer to Henning's first question. "Peru has dozens of islands where millions of birds have deposited it for centuries. Years ago a German naturalist, Baron Alexander von Humboldt, tested it. I can still remember his conclusion." Del Solar switched to his version of a German speaking English. "'Peruvian guano is thirty-five times as concentrated as barnyard manure and more readily absorbed by plants.'" He continued in his normal voice, "Samples sent to England tripled crop yields, and entrepreneurs like myself began exporting it by the shipload. Profits were so remarkable that the government nationalized guano and imposed a tax that raised the price from fifteen to fifty U.S. dollars a ton. I went broke when my former customers started buying in Africa for eight dollars a ton." Angrily he ground his boot heel against the dirt floor.

Having heard little he hadn't previously read, Henning asked, "Why did the government raise the price so high?"

"It doesn't rain on Peru's islands so none of our guano's nutrients get washed away. Compared to other guano, farmers can use half as much and still get far better results. Also the rest of the world has very little guano and without it, farmers can't feed and clothe the world's expanding population. We'd be crazy to sell ours cheap because we'll soon have a monopoly."

"How could an outsider take advantage of this opportunity?"

"Altamira Island has stood idle since I left. Our government is bankrupt and looking for someone to lease it. To do that, you'll need to know a whole lot more than you do now. Give me a week of your time and enough money for a ticket home, and I'll teach you."

"I'll give you half now and the rest when we finish." Henning took out his wallet. "Can we start now?"

CHAPTER TWENTY-SEVEN
A SHAVING MUG OF CASH

Eduardo had sweat blood remodeling his once shabby house. He had made it more functional, but also fashionable—strange for some men perhaps, but understandable for him. Every time Henning and Alcalino went south for merchandise, he entertained female companions. Full of fun and never alone for long, he now wore stylish suits and had trimmed his once full beard to a rakish Vandyke. Wherever he went he was instantly popular with the ladies.

As he and Henning relaxed on his living room couch, Eduardo's body abruptly stiffened.

Concerned, Henning leaned toward him. "What's wrong?"

Face scarlet by the time his expression returned to normal, Eduardo said, "Dr. Mossman can't figure it out. He said to eat regular meals, drink plenty of water, and sleep eight hours a night. But that's not helping."

"With so many women around these days, it's hard to imagine you sleeping eight hours a night," Henning teased.

"You wouldn't say that if you knew how tired I feel these days."

"Let's have Mossman take another look." Henning stood. "I'll go with you."

"I don't have enough money."

"After your volunteer work at the hospital, Mossman will give you a special price."

"Anything he charges will be more than I can afford. I went to make a withdrawal at Mercantile Bank last week and found it locked tight. A sign on the door said accounts will be settled for ten cents on the dollar, but it didn't say when."

Looking down to hide his I-told-you-so look, Henning said, "I'll pay."

He was in dangerous territory, which Eduardo brusquely confirmed by expressing disdain for charity. Almost back to its normal color, his face reddened again—with anger this time.

"At least let me help with your house payments," Henning persisted.

"I'm not a helpless fool who can't look after himself."

"You can repay me after selling your house, which is better than losing it to the bank."

"You warned me to move my account. I should have listened."

"I don't have time to wear you down slowly." Henning sat back down. "I'm leaving for Peru tomorrow morning and won't be returning."

"That's sudden. What happened?"

"I found an opportunity in the guano business. It sounds lucrative and a lot more interesting than transferring merchandise from one set of hands to another. Besides, San Francisco's been taken over by bookkeepers and bankers. I'd rather be someplace where there won't be men with ink-stained fingers until the trail's been blazed."

"Be careful. A few years back Peru's guano trade was more profitable than her silver mines, but sales plummeted when the government tripled the price."

"Yes, but the rest of the world's guano is running out and Peru's customers are coming back. I'm thinking about leasing a guano island. If I do, I'll need a manager. You interested?"

"I'm temporarily out of work," Eduardo said, "but in a month or two, Andrew Larsen will be putting up a passel of brick buildings and I'll be back on the job."

"I'll top what he pays."

"Once my signature's on a contract, I honor it."

"I'll pay Larsen to release you."

"Truth is, I'd rather put up buildings than work with bird shit."

"Well, you have a job with me whenever you want it—no matter what I'm doing at the time." Henning stood. "Can we finish this conversation on the way to Mossman's office?"

"No charity." Eduardo remained seated. "If you must do me a favor, arrange for me to see tonight's performance at the Jenny Lind Theatre. I need the two best seats in the house."

Henning raised his eyebrows. "Who's going with you? A special lady?"

"No. But by coincidence, this is your last night in San Francisco and Eliza Biscaccianti, the world's finest soprano, will be giving her final performance here. When she came, she was supposed to stay a week. Six months later she's still basking in our fair city's adoration. If you don't fall in love with her, you can sit there and admire your damn Ecuadorian mahogany."

******

No one was being admitted to the Jenny Lind without black trousers and frock coat, which Henning had rented and Eduardo already owned. Even the cheapest seats were beyond the means of most, but Henning had abandoned his rigid thriftiness long enough to purchase front row tickets.

In a town where women's chests often bulged above low-cut dresses, Eliza Biscaccianti wore a dark blue, neck-to-ankles dress with a few subtle frills and a sparkling brooch at her throat. The petite singer's strong voice and delicate beauty turned hours into minutes.

As she finished her last scheduled song, the audience rose to its feet applauding. La Biscaccianti responded with three encores. Then, with roses and coins raining down around her, she stood at center stage exuding refinement as welcome in San Francisco as it was rare.

"Apparently you're stingy as ever," Eduardo griped.

Henning pulled a fistful of coins from his pocket. "Take whatever you think is her due," he said, opening his hand.

Eduardo raked Henning's palm clean. Instead of tossing his coins he stepped to the stage, then set them near La Biscaccianti's feet and backed away.

"The first time we threw coins for her," he told Henning, "an editorial in the *Alta California* newspaper criticized our lack of good taste. But in an interview, she praised us for taking such pains not to hit her."

"Maybe San Francisco's bad manners explain her long stay. I doubt coins are thrown in Paris or London."

Eyes scanning her admirers, La Biscaccianti repeatedly nodded, acknowledging their appreciation and generosity. She seemed to look extra long at Eduardo.

They left the theater behind men loudly discussing a late night bar where naked women posed in suggestive positions. Outside on the sidewalk, Eduardo seemed unsteady and Henning took hold of his elbow. Eduardo jerked free and flagged down a carriage.

"I don't understand how those guys go from opera to gaping at naked women," Eduardo said when they were underway. "I need transition time, myself. Every time I see La Biscaccianti I fall in love with her. Did she have that effect on you?"

"My heart's already taken."

"Is your lady in San Francisco?"

"No, Argentina. Her father is Peru's ambassador in Buenos Aires."

"A member of Peru's high society?" Eduardo shook his head. "Forget her. She'll never be yours. You were born poor. Even if you wind up with a fortune, you'll have to be satisfied with admiring her from afar.

"You never know. Given enough time, I might win her heart."

"Who the hell wants to finally be happy after years of loneliness? The trick, my good friend, is to enjoy life early and often. Loving someone you've never met is pathetic, but not surprising in your case. Puritans like you are always under control and never quite sure it's okay to enjoy yourselves. As long as I've known you, you've always chosen duties over pleasures. You'd make a good Christian if only you believed in God."

Their carriage passed through an upscale area with ornate lampposts and horses tied to wrought-iron hitching rails. At this hour, the few ladies on the planked sidewalk were probably prostitutes, but classy and discreet, a far cry from their sisters at the Barbary Coast.

Walking into Eduardo's favorite all-night restaurant, Henning stayed close in case his friend suddenly felt faint. Inside red fabric-covered walls, a waiter recognized Eduardo and took him around waiting customers to a booth.

"Going to an expensive restaurant makes you uncomfortable, doesn't it?" Eduardo asked when they were alone with their menus.

"Any other faults you'd like to call to my attention?"

"Just one." Eduardo stretched his arms along the seatback. "You have as much backbone as any man I've ever met, but you lack confidence where women are concerned. You never take the initiative with them."

Henning opened his mouth to object, but Eduardo had a point. Encinas, Makayla, and Pilar had all made the first move. And he'd never found the nerve to go anywhere near Martine Prado. Too, as a schoolboy attending Maximilian Academy on charity, he'd been so deferential to Professor von Duisburg's daughter, Christiane, that kindly Fräulein Lange, the librarian, had told him, "Your devotion to her makes me wonder if you feel unworthy of female friends."

"Why did you call me a puritan?" he asked Eduardo.

"Because you worship the opposite sex but never get around to enjoying them. And you have a puritan's taste in women. You like them elegant, refined, and proper. The most exciting woman I ever knew was somewhat liberal with her favors. No one—least of all her husband—suspected she was a bit of a whore. You can't imagine how that spurred my appetite. She was the only woman who tired of me before I tired of her. I still miss her at times."

"And while shopping for her replacement, you give auditions to every female in sight."

"What's wrong with that?" Eduardo tracked a passing lady with his eyes. "I'm obviously giving them what they want. Men in this town outnumber women hundreds to one, yet I always have a pretty lady on my arm."

"To you they're all pretty."

"There are very few who don't have some kind of beauty. I know you consider me a womanizing scoundrel, but I'll take my private life over yours any day."

"So would most men. Even me at times." Uncomfortable, Henning changed the subject. "Please don't mention the guano business in front of Alcalino. He sees no virtue in keeping secrets, and there's only one island available. I don't want him blabbing about it."

Face suddenly flushed, Eduardo clenched his jaw and grabbed Henning's shoulder, fingers digging in.

"How can I help?" Henning asked anxiously.

"You can't," Eduardo gasped.

"You need rest. Let's go home."

"No. I'm not going to sleep during our last night together. I'll get my eight hours after your ship leaves."

They lost track of time until dawn, when a man stopped at their booth and said, "The biggest fortunes in San Francisco are based on real estate. When this was a small trading village, prime lots sold for fifteen dollars. Just four years later, they go for forty-three thousand. Let me show you some investment properties before someone else snaps them up."

"I'm leaving and won't be coming back," Henning said.

"That's a mistake." The man turned to Eduardo. "And you, sir?"

"Haven't got a dime to my name."

The man tipped his hat and left.

Thumbs hooked behind his suspenders, Henning said, "Apparently these clothes make us look prosperous."

"Speak for yourself," Eduardo teased. "You're the one who never wears anything but Levis and plaid shirts."

"Well I don't need as many suits as you have, but I think I'll buy one."

"Why don't you start wearing that gray alpaca showpiece you had made in Lima?"

"I'm saving it for special occasions."

"Why? You never have any."

In the light of a new day, Henning hired a driver to take them to Eduardo's house. They changed clothes while Alcalino wolfed down breakfast. Then Henning and Alcalino loaded two heavy travel trunks aboard the waiting cab.

On the way to Clark's Point Henning had the driver stop twice, first to return his rented suit, then at the post office. He still hadn't heard from his grandfather, but mailed the old man yet another letter. Several pages long, it said he was leaving San Francisco and gave his Lima post office box number. If it brought no response, he wouldn't write again.

******

Too soon, the final call forced Henning and Alcalino to board *George Washington*, a side-wheel steamer. At the rail trying to find Eduardo on the crowded dock, they waited as her crew prepared to shove off.

"Hope this helps someone who's down on his luck." A passenger on the upper deck launched a fifty dollar gold piece with his thumb.

It cartwheeled higher, then lower, then disappeared into the crowd, producing a scuffle. The fist triumphantly thrust in the air couldn't have been Eduardo's. He was too proud to scramble for coins.

As a boy Henning had once told his mother, "It doesn't hurt anywhere when I'm sad. I just know I'm sad."

He felt that way as *George Washington* inched away from the pier. Taking one last look, he saw the city as it was but remembered how it had been. He'd seen a shantytown become a metropolis where a cigar stand in a fine hotel rented for more than mansions in most cities. A boomtown that once imported everything it needed was now exporting products with worldwide reputations, including Domenico Ghirardelli's chocolates and Levi Strauss's canvas trousers.

A young lady on the dock strongly resembled Makayla Santa María but couldn't have been her. According to the attorney who'd represented *Don* Domingo before the Land Commission, her family had gone to Mexico after vowing to never again set foot in the United States. The only hint of justice had come when a court ruled that Navarro Lydecker couldn't foreclose because *Don* Domingo had no legal right to mortgage land that wasn't his.

"No doubt Don Domingo's grant would've been upheld," the attorney had told Henning, "if he could have raised money to pursue the matter in court. But he was up to his eyeballs in debt after splurging on race horses, silk suits, carriages, and God knows what else."

With a tiny fraction of his savings, Henning could—and would—have financed *Don* Domingo's appeal. But even though he should have known trouble was imminent, he'd been too busy chasing money.

At least he'd done better next time a friend was in trouble. When Eduardo found the roll of bills in his shaving mug he'd grumble but wouldn't lose his home or go hungry. And he'd be further surprised by Dr. Mossman's house call. Mossman had refused payment, but Henning had forced a stack of fifty dollar gold pieces into his hand, saying, "Consider this a contribution toward the medicine you give the poor."

Mossman had praised his concern for the needy. But in truth, Henning had been obligating the good doctor to do whatever Eduardo needed for as long as he needed it.

CHAPTER TWENTY-EIGHT
THE WORST KIND OF SLAVERY

Henning seldom left his cabin during the voyage to Peru. For hours he pored over and digested a report commissioned by Peru's government and authored by Antonio Raimondi. Knowing its value, Francisco del Solar had brought this treasured document to California in case he didn't return to Peru. It had cost Henning dearly and its detailed discussion of Peru's major guano islands was worth every penny.

Meanwhile Alcalino roamed the deck talking with Spanish-speaking servants who were traveling with their employers. *George Washington* was off Peru's coast when Henning first noticed distress on his employee's normally stoic face.

When they were alone at the rail, he asked, "What's troubling you?"

"I don't know where we're going or why," Alcalino replied. "I don't even know if I still have a job."

"You'll work for me as long as you want to."

"What will I be doing next?"

Henning didn't want Alcalino divulging his plans to anyone who might be looking for opportunity. But their fellow passengers were from Peru, and that country's newspapers had thoroughly publicized the government's desire to lease Altamira Island. Fortunately, Peruvians with enough money weren't interested. They didn't trust the politicians who'd driven buyers away by nationalizing guano and tripling its price.

"If we're lucky," Henning told Alcalino, "tomorrow morning I'll show you what we'll be doing next."

******

Henning and Alcalino were back at the ship's rail as the rising sun revealed gray water under a cloudy sky. Out of nowhere, thousands upon thousands of dark-colored seabirds appeared, wingtip to wingtip, layer upon layer, blocking the sun and casting an enormous shadow. Their excited cries and beating wings drowned out *George Washington's* engines and brought more passengers on deck.

"I've never seen that many birds," Alcalino said after the flock had been overhead for several minutes with no end in sight.

"They're called *guanay* and their droppings are worth a fortune."

"What brought them out here?"

Henning pointed at a dark mass beneath the ocean's surface.

Squinting Alcalino asked, "What is that?"

"You'll see."

Clusters of *guanay* dived into the ocean, avoiding collisions by virtue of some unknown instinct. As they emerged with small fish struggling to escape their hook-tipped beaks, others stopped circling and knifed into the water. The flock was feeding on anchovies packed so tightly that waves broke over them as if they were a reef.

"British naturalists," Henning said, "estimate this area has millions of birds and billions of anchovies per square mile."

"The British must be rich if they have the leisure to study such matters," Alcalino said.

"The things they learn are one of the reasons they're rich. Those birds' manure is the world's finest fertilizer." As the flock flew toward a yellowish tan island, Henning added, "That's one of the Lobos Islands. Its distinctive color comes from being covered with dung piled five times higher than this ship. Men will make fortunes selling it."

"And you'd like to be one of them?"

"It wouldn't upset me."

******

Buildings housing the government were constructed centuries earlier when Lima was the City of Kings. Spanish *conquistadores* had forced the most talented of the conquered Indians to learn European arts and crafts, and then had them construct stately palaces. Entering one in his new cream colored suit, Henning passed a shield adorned with Francisco Pizarro's coat-of-arms.

A wooden spiral staircase provided access to the balcony along one inside wall. Railings along both contained hundreds of intricate spindles, which must have taken years to carve. Here and there, Indians polished the woodwork and tile floor with cloth superior to what they wore.

The old world elegance was impressive but sad. Streets outside were crowded with beggars, and Peru's bankrupt government hadn't paid secretaries or janitors for months. Henning crossed a courtyard and passed under a sign that said Ministry of Guano, a dignified title considering what was being administered.

At a counter he filled out an application to lease Altamira Island, and then followed a clerk to an office where Minister Raul Rubio sat behind an Italian Renaissance desk. Its polished marble top displayed blank paper, an inkwell, and a gold cup full of pens. Rubio looked important—as indeed he was, being in charge of the world's most sought-after resource.

Carefully, to avoid smearing the still-wet ink, Rubio reviewed the application then looked up and waited for Henning to speak. But Henning knew better then to seem overly eager.

"I can't lease this island to someone who's inexperienced," Rubio finally said. "We need a man who'll increase tax revenues by shipping a maximum of guano in a minimum of time."

"My inexperience will be an advantage," Henning replied. "I'll see things with fresh eyes. Rather than simply copy old excavating and loading procedures, I'll devise better ones."

"How can you improve something you know nothing about?"

"I spent a great deal of time with Francisco del Solar, the man who formerly operated Altamira Island. He drew these sketches of the installations." Henning handed over a folder and Rubio thumbed through it. Then Henning offered more drawings, explaining, "These are a few of the improvements I have in mind."

Still no reaction.

"This third folder," Henning said, "contains bank statements to show I have funds to lease and operate Altamira Island. As you already know, it won't be easy to find anyone willing and able to do that while most of Peru's former customers are buying elsewhere."

"Altamira has been shut down since del Solar left," Rubio said, "but the same methods are used on the Chincha Islands, which are still in operation. Before I can consider your application, you'll have to go there with my vice minister, Jorge Villegas, and explain your improvements. You'll also have to pay his expenses and a fee for his time. Don't worry. The government won't steal your ideas. We don't have enough money to do anything with them."

******

Henning gave Alcalino the week off and met Jorge Villegas, the Vice Minister of Guano, on one of Callao's docks the following morning. Round-faced with black, combed-back hair, Villegas wore a shapeless brown suit. His questions soon marked him as a communist. Like many such men, he was obviously austere and convinced he might have to die for his cause.

As *Diosa del Mar*—a small fast sailing ship—left the dock, Villegas stood on its gently rocking deck, asking carefully phrased questions. These were clearly designed to evaluate Henning's potential and became personal as they cleared the harbor.

"It's unusual," he said, "for someone your age to have enough money for a guano island. You inherited it, of course."

"A typical communist assumption," Henning joked, "but inaccurate. I earned every cent."

"Where and how?"

"In California during the gold rush. First I was a prospector, then an entrepreneur."

"So you're a soldier of fortune with no rifle? Too bad. Guano excavating is no business for adventurous men. In fact, it's downright dull."

"Only because it's boring to do things as they've always been done," Henning said.

"For someone who plans to revolutionize the guano business, you don't know much about it."

"Before I went to California I didn't know anything about gold or being a merchant, but I learn fast."

"You seem to move from one thing to another—not that I disapprove. Men, like air and water, become stale if they stand still too long. I take it you did well in California?"

"I was fortunate."

"Do you think your humility will be helpful in the guano business?"

"Not as helpful as hard work. If I decide to go into the guano business, I—"

"If you decide?" Villegas looked astonished. "Do you have any idea how lucky you are that the minister is willing to consider leasing Altamira Island to you? You're inexperienced. You have no connections. No big company stands behind you. The world's best guano comes from our islands, and we need men who'll make them productive."

"I'm such a man. Give me a chance and I'll prove it."

"Your only hope of leasing Altamira is to get my recommendation, unless you've bribed someone more important than I."

"I haven't bribed anyone and I'm not going to."

"No doubt you've noticed I have both Indian and European blood. My Inca ancestors respected guano as a necessity of life. Everyone left the islands during nesting season, and killing guano birds was punishable by death." He slashed a finger across his throat. "Nowadays, authorities permit year-round extraction and allow *guanay* to be shot for sport."

"Humans often waste nature's gifts. The cinchona forests for example."

Coming in view, the main Chincha Island looked like a vast snow-capped plateau.

"You're looking at the largest concentration of guano on earth," Villegas said. "Its height never seems to go down no matter how many ships are loaded."

As waves rolled in and exploded against sheer rock, Henning said, "Magnificent cliffs."

"But deadly. Scarcely a week goes by without at least one digger throwing himself on the rocks below to end his miserable existence."

"Are conditions that bad?"

"If there's a worse kind of slavery, I hope I never see it."

CHAPTER TWENTY-NINE
WASTE NOT

North Island—a mile long and half as wide—was the largest of the Chinchas. Canvas chutes hung from its cliffs, discharging guano into barges called lighters. These took their cargo out to a British freighter, where the crew winched it aboard in baskets and poured it into the hold. Between lighters, sailors climbed the masts and sat on horizontal timbers.

"Even someone who learned about guano from books should be able to answer this," Villegas declared. "Why is that crew up in the rigging?"

Henning had parried Villegas's previous thrusts designed to emphasize his inexperience. The best he could do this time was, "You tell me."

"Working with guano releases ammonia fumes. Men can tolerate them only briefly."

"How long does it take to fill a ship with those barges?" Henning asked.

"An average of six months. It used to take eight."

"I plan to eliminate the lighters and load directly from the island."

"Impossible," Villegas scoffed. "The water near shore is too shallow."

"I shy away from the word impossible."

"God doesn't need it, but humans do."

"I thought communists didn't believe in God."

"Not officially perhaps, but some do. We also believe He intends for His bounty to be shared by all—not hoarded by a few."

Diosa del Mar anchored near a flotilla of boats unloading the day's catch of sea bass, lobster, and shrimp. A small launch took Henning and Villegas to the base of a sheer rock wall. They climbed to the top avoiding the outer edge of a narrow trail with no handrail, then hiked toward distant workers on what Henning had read was ninety-foot-deep guano.

"Those holes are *guanay* nests," Villegas said. "Crews from freighters gather breakfast from them." Pointing to a knee-high mound of eggs, broken shells, and dead embryos, he added, "They dumped those when they found chicks inside."

Henning picked up a whole egg and touched it to his cheek, then set it down—being careful not to crack the shell even though it didn't matter.

"I thought we might keep some of them warm and hatch them," he said, "but they're cold. The chicks inside have come to a bad end."

"Are you a naturalist?" Villegas asked, continuing toward the diggers.

"No," Henning replied, "but I read their writings and respect their beliefs."

The diggers were *Serranos* from the Andes Mountains. As they broke into the guano with picks and shovels, harsh ammonia fumes stung Henning's nostrils and throat. Trying to cough away the discomfort, he gagged instead.

"These will filter the dust. There's nothing we can do about the fumes." Villegas handed a cloth mask to Henning, then put one on.

Workers on the island's other side had sent lighters of guano to be shoveled into baskets and winched aboard ships. The ones here put it in gunny sacks.

"I've devised a superior way to load," Henning said. "The sketches I showed Minister Rubio are in my luggage. If you like, you can see them when we get back to the ship."

Under a hot sun, the diggers were barefoot and shirtless with knee-length trousers. Their skin was splashed with scarlet inflammations.

"Those ammonia burns," Villegas said, "are the most obvious but the least serious of the diggers' problems. The fumes have also damaged their lungs, and most will eventually go blind. When they can no longer work they'll be sent away to die before their time, and the goddamn capitalists will bring the next victims."

Periodically *Serranos* spit out wads of well-chewed vegetable matter and refilled their mouths with dry leaves and gray powder from belt pouches.

"Coca lessens their suffering," Villegas said, "and the ashes release its tonic properties."

On their way back to *Diosa del Mar*, a breeze dispersed the fumes. Henning picked up a tag that had fallen from a sack being wheelbarrowed to waiting lighters. It said, 'Genuine Peruvian Guano. Doubles Fertility & Remuneration. Chemists Analysis: 18% Ammonium.'

"That's the most famous trademark on earth," Villegas boasted. "Not even the emblems of the finest sword and violin makers command more respect."

"I'll take better care of my workers," Henning said, unable to stop thinking about the horrendous fate waiting for the men he'd just seen.

"How?"

"What are other extractors doing?"

"Nothing. They're in business to earn money—not spend it."

"I won't jeopardize people's health to save a few dollars."

"My father taught me that men with blue eyes are natural-born liars," Villegas's tone was suddenly gentler. "But maybe you're the right man for Altamira Island after all."

"I thought you were unhappy with my inexperience."

"It doesn't take a whole lot of experience to dig shit and put it on ships."

"Then why have you been asking so many questions?"

"Because your answers tell me what kind of man you are. You seem to love nature and be concerned for your brothers no matter what their race. And you're honest or you would have tried to bribe me when I gave you an opening. You're different from most capitalists."

"I try to avoid their excesses, but all in all I think capitalists are building a better world. In *Wealth of Nations* Adam Smith advocated private ownership and letting supply and demand—not government—control prices and wages. When Britain put his theories in practice its economy boomed, turning paupers into wage earners and—"

"And creating vast wealth for the privileged few. Read *The Communist Manifesto* and you'll see that private ownership is inherently immoral because it always leads to exploitation."

"If communism is ever tried on a large scale," Henning replied, "I suspect it won't be as moral as you think—not with bureaucrats controlling every aspect of people's lives."

"So your answer to capitalist abuses is to look the other way?"

"No. The solution is for capitalists to honor the moral code Adam Smith called rational self-interest."

"What about men whose self-interest forces diggers to die before their time?"

"The government should pass laws that make exploiters choose between changing their behavior and going to jail."

"Shall I show you an island where your enlightened management could create utopia?"

"No, thank you." Henning rubbed his palms together. "Show me one where I can ethically earn a fortune."

******

They slept aboard *Diosa del Mar* and at first light Villegas had the crew set sail.

"Altamira Island is south of here," he told Henning as they got underway. "Even with a favorable wind it'll take most of the day to get there."

"Good." Henning handed Villegas a sheaf of sketches. "That will give me time to explain the advantages of the loading platform I've designed. With it, I'll be able to fill ships in far less time than it takes at the Chinchas."

After lunch Henning explained his budding plans for protecting diggers and loaders from ammonia's ill effects.

When sighted, Altamira Island resembled a distant domed coliseum. Closer, the apparent walls became cliffs and the roof a gigantic guano mound. A reef forced *Diosa del Mar* close to the island. Its steep stone walls blotted out the sun, revealing birds nesting in crags. Loud thuds came from a dark, shallow cave where incoming waves were compressed and exploded back into the light with a halo of spray.

In water barely deep enough for their small ship, the crew tied up at an abandoned dock on a pebble-covered beach.

Overheated during the brisk walk to a nearby clifftop, Henning shrugged off his jacket and slung it over his shoulder.

"Appears you're not afraid of hard labor." Villegas said, his gaze lingering on Henning's calloused hands and scarred arms.

"I enjoy working with my hands but prefer using my mind." Henning looked at the ocean below. "This would be a perfect place for my loading platform."

"Which will be an excellent investment no matter how much it costs. I measured these deposits last year. They're worth a fortune. Say the word and I'll have your lease drawn up as soon as we get back to Lima."

Henning offered his hand. Villegas shook it.

******

In Callao, Villegas hired a *calesa*. An hour later he and Henning passed through Lima's dilapidated adobe wall and six-foot-high ring of trash.

"Stop here," Villegas told the driver near a woman with two children grasping her skirt as she sifted through garbage. Villegas threw a coin and she it picked up. Henning jumped down and handed her several more. Her *gracias* was barely audible above the buzzing of flies.

"This was once the City of Kings," Villegas said as Henning rejoined him. "Look at it now. The barrier built to protect us from pirates is obstructing our growth. And every day this stinking dump becomes more of an eyesore and health hazard."

"Why doesn't the government tear down the wall and haul the trash away?" Henning asked.

"Because the treasury's empty."

"Being a communist you see that as a problem," Henning teased. "Being a capitalist I see it as an opportunity. I'll loan you the money. Go to the mayor and offer to clean up this mess in exchange for a percentage of the land you redeem. Then divide your property into building lots and sell them. At the very least, the profits will educate your children and provide you with a decent retirement. And if you find beggars who want to work, you can provide them with an income by hiring them."

"Who'd buy land that used to be a dump?" Villegas scoffed.

"Lots of people if you put in tree lined streets and a park."

"Why help me instead of doing it yourself?"

"I have enough to keep me busy on Altamira Island. Besides, honest vice ministers get paid too little to finance the comfortable old age you deserve."

"If the city accepts, I'll give you a share of the profits," Villegas insisted. "I prefer a business deal to a favor."

"Why?"

"Because I'm a vice minister in a position to help you, and I don't want to be in your debt if the time comes when I have to tell you no."

******

Two days after Henning signed his lease, a somber Jorge Villegas invited him to lunch.

"I'll pay," Henning said. "Pick a restaurant where you've always wanted to go."

Villegas chose one with bookcases of leather-bound volumes along its walls. They waited an hour for a table.

"The mayor accepted my proposal," Villegas began when they were finally seated. "I'm ready to tear down the wall and haul away the trash if you're still willing to finance me after you hear the bad news." He sniffed, then plunged ahead, "You can only have half of Altamira Island. Someone else will work the rest."

"What are you talking about? I already have a lease on the entire island."

"Not any longer. A rascal named Felipe Marchena has been lurking in the shadows, waiting for the ministry to lower its lease fee. He insisted Minister Rubio and I cancel your lease and reissue it to him. We refused but his government connections outrank us. The best we could do was negotiate a compromise giving you the southern half and him the northern."

"My lease is in writing. I'll have an attorney enforce it."

"If you take this to court, Marchena will wind up with the whole island."

"How?"

"Most likely by coming up with a lease dated before yours."

"He's that powerful?"

"His friends are, and your admirable distaste for bribery puts you at a disadvantage against him. Your best bet is to settle for half of millions of dollars."

"Sounds like buying and selling favors is common here."

"Not only in the government. Did you notice how many customers came into this restaurant after we did, then tipped the maître d' and were seated before us?"

"How much do you need to start tearing down the wall?" Henning asked after the waiter brought menus.

"You sure you want to go ahead after what happened?"

"It would have been worse if not for you."

"You were right about beggars," Villegas said. "Few took the jobs I offered, but don't worry. We won't be competing for workers. Laborers in Lima are mostly half-breeds who'll happily work for me but know better than to take jobs on guano islands. You'll have to hire pureblood Indians, and getting as many as you'll need means bringing them from the highlands."

They sat lost in thought while the waiter served their lunch.

Salting his food without first tasting it, Villegas said, "Marchena is already hiring workers. You should do the same. You'll need five hundred and Peru has a centuries-old labor shortage. With their customers coming back, guano extractors need thousands of new workers. The Ministry of Labor gave Domingo Elias the right to bring Chinese coolies, but he already has more orders than he can fill. The Indians we call *Serranos* are the only workers available, and it's almost impossible to get them to leave their ancestral homeland in the Andes. Labor contractors do it by resorting to deception, intimidation, and kidnapping."

"I want workers—not slaves."

"Talk to José Geldres. He's the only labor agent the *Serranos* trust. He tells them the truth, looks out for their interests, and supplies more workers than any four competitors."

"Where can I find him?"

"When he's in Lima, which he is now, Geldres passes through the *Alameda de los Descalzos* every afternoon. You'll easily recognize his gray stallion, Goliat. Geldres disfigured him to get the best of a horse trader."

With relish, Villegas described how Geldres had expressed interest in Goliat, offered for sale by Valeriano García. After García named his price, Geldres pulled a razor-sharp knife from his belt pouch and sliced the tip from Goliat's ear.

"Why did you do that to my horse?" García blustered.

"Not yours. Mine. You just sold him to me." Geldres ambled over to a mule in his pack train and returned with a leather purse, then handed over the asking price.

"Why mutilate such a handsome animal?" García demanded.

"To make sure you don't change your mind," Geldres had replied.

"Geldres is a half-breed," Villegas explained to Henning. "His Indian blood led García to assume he was backward. White people forget that Inca physicians performed brain surgery back when Europe's doctors still used leeches and let blood. Geldres knew García routinely reneged on sales in order to negotiate higher prices. So he disfigured Goliat to reduce his value and force García to honor their bargain."

"Obviously a student of human nature," Henning said.

"One of the best."

"What else I should know about him?"

"Don't give him reason to think you look down on part Indians. And address him as *Don*. He likes that title because it's reserved for highborn gentlemen. I've never heard a white man use it to address any other half-breed, which tells you how badly employers need his *Serranos*." Villegas cleared his throat. "You need to make a good impression because *Don* José refuses to provide diggers for guano islands."

"Why would he bring me workers if he won't do it for anyone else?"

"He'll be impressed that you intend to pay well and take care of your people."

CHAPTER THIRTY
RACIALLY INFERIOR

It was noon at the *Alameda de los Descalzos*. Henning had waited since mid-morning, clean-shaven as usual and wearing his linen suit. On the alert for a half-breed riding a gray stallion, he paced the wide walkway admiring flower beds, painted iron urns, and marble statues.

Henning couldn't imagine why this place—full of men wearing expensive clothes and shoes—was called Promenade of the Shoeless. But the reason seemed obvious when barefoot vagrants came for free lunches at a nearby convent.

He asked a well-dressed man to confirm his guess.

"We don't name plazas after Indians," the man said. "This one honors the *Descalzos de San Francisco*, a Franciscan order that wears sandals and is dedicated to helping the poor."

Knowing that, Henning was even more offended by the nearby Roman-style aqueduct, built to bring water for the private reflecting pool of a viceroy's mistress. In its shadow a beggar—legs amputated above the knees—sat on a portable wooden platform with what remained of his thighs forming a small lap. To change locations he pushed the sidewalk with his hands until his platform inched forward on wooden rollers. Passersby pretended not to notice his upturned palm. Henning pressed a handful of coins into it and was besieged by beggars.

The missing arm of the one with an empty sleeve was inside his shirt, behind his back. Ignoring him, Henning gave money to the others before a policeman ordered them to move on. Lima's elite were arriving for the parade of *Limeñas* who would soon begin their afternoon display of beauty and feminine finery. Paupers displaying their misery would spoil the occasion.

A gray horse missing the tip of one ear came around a corner, ridden by a willowy half-breed who sat ramrod straight and defiant, as if ready to contradict anyone who suggested he didn't belong.

Henning stepped in front of him and said, "You must be *Don* José Geldres. My name is Henning Dietzel. I need *Serranos* for my guano concession. I'll pay twice as much as—"

"I'm not interested in sending men to suffer and die," Geldres snapped, ignoring Henning's proffered handshake.

"Nor am I—"

"Then you should go into another business."

Henning reached into his haversack and brought forth goggles with clear glass lenses. Handing them to Geldres, he said, "These are based on ancient Persian goggles made with transparent tortoise shell and used for swimming underwater. My diggers will wear them to shield their eyes from ammonia fumes and dust."

Geldres took a cursory look. "And what about their lungs?"

Henning handed him a cloth mask. "This is woven so tightly that it filters even powder."

"Ammonia fumes will cut right through it."

"Not after it's soaked in vinegar water." Henning held up two bottles. "The clear liquid is diluted vinegar and the yellow one is horse urine, distilled to concentrate the ammonia."

Henning poured urine into a tin cup. Geldres raised it to his nose and breathed in. His eyes widened and watered. Next Henning dunked the mask in a cup of vinegar solution, gently squeezed, then returned it to Geldres. "Wear this and try again. Vinegar neutralizes ammonia."

Mask on, Geldres raised the cup to his nose and tentatively sniffed, then inhaled deeply.

"It works." He sounded surprised. "But now I smell vinegar."

"Which is sufficiently diluted to render it harmless. I'll have barrels of vinegar water available at all times. My diggers will be able to wet their masks and cleanse their skin at will."

"Why are you so concerned for your workers?"

"Why not? I have a conscience," Henning replied. "Besides, it's stupid to use up men and throw them away during a manpower shortage. Bring me *Serranos* and they'll get better pay and conditions than anywhere else. I'll sign a contract to guarantee it."

"Written contracts are unnecessary among gentlemen," Geldres said stiffly. "I don't need judges to make me keep my word, and I don't deal with people who do."

"Tell you what," Henning proposed. "You can find another job for anyone who wants to leave after thirty days, and I'll pay your fee on every man you bring whether he stays or not."

"Let's find a place where we can talk in private." The crowd attracted by Henning's demonstration had made Geldres the center of clearly unwanted attention.

When they shook hands later on a quiet side street, Henning was confident Geldres would deliver as promised. But despite Geldres's assurances, he wasn't sure *Serranos* were the workers he needed. According to other extractors, they brought more problems than they solved.

******

Felipe Marchena, who'd leased Altamira Island's other half, looked young for a man with so much influence. He had black, brushed-back hair and a nose like a hawk's beak. Suggesting an elevated opinion of himself, he held his head high, chin tipped up—whether giving orders to his shorter employees or talking with the taller Henning.

"Most of our coastal Indians, *cholos*, have European blood," he had told Henning the first time they met. "Very few mountain Indians, *Serranos*, can say the same. That explains their differences to my satisfaction. *Cholos* are none too good, but their Caucasian blood makes them superior to *Serranos*. Unfortunately they can find better jobs than we offer, so we're stuck with *Serranos* until we can get coolies."

Henning's reaction was to disapprove of Marchena—not *Serranos*. Suspecting as much, Marchena had asked, "If they're not inferior, how did Francisco Pizarro and less than two hundred Spaniards conquer millions of the ignorant bastards?"

A month after that first meeting, the two stood between dark brown cliffs on Altamira Island's dock.

"That's the first schooner I've seen that has a flat-bottomed hull," Henning said, watching *Intrepido* slowly approach the dock in water too shallow for any but the smallest ships.

"Too bad it's so slow," Marchena complained. "I have better things to do than stand around."

So did Henning, but both had to make sure they received all the supplies they'd ordered. An incomplete shipment would have dire consequences. Between them, they had a thousand workers on an island self-sufficient in absolutely nothing—not even firewood or drinking water.

Decades earlier, Francisco del Solar's *Serranos* had excavated guano behind the dock, leveling an area where they built two huge warehouses and row housing for workers. These facilities—except for one warehouse—were now Henning's. He'd had them renovated—inside and out—with fresh white plaster. They were a stark contrast to Marchena's rundown warehouse and the grim structures on his side of the island.

Intrepido's captain, Gustavo Medina, came down the gangplank, gentle brown eyes cheerful, hair combed across his bald spot. He greeted Henning and Marchena, then stood—hands behind his back—as *cholos* carried his cargo past the warehouses' propped-open doors.

With a plateau of eighty-foot-deep guano in the background, Henning and Marchena personally checked off each item as it went by—making sure they wouldn't run out of food before Intrepido brought more.

After the delivery, Captain Medina met Henning and Marchena between the warehouses.

"So far my workers have done nothing to contradict your low opinion of *Serranos*," Henning told Marchena as they signed Medina's delivery receipts. "At first I gave them the benefit of the doubt because they speak only *Quechua*. But Alcalino is fluent in that language, thanks to his mother, and nonetheless my workers listen with blank faces and then do precisely what he asked them to stop."

"After centuries of inbreeding," Marchena said, "they're simpleminded."

"Are the *Serranos* on other islands any better?" Henning asked Medina.

"I don't know what I'd do if I had to hire *Serranos* instead of *cholos*,"

Medina replied. "I've never seen one who was a good worker."

"How do the other extractors motivate them?" Henning asked.

Medina filled his pipe. Finally he tired of waiting for Marchena's answer and said, "Their overseers use whips. *Serranos* don't respond to kindness. If you want yours to do a good job, put the fear of God in them."

Marchena agreed but held his tongue. He wanted all of Altamira Island and wasn't about to say anything that might help Henning hold on to his half.

******

Instead of clamping down on his *Serranos,* Henning tried more kindness. With temperatures soaring, he ordered *chicha de jora,* a corn beer popular in their Andean homeland. Unlike *chicha morada* it was fermented and alcoholic. The morning after Captain Medina delivered several kegs, Henning found most of his workers scattered on the ground like battlefield casualties. They'd broken into the warehouse and guzzled all they could before passing out.

"I warned you not to bring *chicha,*" Medina said when Henning returned the empty kegs. "Alcohol is an Indian's worst weakness."

A wagon careened onto the dock, going too fast. Henning raised his hand and patted the air. When the driver ignored this signal to slow down, Medina flung the apple he'd been eating, hitting the *Serrano's* chest. Only then did the man pull back on the reins.

"*Serranos* take advantage of kindness," Medina said. "*Señor* Marchena has as much experience with them as anyone. His *Serranos* work hard and follow orders. Watch what he does and do the same."

"I can't treat human beings like that," Henning said, making no attempt to hide his strong disapproval of Marchena's brutish overseers and their whips.

"Then why did you hire overseers?"

"To organize my workers and ensure they use their safety equipment— not beat them."

In bed that night Henning had a promising inspiration. In morning's clear light he liked it even more. Marchena's overseers couldn't have pushed California's prospectors harder than they pushed themselves. Not even whips could've gotten more from the *cholo* boys who'd caught cats for him in Callao. Why? Because the prospectors' income—and the boys'—had increased when they worked harder. All Henning had to do was pay his *Serranos* based on production.

Because José Geldres had reserved the right to approve changes in the *Serranos*' wages, Henning sailed with Captain Medina to Callao. From there he went straight to the *Alameda de los Descalzos*, where he intercepted Geldres near one of the bougainvillea covered columns that supported the aqueduct. Geldres objected vehemently to his proposal.

"Every time *Serranos'* income gets tied to their performance," he groused, "they wind up working harder and longer for less money."

"That's not my intention and I'll prove it by paying each man's current wage or a sum based on the amount of guano he excavates, whichever is more."

"Fair enough."

******

From a clifftop, Henning and Captain Medina watched British engineers and construction barges add to the parallel lines of pilings for Henning's loading platform.

"After I announced my new pay plan, production increased and then fell back to previous levels," Henning said, taking his sombrero off during a gust of wind.

"This is the only way to speed up *Serranos*." Medina made a fist. "They've been exposed to a faster-moving culture for centuries and still do things at their ancestors' pace. They don't understand our need to hurry any more than fish understand our fear of drowning."

"Nonetheless, my incentive plan worked perfectly for a few days," Henning said. "I can't figure out what went wrong."

"The friars at Mission San Miguel have a history of motivating Indians without overt force. If anyone can help you they can. I'll take you there if you like. It's on my way."

Founded soon after the Spanish conquered Peru, Mission San Miguel was south of Lima on a clifftop overlooking the Pacific Ocean. It was self-sufficient. Under the friars' guidance, the first Indian converts had built the rectory, dammed a creek, completed an aqueduct, and planted crops. Their successors added a mill, bell tower, botanic garden, tanning vat, pottery kiln, and a library that now contained hundreds of manuscripts written by generations of San Miguel's scholars—two of them Indians.

Although small, Father Cornelio Aranda had a commanding presence. The walls of his office were painted to look like marble and the floor was paved with dull red terracotta tile. He and Henning sat on opposite sides of a well-worn desk, Aranda politely listening as Henning described his problem.

Drawing his eyebrows together Aranda then asked, "How often do you pay your *Serranos?*"

"I provide everything they need," Henning replied, "and when they want to send money home, I do it for them. I'll pay the rest of what they've earned when they leave after fulfilling their contracts."

"To a *Serrano's* way of thinking, you promised more pay if they sped up but nothing happened when they did. They can't grasp the concept of a future reward. They need immediate results."

"It must be difficult to get them interested in heaven."

Chuckling, Aranda said, "Difficult but not impossible. If you pay your *Serranos* daily they'll work harder."

"That would create thieves and gamblers. I'd wind up mediating disputes and investigating theft."

"Come to our religious instruction class in the chapel this afternoon. Perhaps you'll benefit from seeing how we motivate our Indians."

When Henning arrived, Aranda was displaying paintings on easels in front of the pews. One showed a priest carrying a *chakana* or Inca cross, a symbol that pre-dated Catholicism's arrival in South America. Another depicted the Last Supper with Christ and his disciples dining on guinea pig, a *Serrano* delicacy.

"These were done by Indian artists," Aranda said. "They use what our students already know to convey the lessons we want them to learn."

For hours Henning watched Aranda and another friar teach their faith to men they called heathens but treated with remarkable patience and gentleness. Again and again the fathers used Inca parables to explain

Catholic dogma, a radical departure from the past. Spanish *conquistadores* had brutally attempted to eradicate the Inca religion and culture. The Catholic Church had followed up during the Inquisition. But San Miguel's friars took *Serrano* reverence for their traditions and transferred it to what they called Christ's beloved Church.

That night dinner was served in two shifts. After the Indians left the dining room, the friars shared what remained in the cooking pot with Henning. The tasty sweet and sour stew contained beef, potatoes, onions, beans, corn, squash, apples, pears, and raisins. Its unique flavor had been sharpened with chilies.

As they ate, Aranda told Henning, "Peru's natives had a barter system when the *conquistadores* arrived. Unfamiliar with money, they thought it had magical powers and they still do. Before plowing they drape their draft animals in cloth with banknotes pinned to it as supplication for a bountiful harvest. The more I think about it, the more certain I am that giving them cash at the end of the day will encourage them to work harder."

That night Henning tossed to and fro in the mission's guest bed, trying to think of a way to pay his workers daily without encouraging the vices associated with ready cash.

By morning he had a plan that might work.

******

From the mission, Henning sailed to Lima and bought a small printing press. Back on Altamira Island, he produced scrip certificates similar to Peruvian banknotes but bearing a likeness of Ekeko, the Indian god of prosperity and abundance.

Every night after work, Henning and Alcalino handed out these certificates to represent each man's earnings, making it clear that increased effort brought more pay. Within a week, *Serranos* were reporting for work before the morning bell sounded. And when the evening bell gave them permission to stop, most kept going. Soon diggers were excavating twice the guano, loaders were putting it aboard ships twice as fast, and both were earning sums that brought smiles to their normally unreadable faces.

Henning's workers saw scrip as the equivalent of banknotes. Repeatedly Henning had Alcalino explain the difference, always in vain. And because his *Serranos* saw scrip as real money, Henning was soon faced with the problems he'd hoped to avoid. To prevent theft he opened a so-called bank where employees could make deposits and withdrawals. But love of gambling was the main reason his *Serranos* were working harder, and Henning didn't discourage it because nothing of value was being lost. When workers left he'd pay what they'd earned rather than cash in their scrip.

Marchena's efforts to keep his *Serranos* from finding out how much Henning's were earning were no more effective than most attempts to contain the spread of news. After his workers complained about the pittance he paid, he confronted Henning on the dock following Captain Medina's next delivery.

"If you try to lure my workers away with higher pay," Marchena fumed, poking Henning's chest for emphasis, "I'll send you down the road to perdition."

Henning slapped his hand away. Outraged, Marchena raised his eyes while Henning did the reverse. From opposite sides, they saw only the brim of Marchena's hat. He whipped it off, releasing the full fury of his glare before clambering aboard his carriage and speeding away.

Having witnessed this confrontation, Captain Medina told Henning. "I'm glad you didn't let your overseers beat your workers. You showed me a side of *Serranos* I never imagined. I've always thought Indians are shaped by heredities and experiences that inevitably make them lazy."

"History books tell the stories of many men who overcame inherited shortcomings and bad upbringings."

"Surely you don't think *Serranos* are the equal of those men?"

"Not as they are now. But they could be."

"Do you think that's what God intended?"

"To be honest, I don't see myself or anyone else as God's puppets. That kind of thinking gives too much power to the people who tell us what He wants."

CHAPTER THIRTY-ONE
THE BRITISH MAKE THE RULES

The ocean around Altamira Island was too shallow for freighters, so Marchena's lighters took guano out to them. Henning's operation began that way while a British contractor built an elevated pier, starting at the top of a cliff and ending where the water was deeper. There a towering dock with berths for ships along its bottom gave the structure a t-shape. Twice the height of the tallest ship's deck, this facility's upper platform was wide enough for two lanes of wagons, one going to cube-shaped storage bins above the berths, the other returning to the island.

"Ingenious," Captain Lewis Eddings told Henning admiringly. "If you can't get ships close to the island, bring the island to them."

Eddings commanded the American freighter *Andrew Chesterton*, tied up at the newly completed loading platform. High above his ship, guano from a storage bin was being shoveled into canvas chutes that emptied into *Chesterton's* hold. Like all ships Henning's men loaded, she'd been engaged by Antony Gibbs & Sons, a British trading company.

For years, *Chesterton* had loaded at the Chincha Islands, where lighters brought guano that had to be winched aboard by her crew. But at Altamira Island, they hooked chutes to *Chesterton's* hatches and relaxed while their cargo flowed aboard. They were further astonished when a second shift of workers loaded all night under giant lanterns with reflectors.

Chesterton's hold was full in a month, a fraction of the time it took at the Chinchas. When she returned for her next load, Henning was invited to an onboard dinner. Following the first mate past the mess hall, he saw the crew eating dull-gray salted fish, barley, onions, and hardtack— hard, mold-resistant bread that had to be soaked before teeth could penetrate it.

Grinning, the mate said, "Don't worry. Captain Eddings intends for you to eat better than that."

They found Eddings standing at the dining table in his quarters, alone. The map spread out in front of him was coming apart at the folds.

"I thought we'd eat in what the French call small committee," he said with the soft musical drawl common to southerners. "I'd like to talk to y'all without interruptions."

Y'all was a contraction for you all, but this wasn't the first time Henning had heard it refer to only one person. "That's fine with me," he replied.

Though plainly eager to get down to business, Eddings relaxed as they ate richly browned steak, buttery yellow potatoes, and a compote of pineapple and purple corn.

"Y'all like *chirimoyas*, custard apples?" he asked as a man cleared the table.

"Never tried them," Henning replied.

"You're in for a treat. Mark Twain calls them 'deliciousness itself.'" Eddings sliced one in half, scooped out the seeds, and passed Henning a spoonful.

After an exploratory nibble Henning slid the creamy white fruit into his mouth and pulled the spoon out, clean.

Handing him a glass of red wine, Eddings said, "Peru's current guano production is insufficient for the world's needs."

"Tell me something I don't already know," Henning teased.

"I'm not trying to educate you. I'm opening a subject dear to my heart. Peru's guano is marketed in Europe and the United States, which requires hiring ships, paying duties, renting warehouses, finding buyers, and extending credit. Lacking the necessary expertise and capital, Peru's government sells its guano through British trading companies that manipulate sales so England's farmers and munitions factories get all they need while the United States suffers shortages. We desperately need guano for the exhausted soil on our plantations. The man I work for, Oliver Barnikow, wants to deal in it rather than simply transport it. If you sell directly to him, he'll send all twelve of his freighters here instead of to the Chinchas. And y'all can pocket the fifteen percent commission normally paid to Gibbs & Sons."

"If I do that, Gibbs will stop assigning me ships, and they send more than twelve."

"Screw Gibbs. I can get you enough buyers to triple your income." Eddings was full of enthusiasm.

Henning was interested, but skeptical.

******

Henning stopped his carriage on a clifftop, then put his spotting scope to his eye and saw a British man-of-war bearing down on Altamira Island. When closer, *H.M.S. Gibraltar* lowered her sails and glided to a stop, blocking the channel that led to the loading platform. Her gunports were thrown open, and fifty of her hundred cannons were run forward into firing position.

A row of red-coated marines lined up on deck. Dropping to one knee they faced *Andrew Chesterton*. Her crew scrambled for cover. Henning relaxed when the British ship lowered a launch, then felt renewed tension as armed soldiers descended rope ladders. With military precision, they rowed to shore. *Gibraltar's* captain and twelve riflemen were a hundred yards inland by the time Henning intercepted them and stepped down from his vehicle.

"I'm Charles Farland," the captain said, hands clasped behind him. "You must be Henning Dietzel. My superiors have cause to believe you're planning to sell guano directly to Americans."

"How is that your concern?" Henning asked, angry over the intimidation of *Chesterton's* crew.

"Guano is more important to England's economy than gold and is essential to our security," Farland's voice was arrogant and condescending. "We defeated France in the Seven Years War by cutting off her supply of saltpeter, which in those days was the basic ingredient in gunpowder. Now we make gunpowder from guano and could lose our empire if we don't get all we need. I can't and won't allow you set a precedent that might encourage other extractors to sell outside our trading companies."

"So far, my sales have all been made through Gibbs & Sons."

"So far? Then you admit you're considering direct sales to Americans? " Farland stepped closer. "Sometimes those barbarians need a paddling before they'll follow the rules. Copy them and you'll end up with your head in the British lion's mouth."

"When you say rules, you're obviously referring to the ones the British make."

"They're the only ones that matter. If you need convincing, I can arrange it." Eyes narrowed, lips clamped together, Farland turned and began his return to the beach. His men followed, walking backward, rifles hip high and pointed at Henning.

By the time the marines reached their launch, Henning had figured out how Farland knew he was considering direct sales. An hour after Captain Eddings offered to buy directly from Felipe Marchena, the man had sailed for Lima in an untypical hurry.

H.M.S. Gibraltar's visit so soon afterward was no coincidence.

******

A week later, another unexpected but much smaller ship approached Altamira Island, and the dockmaster sent word to Henning and Marchena. They arrived as a well dressed man came ashore followed by a bodyguard. The visitor and Marchena greeted each other like old friends, which they obviously were.

The man offered Henning a limp handshake and said, "Luis Sarmiento, Assistant Vice Minister of Peru's National Treasury. From time to time I inspect guano extractors' ledgers, which is why I'm here today."

"First things first," Marchena interrupted. "By fortunate coincidence my cook prepared your favorite meal. You and your bodyguard can ride with me. Henning is welcome to follow in his carriage, if he wants."

The halfhearted invitation was clearly designed to be turned down.

Suspicious, Henning said, "Thank you. I accept."

The horses were winded after pulling carriages up the steep incline to Marchena's elegant new clifftop house. Henning had often seen him watching his diggings from its second story windows and dispatching runners with instructions for overseers. This unorthodox practice had inspired Alcalino to nickname him *El Comodón*, the lover of comfort. For Henning, lazy would have been a more accurate description. But today, Sarmiento's arrival had brought out Marchena's best behavior, and he seemed full of energy.

While waiting for lunch, Henning and the bodyguard watched Marchena and the Assistant Vice Minister play ground billiards, using mallets to hit wooden balls through a suspended iron ring. Marchena's lavish post-game congratulations gave the impression he'd let Sarmiento win.

On the house's rear patio, the men washed their hands in a metal basin. Then Marchena pointed to a table surrounded by yellow-blossomed oleander, the island's only vegetation.

"If these bushes look familiar," he told Sarmiento, "it's because I transplanted them from my farm where I grew them from cuttings you so generously gave me years ago. Remember?"

This fawning disgusted Henning, but Sarmiento accepted it as his due.

A uniformed servant dished out *pallares*—pureed lima beans mixed with bits of onion, green chili, and tomato, then garnished with lime juice, oil, salt, and vinegar. Next came broiled tenderloin beef medallions béarnaise with sea scallops. The quantities in serving dishes confirmed Henning's hunch. This meal hadn't been prepared for a man planning to dine alone.

After lunch, Marchena drove his guest to offices on the dock with Henning close behind. Without asking for Marchena's books Sarmiento went through Henning's twice, using a comb with finer teeth the second time.

"Come back in an hour, *Señor* Dietzel," he said when finished. "I need to talk privately with your manager…I believe his name is Alcalino Valdivia?"

Later Sarmiento summoned Henning and met him at the door waving a handful of scrip and growling, "What kind of man pays workers with worthless paper?"

"I give them that so they'll know how much they're earning," Henning replied, "but it's not their pay. They'll get legal tender when they leave."

"So you say. But only banks can issue paper money. This is counterfeit."

"Why would I print such obvious fakes? Anyone can see they're not real."

"Except your *Serranos*. They reacted as though they were losing something of great value when my bodyguard confiscated it. And if you've told them it's worthless, why do you have a bank where they deposit it?"

Henning studied his accuser uneasily. His *Serranos* hadn't understood scrip, even after his and Alcalino's repeated explanations. Finally, he'd given up and let them believe what they wanted.

Sarmiento took sworn statements from several of Henning's workers and was full of good cheer by the time he and his bodyguard left. Evidently he'd been searching for irregularities so Marchena could take Henning's half of the island.

And he'd found one, thanks to a villain who reached his goals with minimum effort and maximum inherited money. And who advanced himself with bribes, flattery, and social cunning.

******

Henning continued paying his *Serranos* daily, but with banknotes. Visibly upset because legal tender bore likenesses of the white devils who abused their people, his workers demanded scrip with its image of their god, Ekeko. But Henning faced counterfeiting charges, and continuing to pay with scrip would increase the difficulty of defending himself.

When production plummeted, he went to Lima's *Alameda de los Descalzos* and paced restlessly until he spotted the familiar gray stallion with a squared-off ear. Seeing Henning, José Geldres allowed a smile to crease his normally stoic mask.

They observed the niceties appropriate when people haven't seen one another for a while, and then Henning explained his dilemma.

"My *Serranos* refuse to believe banknotes are better than scrip," he concluded.

"Your *Serranos*?" Villegas asked, eyebrows raised. "They're people—not property."

"Sorry. I know you don't like them referred to that way. That's one of the reasons they trust you. Can you please come to Altamira and verify what I told them? I'll pay for your time."

"I don't charge for telling the truth."

After Geldres's visit, Altamira Island's production went back up.

Henning kept his private bank open so the *Serranos* would have a safe place for their money. And he did everything he could to prevent gambling.

But in a newspaper interview, Assistant Vice Minister Luis Sarmiento was cited as having said, "Don't be misled by this man's recent actions. He's an unscrupulous foreigner profiting from a national resource that should be in Peruvian hands. And this morning I officially charged him with counterfeiting."

In response to these accusations, the trading companies blacklisted Henning and stopped sending ships. It didn't matter that he'd made his sales through Gibbs & Sons...promptly and honestly paid taxes and fees...and invested heavily in equipment and facilities, delaying his profits in order to multiply them. Felipe Marchena—who'd shown more interest in intrigue and comfort than in work—was poised to take his half of Altamira Island and reap everything he'd sown.

What did that say about Herr Becker's guarantee? During a memorable hunting trip with the owner of the land Grandpa Dietzel farmed, the rest of their party had spent much of the week in camp, playing cards and drinking. But the grizzled Becker and youthful Henning had hunted from sunup to sundown every day. And during the final hour of the last day Henning had bagged a red stag with trophy antlers.

"Your determination and dedication will bring many such successes," Becker had promised.

And he'd been right. But now the fruits of his adult labors would likely accrue to Felipe Marchena, who'd casually sent orders from cool rooms behind windows while Henning toiled under a hot sun at top speed. Without taking breaks.

'To hell with Marchena,' he wrote in his next letter to Eduardo Vásquez. 'Damn Gibbs & Sons and their exorbitant commission. Screw Captain Farland and *H.M.S. Gibraltar*. During my remaining time in this business, I'll sell directly to Oliver Barnikow and every other American that Captain Eddings sends my way.'

CHAPTER THIRTY-TWO
THE WORLD'S FINEST NAVY

The first explosion was distant, muffled. The next—much closer—tore into Henning's dream. Instantly wide-awake, he sprang out of bed and dashed outside, still buttoning his trousers. A glimmer and dull thud far offshore was followed by a blinding flash and a thunderous boom at the island's edge.

Cannon fire.

A salvo ripped Henning's loading platform apart, splintering beams and shattering storage bins. Clouds of guano billowed toward the waves below. Such pinpoint gunnery meant the unseen ship was from the world's finest navy. Looking out to sea, Henning saw only blackness. But he didn't need to see *H.M.S. Gibraltar* to know Captain Farland was reprimanding him for selling to Americans.

He ran down the road that curved around the cliffs. At the dock, off-duty workers stood outside their barracks in underclothes, slack jawed, eyes reflecting firelight.

The bombardment stopped.

"See if anyone was hurt," Henning bellowed to Alcalino.

The mansion on the cliffs across from Henning's house was dark. Marchena had left the previous day, rather conveniently as it turned out.

The sun was up when Alcalino returned. Over the heads of men between them, Henning shouted, "Is everyone accounted for?"

"Yes. And no one was injured," Alcalino replied.

"Go ahead and eat when breakfast is ready. I'll be a while."

"I'll eat when you do. I should be here in case you need help."

With fire slowly reducing Peru's most expensive guano loading facility to smoke, embers, and ash, Henning controlled his outrage. The overseers clamoring for instructions needed to see him calm and in charge. But that façade was difficult to maintain because every time he sent one away with instructions, another brought his seemingly unsolvable problem.

"How long will it take to rebuild the loading platform?" Alcalino asked after the flood of questions dried up and the kitchen's bell announced breakfast.

"Why should I spend hundreds of thousands of *reales* replacing something the British can destroy at will?" Henning grumbled. "Especially since Marchena will get my half of the island if I'm jailed for counterfeiting."

Alcalino went to breakfast leaving Henning to pace the new sports field, his usually disciplined mind wandering. He'd been horrified after two of Marchena's diggers leapt from cliffs to their deaths. To provide his *Serranos* with a place to socialize and an activity that would make their difficult lives more tolerable, he'd assigned a crew to level this area and surround it with benches. Next he'd had goals built for the sport known as football because it involved guiding an inflated ball with the feet. Played by Europeans with tremendous enthusiasm, the game didn't appeal to *Serranos*.

Henning had read that in their Andean homeland *Serranos* enjoyed a sport that involved throwing a ball through a small hoop attached vertically to a wall. He replaced his field's large, rectangular wood and net goal with a small, round, metal one and football had become popular.

The solution to today's problem was more elusive. Logic said he shouldn't spend a fortune to replace a loading platform Marchena might take over if the British didn't destroy it first. But his heart disagreed because waiting for guarantees would involve months of idleness.

At midnight he hiked up to his house and stretched out on his new, extra long bed. By that time he was inclined to rebuild. Then after hours of turning this way and that, he decided against it and drifted into restless sleep.

At dawn Henning was instantly awake, mind racing. Called *mangueras* in Spanish and mongaries in English, the cube-shaped storage bins on his old platform had level floors. It took a hundred twenty men—working day and night—to shovel guano from them into chutes that took it to freighters below.

This greatly slowed the loading of ships. But if the mongaries were rebuilt with sloping floors, gravity would pull guano into the chutes. Loading would be much faster—enough so to quickly recuperate the cost of a new platform.

He hurried through the dining hall to the kitchen where the cook heaped a plate with scrambled eggs and fried potatoes. Hungry for the first time in twenty-four hours he carried this meal to his office, then gathered a pen, ruler, and paper. Humming between bites, he began designing new mongaries.

He'd use this setback to his advantage and thumb his nose at the British. England wasn't to be taken lightly but would find it difficult to repeat the previous night's attack, made when he had no ships to load. By the time his new platform was ready, Oliver Barnikow's four-masted barques would be waiting in line. Another bombardment would jeopardize them and could ignite a war the British didn't want. America's navy was growing and England's was spread thin.

******

Sunday was a day of rest for everyone but Henning. Through his office window, he saw Alcalino stop his new two-wheel cycle. For years, riders had propelled these by pushing the ground with their feet. The latest model had pedals. Henning had replaced Alcalino's mule with one, hoping to increase his mediocre employee's productivity. The pedals had proven better than expected. But Alcalino had been disappointing.

Alcalino stood, one foot on the ground, chatting with workers fishing from the dock. He was probably trying, as usual on Sundays, to interest them in a game of football. But they didn't follow when he rode away, his cycle leaving a single track that became two as he turned a corner and one again on the next straightaway.

Henning tried to refocus on his ledger, but his mind was elsewhere. Altamira Island's new loading dock had ten berths. Months after completion, most had never been used. The day Henning agreed to make direct sales, Captain Eddings had promised more buyers than he could handle. But so far only Oliver Barnikow had sent ships.

The bulk of Peru's guano exports came from the Chincha Islands, where freighters waited their turns before finally being loaded with an excruciating lack of urgency. Paying captains and crews to do nothing for eight months per trip had made American ship owners more eager to purchase and sell guano rather then simply transport it. But Eddings had done a poor job of spreading the word that Henning was willing to make direct sales and usually turned ships around in thirty days.

Henning could effectively spread that news at the Chincha Islands. Problem was, going there meant leaving Alcalino in charge. And he was prone to costly mistakes. Last week a water tank had burst after he neglected its maintenance. Twice he'd charged for less guano than his men loaded. Another time he hadn't ordered enough supplies and the cook had run out of food.

But Henning had no other way to get badly needed income. He returned the ledger to his safe and headed for the football field. There, *Serranos* on a bench squeezed together to make room for him beside Alcalino. They liked having Henning as a spectator, and he enjoyed vicariously reliving his days at Maximilian Academy. But today's visit had another purpose.

As two teams warmed up, Henning told Alcalino, "I'm going to the Chincha Islands. You'll be in charge while I'm there."

"How long will that be?" Alcalino asked, clearly taken unaware.

"Two or three weeks."

"Can't someone else oversee things while you're gone?"

"Who?" Henning asked with pent-up frustration. "If you don't like being accountable for mistakes, stop making them."

Later that week, a panic-stricken Alcalino followed Henning to the schooner *Intrepido*, about to leave for the Chincha Islands after its latest delivery. Before boarding Henning leaned close and whispered, "Your buttons—the ones most important to a man—are undone."

Rather than do them up in front of people, Alcalino pulled his shirt from his trousers and let it hang.

"Avoiding mistakes is better than hiding them," Henning teased, using one of his grandfather's home-grown proverbs.

******

With the Chinchas's North Island in view, Henning counted sixty-three waiting freighters.

"There's a like number off the opposite shore," Captain Medina said as his crew lowered the sails. "Any day of the year there are more ships here than at London, New York, or any other port on earth. Peru's guano is the best-selling commodity in history."

Henning saw the familiar silhouette of *H.M.S. Gibraltar*, her three rows of cannon—one above the other—looking ominous. He was comforted by the presence of an American warship of similar size and armament.

"I didn't expect military vessels here," he said.

"The Americans," Medina replied, "are doing everything they can to get more guano, increasing the tension between them and the Brits. Both have a ship of the line here at all times."

"I offered to sell Americans all the guano they want, but so far I have only one buyer. If they're so anxious, why—"

"Appears to me your friend Captain Eddings hasn't done much to make that known. Apparently he doesn't care if anyone besides his boss buys from you."

After *Intrepido* dropped anchor, a launch came alongside and an American captain climbed aboard.

Handing Medina a list he said, "I'm still waiting my turn and need more supplies."

"How long have you been here?" Medina asked.

"Five months. It's an easy life. Some captains even bring their wives, but I'm not married and I get paid by the load. It's frustrating to sit idle for months."

"Meet Henning Dietzel," Medina said. "He has the guano concession on Altamira Island and sells directly—not through trading companies. With his loading system, he'll have you on your way a month after you tie up."

Looking skeptical, the American told Henning, "I'm Mark Smith and I'm late for an appointment. Care to come along so we can discuss this further?"

On North Island, Smith went about his business while Henning wandered through a cluster of structures. Oversize windows in the governor's residence revealed a ballroom for entertaining visitors. The nearby British and American consul's homes were smaller and less grand. Though occupied by the island's most powerful men, the trading companies looked insignificant. But they were palaces compared to the hovels that housed diggers and loaders.

"Aren't there any hotels or restaurants?" Henning asked a man who sold snacks and beverages from a cart.

"None," the man replied. "Crews live, eat, and entertain themselves on their ships. Dignitaries stay with the governor or consuls. Other visitors stay in mainland hotels."

While Medina and *Intrepido* picked up supplies at the coastal town of Pisco, Henning would have no place to stay.

******

After lunch on his freighter, Captain Smith lit a cigar and said, "My ship delivers guano for Gibbs & Sons, but the owner would much rather buy and sell. What do you charge?"

"I match Gibbs's price," Henning replied.

"In that case you'll soon have all the buyers you can handle." Smith sucked his cigar and released a smoke ring. "The captains' wives have scheduled a picnic for tomorrow on South Island. You're welcome to sleep on my ship and go with me. Several of the Americans on hand will be delighted to meet someone who makes direct sales."

Early next afternoon, rowers took Smith and Henning to South Island, desolate and uninhabited because its guano wasn't yet being mined. Except for a fenced-off rectangle where the picnic would be held, the island was covered by guano birds, thick as flies and tame as chickens. The nearest flew away after a man shot one. To Henning's disgust the gunman's next victim was a sea lion sunning himself at the island's edge. The magnificent bull was left where he'd breathed his last, killed for sport—not meat or blubber.

Smith introduced Henning to three American captains who worked for companies interested in buying guano.

"I guarantee my employer will buy from you," one declared after Henning showed him Altamira Island on a nautical chart.

"Mine will probably send every vessel he owns," another offered.

Henning wound up with tentative commitments for twenty-one ships.

When they were alone again, Smith said, "There are other captains you can talk to when they return from digging up mummies on the mainland."

"Isn't that illegal?"

"Sure, but mummies and the artifacts they're buried with bring big money and smuggling them in shipments of guano is easy. Don't worry. There's no danger of getting caught, and these guys will pay you to look the other way."

"I won't have grave robbers bringing loot to my island," Henning declared. "How would your friends feel if someone raided American graveyards?"

"I don't see anything wrong with supplying articles of historical significance to museums and collectors, but I admire your integrity. Most people pick money over principle every time."

Henning, Smith, and others removed their shoes before wading out to a rowboat full of picnic supplies. Carrying a box ashore, Henning looked down as surf washed over his feet and retreated across quivering sand, leaving him momentarily dizzy. After the whirling sensation passed, he caught up with Smith.

His box now on a table, Smith patted the shoulder of a man so formal he'd worn a suit to the picnic and said, "Allow me to introduce Santander Gómez. As far as we Americans are concerned, this man walks on water. He loads ships twice as fast as anyone else."

Smith was called away.

"As a new extractor," Henning told Gómez, "I have a lot to learn and will be grateful for any advice you'd care to offer."

Gómez's homely face lit up beneath reddish-blonde hair and pale red eyelashes.

"It's a pleasure to meet someone who's searching for knowledge," he said. "Most men of your generation have no respect for their elders. My son wants to teach me rather than benefit from my experience. He forgets I've been his age while he's never been mine."

After answering a few of Henning questions, Gómez remarked, "You don't say much."

"I learn more by listening than talking."

Though Peruvian, Gómez chuckled like an Englishmen—in an unenthusiastic monotone. Then he said, "My operation is on Middle Island. You're welcome to come and see it."

"I'd love to but I'm going to sell directly to Americans, which could mean some of your customers will buy from me."

"How much do you charge?"

"The same as trading companies."

"As long as you don't undercut the price, I don't care who your customers are. I have more than I can handle. But how will you get around the trading companies?"

Avoiding this sensitive subject, Henning asked, "Is your invitation still open?"

"Absolutely. You can stay in my guest room tonight."

"Thank you," Henning said as ladies began cooking over open fires.

When lunch was ready Captain Smith joined Gómez and Henning in line. At the buffet table, they served themselves cooked carrots, Chinese-style rice, and steaming slices of blackened *corvina*—sea bass coated with butter, paprika, black pepper, and other spices, then barbecued until the color of charcoal.

******

The next day, an extremely courteous overseer showed Henning an operation that was much larger but less efficient than Altamira Island. Henning's incentive plan had made his workers more productive. And with outdoor lighting, his diggings operated around the clock while Gómez's shut down at night.

Nonetheless, Henning found something worth copying. Gómez's wagons could be unloaded more efficiently because they had removable sides instead of tailgates. Henning opened his sketchbook and drew one so he could have them duplicated.

Next he had an idea that would make unloading faster yet. Turning the page he designed a method for mounting a wagon bed like a seesaw—but unbalanced so it would tip and dump its contents when untied. That inspiration led to another. He'd put his mongaries beneath the loading platform's deck rather than on top. That way his new wagons could dump into them through trap doors, eliminating the need for shoveling.

Gómez served aperitifs on his veranda late that afternoon and seemed bored when shown the plans for Henning's new wagons.

"I'll be glad to show you some of my other innovations if you'd like to visit Altamira Island," Henning offered as they seated themselves at a table with a round, polished granite top.

"We'll see." Gómez clearly enjoyed teaching more than learning.

Again Henning slept unusually well in the guest room. In the morning, a *Serrano* houseboy told him the *patrón* had been called away. Surprised when not offered breakfast, he stepped outside and crossed the island's barren surface toward the diggings he'd seen yesterday. He was almost there when the overseer—minus yesterday's courtesy—stepped in front of him.

"The *patrón* is unavailable today," the man said icily.

"He told me I can take another look at his facilities." Henning started to go around.

"Things gave changed," the overseer said, blocking him again. "Señor Gómez is attending a meeting called by Don Felipe Marchena, and he wants you kept away from his workers."

"Why?"

"*Señor* Marchena says you're trying to steal his people. *Señor* Gómez doesn't mind if you take a few customers, but he spent a fortune on Chinese coolies and can't spare any."

CHAPTER THIRTY-THREE
ENCOUNTER ON THE *DAPHNE*

No longer welcome on Middle Island, Henning paced its dock. Mark Smith had promised to pick him up and was late. For hours, seagulls had swirled above South Island's picnic area across the channel. By now the gulls would have eaten all the scraps of leftover food. They must be feeding on the huge, gratuitously shot sea lion.

"Sorry I'm late," Smith said as his rowers helped Henning board his bobbing launch. "I was spying on your friend Marchena. He called a meeting and told the extractors you tried to lure his workers away with higher wages, which you can afford because you pay with counterfeit banknotes. In light of your distaste for smuggling mummies, I don't believe that. But all the extractors signed his petition to have the government cancel your lease."

Henning willed his face to stay calm. "Will all this fuss stop you and the other captains from recommending that your employers buy from me?"

"Absolutely not. But by the time we deliver our current cargoes and get to your island, you might be out of business. You shouldn't have told Gómez you're going to sell to us. When he told the other extractors, they didn't take it well."

"I'll leave on tomorrow's supply ship. With me gone, things should calm down."

"I've been asked to invite you to tonight's *fiesta* aboard *Daphne*."

"Thanks, but I'd better keep my head down."

"There won't be any extractors there—just Americans, including our ambassador. You should take advantage of the chance to get him on your side. He could be an important ally."

Aboard Smith's ship Henning changed into the best clothes he'd brought, brown corduroy pants and a blue bib-front shirt.

******

With lanterns hanging from its lower rigging, *Daphne* stood out in the dark. Henning and Smith waited in a line of launches while guests who'd arrived before them climbed rope ladders.

Onboard, Henning was introduced to the American Ambassador, Glen Mason, under a sailcloth awning that kept mist from settling on a section of deck polished for dancing. Tall and square-jawed, Mason seemed unusually direct for a diplomat.

"I understand you're going to sell us guano," he told Henning with a firm handshake. "As you undoubtedly know, British trading companies will stop at nothing to prevent that. My government and I will assist you in every possible way. I've already asked for more American warships. If I can do anything else, don't hesitate to ask."

"Thank you," Henning said. "I've already had one run-in too many with the British."

"I heard about that."

Mason's aide interrupted to whisper something.

"Duty calls," the ambassador told Henning. "Let's talk more after the party."

Daphne's captain invited Captain Smith below deck, leaving Henning alone among strangers. Three fiddlers and a piano man played music in triple time while sailors in black breeches and striped shirts danced without partners, palms slapping against thighs, heels clicking on the deck.

The bartender was serving an outstanding *pisco*. He gave it to men straight or blended with egg white, sugar, lemon juice, and bitters. For captains' wives, he mixed it with sweet syrup from the seed pods of *algarrobo* trees. Normally men sailing with their wives struck Henning as frivolous, but not when he felt this lonely.

No one reacted when someone said a Chinaman had leapt to his death from a North Island cliff, but the arrival of a launch caused a stir.

"Peru's ambassador to Argentina," someone said. "He's on his way to Lima and stopped here to hobnob with Ambassador Mason."

Henning's *pisco* went down the wrong way. Eyes watering, he coughed repeatedly as he joined the reception line. *Don* Manuel Prado stepped over the ship's rail, wearing a top hat and black dinner suit. Regal as ever, he was ceremoniously welcomed. Then his daughter, Martine, reached the top of the boarding ladder and replaced him as the center of attention.

Her gown was simpler than those worn by captain's wives. Ivory with black trim, it had a low off-the-shoulder neckline and sheer sleeves, gathered at the wrists. Below her fitted bodice, a cascade of silk hung from her hips without the usual hoop, bustle, or petticoats.

Henning's memory carried a well-preserved image of her, but she'd changed. Her hair was half as long and her features were no longer a girl's. Up close, he saw an upper tooth that slightly overlapped its neighbor, an imperfection that somehow made her more perfect.

Henning heard *Daphne's* captain introduce him as the owner of Altamira Island.

"I feel as if I already know you," she said in a voice as sweet as any Henning had heard.

Prepared to say meeting her was a pleasure, he felt the now-inappropriate words freeze in his throat.

She had offered her hand—palm down—so other men could gently squeeze it. When she leaned toward Henning, he wasn't sure it meant what he hoped until she raised her chin. He bent at the waist. They touched cheeks and silently kissed air. Her hair smelled like lilacs.

"My father and I owe you a debt of gratitude for the hospitality we received at your island," she said.

"I don't own Altamira Island," he replied. "I just have a guano concession there."

"Is it managed by a man named Alcalino Valdivia?"

"Yes."

"Then it was your hospitality we enjoyed. Our ship needed repairs and *Señor* Valdivia was immensely helpful."

Señor Valdivia. Henning was impressed. Few aristocrats extended respect to half-breeds.

"I'm glad to hear that," he said.

"I'm sure the workers and material he provided cost you more than enough to deserve our eternal gratitude."

She moved on. If *Daphne* had begun sinking, Henning could've dived into the ocean, kept her afloat with one hand, and patched the leak with the other.

Conversations paused as Martine and *Daphne's* captain inaugurated the dancing with a fast-paced mazurka. Guests gathered to watch her supple footwork, hips, and bare shoulders. When the music stopped, damp curls were plastered to her forehead. She scraped them away with her fingertips while men crowded around, eager to be her next partner. In time she accommodated them all, making Henning wish he'd let Makayla teach him to dance.

At midnight a launch came for Martine and her father. Henning positioned himself where she'd pass close by. Seeing him, she stopped, gown in sweet disarray, green eyes shining. Unsteady after several cocktails she looked both sensual and innocent. Henning regretted being absent during her visit to Altamira Island, where he would've had her to himself.

"On your island," she said, "my father and I had a tête-à-tête with your neighbor, *Señor* Marchena. He said he's having worker problems because you overpay yours. As the daughter of an ambassador, I officially congratulate you. You don't pay too much. Marchena pays too little. Like you, I believe in treating workers well.

"By the way, *Señor* Marchena told my father you're trying to steal his workers, but *Señor* Valdivia insisted you've done nothing of the sort. Marchena also said you're paying your workers with counterfeit banknotes, but Valdivia explained that it's scrip. My father believed him and declined to help Marchena against you."

For once, Henning was grateful for Alcalino's chattiness. His gaze was pulled where he dared not let it linger, the top of Martine's gown where shadows emphasized her cleavage.

Her pink lips parted to show white teeth. She raised her heels from the deck and touched her warm, damp mouth to his cheek. The gesture—though formal—brought heat to his face. Looking down while she was on tiptoes, he imagined the tightening of calves, thighs, and buttocks under her gown.

"Sorry to embarrass you, but I couldn't resist a little kiss," she said, eyes twinkling. "That blue shirt emphasizes your eyes and tan. But that's not news to you, is it? When men are handsome, they know it."

Martine's father gripped her arm and steered her to the rail. Impeded by her long dress, she started down the rope ladder toward a waiting launch. Wishing she'd seen him in his gray alpaca suit, Henning again bid her a silent *adiós*, six years after the first time.

He was still watching her launch when Ambassador Mason renewed their conversation.

******

"You'll never guess who was here," Alcalino called as Henning descended the gangplank at Altamira Island.

"Martine Prado." Shading his eyes, Henning enjoyed Alcalino's puzzled expression, then added, "She and her father stopped at the Chincha Islands after they left here."

"You must have been pleasantly surprised."

"Unfortunately there was also a sour note. Felipe Marchena was at North Island with a petition demanding that the Ministry of Guano revoke my lease. After the extractors signed, he took it to the Ministry of Guano in Lima. Between that and the counterfeiting allegations, I could lose my lease and even get thrown in jail. But your defense of me convinced *Don* Manuel Prado not to support Marchena's petition. Thank you."

"I have bad news," Alcalino said, obviously reluctant to lose Henning's approval as they walked toward the office. "While you were gone, three diggers nearly suffocated in a cave-in while working in a trench on a hillside."

"That requires special training. Did you give it to them?"

"No. I'm sorry."

"Are they all right?"

"They're still recuperating."

Henning changed directions and rushed to the infirmary. As usual the doctor was out among the diggers. Before the trench collapsed his most serious cases had involved sprains, cuts, and mild fevers. But now—for the first time—cots in his simple white-walled recovery room were occupied by men whose lives he'd likely saved.

"How are you feeling?" Henning quietly asked the nearest, kneeling beside his bed.

The only answer was a glance from lackluster eyes. *Serrano* men were under a cultural obligation to suffer in silence.

"Don't worry about anything," Henning said. "Your wages will continue while you recover, no matter how long it takes."

Twice more Henning knelt, struggling to find different words for each man. *Serranos* weren't offended by lack of originality the way white people were. But he wanted them to know he saw them as individuals. After all, they had nearly died serving him.

Leaving the infirmary, Henning paused at a glass case containing three pieces of orange-brown earthenware. Crude pottery from ancient Indian temples and tombs, *huacos* portrayed anything from animals and people to scenes and erotica. In the absence of written language, they portrayed the history of Peru's indigenous peoples.

Henning's three pieces showed medicine men, one assisting a woman during a breech birth, another treating a man for burrowing sand fleas, and a third trepanning a patient's skull in preparation for brain surgery. He'd bought these to remind Altamira Island's white doctor that his patients' ancestors had been more advanced than their European contemporaries.

Their people's glory days long gone, his workers had left families and friends in beautiful Andean Valleys in order to work on Henning's desolate eyesore of an island. Far away from the comfort of their women and the joy of their children, they did little besides eat, sleep, and labor under harsh conditions. They didn't suffer as much as workers in Peru's silver mines or on other guano islands. And not one had committed suicide. But still, how did they stand it?

From behind a wagon at the diggings, Henning watched three diggers he'd chosen because they spoke Spanish more often than *Quechua*. Stoic when he was around, they didn't know he was there. Normally he'd have been pleased to see them working so hard, but today he was looking for something else.

Their silent toil was interrupted when they stopped to wet their masks in a barrel of vinegar solution. Washing down his exposed skin, one asked, "You have any pictures of your wife naked?"

"Of course not," another replied, clearly offended.

Opening his belt pouch, the first man asked, "Wanna buy some?"

The butt of the joke joined the laughter. His unexpected sense of humor put Henning's mind at rest. The dreary monotony of these men's jobs hadn't shriveled their souls. And from now on he'd give them annual paid vacations to spend with their families. Expensive? Yes. And he'd have to replace those who didn't return. But that was preferable to scraping up human remains at the base of a cliff.

He set out to find Alcalino, determined to make sure none of his workers ever again dug on hillsides without proper training. How had Alcalino forgotten something that important? Though he'd proven surprisingly helpful with the Prados, his carelessness had shown he still wasn't protégé material. Was it time to give up on him and find another manager?

No, not yet. Deep inside, he still had the qualities that had been so helpful during Henning's first shipment from Peru. There had to be a way to bring those out again.

******

Months later, Henning waited for Jorge Villegas at their project in Lima. The city's surrounding wall and dump were gone, leaving clean, level ground. Villegas had divided his and Henning's share into building sites, long since sold out. Bricklayers were putting up houses.

A carriage stopped and Villegas got out. Despite his much improved finances, his old brown suit still billowed around his slender body.

"On time as always," Henning greeted.

"Your share of the profits." Villegas handed over an envelope.

"You may be a communist, but your cheerfulness says you enjoy making money."

"When it's for good purposes."

"What's the latest on Felipe Marchena's *Serranos*?" Henning asked. "You always know more than I can find in newspapers."

Weeks ago, Marchena's workers had demanded he raise their wages or allow them to leave. His response had been to stop feeding them. Not until an exposé on the *Lima Correo's* front page reported them on the verge of starvation had he let them go home.

"He's going to replace them with Chinese coolies," Villegas said.

"Evidently he's not as good at motivating workers as he thought. When will his coolies arrive?"

"In eight months at best, and there's no way the bastard can speed up the process. President Castilla just initiated a stringent anti-corruption campaign. For once Marchena will have to wait his turn rather than bribe his way to the head of the line."

"What's delaying my counterfeiting trial and the Ministry of Guano's response to Marchena's petition?"

"Ask your lawyer. All I know is someone important has taken your side."

"The American ambassador?"

"Someone even more powerful."

Villegas was called away and Henning opened his envelope. The check inside was for an astonishing sum. His luck had never been so good. Americans were buying Altamira Island's guano as fast as his workers could load it. Courts had twice postponed his counterfeiting trial. The British navy was keeping its distance. And Marchena's petition was in limbo. Could Villegas be right? Did someone more influential than Marchena wish him well? And if so, why?

Possibly because two-thirds of Peru's guano sales went into the treasury as taxes. Before the strike shut Marchena down, Henning had shipped five times as much. Since then, Marchena's side of the island had been idle.

******

An ordinary day became memorable when a stranger barged into Henning's Altamira Island office. The amount of white surrounding his blue irises gave him an energetic—if slightly crazed—look. Henning stood, prepared to welcome his visitor or confront him, depending on whether he'd come to pursue Sarmiento's counterfeiting allegations.

"I'm on my way to Chile," the man said, "and since I was in your neighborhood, I decided we should meet. Looks like you're doing well. Hard to believe so much money comes from the assholes of birds, isn't it?" From such a courtly gentleman, the obscenity was jarring. "You've made powerful enemies. When you have those, you need influential friends. Does Alcalino Valdivia still work for you?"

"Yes, but he's not what I'd call influential."

"Well I am, and he was my maid's son. My wife didn't bear children, so I put a lot of effort into Alcalino and kept an eye on him after he ran away. You gave him opportunities no one else would have." The visitor's nose and mouth were identical to Alcalino's.

"He earned everything I gave him," Henning said.

"I believe that, but then again I don't. He's a hard worker but short on initiative and without the balls to stand up for himself."

The stranger crossed the room as if he owned it. Studying the contents of Henning's bookcase, he said, "I'm not here to discuss Alcalino. Recently Raul Rubio, the Minister of Guano, was pressured to revoke your lease. I helped him put a damper on those efforts. Let me know if they flare up again."

He took out a business card that bore four words, Diego de la Torre. Cards with only a name were favored in Peru because they allowed for the personal touch of adding information by hand. De la Torre pulled a pen from Henning's inkwell and carefully printed his address.

"Felipe Marchena has done things," he continued, "that are about to bite him in the ass. He'll be his own worst enemy when he tries to explain, and you'll wind up with both halves of this island."

"I thought I'd be the one losing his lease," Henning said, relaxing just a bit.

"You came close until I showed Minister Rubio that you pay ten times the taxes Marchena does. Stupid bastard. You showed him how businesses should be run, but he stuck with outdated methods and spent almost nothing on facilities while you built the best there are."

"I hope you realize how much I appreciate—"

"I had a score to settle with the son of a bitch." *Don* Diego smirked. "Besides, these matters were simple enough to be handled by my assistant. However, your run-in with the British navy required my personal attention.

Don't look so surprised. The only things that escape my notice are those I don't care about."

"Would you like something to eat or drink while I have someone fetch Alcalino?"

"Don't bother. He blames me for things so ridiculous that I can't possibly defend myself. And instead of confronting me, he chose to slink off in the middle of the night. Damned if I'll chase after him."

After *Don* Diego left, Alcalino came to Henning's office, looking concerned. "Heard you had a visitor," he said "Bad news?"

"On the contrary. He was your mother's *patrón*. I'm sure you're right about his being your father, but you're wrong to think he doesn't love you. He kept track of you after you ran away and more than once saved me from my enemies to protect your job."

"Well, I don't love him." Alcalino crisply bit off each word.

"You should give him another chance."

"Not until he apologizes for what he did to my mother."

"An apology from a man like him is a lot to ask for. He's very proud."

"So am I. It must be hereditary."

Who is this guy with all the backbone?' Henning hid his surprise. *And how can I get him to drop anchor more often?*

✳✳✳✳✳✳

The instant *Intrepido's* gangplank touched Altamira Island's dock, Captain Medina rushed ashore. As the crew began unloading, he followed Henning into the warehouse where they watched as gunnysacks went on the scale.

"Ten sacks containing four hundred seventy-one kilos of rice," the weighmaster said.

Henning wrote 471 next to 'rice' on the bill of lading and the bags were stacked against a wall. The next sacks contained four hundred ninety-two kilos of oranges that were carried to a cool, dark, insulated room in a corner.

"I understand you're taking over the rest of the island," Medina said.

"There's a rumor to that effect," Henning replied, "but I haven't heard anything reliable."

"Allow me to remedy that." Medina reached into the leather bag hanging from his shoulder. Unfolding a well-worn *Lima Correo,* he pointed to an article that said Marchena's lease was being been transferred to Henning.

"I'll celebrate when the news is official."

"It already is." Medina handed Henning an envelope with a red wax seal securing its flap. The contract inside bore Minister Raul Rubio's signature and granted a lease on the entire island.

"Take over please," Henning said, handing the bill of lading to his weighmaster.

Seated on a crate of lettuce, he made certain the contract's copies were identical, then signed both and returned one to Medina for delivery.

"Congratulations." Medina smiled. "You deserve this. You're a better businessman and a far better person than Marchena. Now that you'll be shipping twice the guano, you'll have to enlarge your loading platform. Shall I bring the engineer who built it?"

"Find me an underwater demolition expert instead," Henning replied. "Rather than create too much traffic in one area, I'm going to build a second loading facility on the island's other side. And I've devised a better way to do that."

CHAPTER THIRTY-FOUR

THE PATCHWORK QUILT

Guano extractors had large accumulations of capital and received frequent loan requests. Henning automatically denied these until Alcalino's father intervened on behalf of a friend. Normally brusque in speech and manner, Diego de la Torre involved himself tactfully, beginning with an invitation to his palatial Lima home.

"As you know from his application, Belisario Lorca needs to build a sugar mill," he said as a maid ladled out bowls of *chupe de camarones*, shrimp chowder. "His hacienda is worth several times what he wants to borrow, and he's offering it as security. I'd make the loan myself if my money wasn't tied up. Any chance you can help him?"

Unable to flatly refuse someone who'd done so much for him, Henning said, "My aversion to lending began when a friend lost his ranch because be borrowed a fortune to buy things he didn't need."

A second maid silently appeared and stirred a pinch of salt into *Don Diego's* soup. Tasting the results, he nodded his approval. The maid had a pretty smile, but when leaving the room she struggled with a knee that bent in both directions.

"Alcalino's mother?" Henning asked.

"She died. That's her sister. She can't hold a job with that knee so I'm helping her." He cleared his throat. "Getting back to the subject at hand, borrowing to invest isn't the same as borrowing to squander. A loan from you to *Señor* Lorca would be an ideal transaction because it would benefit you both."

A week later, Lorca sent Henning a financial statement clearly prepared by an amateur. After poring over it, Henning suspected the man's hacienda wasn't doing well and requested more information. Lorca responded with rosy prose rather than numbers, meaning he had no records beyond those already provided.

Henning granted the loan after Lorca agreed to let him disburse funds in increments as the mill was built. The remaining details fell in place until only Henning's personal inspection of the property remained. Prepared to forego that, he changed his mind when he heard that Lorca's hacienda was near Hacienda Toledo, owned by Martine Prado's father. The ambassador had recently retired there with his daughter, still unmarried a year after Henning met her on *Daphne*.

******

The sky was clear and the early morning temperature high when Henning's ship docked at Cortéz. The sun pounded him like a blacksmith's hammer as he came down the gangplank. From the dock below, a man and young boy—both with blond hair and blue eyes—expectantly watched him.

"You must be Henning Dietzel," the man said. "I had pictured someone older. I'm Belisario Lorca. This is my son, Marco Venicio." Lorca's angular face was ruggedly handsome, but his profile was spoiled by a protruding nose.

Pale and unhealthy looking, the boy offered his hand. Henning grasped it gently. "You have wonderful manners." He smiled. "Your mother must be proud of you."

Marco Venicio examined his shoes and Lorca rescued him. "His mother passed away."

"Sorry. I didn't mean to—"

"Don't worry. We like being reminded of her. She left wonderful memories."

On the way to Lorca's carriage Marco lagged behind and his father took advantage to say, "My wife died during our son's birth. I talk about her so much that he thinks he remembers her, which is better than blaming himself because she died bringing him into the world. I couldn't bear to have him think he's responsible for something that's not his fault in any way."

"You love him a great deal, don't you?"

"In direct proportion to the high price I paid. Oh, that sounded selfish, didn't it? Marco paid part of that price. He lost his mother." Lorca cleared his throat. "I don't imagine they fed you on the ship. Would you like to eat before we set out?"

Henning soon regretted having accepted. The meal would have been enjoyable if he hadn't been impatient to get to where he might see Martine Prado. He ate quickly, then squirmed while Lorca methodically chewed, pausing between bites for conversation. The old aristocrat's shrimp, oysters, halibut, fried yellow potatoes, and seared asparagus slowly disappeared—only to be replaced by pastries and coffee. Next, Lorca ordered a drink of American rye whiskey from a cut-glass bottle with a label reading, 'It was impossible to make the contents better, so we improved the container.'

When they were back in the carriage and underway, neither had yet mentioned the loan.

With no other sign of being in a hurry, Belisario drove fast along the flat coastal road. Later the climb into steep, barren coastal mountains forced a slower pace.

Belisario paused his vehicle where the summit provided a panoramic view of the ocean behind them. Farther along, he stopped to admire an even more remarkable scene. Below and to the east, an immense flat valley stretched to the distant Andes. Both edges extended beyond their respective horizons and a silvery river divided its rippling, green fields.

"The Chiriaco Valley is being concentrated in fewer hands," Belisario said. "There are barely a hundred haciendas left. There used to be five times that many. In those days, the fields were smaller and colored different shades of green because we raised a variety of crops. Seen from up here, they looked like an immense patchwork quilt. But now most of us grow sugarcane and the view is monotonous."

Reaching flat land, Belisario's carriage sped along a narrow lane between towering walls of sugarcane. From the summit, the Valley had looked like an uninterrupted green sea. Now Henning caught occasional glances of roads, windbreaks, corrals, and workers.

Approaching an oncoming rider, Belisario slowed until dust no longer boiled from beneath his vehicle's wheels.

"Federico García," he said quietly. "He manages the Valley's largest hacienda and can eat garlic whenever he likes." Seeing Henning's perplexed reaction, he clarified, "In other words, he does things that are only done by men who have no need of friends. I steer clear of him. You should do the same."

Belisario and García tipped their hats as they passed. The carriage accelerated past three Indian women, trudging along the shoulder, wearing white *sombreros* with black hatbands. Dressed in rainbow-colored skirts, they had infants tied to their backs with sashes. The babies' heads nodded with their mothers' movements. After slowing for García—a man he plainly disliked—Belisario passed the ladies at full speed, spraying them with dust.

"Valencia," he announced as the cane gave way to an orchard followed by paddocks where horses dozed beneath trees with thorns and fern-like leaves. A layer of their yellow seedpods gave off a sweet smell as the carriage rolled over them.

"*Algarrobo* trees," Belisario said. "Depending on who you ask, they're a native mesquite, carob, or acacia. The seedpods make terrific livestock fodder, beer, flour, and syrup. Our Nazca Indians once lived in an Eden of them. But they cut down so many that wind and flash floods carried off the topsoil, creating a desert. And because *algarrobo* is ideal for charcoal, producers are greedily harvesting Peru's remaining trees, usually on private land under cover of night. Then they disappear, leaving us landowners to deal with the consequences."

"Too bad so much of nature is..." Henning switched to English, "... dollarable."

"Dollarable. What a great word." Still chuckling, Belisario turned into a lane leading to a solid gate in a wall covered by thorny vines. "That's the finest growth of cat's claw in Peru. It discourages trespassers better than anything else I've tried."

The gate swung open before Belisario could ring the bell hanging from a metal pole's curved tip. As they drove through, Henning saw an elderly peon, brown cheeks a mass of corduroy-like puckers, shins muddy below trousers that ended at his calves. Evidently he'd been cleaning an irrigation ditch when he'd heard them and opened the gate.

The old man watched, clearly hoping for some expression of gratitude. Henning smiled and waved. Belisario didn't even turn his head.

CHAPTER THIRTY-FIVE
TABLE FOR ONE

Next morning at breakfast, Henning speared his last mouthful of pancakes and used it to clean the remaining butter and *algarrobo* syrup from his plate. Within seconds, Belisario's cook brought him another helping on a clean plate.

"How'd he know I was still hungry?" Henning asked.

Belisario grinned. "I saw you looking at the empty serving dish and told him."

Later they relaxed on padded chairs in the garden, surrounded by shade trees. Fresh from Altamira Island's frantic pace, Henning had difficulty beginning his day sitting down, but found it easier after Belisario asked, "Do you know anything about military tactics?"

"Few subjects interest me more. I studied every famous general from Alexander the Great to Napoleon at a Prussian Academy."

"This is my lucky day." Belisario pounded his right fist into his left palm. "What can you tell me about Napoleon's tactics at Waterloo?"

Later they detoured into a discussion of death that ended with Belisario chuckling as he said, "I don't worry about what will happen after I die. I didn't exist before I was born and it wasn't all that bad."

Next they delved into Darwin's theory of evolution, then the amazing effectiveness of cinchona and quinine. They were in the same chairs talking about horses as the sun went down. There had been no awkward silences— no silences of any kind. Seeing them so engrossed, the maid had brought lunch and later tea rather than call them to the dining room.

******

A chance meeting with Martine Prado was unlikely. To be sure of seeing her, Henning would have to go to her father's hacienda. For a week he woke up thinking *I'll do it today*, after which Belisario outlined schedules that left no free time.

A routine developed. Every morning Belisario drove Henning around, introducing neighbors and showing off Valencia's fields, warehouses, irrigation system, and the site where engineers would soon lay out the new mill's foundation. In the afternoons their wide-ranging talks in Valencia's garden were pure heaven.

Henning's most enjoyable conversations had always been with people who were passionate about the topic. Belisario was that way about everything. Sometimes he threw his head back, bellowing with laughter. Or slapped his knee. And when he could resist no longer during meals, he pounded his fist on the table, after which his maid peeked into the room and—if necessary— wiped up whatever he'd spilled.

"Is there a subject that doesn't interest you?" Henning asked from his garden chair as the sun set at the end of their first week together.

"I don't much care for anything a woman brings up after saying, 'We need to talk.'"

Henning chuckled. "We barely know each other, yet I feel like we're old friends."

"Barely know each other?" Belisario repeated incredulously. "We've been together fourteen hours a day for a week. Would you know me better if we'd eaten lunch together ninety-eight times? Either way we'd have shared the same amount of time."

Pleasant though it was, Belisario's dawn-to-dusk companionship was preventing Henning from visiting Martine. He might never see her again if he didn't do it soon. It was time to gather his courage and go to Toledo. But first he needed to come up with a reason that wouldn't reveal the depth of his interest to Belisario, who didn't seem fond of her.

******

Belisario's Hacienda Valencia appeared on maps, had its own legal and economic systems, and was self-sufficient. Its fields, pastures, and orchards fed two thousand inhabitants. Resident craftsmen produced life's necessities and luxuries. A stable supplied horses for legions of overseers who supervised planting and harvesting. Profits had built a church, cemetery, school, post office, and hospital.

During his stay, Henning had finalized but not yet revealed his decision to finance the mill that seemed certain to make Valencia's future even brighter than its past.

"I've never enjoyed a house this much," he told Belisario as they finished breakfast on the tranquil patio. "It's the most beautiful example of Moorish architecture I've ever seen."

"It's my favorite place," Belisario responded. "But to my eternal surprise, it doesn't provoke as much jealousy as Emiliano Cabrera's residence on Hacienda Noya. I'll take you there this morning."

In the Chiriaco Valley's flat vastness, Cabrera's French-style chateau was conspicuous atop a manmade eighty-foot mound of rock and compacted dirt.

"From its windows," Belisario said, stopping his carriage on the nearest road, "Cabrera can see for miles in any direction, all the way to the borders of his empire back before its size doubled. To me, those two towers belong in a dark fairytale. Every time I get close, I expect to be stopped by a knight on horseback. And the interior is equally ostentatious. The vestibule has water fountains, ivy crawling up rock walls, and a life-size bronze statue of... guess who. I'd take you to see it, but Cabrera doesn't welcome visitors—not that he'd have any if he did. The methods he uses to expand his holdings got him ostracized, which is less than he deserves."

"I'd find it very painful," Henning said, "to be denied the company of people here."

Henning was lost in fond memories as they began the drive back to Valencia. Belisario's neighbors reminded him of *Californios*. They treated one another with a subtle blend of formality and friendliness. He found their relaxed manner calming and their knowledge interesting. Their exquisite courtesy made him feel accepted. He could have happily lived and worked among them. As a boy on his grandfather's farm, he'd detested agriculture. But in Peru he could hire people for the drudgery and afford enough land to raise crops on a scale impossible in Prussia.

After exporting most of his annual harvest as raw sugar, Belisario made the rest into cone-shaped loaves marketed in Peru. Those sold wholesale weighed thirty pounds and were three feet tall. The ones used in people's homes were smaller. A dazzling white example sat in the middle of Valencia's dining table. Having grown up poor, Henning used the expensive sweetener sparingly. But like Domingo Santa María at Rancho Salamanca, Belisario frequently indulged his sweet tooth after cutting off a generous chunk with tong-like sugar nips.

******

Henning's visit had lasted two weeks when Belisario invited him to the stable.

"You've seen the rest of Valencia," he said as they exited the back door after dinner. "Now I'll show you my private passion. Are you familiar with Peruvian Paso horses?"

"Years ago in Lima, I saw two of *Don* Manuel Prado's. He was taking them to Argentina as a gift for its president."

"My horses aren't as excellent as *Don* Manuel's but I think you'll like them." Despite his gracious words, Belisario's tone said Valencia's horses were second to none.

All week Belisario's son had followed them when permitted, but at a respectful distance. Tonight, finally comfortable in Henning's presence, Marco Venicio ran circles around them chattering incessantly.

"All this exertion concerns me," Belisario said, holding the back of his fingers against his son's forehead until apparently satisfied the boy wasn't overheated.

"Marco, time for your syrup," a female voice called. "Where are you?"

"Over here, Chabuca," Belisario answered.

A short, heavyset Indian maid with a heart-shaped face came out of the rose garden and minced toward them with a bottle and tablespoon.

"Can't I go without my syrup just this once?" Marco pleaded. "Please."

"You have to take three spoonsful after every meal," Belisario said. "It'll help you grow big and strong."

Marco kicked dirt, clearly unhappy that Henning now knew he needed help growing up.

"Why don't you take your syrup by yourself tonight," Belisario offered.

Chabuca handed Marco the bottle and spoon. He glanced around to see who was watching. Henning looked away.

Later Belisario opened the top half of yet another stall door and said, "You like horses more than I would have guessed. Along with everything else here, these will be yours if I default on my loan."

They were scheduled to sign the documents tomorrow. Belisario was clearly dangling bait to make sure Henning didn't change his mind.

"I wouldn't want to acquire your horses that way," Henning replied, "but perhaps I'll buy one when I have a place to keep it."

"I don't sell horses, but I'll give you one. You can leave him here as long as you like. That way you'll have a reason to visit often."

"I can't—"

"You can't say no unless you want to insult me."

"You're like the *Californios*. They're descendants of California's original settlers and just as openhanded as you. Thanks to their generosity men can start in San Diego, ride a thousand miles north, and never spend a penny for lodging, food, or fresh horses."

"It's that way in Peru too. With my letter of introduction, you can ride from Ecuador to Chile without taking out your wallet. But not without a horse. Let me give you one. Please."

Twice Henning had mentioned his desire to visit *Don* Manuel and *Doña* Martine Prado, but Belisario hadn't offered to take him. With his own horse, he could ride there and Belisario would never know.

"Okay," Henning said. "You win."

"No, you win. I have a phenomenal horse for you. His name is Maximo."

CHAPTER THIRTY-SIX
GARDEN WITH NO PATHS

Following Belisario to Maximo's stall, Henning stopped to look at a rust-red stallion in a corral.

"Sultán isn't good enough for you," Belisario volunteered. "If he was he'd be in a stall instead of out here."

"May I ride him?" Henning asked.

"What do you like about him?"

"He isn't fooled by our pretence that we're not predators."

The stallion had backed into a corner and would have kept going if the fence hadn't stopped him. Henning's preference in horses resembled his taste in women. He liked them proud and a bit standoffish—not slavishly devoted as if they were pet dogs.

"Maximo is a far better horse," Belisario said. "I'll have him saddled so you can try him."

Maximo, a bay, was flashy—ideal for attracting attention but not for working. He wasted energy, and riding him didn't change Henning's opinion. But when he settled in the saddle and touched Sultán with his heels, an equally energetic and far more efficient response said this was his kind of horse. The unbelievably smooth ride was like floating on a magic carpet. The power and energy brought to mind Spanish cavalry stampeding numerically superior Inca warriors, thanks to horses so magnificent they seemed heaven-sent.

Henning had ridden many horses, but never one like this. In the end he got the gift he wanted rather than the one Belisario wanted him to have.

******

After Marco Venicio left the breakfast table, Henning mentioned his interest in visiting the Prados.

His son now beyond earshot, *Don* Belisario spoke his mind. "If I'm correct in detecting an interest in Martine Prado, you should know that such an alluring woman is unmarried for good reason. She might be described as well-balanced, I suppose, but only because she has a chip on each shoulder." Seeing Henning's expression he added, "My apologies for offering an unsolicited opinion. Do you know anyone else in our valley?"

"Only José Geldres."

"The *mestizo?*" Belisario frowned.

"Why do you call him a half-breed?" Henning asked.

"Because that's exactly what he is. But even though the word *mestizo* usually suggests a mongrel, it carries a large measure of respect in Geldres's case. He's gone far in life for someone of humble origin. How do you know him?"

"He supplies workers for my guano concession."

"Really? He's always refused to send men to the diggings. You must have made a good impression."

"He impressed me, that's for sure. I'd like to visit him while I'm here."

"His place is in the foothills. I'll draw you a map. However, you'll have to call on him some other time. He's in the highlands looking for workers."

"Do you mind if I take a ride on Sultán this afternoon?"

"Of course not. He's yours to do with as you please."

******

His gray alpaca suit would tell Belisario that Henning was eager to make a good impression so he wore the tan linen one. Five miles down the Valley's main road, he began reversing directions periodically so he could again pass the entrance to Manuel Prado's Hacienda Toledo. After two hours of this failed to produce a chance encounter with Martine Prado, he steeled himself and rode under the iron arch bearing the words 'Toledo – Prado.'

He was soon surrounded by an astonishing variety of trees. Those lining the road shaded him with long intermingling branches. Their leaves ranged from huge and rubbery to tiny and delicate. Some were so vividly colored that Henning initially mistook them for blossoms.

Rounding a curve, he saw a stately two-story house with a porch wrapped around it. A man and woman were gesturing angrily on the landing above the front steps. The door slammed. Now alone, the woman kicked the railing. Martine Prado.

Henning stopped Sultán. Better to return some other day. Too late. She'd seen him and was coming down the stairs, a simple white cotton dress hanging loosely from a gathered waist. She didn't wear the full-skirts currently fashionable, but preferred a narrower, more shallow silhouette and clearly had her clothes custom-made. Henning was glad. She was far too elegant for those billowing monstrosities most women wore.

Henning rode up to her and waited for an invitation to dismount. When none came, he took off his broad-brimmed planter's hat and said, "Thought I'd stop by and say hello."

"I'm Martine Prado," she said.

Only a year after their encounter at the Chincha Islands, her failure to recognize him was disheartening—but understandable. Her mind was elsewhere, and aboard *Daphne* she'd seen him only briefly in dim light. As he dismounted, she focused on Sultán.

"Pretty horse," she said. Another disappointment. Peruvians thought stallions should be masculine—not pretty.

"He was a gift from Belisario Lorca," Henning explained. "I chose him over *Don* Belisario's objections."

"That explains the four white stockings. Knowing Belisario, I'm sure he wanted to give you a better token of his esteem." Henning overlooked her tactless remark. The anger behind it had been provoked before his arrival.

Confidently picking up Sultán's forehoof she inspected it, then lectured, "White stockings mean white hooves, which are less durable than dark ones. That's a serious fault in Peru because we don't shoe our horses. If you ride this one in rough country he'll go lame."

Unable to quietly accept her assumption of his ignorance, Henning said, "Light-colored hooves aren't frowned on in Prussia. We shoe our riding horses, and I've already made an appointment with a blacksmith."

"Extra weight on his feet will spoil his gait. I didn't catch your name."

"Henning Dietzel."

"From?"

"I was born in Prussia but live in Peru and could very happily live in this valley."

"You might want to think twice. Outsiders don't fit in here."

"Doesn't that depend on the kind of people they are?"

"What kind of person are you?"

"I doubt I'd fare well if evaluated by someone with as sharp a tongue as yours."

Her tone changed. "I deserve that. Regrettably, you've come at a bad time. My father wants me to marry the man who'll inherit the hacienda to our north. But no matter how highly he approves of that gentleman, I won't marry him. Poor daddy will have a devil of a time finding another potential husband for his old maid daughter."

Annoyance draining, Henning felt as he had when he'd first seen her. No longer the most pursued female in Peru, she was a spinster pushing thirty in a land where men had a fetish for women half her age. But to him, she was gorgeous without makeup and fancy clothes. He preferred her cheeks naturally rosy and her hair down. And up close, he was struck by the emerald green irises in those startlingly clear white eyes.

"You look familiar. Have we met before?" Martine asked.

"You were my guest once, but I wasn't home at the time." Seeing her puzzled frown, he offered another clue. "A few days later we saw each other on a freighter at the Chincha Islands."

"And I kissed you on the cheek." Martine bumped the heel of one hand against her forehead. "You're the guano extractor who treats his workers too well and I've treated you badly. Can we start again?"

Henning put his hat on, took it off with a flourish, and bowed. "Good morning, *señorita*."

She curtsied. "Does your wife find our valley as appealing as you do?"

"I'm not married."

"I see. What makes you want to live here?"

"It's heaven on earth, and I feel like I belong." Explaining why would've shocked her.

"Then we have something in common," she said. "Will you buy property?"

"I'm not sure. Big changes are coming and I like things as they are."

"This valley doesn't change. That's part of its charm."

"It will evolve along with the rest of the world, thanks to capitalists."

"And what are they?"

"Businessmen who have capital instead of money."

"Sounds clever. What does it mean?"

"Capital is money used exclusively to earn more money," Henning said. "It's never spent on luxuries such as Toledo's forest—which, by the way, is delightful."

"I designed it. It's my somewhat oversize garden. Most people find it lacking because it doesn't have little paths lined with whitewashed stones, leading to the best views."

"Once you make paths, rules requiring people to stay on them are inevitable," Henning said. "I don't care for those kinds of restrictions."

"I feel the same. The way I see it, if I tell others where to go and what to appreciate, they have the right to do the same with me. Would you like a tour of my garden?"

They walked into a grove where tiny leaves filtered sunlight into pencil-thin shafts. Hands clasped behind his back, Henning held himself to half his normal pace while listening to the stories behind her acquisition of certain trees.

Later in a clearing, Martine stopped and faced him. Dressed in white, standing in bright sunshine, she looked like a painting.

"Miguel de Cervantes is *Don* Belisario's favorite author and preferred topic of conversation," she said. "When you want to please him, you should start a conversation about *Don Quixote*. Have you read it?

"Yes. Several times."

"You don't strike me as someone who enjoys classical novels."

"I prefer the works of naturalists like Charles Darwin and Alexander von Humboldt."

"I've read every book they wrote. We may also have something else in common. People are forever telling me I should smile more. I suspect they do that to you too?"

"And for good reason, I'm afraid." Hoping she liked it, Henning flashed his smile,

"Shall we continue your tour?" she asked.

"Perhaps another day? I have an appointment this afternoon with Belisario."

"Come back whenever you like," she said, giving the invitation Henning had sought. "May I bring you some *chicha morada* before you leave?"

"Please. It's my favorite beverage, though I suspect it brings me bad luck with women."

"Is there a joke in there somewhere?" she asked. Their eyes met, hers puzzled, his blue, both squinting as they stepped into bright sunshine. She stared as if her mind was elsewhere. Perhaps she—like Makayla—had noticed that his eyes got bluer as the pupils contracted.

"I'm not much for kidding around," Henning replied.

"I noticed. That's something else we have in common. It probably explains why we're both single. Most people want mates skilled at easing life's pains."

"That's not your kind of man?" Henning asked.

"Heavens, no. I don't want someone who jokes and laughs when things go wrong. The only man who ever interested me was a rock I could hold on to in bad times...or so I thought."

To Henning's disappointment, she quickly changed subjects.

CHAPTER THIRTY-SEVEN
A PREDICTABLE OLD FOOL

Peru's guano had seemed inexhaustible before demand quadrupled. Now extractors on small islands were diluting what was left with sand and dirt, increasing its bulk but decreasing its effectiveness.

"Will you do the same?" Alcalino asked at lunch the day after Henning's return from the Chiriaco Valley.

"What do you think?" Henning took a sip of lemonade.

"I doubt it."

"Business requires a fundamental choice," Henning said. "You can cheat and briefly make exorbitant profits. Or you can give fair value and earn a reputation that brings repeat customers and follows you to whatever you do next."

"You're going to recite one of your grandfather's platitudes, aren't you?"

Despite his raw, inborn intelligence, Alcalino hadn't used words like platitude until after they met. It pleased Henning to have elevated him, if only in small ways.

"Actually, I'm going to recite two platitudes, both mine," Henning replied. "'Doing wrong is never right, and doing right is never wrong…and 'Integrity trumps financial reward.'"

"But integrity's biggest reward comes after we're dead and hopefully in heaven."

"I disagree. The effects are immediate because our behavior affects the way we feel about ourselves."

Henning's reputation for honesty and efficiency was spreading. Annually his sales increased, his workers become more productive, and his profits multiplied. This year, 1859, promised to be his best yet. But other small extractors had run out of guano, and knowing his turn would come, he focused his attention on the nitrate deposits in southern Peru's Atacama Desert.

Nitrate's prospects were better than guano's had ever been. Both were ideal as fertilizers and for explosives. The difference was, nitrate could be privately owned while guano—and the land where it was found—belonged to the government. When people left the guano business, their replacements paid the Ministry of Guano for the right to take their places. Nitrate mines, on the other hand, could be sold for good money.

The writings of naturalist Mariano Eduardo de Rivero had taught Henning that nitrate formed in hot, dry areas. And that Peru's Atacama, the world's driest desert, had unequaled deposits. But to see that area firsthand he'd have to leave Alcalino unsupervised again, which was unthinkable.

As *Intrepido's* crew unloaded a delivery months later, Henning was astonished to see Eduardo Vásquez stride down the gangplank. Five years had thinned his hair and thickened his waist. But as his occasional letters had shown, his bluster was unchanged.

"The manager of your Lima office told me you'd be on this stinking island," he said.

They hugged, slapped backs, and stepped apart—at a loss for words until Eduardo wrinkled his nose and asked, "Does this place always smell so bad?"

"No," Henning replied. "It's usually worse, but you'll get used to it."

"You think I'll stay that long?"

"I hope so. How are you?"

"Lucky to be alive. After you left San Francisco, I was diagnosed with malaria. But my symptoms were unusual. If you hadn't sent Dr. Mossman, I would've died and you'd never have gotten reimbursed for that money you left in my shaving mug."

"You earned that money a hundred ways," Henning said. In his mirror these days, he saw a confident man in his prime. What did Eduardo see? The pup he'd known in California?

"Would you like a glass of *chicha morada*?" Henning asked. "I have some in my office."

The cobalt blue ocean behind them, they started toward a simple wood structure outlined against a yellowish plateau that was a third as high as when Henning first harvested its guano.

"Have you had second thoughts about that job you offered?" Eduardo asked.

"Absolutely not. Can you start today?"

"I won't take orders from Alcalino."

"You won't have to. You'll be in charge of him."

"I heard you might go into the nitrate business."

"Not necessarily." Henning made a mental note to explain the virtues of discretion to the manager of his Lima office. "But I plan to explore that possibility as soon as you settle in."

"The sooner the better. Nitrate's future is far more promising than guano's."

"Sounds like you're still the custodian of all truth," Henning teased.

"The owner," Eduardo corrected with an expressive wink.

"Still the same old Eduardo, always joking around."

"It's my way of letting off steam. I don't know how you survive without doing the same. If you can't manage it sober, try getting drunk."

"I've never been in that condition."

"I wouldn't believe any other man who said that."

******

Twelve hours after leaving Altamira Island, Henning reached Iquique, a Peruvian port that was home to nitrate's important pioneers. He made inquiries until satisfied the ultimate authority was a Chilean, Bernardo Armstrong.

Next morning Henning waited on a barstool in The King's Hideaway, an English-style pub with the traditional dartboards and brass spittoons. And some not-so-traditional girls who charged five *centavos* for a dance or twenty an hour to sit at customers' tables.

Armstrong's arrival revealed a large man with enough eccentricities to make him typically English. As he sat alone at a table two men tramped across the floor to pay their respects, then reseated themselves near Henning.

"Good old Bernardo," one said quietly. "He talks but never listens, which inevitably deprives him of the opportunity to do either."

Most of the bar's patrons descended from English immigrants. They were Chilean citizens but remained English in other ways. Like most of them, Armstrong smoked a briar pipe and wore a tweed suit. Clearly bored, he fiddled with the thick sideburns joining his handlebar moustache and bushy hair.

He perked up when Henning approached to ask, "What got you interested in nitrate?"

Gesturing to the chair beside him Armstrong took a deep breath and said, "The Spanish ruled Chile when my father came from Great Britain and fought in the Wars of Independence. After being rewarded with citizenship he exported nitrate to England and France, trying to create a market. Compared to guano, nitrate is easier to handle, more effective, and more available. The Atacama has veins fifteen feet deep, fifteen miles wide, and hundreds of miles long. These contain concrete-like strata of gravel, rock, calcium carbonate, and nitrate. Removing the impurities by hand is slow. Someday the British will develop machines that do it faster, but that will cost more than they're willing to invest right now. When the guano runs out, however, England's farmers will need another fertilizer and her military will still require gunpowder. Then the Brits will loosen up on development money and control nitrate as they now do guano. Did I mention that nitrate is an excellent source of iodine and is also used in curing salt for meat? Well let me tell you…"

Henning waited for a pause that never came as Armstrong—red faced with enthusiasm—continued a speech he'd obviously delivered many times.

"Maybe someone here will develop the machinery," Henning broke in.

Still performing for an unseen audience, Armstrong blew a burst of air. "There's no significant capital in South America, my boy. Why? Because our sainted Peruvian leaders—being good Catholics—discourage banks from lending. Their attitude toward charging interest is best seen in Dante's *Inferno*, where money lenders were consigned to an even worse part of hell than murderers. The British astutely concluded that money lent at moderate rates spawns industries that provide employment and profits. As a result they have the world's largest accumulation of capital. Once they develop the needed machinery, it'll be *adiós* guano, *buenos días* nitrate. Get involved now and you could wind up as one of the world's richest men. There are damn few seats at that table. Of course, not even nitrate is guaranteed to make you wealthy. It's like—"

"Playing chess with God?" Henning had heard that memorable expression twice. Armstrong had used it earlier that morning. And years ago, Eduardo had employed it to describe the uncertainties of prospecting for gold.

"How'd you know I was gonna say that?" Armstrong frowned. "Damn. I must seem like a predictable old fool."

"Barely predictable and definitely not a fool."

Later Henning questioned accountants who kept books for nitrate mines. Happy with their answers, he visited some of their clients' operations. Everything he saw and heard pointed to the same conclusion. Guano was the past and nitrate was the future.

Again Henning prepared to leave a declining business for an uncertain one. This time though, his transition would be gradual. In a costly enterprise such as nitrate, he couldn't prevail by simply refusing to quit.

He'd driven his stake in the ground and overcome all obstacles with his cinchona shipment, in the importing business, and on Altamira Island. Time and again unexpected twists and turns had almost derailed him. But his knack for finding ways out of difficult situations wouldn't be enough with nitrate. He couldn't simply plunge in. First, he needed to understand the business, inside and out so he could avoid fatally expensive problems.

******

Back on Altamira Island, Henning measured the length and breadth of his remaining guano. Forced to estimate its depth because no one knew the height of the land beneath it, he calculated his guano would last as little as a year or as long as four.

He had enough savings for a down payment on a nitrate mine. But if his guano diggers hit bedrock, he wouldn't be able to make the monthly payments. He'd do better to start a business that supported the mines. That way he'd see the industry up close and at the same time increase his financial reserves.

A week later Henning rented a room in Iquique. Known as the Queen of the Coast it was a quaint town on a shelf between the Pacific Ocean and a palisade of cliffs. Most Peruvian cities featured Spanish architecture and were made of mud bricks. But without clay—and therefore adobe—Iquique had imported lumber from the same Oregon forests that helped build San Francisco. The residents were mostly British or Chilean. Streets had English names. Houses and shops were Georgian in design, giving the appearance of an English hamlet.

Little had changed since Henning's days as a sailor when he'd occasionally gone ashore there. Water for the five thousand inhabitants still came south by ship from Pisagua, a name created by combining *pis* with *agua*. Pisswater was a fair description of the liquid from that town's heavily mineralized wells. Pedro Casas sold it in Iquique. Short, fat, and good-humored, he was prospering but was no longer the town's most popular man.

Back when Casas transported water in goatskin bags on llamas, his customers had been guano excavators on the Atacama's peninsulas. After the guano ran out he bought wagons and mules in order to sell water in Iquique and at inland nitrate mines. He drove his competitors out of business, then failed to maintain his equipment or replace his aging mules. Now his wagons often broke down, his mules dropped dead along the trail, and his deliveries were always late.

As Iquique grew, Casas's problems had increased to where they seemed insurmountable. His mules—the largest available—were too small to pull heavy loads. His wagons—built of hardwood as good as any in Peru—weren't sturdy enough to carry fifty gallon, four hundred pound barrels of water. So he used eighteen-gallon casks instead, but had too few. The cheerfulness that once made him popular now added to the impression he was incompetent.

When Casas's best customers told Henning they'd buy elsewhere if only they could, he arranged for *Andrew Chesterton* to bring white oak and mammoth mules from Louisiana. While the shipment was en route he hired craftsmen to refurbish the schooner he'd bought to bring sweeter water from beyond Pisagua.

When the enormous mules arrived, they caused a sensation.

"I would've been less amazed by unicorns," the mayor said, when they were unloaded and led to Henning's new stable.

With the oak, craftsmen made oversize wagons and fifty gallon barrels. Next Henning hired muleskinners and based their wages on the amount of water delivered. To maximize their pay they worked fast. But they also took good care of Henning's equipment and animals because their income declined when wagons broke down or mules weren't at their best.

Each morning Henning's bright green water wagons climbed the switchbacks behind town toward the mines. In a land where nothing happened on schedule, he soon earned a reputation for reliability. Unable to compete, Pedro Casas shut down.

******

Sitting on the beach, sleeves rolled up, Henning counted the ships anchored in Iquique's bay—twice as many as last week. The latest arrivals—like guano freighters of bygone days—would wait their turns for months. Then they'd be loaded by lighters that brought bags of nitrate from dilapidated docks in water too shallow for cargo ships.

Figuratively, Iquique's primitive harbor resembled a narrow neck on a large jug. And being the only port that exported Peru's nitrate, it hampered the trade's growth. But not for long. Henning's success on Altamira Island had been based on ultra-efficient loading procedures, a formula he was ready to repeat.

Months ago, he'd bought a waterfront property, then hired an English company to dredge the seabed in front until it was deep enough for cargo ships. Next he'd hired a contractor to build a wharf and warehouses with conveyor belts. Tomorrow, Henning's new facility would begin loading nitrate directly into freighters' holds.

******

A few months later, Henning's new dock had eliminated the congestion in Iquique's harbor and was still operating at only half capacity. Looking ahead, he'd built a large, ultra-modern facility he believed would be adequate for the foreseeable future. The wisdom of spending that much money had been questionable before Lammot du Pont solved the problem that had made

Peru's nitrate unsuitable for explosives. But now it appeared to have been a stroke of genius.

Before duPont's discovery, both gunpowder and blasting powder had been made with potassium nitrate because Peru's less expensive sodium nitrate absorbed moisture from the air, limiting its explosive power. Du Pont's process corrected this, and his company now bought enormous amounts of Peruvian nitrate for its type B blasting powder. This was the preferred explosive of miners, men clearing farmland, the United States military, and builders of roads, canals, and railways. In a hurry to receive its nitrate shipments, DuPont Explosives selected Henning's facility to load its ships.

After a few months of loading other people's nitrate for du Pont, Henning set out to buy a mine of his own.

CHAPTER THIRTY-EIGHT
A NEW LIFE

Once Henning bought a mine, he wouldn't have time for anything else. So he put Eduardo in charge of his dock and loading facility in Iquique. And with trepidation, he gave Alcalino authority to make decisions without his approval. But no one in Iquique was both available and suitable to run his water business. He'd have to look elsewhere.

Eleven years ago, his first true love hadn't answered his letters. But his infatuation with Martine Prado had diminished the pain of Encinas Peralta's rejection. He thought of her now only because her business instincts were better than most men's. He'd seen her go from prostitute to manager of the House of Smiles, where she'd doubled and redoubled profits.

Encinas had abandoned chastity at a young age—but was honest, competent, hardworking, and trustworthy. Buyers wouldn't like dealing with a woman and the proud, masculine workers at his water business wouldn't appreciate a female boss. But his customers had to have water and his employees would forget their male pride when she started handing out pay envelopes.

Encinas might not be happy to see him, or be interested in his offer. But if she turned him down, it wouldn't hurt the way her first dismissal had. He'd replaced her in his personal life.

******

In a face that was now less round, her features seemed chiseled and her eyes more prominent and expressive. A few fine lines added character more than age. As did the pucker between perfectly plucked eyebrows. Eleven years older, she continued to braid her hair in the trademark House of Smiles pigtails. Changes, if any, in her body were kept in check by a tight corset.

The tidy room said she was still organized and responsible. An overstuffed couch and coffee table with cigars, rum, and sweets reminded of her talents as a hostess. Henning had been with her the day she bought the painting on the wall behind her. It showed a naked girl—around fourteen, not fully developed—studying herself in a mirror. Seeing that image years ago, a young and naïve Henning had realized that girls too wondered if they were attractive. This one's innocence was out of place in a brothel, but few were run by madams as sensitive as Encinas.

He nudged the door open. She looked up and her gemlike eyes sparkled. Taken by surprise, she was remarkably composed. Only her smile was out of control as she came around the desk, curling a forefinger to beckon him closer. When he obeyed, she grabbed and hugged him. As she let go, Henning couldn't remember what he'd planned to say.

With a sensuous grin, she said, "Apparently you don't smile any more than you used to."

"Not when I'm this nervous. Did you receive my letters from California?"

"Yes. What finally happened to your *Californio* friends, the Santa Marías? Your last letters were full of them."

"They lost their ranch."

"The moneylender wound up with it?"

"No, the government declared their grant invalid. Why didn't you answer my letters?"

"I did as soon as I received the number of your San Francisco post office box. When you stopped writing, I figured you'd found someone else."

"I didn't receive a single letter from you."

Encinas's eyes brimmed with tears. "If I had known that, I would have found another way to send them. Why did you wait so long to visit me?"

"Because nothing is as pathetic as a man holding on when he's not wanted. I'm glad you're still here."

"I probably shouldn't be. I'm not exactly prime meat these days." She sat on the couch.

He sat beside her and said, "The years have treated you well."

"My mirror tells me otherwise, but you're more handsome than ever. Look at you…in a suit, dashing and dangerous like that photograph of your father. I have a nice house and a real bed these days. Would you care to spend the night or do you prefer younger girls?"

"I'm here to offer you a job."

"Doing what? It's difficult to imagine you involved in the only business I know."

"It's easy to imagine you in another line of work."

"You're serious?" she asked. "What would I be doing?"

"Managing a water business in Iquique."

"What do I know about that? You might as well ask me to live on the moon."

"You know how to run a business. I'll teach you the rest. And I'll guarantee a minimum of twenty percent more than you earn here."

This was where Henning had intended to say their relationship would be strictly professional. But he could no longer promise that in good faith.

Encinas got up to answer a knock on the door.

"I'll be right back," she said over her shoulder, leaving the room.

Henning hurried to the water closet and combed his hair at its mirror. He was back on the sofa when Encinas returned.

"How soon do you need an answer?" She sat beside him.

"Now would be nice. My ship leaves for Iquique tonight. You could come with me."

"In that case the answer is yes." She glowed like a long neglected girl who'd suddenly become the center of attention.

Impressed she'd made a life-changing decision so easily, Henning was also uneasy. His decade long devotion to Martine Prado had wavered only once, on that lonely *Carnaval* night when Pilar came to his hotel room after their water fight.

"Do you mind combing out your hair?" he asked.

Encinas's voice turned wintry. "Because you don't want anyone to see my pigtails and know what I do for a living?"

"What you did for a living."

"Wearing my hair differently won't fool the officers on our ship if I fucked any of them."

Henning flinched. "Why use that kind of language?"

"To make you think twice about hiring me. If you can't stomach the possibility that someone might recognize me, leave me here."

Encinas's hard shell was gone by the time she and Henning boarded *Portales*. But on her way to a new future she wore a remnant of her past—a shiny red gown, slit from ankle to mid-thigh. It embarrassed Henning but delighted the crew even though she carefully held its opening shut.

******

Listening to the swoosh of water along the hull, Henning stood at *Portales's* rail watching the pink, gray, and blue sunset. He'd tiptoed from their cabin after Encinas—drained following weeks without a day off—fell asleep before finishing dinner. Eager for her company in more ways than one, he'd been a gentleman and removed only her shoes before covering her with a blanket and coming on deck.

These tender feelings for Encinas were unfathomable so soon after his marvelous conversation with Martine Prado at Toledo. Simultaneous interest in two women was a recipe for losing both. But if he had to pick between them today, his choice wouldn't be the one he'd have made yesterday. Martine hadn't recognized him after only a year. And after eleven times that long, Encinas had left the only life she'd ever known to be with him.

On the way back to their cabin, Henning pledged he wouldn't let his and Encinas's renewed relationship go to the next level until certain of his feelings. The last thing he wanted was to mislead or hurt her. Turning the knob and holding it to prevent clicking, he opened the door. Encinas was under the covers, and her gown hung from a clothes hook.

When the hinges squawked, her eyes fluttered. Encinas lay more than half asleep as he undressed. After she patted the bed beside her, he slid beneath the covers. Turning her back didn't make her less arousing. Abstaining while sharing a bed would be difficult.

Henning seldom allowed himself to think about intimacy with Martine, but often imagined it with Encinas. Perhaps the expression 'making love' was more than a discreet reference to sex. Maybe it had originated because love announced itself by increasing sexual attraction.

******

Neither Henning nor Encinas had moved when they woke the next morning. If Encinas wondered why he got out of bed so quickly, she didn't show it. After breakfast, they relaxed in reclining chairs on deck, her reading and him staring at the seascape.

"If memory serves me correctly," he said, "it's eleven years to the day since we met."

Moving her glasses from her nose to the top of her head, she exclaimed, "I can't believe you remember."

"Better than that, I arranged to have your favorite dinner served in our cabin."

"Scallops?"

"With all the trimmings."

"Then you'll get all the trimmings too, but first I'll wrap them in that new dress you bought me."

All morning *Portales* had glided across a vast blue plain. Out of nowhere, a sudden storm created hills and valleys. Dashing to safety, Henning and Encinas were pelted with spray that made the deck look freshly varnished.

They staggered down the rocking hallway. Inside their cabin, Henning plopped down beside Encinas on the sofa. They clutched the arm rests, firmly at first, then hard enough to whiten their knuckles. In danger of being flung across the room, Henning stood and caught the wildly swinging kerosene lantern. He turned the knob to retract the wick, extinguishing its flame. The danger of fire eliminated, he went limp and gravity slammed him back to the couch.

With surprising strength Encinas clung to him to avoid being catapulted into the inky blackness. For what seemed an eternity the ship violently pitched and rolled, rose with neck-snapping surges and fell with loud, jarring thuds.

When the bucking and rearing finally subsided, Henning touched a match to the lantern's wick expecting to find Encinas terrified. Face flushed, chest heaving, clothes damp with perspiration, she was invigorated more than frightened.

"It's crazy," she purred huskily, "but that was unbelievably arousing."

"You're teasing, right?"

She lifted her shoulders and let them fall. "Maybe that's why daredevils love danger."

Henning lit the wall lamp. Backlit, the space between Encinas's shapely legs showed through her thin dress. They'd last made love in the final year of their teens. Since then Henning had heard men brag about the intensity— but never the quantity—of their partners' climaxes. Based on his limited experience he doubted many women gasped, stiffened, and writhed in slow-moving ecstasy as intensely or often as Encinas.

Caressed properly, her body—like a fine violin—produced enchanting rhythms, sweet and lilting now, then powerful and resonant. Often they trailed off as if she was satisfied, then built to new crescendos. And on this night, her powerful responses excited Henning to where his enjoyment matched hers twice in an hour.

"We're going to sea every time there's a storm within a hundred miles," he teased as they lay on their backs afterward.

"It wasn't the storm that made this special—not for me at least," she said. "I haven't felt like I just did since the last time I was with you."

The ship's bell rang on the hour as they talked and traced each other's bodies with their fingers. Encinas couldn't remember another man who'd shown interest in her after sex. And Henning—who usually saw relaxation as decadent—now found it an unimaginable luxury, one he'd probably never have with Martine. But he shouldn't think about her. He and Encinas were lovers again, and he should be hers—completely, without misgivings or reservations.

"Did I convince you to go to California during the gold rush?" she asked. "Or am I flattering myself?"

"I wouldn't have gone if it hadn't been for you. And Henning—who usually saw relaxation as decadent—now found it a delicious luxury, one that was natural with a warm woman like Encinas and probably not possible with one as chilly as Martine.

Having a history made conversation easy. Encinas was fascinated as Henning told her about the savage winter he'd struck it rich. Then he described his twenty mile, twenty-four-hour pursuit and gun fight with Mexican bandits. Engrossed in the story of his cinchona shipment to New York, they didn't stop for lunch.

After enjoying the special anniversary dinner in their room they yawned continuously, fighting to stay awake and keep a perfect day from ending.

"See you in the morning," she finally said, then rolled on her side and was asleep.

The tailored, conservative gray dress he'd bought her hung from a wall hook. She'd worn it but didn't seem to like it.

******

"The man waving from the dock is Eduardo Vásquez," Henning said as *Portales* was tied up in Iquique. "We were in California together during the gold rush. Now he runs my dock."

"This dock is yours?" she exclaimed, eyes wide. "You didn't tell me…"

"Just wanted to be sure you love me for who I am and not what I have," he teased, then was instantly concerned that she might have taken his quip seriously.

Eduardo winked when Henning and Encinas came down the gangplank together. "Now I know why you were gone so long," he boomed, spreading his arms.

After their backslapping *abrazo*, Henning said, "You ready for some time off?"

"That's why I'm so happy to see you," Eduardo replied gruffly.

"I brought someone to run the water business. You can take a month off after you show her what she needs to know. Eduardo Vásquez, meet Encinas Peralta."

Henning wanted them to like each other. But studying the dress that covered Encinas's body too tightly to hide it, Eduardo clearly thought she'd won her new job with feminine wiles.

Detecting and mirroring his hostility, Encinas asked, "Where's the washroom?"

"Over there." Henning pointed then took her arm.

She pulled away. "I'll find it. Stay here so you two can talk freely."

When she was out of earshot, Eduardo asked, "I didn't recognize her until I got a closer look. Are you aware she was the madam at Talcahuano's House of Smiles?"

"Yes. That's where I met her."

"Doesn't that give you pause?"

"No more than it bothers her that I was there as a customer. And please don't say it's different for men."

"Did you settle for her because Martine Prado is beyond your reach?"

"This isn't a fling. I love her and want her treated with respect."

Eduardo stifled an undoubtedly sarcastic retort.

"How's the water business doing?" Henning asked as Encinas rejoined them.

"Better that ever," Eduardo replied, "and we're shipping twice as much nitrate as the rest of the waterfront combined. Consider yourself up-to-date."

"Eduardo's a man of few words," Henning told Encinas, "except when giving advice."

Before going to the hotel, Henning looked at that month's books. Delighted with what he saw, he doubled Eduardo's usual bonus, then said, "Tomorrow I'll go and see how Alcalino's doing. While I'm gone, please show Encinas the ropes."

Henning seldom used slang, but that expression came naturally. It had originated on sailing ships where new crewmen were said to know the ropes if they could tie sailor's knots and identify what lines hauled up which sails.

******

By the time Henning returned from Altamira Island, Encinas had a remarkable understanding of the water business and had transformed her appearance. He scarcely recognized her without makeup, her hair pulled into a severe bun, wearing a loose ruffled blouse and a skirt over petticoats that hid her curves.

"Eduardo is forever looking over my shoulder," she told Henning. "He's obviously afraid Iquique's men won't buy anything but pussy from a woman.

But they will after I win over their wives. What do you think of the new me?" She presented herself for approval—rotating in a circle, arms spread. "Do I look like an old maid schoolteacher?"

"I never saw one as pretty as you."

"That's not what I want to hear." A pleased smile belied her words. "I'm trying to look plain for your buyers' wives."

When Eduardo returned from his vacation, Encinas was selling more water than he had. Impressed by her gracious efficiency, Iquique's men had accepted her. And their wives—far from being jealous—took pride in seeing a plain and simple woman do well in a man's world.

CHAPTER THIRTY-NINE
SALAMANCA REBORN

Cracked lips, thumbs, and elbows were an epidemic in Peru's bone-dry Atacama. No rain had fallen during Henning's year there, and in places none had ever been recorded. Even peaks above twenty thousand feet had no glaciers and little snow.

Tests showed Antarctica was even more arid because its sub-zero temperatures froze even the air's humidity. But the Atacama was the world's driest non-polar desert. Its chilly offshore current resisted evaporation. And on those rare occasions when clouds formed, towering mountains blocked them.

The Atacama's moistureless heat provided a perfect environment for nitrate. And with demand exceeding production, Henning's search for a mine had become urgent. The latest candidate was Oficina Oasis, east of Iquique.

With the sun still below the horizon Henning and Encinas left the assistant manager in charge of water sales and rented a buckboard at Iquique's livery stable. All day they drove east and then spent the night in a boarding house run by the vivacious Raquel Vargas.

"This may not be to your taste," Vargas apologized as she dished out goat stew for dinner. "But cows and pigs do poorly out here."

"No need to explain," Henning said. "We're glad to get any kind of meat in a desert."

Weary after their long drive, Henning and Encinas chewed the tough, stringy cubes in silence occasionally punctuated by what sounded like moans.

"Is that wind we hear?" Encinas asked when *Señorita* Vargas brought coffee.

"No," she replied. "For centuries this building was a mission where *Atacameño* Indians were forced to learn white men's ways. Don't let their ghosts bother you. I've come to love them. They're not looking for revenge."

And with that, the enigmatic spinster bid them goodnight.

******

All morning Henning had followed the faint wagon tracks that led to Oficina Oasis. In the midst of barren, brutally hot flatland, these disappeared into drifted sand.

"Which way to Oficina Oasis," he called to an Indian passing in the opposite direction behind llamas.

"It's easy to find." Leaving his dog in charge, the man came closer and sketched a map in the sand with his fingertip.

"How much farther?" Henning asked.

"Not far. Just beyond the *tamarugo* trees."

"Oh, good." Encinas sounded relieved.

"Not necessarily," Henning cautioned, staring at the distant horizon. "I don't see any *tamarugo* trees, do you? *Atacameño* Indians consider it unkind to discourage travelers. Those *tamarugos* are probably very far away."

Hours later Henning and Encinas passed a *tamarugo* grove and entered a town he very much hoped was Oficina Oasis. On its bad side—going toward nicer buildings—they passed rows of connected one-room shelters with corroded sheet metal roofs and walls.

Indians lounged in doorways. Typical nitrate workers, they were *Atacameños*. Different from the one who'd given Henning directions, these were new to the white man's world and had clearly come from the mountains. Despite the desert heat, they wore wool ponchos and had knitted skullcaps under their *sombreros*.

"Their faces show no resentment," Encinas said. "But they must feel it, living and working as they do."

Henning asked several men before one finally answered. "Yes, this is Oficina Oasis."

"Finally, someone who'll talk to me," Henning responded, smiling.

"Don't be insulted," the man said earnestly. "I'm the only person on this side of town who speaks Spanish in addition to our native language. That's why I'm the foreman."

Not a typical nitrate town, Oasis offered luxuries. But the ornate mausoleums and wrought-iron gates at the British Cemetery added to Oasis's price without increasing its value. The same was true of the opera house. Inside, Henning and Encinas sat in red velvet seats and watched a man jump onstage. The lady he'd left in the front row applauded after he'd given his rendition of the 'Alas, poor Yorick' speech from *Hamlet*.

At the outdoor market, Colonel John Cowden's profile on rubber coins reminded Oasis's inhabitants that their town was dominated by the Nitrate King. Beneath a hipped roof and dormers, his imposing Queen Anne style house added to his aura. In England such a mansion would have had a carved stone doorframe. But with no quarries within hundreds of miles, workmen had created a reasonable facsimile with plaster-covered adobe.

Under the stern gaze of an armed guard on the porch, Henning parked at the head of the circular driveway and quietly told Encinas, "Most nitrate towns offer only the bare necessities. But Colonel Cowden has a grand vision for nitrate's future. So he spent a fortune on an opera house, fancy cemetery, and mansion. Those luxuries won't make sense until nitrate's price goes up. He moved too fast too soon, but the price he's asking says he doesn't realize that or can't resist driving a hard bargain."

******

"Come in," Cowden's butler greeted, stepping back from the door. "We held lunch. I'll tell the colonel you've finally arrived."

"I didn't think our appointment was for a specific time," Henning said.

"The colonel is always specific and extremely punctual."

Not without manners, the butler soon returned and showed them the ballroom while they waited. In the library, he introduced them to a ramrod straight, suntanned man with a stiff military bearing and thick white hair.

Colonel Cowden herded them to the dining room. Like the rest of his house, it delighted the senses—the ear with delicate piano music, the palate with hors d'oeuvres, and the eye with crystal, silver, and a sideboard displaying decorated pastries.

Cowden's wife seemed to confirm Henning's theory about rich men's often disappointing offspring. With a wide selection of women available, they often chose wives based almost entirely on beauty.

Glasses of dry sherry were passed out and Cowden proposed a toast, "To Mother England, the land that gave me birth and prepared me for the world's opportunities."

The piano player filled the room with *God Save the King*, which Henning had heard in California as *My Country, 'tis of Thee*. After Cowden called dinner to order and said grace, metal covers were lifted from platters. An *Atacameño* maid served ladies first, then Henning, and finally the host, who suddenly became gracious and congenial.

After dinner Cowden's wife escorted Encinas from the room, and a tray of cigars was laid between Henning and the colonel.

"Before we tour the mine," Cowden said, his presence and voice now commanding, "let's see if we're close on price, shall we?"

"That will be difficult until I know exactly what I'm bidding on," Henning replied.

"I sent the production records, and you surely know how much you can spend."

Negotiating with Cowden quickly revealed his aversion to concessions.

Opposed to establishing a preliminary value, Henning finally declared, "The amenities you use to justify your asking price are pleasing but without economic value."

"May I show you the mine?" Cowden started for the door. "That's where the value is."

"Is it okay if I bring Encinas?"

"If you must."

After a dusty carriage ride, the three dismounted beside an open pit swarming with men and mules. In its depths workers blasted caliche into jagged chunks, then sledgehammered these into smaller pieces that were tossed into wagons.

"From here, the ore goes to the Atacama's most modern crushing plant," the colonel said, leading the way back to his vehicle.

Inside the ball mill's metal walls, sweaty workers shoveled pieces of caliche into rotating drums where heavy steel balls reduced it to gravel, rocks, and powder. Next the rocks were picked out and the gravel was strained away.

"From here the powder goes to that industrial laboratory," Cowden explained, pointing to another large structure. "There it's dissolved and left to crystallize. As you can see I didn't cut corners. Compared to this area's other processing operations, Oficina Oasis produces twice the nitrate per employee. Excuse me please."

As Cowden spoke with his foreman, Encinas whispered, "Your nitrate will cost more to process than his does."

Henning raised an eyebrow. "How so?"

"Didn't you notice? None of his workers have helmets, goggles, respirators, gloves, or boots. He hasn't spent a penny on safety, but you'll spare no expense."

"If I buy Oasis…which I won't unless he reduces the price. He's losing money. Transporting his nitrate to the railroad is too costly."

"If you can solve that problem, why can't he?"

"Apparently he doesn't know there are bigger, more durable wagons available in California. With the same number of drivers and mules, they handle four times the weight. Their wheels are taller than a man and a foot wide with inch-thick iron rims. With wagons like that, Salamanca," he emphasized the word, "can cut its shipping costs in half."

"Salamanca," she repeated. "You'll rename Oasis if you buy it?"

"Can you guess why?"

"I don't have to guess. I listened to your gold rush stories very carefully. Salamanca was Domingo Santa María's *rancho* in California."

"Exactly. Hearing that name daily will remind me to never fail another friend."

Her pink tongue flicked across dry lips. "If Cowden is losing money, why doesn't he ask a reasonable price?"

"Foolish pride. His other mines are closer to the railroad and can easily subsidize Oasis."

"Does that somehow justify wasting money?"

"If I tread lightly, maybe I can get the good colonel to ask himself that question."

******

Back at the mansion after tea, an unspoken code again banished Colonel Cowden's wife and Encinas to the sitting room. After an hour of frustrating wrangling, Henning leaned forward in his chair and politely declared, "That's my best offer."

"But it's ridiculous," Cowden declared. "Buying the land and building this facility cost more than that and claimed two lives to boot."

"You spent too much on touches that add no value."

"My financial records clearly show a substantial profit."

Only the ones you showed me. And your accountant must have worn out a box of erasers making changes, Henning thought, then said, "Sometimes the return *of* your money is more important than the return *on* your money."

"I'm afraid you've wasted our time," Cowden dug both hands into his pockets.

Henning saw negotiating as a waltz. The trick was to get in step—not stomp on each other's feet. But Cowden bargained as he'd been trained to fight battles, looking for total victory. Henning knew better than to emphasize that Oasis had been on offer for a year and he was the last potential buyer. The colonel would have to acknowledge that on his own and had resisted all efforts to nudge him in that direction.

"Maybe some other time," Henning said.

"I'm in no rush. I can almost hear God telling me not to sell."

"With His advice you can't go wrong." Henning flashed a smile he hoped was disarming.

They joined Mrs. Cowden and Encinas in the sitting room. Lost in thought, the colonel remained standing.

As previously planned, Encinas stoked a lengthy conversation, followed by a gracious thank you and a drawn-out goodbye. Finally, handbag strap over one shoulder, she stood and said, "Thank you again for your stellar hospitality."

The butler showed her and Henning to the door.

"Is the price anywhere near reasonable yet?" she quietly asked as they crossed the porch.

"Walk slower," Henning said, without moving his lips. "He's still thinking."

"You devil, I—"

"Stop smiling. He can see us through the window."

They meandered toward steps that descended to the driveway.

"Would you care to take another shot at this?" Cowden called from the doorway.

"Time for a face-saving concession," Henning whispered, then raised his voice. "Will my offer look better if you keep the theater?"

"Let's write it up," Cowden said, going back inside.

Suppressing a grin as she and Henning reversed course, Encinas whispered, "I bet a check of your ancestors would turn up more than one extremely polite pirate."

CHAPTER FORTY

TIDAL WAVE

Two years later a three-foot-high, twenty-mile-long underwater wave sped away from a violent earthquake beneath the Pacific Ocean. Racing toward southern Peru at twenty times the speed of the fastest train, it stealthily passed beneath ships. Crews noticed a slight swell, if anything.

Approaching Iquique, the wave's leading edge slammed into the continental shelf. Friction braked it while water behind caught up, piling higher. The sea in front of Henning's dock receded with an eerie sucking sound, and two workers strolled out to examine the ocean floor.

"You don't often see those around here." The shorter man pointed at an octopus slithering in mud.

Unable to conceal itself in a cloud of ink as it would have done underwater, the octopus gnashed its beak. When they came closer, it curled into a tight package the size of a rugby ball.

"Doesn't seem uncomfortable out of water, does it?" the taller man asked.

"I've seen them leave the ocean for as long as five minutes," his companion replied.

The seabed trembled as a thunderous roar tore their attention from the octopus. Terrified by an onrushing white-water avalanche, they sprinted for shore too late. Both were mangled as the wall of water smashed into Iquique.

Twenty feet tall and chocolate-brown with mud, the wave crushed wharves and churned inland. The writhing, grinding ridge of water, rubble, and bodies erased every trace of structures, even foundations. Railroad tracks were ripped from ties and twisted into bizarre shapes. The carcass of a freighter was dumped among sand dunes and cactus beyond town.

Empty lighters were shattered against cliffs before receding water pulled their remains back across town. Debris, drinking water, food, and countless tons of nitrate were flushed out to sea, along with the corpses of pets, livestock, sea creatures, and human beings.

******

Miles away and hours behind schedule, a train stopped. Coughing in the smokestack's discharge, the engineer lowered the v-shaped snow blade. Beside him a sweaty fireman shoveled coal into flames under the boiler, pushing the steam gauge's needle as high as it would go. Even then the locomotive struggled to pull its heavy cargo while also plowing through drifted sand.

After the train cleared that obstacle and accelerated, Henning sat at a window estimating the speed by timing intervals between telegraph poles. During the last two years he'd increased his mine's output, and the railway had built a spur line to Oficina Salamanca. This had reduced travel time to Iquique, making it possible to visit Encinas more frequently. But hours lost during frustrating delays and breakdowns too often cut into their time together.

Recently Encinas had come to Salamanca on weekends. But he preferred being with her in Iquique where Salamanca's merciless demands couldn't interrupt them. True enough, limited time together had kept their relationship fresh. But that provided little comfort when he missed her, something he did surprisingly often.

Suddenly concerned with a new problem, Henning opened the car's rear door and stepped onto its platform. The long tail of low-sided, open-topped gondola cars contained hundreds of cubic yards of his nitrate, under canvas to prevent the wind from stealing it. Not intended to protect from rain, the tarps' edges were inside the cars. The white, crystalline powder beneath would be ruined if it got wet. And something had altered the Atacama's perpetually clear skies.

As distant black clouds boiled toward the train, their murmuring became thunder and white flickers grew into lightning. In fast-fading twilight,

Henning saw rodents scurrying along the ground. Neither they nor a century of predecessors had experienced a thunderstorm, but they sensed impending violence.

Henning found the conductor in the dining car and told him, "It's going to rain…hard. The tarps need to be retied with their edges outside the gondola cars."

"Makes better sense to keep going," the conductor snapped. "Your nitrate will be nice and dry under the station roof in Iquique."

"It'll rain long before we get there."

"Doesn't look that way to me."

"Have you ever seen a thunderstorm?"

"No, but we're not stopping and that's final."

Flashes brightened the car's dimly lit interior. Eyes wide, the lady across the aisle stuck fingers in her ears as thunderclaps rattled steins and glasses behind the bar. Huge raindrops pelted the roof and windows, then abruptly became sheets of water.

Beside the track ahead, a man frantically swung two lanterns. The engineer applied the brakes. Pushed by countless tons, the train screeched past the signalman on wet, slippery tracks.

"What's wrong?" the engineer asked as the signalman caught up, Henning close behind.

Making himself heard over the shriek of wind shredded by telegraph wires, the signalman bellowed, "According to the latest message, Iquique was destroyed by a tidal wave."

Destroyed? Henning's chest convulsed. "How soon can we get there?"

"I can't let the train continue at night in this weather," the signalman declared.

"People in Iquique need our help," Henning protested.

"Sorry, but you'll have to sit tight until at least morning."

"Are our lives more important than those in Iquique?"

"We don't even know if anyone survived."

"Let's take a vote," Henning suggested.

"Even if everyone votes yes," the engineer chimed in, "I won't go on in this weather."

Having tried every argument he could think of, Henning stomped off. A hundred yards later he came to his senses and turned back. Better to save his strength. The train would pass him long before he could walk to Iquique.

CHAPTER FORTY-ONE
HENNING'S MOST IMPORTANT DAY

*"The two most important days in your life are the day
you are born and the day you find out why."*
-Mark Twain

Asleep in his seat at midnight, Henning was wakened by approaching hoofbeats. As he rushed outside, the signalman shouted, "Halt. Danger ahead."

Cloaked in driving rain, the oncoming vehicle slid to a stop. It was one of Henning's water wagons—springs fully extended, barrels obviously empty. Energized by the storm, the mammoth mules pulling it pranced in place.

Doffing his hat and ignoring the sting of wind-driven rain the Negro driver said, "*Señor* Henning, I can't find shelter for your mules."

"Bring them closer to the train, Guillermo."

Guillermo parked beside a gondola car, avoiding cloudy nitrate-saturated rainwater gushing from between its wall and floor.

When the rain let up, the engineer announced, "We'll stay here until morning."

To lighten the water wagon Henning and Guillermo climbed aboard, then grabbed the opposite ends of empty oak barrels and pitched them—one by one—into a still-draining gondola car. Next Guillermo made sure the harness buckles were securely fastened while Henning rushed into the dining car.

Returning with the bartender's remaining bottles cradled in his arms, Henning noticed his driver's disapproval and felt compelled to explain, "This will be an excellent disinfectant and anesthetic for those injured in Iquique."

To protect the bottles, Henning tucked them among the clothes in one of his bags.

As Guillermo drove them past the train Henning said, "I hope these mules are as fast as I was told. Their mothers were Standardbred mares from New York's harness races."

"They're fast all right," Guillermo said. "That's why God sent them to you tonight."

"If there's a God, why didn't He stop the tidal wave and save Himself all this trouble?"

"You think it's just luck that your mules arrived at the very instant you needed them?"

"Sorry. I shouldn't question your faith."

The mules seemed to enjoy the opportunity to do more than plod along. With flowing strides, they paralleled the track in sand normally powdery and loose, but now wet and firm. Powered by heavily muscled shoulders, their forelegs seemed to pull the ground toward them.

"Don't worry," Guillermo told Henning. "It will take more than water to hurt *Señor* Eduardo and *Señorita* Encinas."

"I won't feel better until I see them alive and well."

The wagon rumbled and quaked for hours before reaching the switchbacks that normally took trains down to Iquique.

The tightness in Henning's chest became euphoria as dawn revealed women—Encinas among them—near the tracks. He vaulted from the wagon and ran to her. Eyes smoldering she held out a hand to stop his embrace.

"You okay?" Henning asked. "Where's Eduardo?"

"I'm fine," she sputtered. "He's in town helping the injured, which is what I'd be doing if this idiot chief of police hadn't forced me up here because ladies shouldn't see blood and guts."

"I've told you a hundred times, ma'am," the chief growled, "there's nothing to do down there but recover bodies, and that's not women's work."

Below them, central Iquique was a swath of tangled rubble, bordered on both sides by heavily damaged buildings. The entire waterfront—including Henning's dock—was gone.

As a boy in Hamburg's Lutheran Cathedral, Henning had found no comfort in 'The Lord giveth and the Lord taketh away.' It still made no sense. God hadn't given what the ocean took. Men had worked for it. If there was a supreme, all-powerful being, Henning hated Him. After bestowing His bounty on Iquique, He had destroyed it. Or equally cruel, had permitted its destruction when He could have saved it.

Unlike the time when bandits stole his gold in California, Henning couldn't simply take back what he'd lost. And with Southern Peru's only port out of commission, he'd soon lose what he had left. Unable to ship nitrate, he couldn't finish paying for his mine or rebuild his dock, warehouses, loading facility, and water business. Banks would take his mine and the land where his businesses had stood. Then they'd petition the courts for the right to take charge of his guano concession.

Seeing that the wave had gouged away the lower part of the road down the cliff, Henning banished these self-centered musings and grabbed his luggage. He steadied Encinas with his other hand as they bolted down the tracks toward town where people's problems were immediate and potentially fatal.

On level ground they skirted an enormous cactus, on its side, root ball dripping sand. What had been a city now resembled an immense dump. They skirted piles of wood mixed with seaweed, wagon wheels, cooking utensils, fishing nets, clothes….

Two men wandered aimlessly, unable to pull themselves together. One was a nitrate baron. The other a janitor. The disaster had leveled their status along with Iquique's structures. Henning helped Encinas across a waist-high ridge of slimy debris. Screams barged into his consciousness. He saw a corpse. Then another. Then Eduardo, using his belt and a stick as a tourniquet to stop blood gushing from a man's crushed knee.

"That doctor needs help," Eduardo shouted, pointing with his chin.

"Why is the man beside him just standing there?" Henning asked, already on his way.

"He's gone mad," Eduardo called out. "Trying to get him to do anything but watch for another wave is a waste of time."

"Tell us what to do," Henning said as he and Encinas knelt beside the doctor.

"Go through the buildings still standing," the doctor told Encinas, "and bring all the alcohol, clean cloth, sewing needles, and thread you find." Turning to Henning, he said, "No one wants to work with that man in prison clothes. Have him hold people still while you clean wounds that need stitching."

The wave must have freed the convict. Henning opened one of his bags, tore shirts into strips, then pulled out a bottle of whiskey. The former inmate held a pain-crazed victim while Henning cleaned and disinfected gaping wounds that looked like meat on a butcher's block.

Responding to screams, Henning and the convict struggled to lift and prop up the corner of a collapsed wall. Then they dragged a woman and boy from underneath and knelt to find out why her leg was sprawled in an impossible position.

"Idiots," the doctor roared. "Broken bones can wait. Give priority to the poor bastards at death's door."

Victim by victim, the three men and Encinas worked their way toward the harbor searching for gravely injured victims.

"We'll come back as soon as we can and help the others," the doctor said.

Kneeling beside a man with both ends of his splintered shin protruding through slashed skin, the doctor cauterized the bleeding's source with silver nitrate solution and barked, "Mesh the ends of the bone and disinfect this wound so I can stitch it."

Punished by their patient's screaming, Henning and the convict fit the shin's jagged ends together as gently as they could and poured a trickle of whiskey on the open wound. Then the doctor returned from another emergency and sewed the skin shut with a sewing needle and common thread.

"Come back and splint this when we run out of emergencies," he said, moving on.

Leaving this victim a cup of drinking whiskey to dull his agony, Henning and the convict followed.

Out beyond floating corpses and capsized ships, a freighter dropped anchor. Captains en route didn't know Iquique was gone. They'd continue to arrive for weeks if not months, expecting to load nitrate.

Beaching a launch with *British Miss* on its prow, the ship's officers rushed ashore.

"God Almighty. I need to busy my hands and forget what I just saw." The captain looked away from a headless corpse. "How can I do the most good?"

"Leave as many men as possible along with your medical supplies, food, and water," Henning rasped. "Then take a skeleton crew and bring more of everything. Start at Pisagua, provided it's still there. If Altamira Island was spared, you can get food, medicine, and blankets from my warehouse behind the pier. Bring me something to write with, and I'll give you a note for my manager."

As the captain hurried away, the chief of police told the convict, "There's a train on the cliff behind town. Help its crew bring anything we can use." He handed over folded clothes and some coins. "Then change into these and disappear. You could have escaped, but stayed to help. That entitles you to a second chance, but Judge Brown won't see it that way."

"Thanks," Henning said. "He earned that."

"I was wrong about women being too tender for emergencies." The chief nodded toward Encinas. "I want that to be my last mistake of the day."

******

The worst was over. A few casualties with injuries that weren't serious still lay on the ground waiting for help. Their wounds weren't bad enough to bring the chills Henning had come to expect. Mercifully, there were lulls when he could rest.

But he couldn't stop his racing mind. So many had died. In the railway station's ruins, he'd seen a friend's corpse. He himself would be dead if the train had arrived on time. What had he done to deserve being spared? That, he'd read somewhere, was a uniquely human question. Survivors of disasters often searched the past for something to justify their good fortune.

Problem was, his good deeds were in among major failings. When he should have been helping the Santa Marías save Rancho Salamanca, he'd been chasing money ... well, not money—but the thrill of earning it. He'd been addicted to that even after becoming a millionaire.

Giving Dr. Mossman a fortune in molasses during San Francisco's cholera epidemic had been too easy to be virtuous. He should have stayed to help the victims. That would have cost some of his precious time, making it a truly meaningful sacrifice. But he'd hurried away, leaving others to care for the sick while he brought more merchandise to sell.

With Eduardo's help, Henning splinted the shin he and the convict had set earlier. From his last bottle he poured a thin trickle of whiskey on the now-sutured wound torn by the bone's jagged ends. As he searched for more people in need of help, a back spasm wrenched him to his knees. Muffling an involuntary yelp, he collapsed on his stomach in sucking mud.

Trying to stand made the pain excruciating. He'd done too much pushing, pulling, twisting, and lifting.

"Stay down. You've done far more than your share," Eduardo said, dropping and leaning back against a boulder brought ashore by the wave. Exhausted, he didn't seem to feel its attached barnacles poking him.

Hair protruding wildly, Encinas knelt and slid her folded jacket between Henning's face and the muck. Her face, hands, and arms were smeared with gore. And her skirt was heavy with mud.

Staring blankly, Eduardo said, "Listening to men who were about to die—or thought they were—taught me something I'll never forget. Not one wished he'd worked harder. But they all regretted not spending more time with loved ones. I'm glad my life didn't end today, but not because I regret how I lived." He turned toward Henning. "Can you say the same? Was being rich in money worth being poor in everything else?"

It was the sort of question Eduardo sometimes asked without being aware of how much they hurt.

"Why are you trying to make Henning feel guilty?" Encinas broke in. "The world would be better if more people applied themselves as he does. His taxes—scrupulously paid to the penny—improved the lives of countless people. He provided thousands of Indians with jobs and good wages that fed their families. He made it possible for Jorge Villegas to send his sons to a university at a time when other government officials could barely afford to clothe their children. And he never once let a friend—you included—want for anything."

When Eduardo started to interrupt, Encinas cut him off. "I'm not finished. I've never yet heard you compliment Henning for his honesty. When most businessmen make deals, they're not happy unless the other guy bleeds. If they hit an artery, so much the better. But Henning has never cheated, broken a promise, or negotiated a deal that didn't benefit all parties.

And not once have I ever heard him tell anyone about his good deeds. He doesn't do them to be known as a Good Samaritan. He does them because it's right."

Her spirited defence surprised Henning. Recently she'd been dropping hints to the effect that he worked too much and spent too little time with her, which was true. But even though she wanted—and deserved—better from him, she'd risen to his defence.

She was special.

"Don't be hard on Eduardo," he told her. "When his friends wouldn't honor a promise to teach me to pan gold, he defended me as fiercely as you just did."

"Other times too," Eduardo said, "but only when you weren't around to hear it."

Henning's back cramped again, harder this time. Reacting to the sharp, almost unbearable pain, his fist closed tight and mud oozed between his fingers, leaving a metal disc behind. He wiped it with his thumb after the spasm stopped, revealing a coin.

"The first step toward rebuilding your fortune," Encinas teased. Turning serious, she added, "Every man goes down at some point in his life. Some are never heard from again. But you'll bounce back. That's who you are."

"But this time," Henning told her, "I want a family and a personal life. And I'll settle for less success to get them."

ACKNOWLEDGMENTS

While writing *Playing Chess with God*, I had considerable help and encouragement. People who should be singled out for extra-special thanks include my brother-in-law, Charles Bazalgette; my friends Mimi Busk-Downey, Henry F. Curry, Jr. M.D., Terry Ellis, Rhonda Hart, Tina Clavelle Meyer, Lucille Rider, Babette Sparr, and Jan Swagerty; my brothers, Deane, Harold, and Ralph, who never stopped believing in this seventeen-year project; my nephew, Michael, who gave generously of his time and talent; my stepdaughter, Krista Weber, who made more contributions over a longer period of time than any other person; my high school classmate, Kay Galbraith, who offered invaluable feedback for many years; my first editor, Michael Parrish, who passed away before the job was done; my Rewrite Specialist Jean Jenkins (it was a rare pleasure to work with someone as competent, conscientious, and kind); and my Peruvian friend Robbie Watson, who helped me accurately portray his country, which I love as much as he does.

And last but not least, I'm grateful to my wife, Laurie, for her patience during the seventeen years I invested in this project. Few would have tolerated what she encouraged.

Verne Albright grew up in the American West. At age nineteen, he took his first of sixty-five trips to Peru. He returned sometimes for business but primarily for the pure pleasure of being there. "Finding a true calling is a miracle many people never experience," he says, "and Peru provided me with two. The first was Peruvian Paso horses, which I have promoted throughout the world. The second was Peru's rich history and culture, which provided material to feed a more recent passion, writing historical fiction set in that nation's fascinating past." Albright makes his home in Calgary, Alberta, Canada, with his wife and five dogs.

Made in the USA
Las Vegas, NV
12 July 2021

26340128R00194